CETUS INSOLITUS

CETUS INSOLITUS

Sea Serpents, Giant Cephalopods,
and Other Marine Monsters in
Classic Science Fiction and Fantasy

CHAD ARMENT, EDITOR

COACHWHIP PUBLICATIONS
Landisville, Pennsylvania

Cetus Insolitus
Published 2008 Coachwhip Publications
Coachwhipbooks.com

ISBN 1-930585-66-7
ISBN-13 978-1-930585-66-9

Front cover image: © Daniel Timiraos

Contents

THE TAIL OF THE BIG SEA-SERPENT
By Captain Jonathan Johnson of the Good Ship "Diddleus"
Edited by William H. G. Kingston, Esq.

I had not attended any of the Ancient Mariner's select Conversaziones for some time, till one evening as I was passing the windows of the Jolly Rover, where he spent the best part of his time, I heard his voice raised in fits of loud laughter above those of several other persons. Of course, I could not resist the temptation of endeavouring to discover what had caused his merriment, and accordingly entered the room. Wreaths of smoke were ascending from the pipes of the party, who usually assembled there to enjoy the fragrant weed, and amid the haze caused by them I could just distinguish Jonathan's nose like a light-house in a fog; his hat was on one side, his waistcoat was unbuttoned, and his feet were on the high fender. In one hand he held his pipe, which he had just withdrawn from his mouth, in the other a newspaper, with the contents of which he was then enlightening his audience.

"And so they call that wonderful," he observed, again renewing his laughter as I entered. "Wonderful, indeed! haugh, haugh, haugh! Why, if I hadn't seen a hundred things a thousand times more wonderful than that, I should be ashamed of myself—that I would; haugh, haugh, haugh! There's nothing that I can make out very wonderful after all compared to the things I have seen. But people who never walk an inch before their noses when they happen to hear of any thing a little out of the way fancy it the most wonderful thing in the world, or else won't believe it at all. Now, for my part, I make it a rule to consider, and to calculate well before I offer an opinion, and I'm not a man very easily imposed upon, let me tell you; and in my deliberate judgment there's nothing in it. It's mere moonshine to what I've seen."

"What is it, Captain Johnson?" I asked, for my curiosity, as I dare say that of the readers, was rather excited by the remarks of the skipper, "What is the wonderful thing you are speaking?"

"Why, the wonderful thing is no wonderful thing at all, youngster," he answered. "But I'll tell you something by-and-by that is wonderful, if you like. This is the trumpery story that astonishes all the good folks who know no better—now listen;" and he read forth, in a loud voice, the following paragraph from the paper he held in his hand:— "Liverpool, April 1, 1828.—The barque *Longbow*, Captain Stretcher, master, has just arrived in this port, with hides and tallow from Valparaiso, belonging to the highly respectable firm of Bam and Boozle, after a remarkably quick passage of two months. Captain Stretcher reports that, after he had rounded the Horn, at three o'clock, p.m., on the 20th of February, in latitude 20 deg. 40 mm. S., and longitude 8 deg. 20 min. W., the weather bright and clear, with a cloudless sky and hot sun, a light breeze from the N. E., and a long ocean swell from the S. E., the ship on the starboard tack heading N. W. by N."

"Then she must have been confoundedly out of her course, and not a few points off the wind!" exclaimed Jonathan; "now for my part I can't for the life of me make out how that was. But let's see how it goes on."

"Jim Taylor, the boatswain's mate, saw something, he couldn't make out what, approaching the ship at a furious rate from before the beam. He immediately sung out to the mate of the watch, Mr. Truelove, who was walking the deck with Captain Stretcher. They immediately brought their glasses to bear upon what had caused Jim Taylor so much astonishment; and if he was astonished, so were they much more, and so were all the ship's company, who tumbled up on deck to see the sight, when they beheld an enormous sea-serpent, with his head and shoulders full twelve if not twenty feet above the surface of the ocean, and as nearly as could be judged by comparing large things with small; it being considered how the main-mast with top-mast and topgallant-mast would look in the water, the master and the mate, Jim Taylor, and the whole ship's company, were of opinion, at least all those who had glasses or had opinions, that it was, at the very least, a quarter of a

mile long—that is to say, the part that was above the water was of
that length—how long the part under the water was, it was impossible to say, became there were no means of calculating, for it
wouldn't even stop to let Jim Taylor take its measure, but considering the considerable length of the part seen, and the power requi-
site to move a body of that size through the water, it is but fair to
suppose that it had a very long tail into the bargain—probably, to
be under the mark, not less than six hundred fathoms. It was going at the rate of about twenty knots an hour, more or less, and
not a fathom of the part seen was employed in impelling it. Some
of the crew were of opinion that it had a tail, others that it must
have feet like a duck or a swan. By whatever means it moved, it
approached the ship very fast, and not a soul on board had the
slightest doubt but that it was the big sea-serpent, of which so much
has been said and so little believed. Its course fortunately carried
it clear of the ship, or the consequences might have been unpleasant, but it passed so near that its features were clearly to be distinguished, and every one remarked the very disagreeable leer it
cast towards them with its left eye. It was evident, however, that it
had other fish to fry, or rather was after some particular game, for
it didn't deviate an inch from its course to the S.E., and probably
wouldn't even if the ship had been in the way. What it was going
after at such a rate it was impossible to say—though there were
various surmises on board—some thought one thing, some thought
another; but the conclusion to which every one arrived was that
they didn't know, and hadn't much chance of learning."

But it is time to describe the monster—that is to say as much of
it as was visible—for its tail not having been seen we are unable to
affirm with any degree of accuracy whether it was forked or barbed,
or, in fact, whether it had a tail at all—the latter is only a surmise,
as all fish have tails, and this animal from having been seen in the
water is supposed to have been a fish (although at the same time a
very odd fish), the conclusion to which all naturalists, and indeed
most scientific men or even unscientific men will arrive is, we conclude, that it could scarcely have been without a tail. If it was not
possessed of a tail, but simply of fins, it is difficult to know how it
could have guided itself, supposing it to have been a serpent; of

which latter supposition no one on board entertained the slightest
doubt, nor will our readers, which as all serpents or snakes, or eels,
have tails, is a further confirmation of it also being possessed of
one. We also do not affirm that it had fins, for no fins were seen,
which would strengthen the supposition that it had a tail. If it had
neither fins nor tail there might have been some truth in Jim
Taylor's idea that it had feet, however much such a supposition
may be against experience or reason, yet because no fins were seen
we cannot conclude that it was not possessed of them, because
neither was a tail seen, yet it may possibly have had a tail, indeed
very probably it had one. Still no one can venture to decide whether
it had or had not a tail, fins, and legs, either all three conjointly or
one only of the three, or whether it had arms, and although the
generality of our readers will incline to the opinion that it had a
tail, it has been suggested by a scientific friend that, partaking of
the nature of the electric eel, it might have been impelled onward
by the mysterious agency of polar attraction.

We will not dwell further at present on the subject of the tail as
it is too long for our pages, but we purpose again to revert to it in
a future number, and we shall now proceed to describe the head of
the monster, and we must confess that were we not fully convinced
of the veracity and high character of Captain Stretcher, and of the
trustworthiness of his officers and crew, including Jim Taylor, all
of whom saw it for at least an hour, during which it never once
dived under the water even to pick up a stray porpoise or shark,
we should ourselves have been somewhat startled by the account
we received. The diameter of the part which is usually denomi-
nated the neck, behind the head, was, as far as an opinion could be
formed, about fourteen or fifteen feet—at all events when it opened
its jaws it would have had little difficulty in griping any small craft
not much exceeding a hundred tons, and very likely in swallowing
her whole. It kept its mouth generally shut, so there were no means
of accurately counting its teeth, but it gave one yawn which was
quite sufficient to convince all who saw it what its powers of mas-
tication would be when tried, for four if not five rows of formidable grinders were seen, and a tongue of proportionable dimensions. Its head was long and precisely such as all serpents are drawn

with, especially in works intended for the edification of youth, while it had a mane which looked like that of a horse or a wild bull, or was not dissimilar to a number of swabs towing overboard, or a quantity of sea-weed washed about a reef of rocks at low tide. Its colour was not black nor green, but rather of a brownish tint, while its neck was something between yellow and white. Altogether it was a customer few would wish to encounter, either on land or sea, and we have to congratulate Captain Stretcher and the officers and ship's company of the good ship the *Longbow*, that it was not as wide awake as they were when it passed them, or the consequences might have been very unpleasant. We leave it to the learned to determine where it had come from, whither it was going, what it was going about and if it had or had not a tail.

"I should think it had a tail, and a much longer tail, too, than most people would suppose," exclaimed Jonathan, laughing loudly; "haugh, haugh, haugh. And this is the story they make so much fuss about; now if the truth was known, I haven't the slightest doubt that what Captain Stretcher saw was far stranger than he ventured to describe, because he knows very well what a set of incredulous, doubting, sceptical people he had to deal with in this world, and he was afraid of not being believed if he told all he saw. I know him well; in fact, there are few people who have sailed on salt-water whom I haven't met somewhere or other, and I know what a sensitive, particular man he is, and he wouldn't for a moment have his word doubted— nor more would I, and that makes me very particular what I say— but as I was observing, I'm going to tell you how I saw the tail of the big sea-serpent, and my adventures relating to it, which happened long before this trumpery thing was so much as thought of."

"Well, out with it, captain," exclaimed several voices.

"Oh do let us hear it," cried the little tailor, "it will be so interesting."

"While you're about it, spin a good'un, messmate," sung out the strange sailor, who, by a wonderful coincidence, had popped into the bar-room of the Jolly Rover that evening, "none of your nine-water-grog yarns, but a rigular stiff'un, strong enough to take away the breath of a port admiral, and make a Yankee look small. That's my notion of a right good yarn."

"I don't care what your notion may be, shipmate," answered Jonathan, puffing and blowing with indignation, which, for certain reasons, he thought it wise not to express in any other way, "but I'll tell you what my notion is, and it is not the first time I've said it, and it won't be the last either, that provided a man sticks to the truth, as I always make a point of doing, he may look Old Nick in the face till he makes him turn white with shame and cut his stick."

"But the yarn—the yarn," repeated several of the company, who valued Jonathan's stories more than his sentiments.

"Well, then, as I was saying," he began, after clearing his throat with numerous loud coughs, taking several long nips from his tumbler, and sending forth some thick clouds of smoke from his mouth, "if I couldn't beat that trumpery newspaper story, I should be ashamed of myself, that I should. I told you how I sailed away from the Coral Island in the *Lady Stiggins*, and left the princess my wife behind me. She wept bitterly at parting from me, and I piped my eye not a little. It is a weakness to which I have given way generally when I have left one of my wives. Poor little Chickchick, it was the last I saw of her, she was eaten by the savages of Blarney Botherum. Well, as I was saying, I sailed away. Now remember what I'm going to say is strictly truth. It is my boast, and I'm proud of it, that though I've done some things I had better not have done, I always have and still do maintain the utmost respect for veracity. I scorn a lie as I do a bad sovereign—none but fools can be taken in by it."

"Come, heave a head, messmate, and tell that to the marines," sung out the strange seaman, who was getting tired of Jonathan's long exordium.

The captain looked at him with one eye, and grunted forth an acknowledgment that he had heard him, and after taking a sip of his liquor continued,—

"After leaving the Coral Island the first land we made was the great Southern Continent, almost chock up with the Pole. We did not stay there long, as we merely went there to get some ice to cool the captains champagne, for he was fond of his bottle, and liked to have his wine in good condition. We killed a prodigious quantity of whales in those seas, so that we were filled up in no time, and with joyful hearts prepared to return home. I very nearly lost my life in whale hunting one day. It is the finest sport there is. Rabbit shooting is nothing to it. 'She spouts, she spouts,' cried the look-out from the mast-head, three, four, five, six, and away we went in the boats after the fish. We were not long in coming up with a cow and a young one beside her. I dug my harpoon into her and away she went like mad, but as the rope ran out a turn caught me round the leg, thanks to the lubber who had coiled it down, and overboard I went. The fish was diving, and so was I in a moment, to my no little discomfort, though I could see every thing clearly around me, and rum looking things I did see, too, let me tell you. I had no fear of being drowned, nor did I lose my presence of mind, but I recollected, that when the whole of the rope had run out my leg would get such a jerk that the chances were, it would be cut clean off, so I whipt out my knife, and stooping down cut the rope below my foot. I had now some prospect of being saved, and I was determined, also, not to lose the fish, and fortunately for me, as she just then began to rise again, I caught hold of the two ends and bent them together again. I had scarcely done this, when up came the fish towards the surface, and I had to strike out pretty hastily to get clear of her. I succeeded, however, and when she shoved her nose above water off she went at a tremendous rate, hauling the boat after her. I, meantime, was working my way upwards, for I had gone down some hundred fathom, and I confess, was sadly in want of a gasp of fresh air. I never heard of any body who went down as deep as I did, and consequently nobody ever saw the strange sights I saw and lived to tell of them. The fact is, though I did not like to say so at first, I went to the very bottom of the ocean into the very middle of a grove of coral, with a broad gravel walk running through it, and what 1 took to be a palace at one end, and benches cut out of granite on either side for the mermaids to rest on when they take their walks on an evening. There were several very pretty-looking girls moving about, with fishes' tails instead of legs, which had a very extraordinary appearance. They certainly glided about much more gracefully than if they had had legs, like swans upon the water without any exertion. I had heard before of

such things, but never believed them. I should have stayed down
longer, since I had got as far, but I confess that I was very hard up
for a mouthful of fresh air. I should have liked, however, to have
asked the mermaids a few questions, but you know if I had opened
my mouth to speak it would have been filled with salt water, and I
should have done nothing but splutter, in fact, my movements were
not a little hastened, also, by seeing a big old fellow with a long
beard and long stick of coral in his hand come out of the palace.
Probably he was the father of the mermaids, and had come out to
see who the stranger was, ogling, as he might suppose, his daughters.

"Well, as I was saying, I struck away to rise upwards, passing as I
rose, whole shoals of strange looking fish. Some had heads with
large goggling eyes and no tails, or bodies for that matter to speak of.
Others, again, had great big fins, and tails like turkey-cocks, with
little twinkling eyes, and snouts like pigs; some had great round
bodies, turn-up noses, and eyes like saucers, while others were for
all the world like the beefeaters one sees in the Tower of London,
of all the colours of the rainbow. Some of them had arms, some
claws, others fins, but none of them had legs, for you see legs are
not of much use in the water, at least tails answer the purpose of
swimming better, which is the reason, I suppose, that mermaids
have tails instead of legs, for the look do ye see, I give the prefer-
ence to a pair of well-shaped legs, and a pair of neat ankles.

"They all came round smelling at me and nudging me, and pok-
ing at me with their snouts, for the fact was they didn't know what
to think of me, but I soon taught them to keep their distance, by
kicking out the left eye of one odd old fish, who was more pertina-
cious than the rest. You must know that I was rising so rapidly all
this time that when I came to the surface I regularly sprung a foot
out of water. It was then I discovered what the whale had been
about. Speaking of that said whale, I have since had reason to believe that she was the pet milch cow of the old gentleman with the
pretty daughters whom I had met at the bottom of the sea.

"Well, most people would have been exceedingly uncomfortable at finding themselves swimming about on the ocean alone,
with the nearest boat two or three miles off, and going still further

away at the rate of ten miles an hour. If I had hailed, the people in her would not have heard me, for they were all so eager in hunting after the whale that nothing would have turned them aside, indeed they would not have supposed that it was me if they had heard me, because they fancied all the time that I was made fast to the harpoon-line without a particle of life left in me. Luckily I had got a water-tight tin tobacco-box in my pocket, so I pulled it out and put a quid in my cheek which much restored me, for as you may suppose, I was not a little tired after my exertions. I then threw myself on my back to consider what I had best do. To swim after the ship was more than even I could do then, whatever I might have done if I had been fresh. The whale-boat, the crew of which had succeeded in killing the whale, was still further off, and I afterwards saw the ship heave too, apparently alongside, to cut her up. The work was quickly performed, and just as the sun set I could distinguish her royals above the horizon. It was the last I saw of the *Lady Stiggins* for a long time.

"When I afterwards met my old messmates they would not believe at first that I was alive, and it was only when I asked them if they had not found the whale-line cut in two and bent together again that I could convince them, and they then confessed, till I explained the matter, that they had never been able to make out how it was done.

"Here was I, then, left perfectly alone on the waters during a long, dark night. It was, without exception, as uncomfortable a night as I ever spent. I luckily, at the beginning of the middle watch, fell in with a small cask, which had been thrown overboard. It served me admirably for a pillow, and, considering the circumstances, I slept as soundly as could be expected. I was awoke just before daybreak by getting a tremendous lick on the head, and looking up to discover what was the matter, I saw a big ship towering above me, and heard a loud voice issuing orders in English. I soon made the people on board hear me, and I was quickly hauled on deck. They at first could not make out whether I was a human being or not, and for a long time would not believe my story, especially the account I gave of my visit to the bottom of the ocean, and of the odd fish I saw on my way back, but truth always, you know, makes its way at last, and so did my statement, knowing which must be a satisfaction to those who have the misfortune to see something wonderful, which is certain to be disbelieved by the dull, incredulous world. I say it is a misfortune to know more and to have seen more than one's neighbours. It is one from which few men have suffered as much as I have.

"The ship, I found, was called the *Diddleus*. She was a fine craft, measuring full six hundred tons. The first mate had a short time before been lost overboard; and the captain, who was a man of discernment, soon discovering my qualifications, asked me to take his place, which I gladly did. The *Diddleus* was a Liverpool whaler, and had just arrived on the ground, nor had she taken a fish. Either through my judgment or good luck, it does not become me to say which, we very soon got a full ship, as you will hear. The captain, poor fellow, was an enormously fat man, and, as he was one day looking into the copper, to see how the blubber was boiling, his foot slipped on the greasy deck, and he fell head foremost in. No one missed him at the moment, and he was stirred up and turned into oil before anybody knew what had happened. The accident was, indeed, only discovered by our finding his buttons and the nails of his shoes at the bottom of the copper. In consequence of this sad catastrophe, I became master of the good ship *Diddleus*.

"This was the first time I had gained a command, which is not surprising, for merit, you know, is often long unperceived, and longer still unrewarded. I immediately set to work to get the ship into what I considered order, and I soon made the people find that they had got some one who knew what's what over them. Among the crew we had a man, Jerry Wilkins by name—a chap who was always boasting of what he had seen and what he had done. To hear him, one would suppose that he'd always been going at the rate of ten knots an hour, and had a patent double-sighted telescope at his eyes all the time; but you may be sure I soon took the shine out of him. He'd never been to the North Pole and seen the bears warming themselves at the aurora borealis, as I had: he had never been over an iceberg in a boat, as I had, or been towed by a bear through the North Seas, or had a pet shark, or married a Patagonian wife, or governed a kingdom, or been capsized in a ship, without any one finding it out, or been in such a gale of wind as I had, or been to the bottom of the sea, not to speak of a thousand other things I hav'n't told you of."

"But what has Jerry Wilkins got to do with the tail of the sea-serpent you were going to tell us about, captain?" exclaimed the little tailor, who was growing impatient, for he knew that his wife wanted him at home to nurse the children, and he was afraid he should not be able to remain to hear the end of it.

"Jerry Wilkins has a great deal to do with it," answered Jonathan. "Because he was the first man on board who saw it. He was at the masthead looking out for whales, when he hailed the deck to say that there was land in sight on our lee-bow. I knew very well enough that there wasn't, but when I went aloft and looked out myself, I was dumfounded, for there I saw a dark, long island, with what I took for a number of trees growing on it like weeping willows. Presently the island began to grow larger and larger, and gradually to extend all round the vessel. As I said, when first seen it was on our lee bow,—it now extended, not only on our lee-beam, but on our weather-quarter, till we were completely embayed. I immediately ordered the lead to be hove, expecting to find that some current or other had been sweeping us into shallow water, but to the surprise of all of us there was no bottom. Just before this extraordinary circumstance had occurred, we had killed a large whale, and two of our boats were engaged in towing it along-side, while the ship was endeavouring to beat up towards it, for it was, I ought to have said, dead to windward of us. I now cracked on all the sail I could set, but the wind was so light that I could do nothing with her. Well, the whale was about a mile off, or so, when suddenly the island seemed to rise close to it, thickly covered, like the other end, with weeping willows, but it was evidently of much greater elevation. While we were watching what would next happen, we saw the boats cast off the towlines, and pull like mad towards us. They had good reason to do so, I can assure you, for, as we were looking, we saw one end rise right out of the water full fifty feet at the least, and quickly approaching the whale, the mighty fish disappeared under it, and the elevation sank to its former level. Directly afterwards one of the crew said he saw a large fire at the end of the island; but when I took my glass, I ascertained beyond a doubt that it was nothing more nor less than an immense eye. To give you an idea of its size, I saw large fish swimming about in its lower lid. I should say, not wishing in any way to exaggerate, that the fish were of the size of full-grown cod. Watching attentively, I perceived that there were lips and a mouth; and before the boats got alongside I had ascertained that it was the head of some mighty monster. The crews of the boats confirmed my belief as soon as they came on board, for they declared that when they were close to what they also believed was land, they saw one end open slowly, and formidable rows of teeth, every one of which was as big as a heavy gun, and a tongue twice the size of the whale they were towing, appeared. As soon as they saw this, they thought it was time to cut and run; nor could I blame them for leaving the whale, for had they not, they would have been swallowed also.

"One may form some slight idea of the size of the monster from its having swallowed a whale whole with half a dozen harpoons in it, and still it did not even blink its eyes. I confess I did not like the position we were in, for having no doubt of its possessing a very considerable appetite, I thought it just possible it might take it into its head to swallow us up also. To our great satisfaction, the monster remained stationary, probably finding the harpoons in the whale's back rather indigestible. I, however, thought it more satisfactory to call a council of war that we might decide as to what was to be done. The result of our deliberation was, that we should by all means avoid the jaws of the monster, and for this purpose keep at the opposite end, or as near his tail as possible.

"The difficulty was to find out where his tail was, for it was so far off it was impossible to make it out. I was not altogether comfortable, I own, for I just considered how very dangerous it would be should the monster, even without any vicious intention, take it into its head to be frisky.

"Our position was as follows:—About a mile on our weather quarter was the animal's left eye, which kept winking at us most ominously—his body extended at about two miles distance along our lee beam, winding round again ahead of us till it was lost in the distance, but as far as we could see it was decidedly a solid body, so that we naturally concluded that it must have a very long tail indeed. What I at first took for rows of willow-trees, were, I found, the tufts of hair which formed the mane on its back, and the hill which appeared rising on a sudden, was its upper jaw when it opened to gulp down the whale.

"You may be sure we were not in a little hurry to get away from the neighbourhood of the animal, but after standing on for half-an-hour or so, we appeared to be no nearer the end of its tail than we were when we were a mile off its head, not only that, but from its bearings by the compass there could be little doubt that it was curling its tail inwards. Now I dare say you have all heard of the dreadful passage between Sicily and the main coast of Italy,—on one side are some frightful rocks over which the sea roars like thunder. They are called the rocks of Scylla, and if a ship gets near them she is dashed to pieces in no time. On the other side is an awful whirlpool, called the whirlpool of Charybdis, and such tremendous power has it that it will draw ships towards it from miles off, and suck them under the water like straws—so that let me tell you it's very sharp work navigating that channel,—so at least an old super-cargo of a merchantman declares whose log I once somewhere read. If I recollect rightly his name was Æneas, and the master's name was Palynurus; but my impression is that there are a good many lies entered in the log, which is a pity, as his accounts are not alto-gether unamusing.

"Well, we were just in the same state as the old chap I'm speak-ing about, when he was sailing between Scylla and Charybdis. If we stood too long on one tack we ran a risk of sailing down the serpent's mouth, if on the other, of getting an ugly slap with his tail—that is to say, supposing he had got a tail to slap us with, of which we were not at all then sure. As I swept the horizon with my glass, on every side the monstrous body appeared except dead to windward, where there was a clear opening, and towards that point we were doing our best to beat up. However, even that small space between the Scylla of his tail and the Charybdis of his mouth ap-peared to be narrowing. I watched it with not a little anxiety, so did the mate, and so did Jerry Wilkins. Well, will you believe it, Jerry was the first to see his tail. 'I see it, I see it,' sung out Jerry;

'for all the world like the Falls of Niagara dancing a hornpipe, and, by Jingo, if he hasn't finished by clapping it into his mouth.' It's a fact, by George. It was a fashion the it had, I suppose, when he wanted to bask in the sun, and there he lay exactly like a big cod-fish in a fishmonger's stall.

"We were thus in a pretty fix, for we couldn't tell how long he might take to sleep; judging by his size, a year or so would be merely a morning's nap, and we should all be starved before we could get out. We were in a complete lake, do ye see, and the *Diddleus* was like a child's toy floating in the middle of it. It made us feel very small, I can assure you. I, however, determined to try and get out, and considered that the best chance would be to heave-to near his head, so that should he let his tail slip from between his teeth in his sleep, we might have time to beat round his jaws. But when we got up near his head the crew were so frightened by the look of his jaws even when closed, and the vast cavern of his eye, that I saw if I did not bear away again they would be in a complete mutiny, and would probably, in their terror, jump overboard.

"We had an old fellow on board, Joe Hobson by name, who was considered an oracle by the crew, and he added to their fears by telling them that he had often heard of these serpents before, though he didn't go so far as to say that he had seen one, but he swore that he knew that they often slept for a dozen years or so on a stretch, so that we should have a good chance of being starved before we could get out again. I knew better than that, however. In the first place I calculated we should be able to catch fish enough to support ourselves if we could not get out, and then I had a plan by which I felt pretty certain that we should be able to make our escape. Well after we kept away we ran down about a mile distant from the serpent's neck, and so along its body till we came again to what might be called the weather shore, when we had to best up along its tail towards its head. This survey, which occupied us three days, with a strong breeze, convinced us that we were completely shut in. I now determined to put into execution a plan I had con-ceived at the first, which was to cut a channel for the ship right through the serpent's back. It would be like a mere scratch on the skin to him, and the chances were, I thought, that it would not wake him. I took, however, a precaution which few would have thought of. The surgeon had a quantity of laudanum on board, so I made him start it into a cask, and then jumping into a boat with a few brave fellows as volunteers we pulled right up to the serpent's mouth; I then let the cask float overboard with line made fast to the bung, and to my great satisfaction it drifted alongside his tail and disappeared down his throat, so I pulled the line and the bung came out—the laudanum, of course, running down his throat.

"Now I do not mean to say that under ordinary circumstances that quantity could have any effect on so large a beast, for there was only a hogshead of it; but as our doctor observed, he placed some hopes of the opiate working from his being probably totally unaccustomed to the dose. I had reason to think that it immediately took effect, for, before an hour had elapsed, he snored so loud that one could scarcely hear oneself speak a mile of him. I therefore returned on board, and we made sail to the northward, for about the middle part of the serpent's body, when I judged there would be more fat and less sense of feeling. We reached the spot in rather more than a day, and heaving the ship to, I pulled off in one of the boats to land for the first time on the serpent's back. It was nervous work, I assure you, at first, and we had no little difficulty in climbing up his sides, which were uncommonly slippery, but we succeeded at last, and forthwith set to work with knives and saws to cut into his back. At first we made little progress through the barnacles which covered his skin to the depth of some feet; but when we got fairly through the skin we found, to our great joy, that there was as fine blubber as we ever cut out of a fat whale. We therefore made up our fires, and as we cut the flesh we sent it on board to be boiled. In ten days, so hard did we work, we had cut a channel deep enough to admit the ship, and had besides got a full cargo of the finest oil that had ever been seen. The outer skins we kept to the last, and now cutting them away we made all sail and ran smack on to the very centre of the serpent's back. We had not got quite over, however, when our keel, I suppose tickling him, somewhat awoke him, and suddenly letting his tail slip out of his mouth, he made off in a northerly direction with us on his back. Away he went on the very course we wished to make at the rate of at least thirty knots an hour. There was no wind at the time, and every thing was clewed up, or our masts would have been carried to a certainty over the side. On he went in this way for three days, when the opium, we supposed, again making him drowsy, he put his tail into his mouth, as a little child does its thumb, and went off to sleep again. The movement made us glide off into the sea and outside of him. There was, fortunately a strong southerly wind, and you may be sure we lost no time in making sail and doing our best to get clear of him. The people set up a shout of joy, as they beheld him, like a large island, floating far astern of the ship, but I told them at the time not to make too sure that they were entirely clear of him, and, as it turned out, I was right.

"For two days we sailed on without any thing unusual happening, and our men had begun to recover their usual spirits, when just as it had gone two bells in the middle watch, the first mate called me up in great alarm, to say that there were two glaring lights right astern of us and coming up fast. For the first moment or so, I thought they were lighthouses, and that the ship had been put about without my knowing it; but on looking at the compass I saw she was on her right course. Besides this, there was a strong hot wind, and a strong smell of sulphur, which convinced me of the dreadful truth. We were pursued by the monster of the ocean—the big sea-serpent. I saw there was nothing to be done but to run for it, so we made all sail the ship could carry, studden sails alow and aloft, and the *Diddleus* was a good one to go, let me tell you, and away we bowled with the beast after us. We guessed that he had been aroused from finding his back smart a little from the scratch we made in it. We thus ran on till daybreak, keeping well ahead of the beast, though we did not drop him astern as we could have wished.

"By George, it was very awful, let me tell you, to see his big rolling eyes, to feel his hot breath, to smell a smell of sulphur, and to hear his loud roaring; for he was in a tremendous rage at the liberty we had taken, and would have swallowed the ship and crew, and his own fat into the bargain, as easily as he had swallowed the whale. If it was a terrible sight to see him at night, it was still worse in the day-time. With our glasses we could see his immense jaws wide open, with a dozen rows of teeth, with his large eyes projecting on either side, and his head lifted sixty feet at least above the surface of the water. As you may by this time have discovered, I was not a man to be daunted, so I loaded our stern chasers, and kept blazing away at the monster to make him turn aside, but to little effect. Most of the shot fell short, though the guns were my own patent, and made to carry ten miles, and the balls which reached him he swallowed as if they were so many pills. Though it was very fearful, I own, it was a fine sight to see him coming along so steady and stately, with the water foaming and curling under his bows and flying high up into the air in showers of spray as he cut through it. It was neck or nothing with us, so we kept blazing away as fast as we could load, every moment, I own, expecting that he would make a spring and grab us; and thus we went on until we reached the Line. Just then, either a shot hit him in some delicate part, or else for some reason or other he did not like to cross the Line, probably because he did not know the navigation of the other side, for we saw his head go right under the water, and soon after a huge pillar appeared up in the air, and down suddenly it came with such a splash into the water, that it sent the sea flying over us, and as near as possible pooped us. We had a quick run to Liverpool, where the oil sold at a very high price, and I got great credit for what I had done, and from that day to this, I'll answer for it, no one has ever seen the tail of the big Sea-Serpent?"*

[* I beg that the gallant officer who, not long ago, was fortunate enough (or shall I say, unfortunate enough, should the ignorant not believe him), to see a living specimen of the icthyosorus long known to naturalists, or as some suppose of a gigantic seal, while he gives me credit for not disbelieving his statements, will excuse me for being unable to resist the temptation of giving Jonathan Johnson's version of a similar story.]

Jim Newman's Yarn: Or, A Sight of the Sea Serpent
John C. Hutcheson

"Was you ever up the Niger, sir?"

"Why, of course not, Jim! you know that I've never been on the African station, or any other for that matter. But why do you ask the question?"

"Don't know 'xactly, sir. P'raps that blessed sea-fog reminds me of it, somehow or other—though there's little likeness, as far as that goes, between the west coast and Portsmouth, is there, sir?"

"I don't suppose there is," I said; "but what puts the Niger, of all places in the world, in your head at the present moment?"

"Ah, that'd tell a tale, sir," he answered, cocking his left eye in a knowing manner, and giving the quid in his mouth a turn. "Ah, that'd tell a tale, sir!"

Jim Newman, an old man-of-war's man—now retired from the navy, and who eked out his pension by letting boats for hire to summer visitors—was leaning against an old coal barge that formed his "office," drawn up high and dry on the beach, midway between Southsea Castle and Portsmouth Harbour, and gazing out steadily across the channel of the Solent, to the Isle of Wight beyond. He and I were old friends of long standing, and I was never so happy as when I could persuade him—albeit it did not need much persuasion—to open the storehouse of his memory, and spin a yarn about his old experiences afloat in the whilom wooden walls of England, when crack frigates were the rage instead of screw steamers with armour-plates. We had been talking of all sorts of service gossip—the war, the weather, what not—when he suddenly asked me the question about the great African river that has given poor Sambo "a local habitation and a name."

24

Although the gushing tears of April had hardly washed away the traces of the wild March winds, the weather had suddenly become almost tropical in its heat. There was not the slightest breath of air stirring, and the sea lay lazily asleep, only throbbing now and then with a faint spasmodic motion, which barely stirred the shingle on the shore, much less plashed on the beach; while a thick, heavy white mist was steadily creeping up from the sea, shutting out, first the island, and then the roadstead at Spithead from view, and overlapping the whole landscape in thick woolly folds, moist yet warm. Jim had said that the sea-fog, coming as it did, was a sign of heat, and that we should have a regular old-fashioned hot summer, unlike those of recent years.

"Ah, sir," he repeated, "I could tell a tale about that deadly Niger river, and the Gaboon, and the whole treacherous coast, if I liked, from Lagos down to the Congo—ay, I could! It was that 'ere sea-fog that put Afriker into my head, Master Charles; I know that blessed white mist, a-rising up like a curtain, well, I do! The 'white man's shroud,' the negroes used to call it—and many a poor beggar it has sarved to shroud, too, in that killing climate, confound it!"

"Well, Jim, tell us about the Niger to begin with," said I, so as to bring him up to the scratch without delay; for, when Jim once got on the moralising or sentimental tack, he generally ended by getting angry with everybody and everything around him; and when he got angry, there was an end to his stories for that day at least.

"All right, your honour," said the old fellow, calming down at once into his usual serenity again, and giving his quid another shift as he braced himself well up against the old barge, on the half-deck of which I was seated with my legs dangling down— "All right, your honour! If it's a yarn you're after, why I had best weigh anchor at once and make an offing, or else we shan't be able to see a handspike afore us!"

"Heave ahead, Jim!" said I impatiently; "you are as long as a three-decker in getting under way!"

With this encouragement, he cleared his throat with his customary hoarse, choking sort of cough, like an old raven, and commenced his narrative without any further demur.

"It's more'n twenty years now since I left the service—ay, thirty years would be more like it; and almost my very last cruise was on the West African station. I had four years of it, and I recollect it well; for, before I left the blessed, murdering coast, with its poisonous lagoons covered with thick green slime, and sickly smells, and burning sands, I seed a sight there that I shall never forget as long as I live, and which would make me recklect Afrikey well enough if nothing else would!"

"That's right, Jim, fire away!" said I, settling myself comfortably on my seat to enjoy the yarn. "What was it that you saw?"

"Steady! Let her go easy, your honour; I'm a-coming to that soon enough. It was in the old Amphitrite I was at the time—she's broken-up and burnt for firewood long ago, poor old thing!—and we was a-lying in the Bight of Benin, alongside of a slaver which we had captured the day before off Whydah. She was a Brazilian schooner with nearly five hundred wretched creatures on board, so closely packed that you could not find space enough to put your foot fairly on her deck in any place. The slaves had only been a night on board her; but the stench was so awful, from so many unfortunate negroes being squeezed so tightly together like herrings in a barrel, and under a hot sun too, that we were longing to send the schooner away to Sierra Leone, and get rid of the horrid smell, which was worse than the swamps ashore! Well, I was in the morning watch after we had towed in the slaver to the Bights, having carried away her foremast with a round shot in making her bring to, and was just going forward to turn in as the next watch came on deck, when who should hail me but my mate, Gil Saul, coming in from the bowsprit, where he had been on the look-out—it was him as was my pardner here when I first started as a shore hand in letting out boats, but he lost the number of his mess long ago like our old ship the *Amphitrite*.

"As he came up to me his face was as white as your shirt, and he was trembling all over as if he was going to have a fit of the fever and ague.

"'Lor', Gil Saul,' sez I, 'what's come over you, mate? are you going on the sick list, or what?'

"'Hush, Jim,' sez he, quite terror-stricken. 'Don't speak like that; I've seen a ghost, and I knows I shall be a dead man afore the day's out!'

"With that I burst into a larf.

"'Bless your eyes, Gil,' sez I, 'tell that to the marines, my bo'! you can't get over me on that tack. You won't find any respectable ghosts leaving dear old England for the sake of this dirty, sweltering west coast, which no Christian would come to from choice, let alone a ghost!'

"'But, Jim,' he sez, leaning his hand on my arm to detain me as I was going down below, 'this wasn't a h'English ghost as I sees just now. It was the most outlandish foreign reptile you ever see. A long, big, black snake like a crocodile, only twice the length of the old corvette; with a head like a bird, and eyes as big and fiery as our side-lights. It was a terrible creature, Jim, and its eyes flamed out like lightning, and it snorted like a horse as it swam by the ship. I've had a warning, old shipmate, and I'll be a dead man before to-morrow morning, I know!'

"The poor chap shook with fright as he spoke, though he was as brave a man as we had aboard; so I knew that he had been drinking and was in a state of delirium tremendibus, or else he was sickening for the African fever, which those who once have never forget. I therefore tried to pacify him and explain away his fancy.

"'That's a good un, Gil Saul,' I sez. 'Don't you let none of the other hands hear what you've told me, that you've seen the great sea sarpint, or you'll never get the end of it.'

"Gil got angry at this, forgetting his fright in his passion at my doubting his word like.

"'But it was the sea sarpint, I tells you, or its own brother if it wasn't. Didn't I see it with my own eyes, and I was as wide awake as you are, and not caulking?'

"'The sea sarpint!' I repeated scornfully, laughing again in a way that made Gil wild. 'Who ever heard tell of such a thing, except in a Yankee yarn?'

"'And why shouldn't there be a big snake in the sea the same as there are big snakes on land like the Bow constrectar, as is read of in books of history, Jim Newman? Some folks are so cocksure, that they won't believe nothing but what they sees for themselves. I wonder who at home, now, would credit that there are some monkeys here in Afrikey that are bigger than a man and walk upright;

and you yourself, Jim, have told me that when you were in Australy you seed rabbits that were more than ten foot high when they stood on their hind-legs, and that could jump a hundred yards at one leap.'

"'So I have, Gil Saul,' sez I, a bit nettled at what he said, and the way he said it, 'and what I says I stick to. I have seen at Port Philip kangaroos, which are just like big rabbits with upright ears, as big as I've said; and I've seen 'em, too, jump more than twice the distance any horse could.'

"'And why then,' sez he, argumentifying on to me like a shot, 'and why then shouldn't there be such a thing as the sea sarpint?'

"This flummuxed me a bit, for I couldn't find an answer handy, so I axed him another question to get out of my quandary.

"'But why, Gil, did you say you had seed a ghost, when it was a sarpint?'

"This time he was bothered for a moment.

"'Because, Jim,' sez he, after a while, 'it appeared so awful to me when I saw it coming out of the white mist with its glaring red eyes and terrible beak. It was a ghost I feels, if it wasn't the sea sarpint; and whether or no it bodes no good to the man wot sees it, I know. I'm a doomed man.'

"I couldn't shake him from that belief, though I thought the whole thing was fancy on his part, and I turned into my hammock soon after we got below, without a thought more about the matter—it didn't stop my caulk, I know. But, ah! that was only in the early morning. Before the day was done, as Gil had said, that conversation was recalled to me in a terrible way—ah, a terrible way!" the old sailor repeated impressively, taking off his tarpaulin hat, and wiping his forehead with his handkerchief, as if the recollection of the past awed him even now. He looked so serious that I could not laugh, inclined as I was to ridicule any such story as that of the fabled sea serpent, which one looks for periodically as a transatlantic myth to crop up in dull seasons in the columns of American newspapers.

"And did you see it too?" I asked; "and Gil Saul's prophecy turns out true?"

"You shall hear," he answered gravely; "I'm not spinning a yarn, as you call it, Master Charles; I'm telling you the truth."

"Go on, Jim," said I, to reassure him. "I'm listening, all attention."

"At eight bells that day, another man-of-war come in, bringing an empty slaver she had taken before she had shipped her cargo. In this vessel we were able to separate some of the poor wretches packed on board our Brazilian schooner, and so send them comfortably on to Sierra Leone, which was what we were waiting to do, as I've told you already; and now being free to go cruising again, we hove up anchor and made our way down the coast to watch for another slaver which we had heard news of by the man-o'-war that came in to relieve us.

"We had a spanking breeze all day, for a wonder, as it generally fails at noon; but towards the evening, when we had made some eighty miles or so from the Bights, it fell suddenly dead calm, as if the wind had been shut off slap without warning. It was bright before, but the moment the calm came a thick white mist rose around the vessel, just like that which came just now from seaward, and has hidden the island and Spithead from view; you see how it's reminded me now of the west coast and the Niger river, Master Charles, don't you?"

"Ay," said I, "Jim, I see what you were driving at."

"Those thick mists," he continued, "always rise on the shores of Afrikey in the early mornings—just as there was a thick one when Gil had seen his ghost, as he said—and they comes up again when the sun sets; but you never sees 'em when the sun's a-shining bright as it was that arternoon. It was the rummiest weather I ever see. By and by, the mist lifted a bit, and then there were clumps of fog dancing about on the surface of the sea, which was oily and calm, just like patches of trees on a lawn. Sometimes these fog curtains would come down and settle round the ship, so that you couldn't see to the t'other side of the deck for a minute, and they brought a fearful bad smell with them, the very smell of the lagoons ashore with a dash of the negroes aboard the slave schooner, only a thousand times worse, and we miles and miles away from the land. It was most unaccountable, and most uncomfortable. I couldn't make it out at all.

"Jest as I was a-puzzling my brains as to the reason of these fog banks and the stench they brought with them, Gil Saul came on deck too, and sheered up alongside of me as I was looking out over the side. His face was a worse sight than the morning; for, instead of his looking white, the colour of his skin was grey and ashy, like the face of a corpse. It alarmed me so that I cried out at once—

"'Go down below, Gil! Go down and report yourself to the doctor!'

"'No,' sez he, 'it ain't the doctor an will cure me, Jim; I feel it coming over me again as I felt this morning. I shall see that sarpint or ghost again, I feel sure.'

"What with his face and his words, and the bad smell from the fog, I confess I began to feel queer myself—not frightened exactly—but I'd have much rather have been on Southsea common in the broad daylight than where I was at that moment, I can tell you."

"Did you see anything, Jim?" I asked the old sailor at this juncture.

"I seed nothing, Master Charles, as yet but I felt something, I can't tell what or how to explain; it was a sort of all-overish feeling, as if something was a-walking over my grave, as folks say, summat uncanny, I do assure you.

"The captain and the first lieutenant was on the quarter-deck, the latter with his telescope to his eye a-gazing at something forward apparently, that he was trying to discern amongst the clumps of fog. I was nigh them, and being to leeward could hear what they said.

"The first lieutenant, I hears him, turns to the captain over his shoulder speaking like, and sez he—

"'Captain Manter, I can't make it out exactly, but it's most curious;' and then turning to me, he sez, 'Newman, go down to my steward and ax him to give you my night-glass.'

"I went down and fetched the glass and handed it to him, he giving me t'other one to hold; and he claps the night-glass to his eye.

"'By Jove, Captain Manter,' sez he presently, 'I was right, it is the greatest marine monster I ever saw!'

"'Pooh!' says the captain, taking the glass from him and looking himself. 'It's only a waterspout, they come sometimes along with this appearance of the sea!' But presently I heard him mutter something under his voice to the lieutenant, and then he said aloud,

'It is best to be prepared;' and a moment after that he gave an order, and the boatswain piped up and we beat to quarters. It was very strange that, wasn't it? And so every man on board thought.

"A very faint breeze was springing up again, and I was on the weather side of the ship, which was towards the land from which the wind came, when suddenly Gil Saul, who was in the same battery and captain of my crew, grips my arm tight. 'It's coming! it's coming!' he said right in my ear, and then the same horrible foul smell wafted right over the ship again, and a noise was heard just as if a herd of wild horses were sucking up water together.

"At this moment the fog lifted for a bit, and we could see clear for about a couple of miles to windward, where the captain and first lieutenant and all the hands had their eyes fixed as if expecting something.

"By George! you could have knocked me down with a feather, I tell you! I never saw such a sight in my life, and may I never see such another again! There, with his head well out of the water, shaped like a big bird, and higher in the air than the main truck of the ship, was a gigantic reptile like a sarpint, only bigger than you ever dreamt of. He was wriggling through the water at a fearful rate, and going nearly the same course as ourselves, with a wake behind him bigger than a line-of-battle ship with paddle-wheels, and his length—judging by what I saw of him—was about half a mile at least, not mentioning what part of his body was below the water; while he must have been broader across than the largest sperm whale, for he showed good five feet of freeboard.

"The captain and first lieutenant were flabbergasted, I could see; but Captain Manter was as brave an officer as ever stepped, and he pulled himself together in a minute, as the fog, which had only lifted for a minute, came down again shutting out everything from view so that we could not see a yard from the side. 'Don't be alarmed, my men,' he sings out in his cheery voice, so that every hand could hear him, 'it's only a waterspout that is magnified by the fog; and as it gets nearer we'll give it the starboard broadside to clear it up and burst it.'

"'Ay! ay!' sez the men with a cheer, while the smell grew more awful and the snorting gushing sound we had heard before so loud that it was quite deafening, just immediately after the captain spoke, when it had stopped awhile.

"As for poor Gil, he had never lost the grip of my arm since we sighted the reptile, although he had the lanyard of his gun in his right hand all the same.

"'Fire!' sez the captain; and, in a moment, the whole starboard broadside was fired off, point blank across the water, in a line with the deck, as Captain Manter had ordered us to depress the guns, the old Amphitrite rocking to her keel with the explosion.

"Well, sir, as true as I'm standing here a-talking to you, at the very instant the guns belched out their fire and smoke, and the cannon-balls with which they were loaded, there was a most treemenjus roar and a dash of water alongside the ship, and the waves came over us as if we were on a lee shore; and then, as the men stood appalled at the things going on around them, which was what no mortal ever seed before, Gil clasped my arm more tightly, loosening his right hand from the lanyard of the gun which he had now fired, and shrieked out, 'There! there!'

"Master Charles, it were awful! A long heavy body seemed to be reared up high in the air right athwart the vessel, and plunged far away in the sea to leeward; and, as the body passed over our heads, I looked up with Gil, and saw the fearful fiery eyes of the biggest snake that ever crawled on the earth, though this was flying in the air, and round his hideous head, that had a long beak like a bird, was a curious fringe or frill all yellowish green, just like what a lizard puffs out under his throat when in a rage. I could see no more, for the thing was over us and gone a mile or more to leeward in a wink of the eye, the fog drifting after it and hiding it from sight. Besides which, I was occupied with Gil, who had sank down on the deck in a dead swoon.

"Whatever it was, the thing carried away our main topmast with the yards, and everything clean from the caps as if it had been shot away, and there wasn't a trace of them floating in the sea around, as we could see.

"'A close thing that!' said the captain, after the shock was over, speaking to the lieutenant, although all hands could hear him, for it was as still as possible now. 'A close thing, Mr. Freemantle. I've known a waterspout do even more damage than this; so let us be thankful!'

"And then all hands were piped to clear the wreck, and make the ship snug; for we had some bad weather afterwards, and had to put into Sierra Leone to refit.

"Gil was in a swoon for a long time after; and then he took the fever bad, and only recovered by the skin of his teeth; but he never forgot what he had seen, nor I either, nor any of the hands, though we never talked about it. We knew we had seen something unearthly; even the captain and Lieutenant Freemantle, though they put down the damage to a waterspout for fear of alarming the men, knew differently, as we did. We had seen the great sea sarpint, if anybody had, every man-jack of us aboard! It was a warning, too, as poor Gil Saul had declared; for, strange to say, except himself and me, not a soul as was on board the Amphitrite when the reptile overhauled us, lived to see Old England again. The bones of all the others were left to bleach on the burning sands of the east coast of Africa, which has killed ten thousand more of our own countrymen with its deadly climate than we have saved slaves from slavery!"

"But, Jim," said I, as the old sailor paused at the end of his yarn. "Do you think it was really the sea serpent? Might it not have been a waterspout, or a bit of floating wreck, which you saw in the fog?"

Jim Newman got grumpy at once, at the bare insinuation of such a thing.

"Waterspouts and bits of wreck," said he sarcastically, "generally travel at the rate of twenty miles an hour when there is no wind to move them along, and a dead calm, don't they? Waterspouts and bits of wreck smell like polecats when you're a hundred miles from land, don't they? Waterspouts and bits of wreck roar like a million wild bulls, and snort and swish as they go through the water like a thousand express trains going through a tunnel, don't they?"

I was silenced by Jim's sarcasm, and humbly begged his pardon for doubting the veracity of his eyesight.

"Besides, Master Charles," he urged, when he had once more been restored to his usual equanimity; "besides, you must remember that nearly in the same parts, and about the same time—in the beginning of the month of August, 1848—the sea sarpint, as people who have never seen it are so fond of joking of, was seen by the captain and crew of HMS *Daedalus* and the event was put down in the ship's log, and reported officially to the Admiralty. I suppose you won't go for to doubt the statement which was made by a captain in the navy, a gentleman, and a man of honour, and supported by the evidence of the lieutenant of the watch, the master, a midshipman, the quartermaster, boatswain's mate, and the man at the wheel—the rest of the ship's company being below at the time?"

"No, Jim," said I, "that's straight enough."

"We was in latitude 5 degrees 30 minutes north, and longitude about 3 degrees east," continued the old sailor, "when we saw it on the 1st of August, 1848, and they in latitude 24 degrees 44 minutes south, and longitude 9 degrees 22 minutes east, when they saw it on the 6th of the same month; so the curious reptile—for reptile he was—must have put the steam on when he left us!"

"Stirred up, probably, by your starboard broadside?" said I.

"Jest so," went on Jim. "But, he steered just in the direction to meet them when he went off from us, keeping a southward and eastward course; and I daresay, if he liked, he could have made a hundred knots an hour as easy as we could sail ten on a bowline with a stiff breeze."

"And so you really have seen the great sea serpent?" said I, when the old man-of-war's man had shifted his quid once more, thus implying that he had finished.

"Not a doubt of it, sir; and by the same token he was as long as from here to the Spit Buoy, and as broad as one of them circular forts out there."

"That's a very good yarn, Jim," said I; "but do you mean to say that you saw the monster with your own eyes, Jim, as well as all the rest of you?"

"I saw him, I tell you, Master Charles, as plain as I see you now; and as true as I am standing by your side the sarpint jumped right over the *Amphitrite* when Gil Saul and I was a-looking up, and carried away our maintopmast and everything belonging to it!"

"Well, it must have been wonderful, Jim," said I.

"Ay, ay, sir," said he, "but you'd ha' thought it a precious sight more wonderful if you had chanced to see it, like me!"

I may add, that, shortly afterwards, I really took the trouble to overhaul a pile of the local papers to see whether Jim's account of the report made by the captain of the *Daedalus* to the Lords of the Admiralty was substantially true; and, strange to say, I discovered amongst the numbers of the *Hampshire Telegraph* for the year 1848, the following copy of a letter forwarded by Captain McQuhae to the admiral in command at Devonport dockyard at the date mentioned:—

"Her Majesty's Ship *Daedalus*

"Hamoaze, October 11th, 1848.

"Sir,—In reply to your letter of this day's date, requiring information as to the truth of a statement published in the *Globe* newspaper, of a sea serpent of extraordinary dimensions having been seen from her Majesty's ship *Daedalus*, under my command, on her passage from the East Indies, I have the honour to acquaint you, for the information of my Lords Commissioners of the Admiralty, that at five o'clock, PM, on the 6th of August last, in latitude 24 degrees 44 minutes south, and longitude 9 degrees 22 minutes east, the weather dark and cloudy, wind fresh from the North West, with a long ocean swell from the South West, the ship on the port tack heading North East by North, something very unusual was seen by Mr. Sartons, midshipman, rapidly approaching the ship from before the beam. The circumstance was immediately reported by him to the officer of the watch, Lieutenant Edgar Drummond, with whom and Mr. William Barrett, the master, I was at the time walking the quarter-deck. The ship's company were at supper.

"On our attention being called to the object it was discovered to be an enormous serpent, with head and shoulders kept about four feet constantly above the surface of the sea, and as nearly as we could approximate by comparing it with the length of what our main-topsail-yard would show in the water, there was at the very least sixty feet of the animal à fleur d'eau, no portion of which was, to our perception, used in propelling it through the water, either by vertical or horizontal undulation. It passed rapidly, but so close under our lee quarter that had it been a man of my acquaintance I should have easily recognised his features with the naked eye; and it did not, either in approaching the ship or after it had passed our wake, deviate in the slightest degree from its course to the South West, which it held on at the pace of from twelve to fifteen miles per hour, apparently on some determined purpose.

"The diameter of the serpent was about fifteen or sixteen inches behind the head, which was, without any doubt, that of a snake, and never, during the twenty minutes that it continued in sight of our glasses once below the surface of the water; its colour a dark brown, with yellowish white about the throat. It had no fins, but something like the mane of a horse, or rather a bunch of sea-weed, washed about its back. It was seen by the quartermaster, the boatswain's mate, and the man at the wheel, in addition to myself and officers above-mentioned.

"I am having a drawing of the serpent made from a sketch taken immediately after it was seen, which I hope to have ready for transmission to my Lords Commissioners of the Admiralty by to-morrow's posts.

"I have, etcetera,

"Peter McQuhae, Captain.

"To Admiral Sir WH Gage, GCH, Devonport."

Consequently, having this testimony, which was amply verified by the other witnesses at the time, I see no reason to doubt the truth of Jim Newman's yarn about THE GREAT SEA SERPENT!

A Real Sea-Serpent
Anonymous

"What's the matter with ye?" shouted a tall, raw-boned fisher-man, seizing a still taller and thinner companion in furs who had staggered in a foggy condition into a Seguin grocery and, in open defiance of the law, called for Medford and molasses. "What d'ye mean," continued the speaker, giving the bewildered individual another shake that caused a rain of navy plug, sinkers, trawl-hooks, and mackerel-plows, "by rushin' intew a law-abidin', quiet section like as ef ye was all stove up?"

"I am stove, Bill," replied the other, in a high key, bringing him-self together with a jerk, and, swallowing a compound that was taken from a stone jar labeled "Arnold's Writing Fluid," he said, "Ef I hain't seen that 'ere blessed sea-sarpint. Wall, no matter; jest a drap more o' that writin' fluid, Amos, and I'll give ye the account as I hev it. I hope this 'ere fluid's been through the custom-house. I ain't meanin' no offense tow yaou, but ef that stuff hain't got a flavor of Gillis's tradin' schooner's bilge,—her that's in the Havana trade, —then I'm losin' my smell. I'll tell ye how I kem to make the remark. I took a voyage in her afore she was hogged. We took in Havana and brought a load of oranges tew New York and several barrels of Spanish cider under the floorin' tew Boothbay, and afore this 'ere cider was put in the market the old man thought he'd water his stock, and draw'd on a water compartment he'd hed rigged, and somehow the bilge leaked in, the old man never found it aout, and for six months arter that queer-tastin' stuff was a-goin' the raounds. Some sold it as forty-year brandy, some as Spanish rum, and the different names that old bilge gev that stuff was a caution; but ef yaou say this ain't the same, all right.

37

"Sea-sarpint? Wall, I was a-goin' tew say when Amos broke in on me, ye know Newagen Ledge? Wall, I struck over there tew see old Faber,—curious old chap a-livin' there and oncet an old mate o' mine. When I seen him I ran along daown shore tew sell some lobsters that was caught daown in Massachusetts waters. I hauled my boat up afore a house, and was a-walkin' up when a feller kem a-runnin' oaut, hair a-flyin', and pintin' oaut tew sea, yells, 'What's that?' I turned and looked, and then we both started down the rock lickity-split, a-watchin' the cussedest-lookin' cuss y' ever see. What was it? Wall, that's jest what I'm arter myself. I never see the like afore. First off I thought it was a school of puffers [*porpoises*] a-comin', but the humps like kept in sight all the time, and we see it belonged tew one and the same critter, and I took it tew be a long snake-like critter. Haow long? Wall, I should say I caounted twenty humps, and they was about three foot apart; that would make it abaout sixty foot. It was amovin' along the rocks abaout as fast as we could run, and me and this 'ere stranger was a-goin' it head over the rocks and so excited he didn't know what his name was when I asked him. 'That's the sea-sarpint!' he yelled when the critter turned aout tew sea, and you could see the form and wake just as plain as I see yaou. 'I'll give yaou five thousand dollars ef yaou'll catch it,' says he. 'I wouldn't tackle it for ten,' says I, and nary I wouldn't. Then he let on tew cuss and swear dretful; said we were lookin' at a fortune and couldn't lay our hands on it. 'Why,' says he, 'ef we could catch the sea-sarpint and show it, we could make a million dollars.' He must hev been a little wrong in his head."

"What did it look like?" asked the aforesaid Amos.

"Wall," was the reply, "it looked tew me like a big snake, black as a whale, and kind o' wriggled along. No, I didn't see no head, but I was so took back and upset that I didn't know where I was, and the head might hev been stickin' up, for all I know. Wall, the first thing I knowed the critter was aout o' sight and I lit aout for hum, and when I was abaout two miles off Seguin, here, I heard a big slosh astarn, and, begorry, there was that selfsame critter a-bowlin' along right astarn.

"Scart? I felt my hair a-risin' and was that took I couldn't move. On it kem, I a-layin' still, and passed clost tew the boat. I see its body a-shinin' and the humps, but no head, no trawl, no shark, no porpoises, no whale nor black fish; it was suthin' what 'ain't been seen raound these parts afore, I'll swan. I was that scart that I couldn't steer the boat, and up she kem in the wind, and I a-layin' there, a-snortin', and I reckon the flap of the sail must hev scart the cuss, for it went daown, and I pulled for the shore for all I was worth, and here I am. Jest a little more o' that writin' fluid, Amos— so."

"Wall," said one of the attentive listeners, "I've heard my old man tell abaout a cur'us critter that us'ter cruise araound here abaout fifty years ago, scarin' folks to death; but I allus thought they was a-foolin' or hed seen a dream or sech."

"There wa'n't no dreamin' abaout this," said the demoralized sight-seer. "It ain't likely I'd git scart over a dream twice in the same day,—broad daylight, too. Why, If I'd hed the fixin's I could 'a' put an iron intew the critter jest as easy as rollin' off a log. I reckon yaou hev seen sech things, Captain Perkins?" said the speaker, addressing himself to an old mariner who had been a close listener and conscientious drinker during the recital.

"Wall, naow ye put a leadin' question," replied the captain; "I'm 'bliged to say I hev; but it wasn't eggzactly the kind o' sarpint yaou mean. You've all hearn tell of my brother Tom, what accumulated such a fortune in the tavern business? Jest so. Wall, when he started in he had a little tavern on the beach,—held abaout twenty, I calkilate,—and every summer he got addin' on and addin' on till he got quite a place, big enough to hold all he could git in. Then he went tew work devisin' haow tew make folks come with a rush. He hed boat-racin' and tub-matches and sech tew bring crowds. One day I kem in. I was a-fishin' for the haouse, and he sed to me, tippin' me a wink, 'Bill, you've seen that sea-sarpint what's been raound here, haven't ye?' 'I believe I hev,' says I. 'Wall,' says he, 'if fifty dollars is any inducement for that old cuss to hang off shore here for a few days next week I know who'll provide the cash;' and dew yaou know," said the captain, stirring up the fluid with the stem of his pipe, "that the sea-sarpint did appear jest at that time, and the crowds that kem daown to see it abaout eat and drinked up the hull place. The hull place was black with folks, swearin' mad 'cause they couldn't git no boat tew go aout and harpoon the critter; for there it was abeout a mile off shore, abaout a hundred foot long, a-rollin' abaout,—see it as plain as nothin' in the glass.

"Haow was it done? Wall, I know it won't git aout here, bein' all neighbors, so I don't mind lettin' on and givin' the rec-i-pe. Tew make a sea-sarpint yaou want about a hundred barrel-hoops and abaout two hundred yards o' tarred muslin. Hev yer muslin sewed intew a funnel abaout sixty foot long and two foot across, and brace it aout with the hoops. Pint off the ends, rig a mane on the head of kelp, put abaout twenty sinkers in it at reg'lar interwals,—that makes the humps; then hire up all the boats abaout so't none o' these 'ere investigaters kin git at it, and anchor it off shore in a long line, and ye'll draw the hull country around; that's jest what old Captain Bob did.

"But," added the captain, "I ain't sayin' but what there's some sech livin' critter in the sea. I've hearn folks tell on 'em, and I knowed 'em to be professors of religion. But what catches me is, if there is sech a critter, why don't they ever git washed in?"

"Haow is it ye never see a puffer washed in?" asked Amos.

"Whoever faound a dead bird or critter in the woods?" asked some one else. "'Cause they git eat up afore they're found; that's the reason."

A Matter of Fact

Rudyard Kipling

And if ye doubt the tale I tell,
    Steer through the South Pacific swell;
Go where the branching coral hives
    Unending strife of endless lives,
Where, leagued about the 'wildered boat,
    The rainbow jellies fill and float;
And, lilting where the laver lingers,
    The starfish trips on all her fingers;
Where, 'neath his myriad spines ashock,
    The sea-egg ripples down the rock;
An orange wonder dimly guessed,
    From darkness where the cuttles rest,
Moored o'er the darker deeps that hide
    The blind white Sea-snake and his bride;
Who, drowsing, nose the long-lost ships
    Let down through darkness to their lips.
—*The Palms.*

Once a priest always a priest; once a Mason always a Mason;
but once a journalist always and for ever a journalist.

There were three of us, all newspaper men, the only passengers on a little tramp-steamer that ran where her owners told her
to go. She had once been in the Bilbao iron ore business, had been
lent to the Spanish Government for service at Manilla; and was
ending her days in the Cape Town coolie-trade, with occasional
trips to Madagascar and even as far as England. We found her going to Southampton in ballast, and shipped in her because the fares

41

were nominal. There was Keller, of an American paper, on his way back to the States from palace executions in Madagascar; there was a burly half Dutchman, called Zuyland, who owned and edited a paper up country near Johannesberg; and there was myself, who had solemnly put away all journalism, vowing to forget that I had ever known the difference between an imprint and a stereo advertisement.

Three minutes after Keller spoke to me, as the *Rathmines* cleared Cape Town, I had forgotten the aloofness I desired to feign, and was in heated discussion on the immorality of expanding telegrams beyond a certain fixed point. Then Zuyland came out of his stateroom, and we were all at home instantly, because we were men of the same profession needing no introduction. We annexed the boat formally, broke open the passengers' bath-room door—on the Manilla lines the Dons do not wash—cleaned out the orange-peel and cigar-ends at the bottom of the bath, hired a Lascar to shave us throughout the voyage, and then asked each other's names.

Three ordinary men would have quarrelled through sheer boredom before they reached Southampton. We, by virtue of our craft, were anything but ordinary men. A large percentage of the tales of the world, the thirty-nine that cannot be told to ladies and the one that can, are common property coming of a common stock. We told them all, as a matter of form, with all their local and specific variants which are surprising. Then came, in the intervals of steady card-play, more personal histories of adventure and things seen and reported; panics among white folk, when the blind terror ran from man to man on the Brooklyn Bridge, and the people crushed each other to death they knew not why; fires, and faces that opened and shut their mouths horribly at red-hot window-frames; wrecks in frost and snow, reported from the sleet-sheathed rescue tug at the risk of frost-bite; long rides after diamond thieves; skirmishes on the veldt and in municipal committees with the Boers; glimpses of lazy, tangled Cape politics and the mule-rule in the Transvaal; card-tales, horse-tales, woman-tales by the score and the half hundred; till the first mate, who had seen more than us all put together, but lacked words to clothe his tales with, sat open-mouthed far into the dawn.

When the tales were done we picked up cards till a curious hand or a chance remark made one or other of us say, "That reminds me of a man who—or a business which—" and the anecdotes would continue while the *Rathmines* kicked her way northward through the warm water.

In the morning of one specially warm night we three were sitting immediately in front of the wheel-house where an old Swedish boatswain whom we called "Frithiof the Dane" was at the wheel pretending that he could not hear our stories. Once or twice Frithiof spun the spokes curiously, and Keller lifted his head from a long chair to ask, "What is it? Can't you get any pull on her?"

"There is a feel in the water," said Frithiof, "that I cannot understand. I think that we run downhills or somethings. She steers bad this morning."

Nobody seems to know the laws that govern the pulse of the big waters. Sometimes even a landsman can tell that the solid ocean is a-tilt, and that the ship is working herself up a long unseen slope; and sometimes the captain says, when neither full steam nor fair wind justify the length of a day's run, that the ship is sagging downhill; but how these ups and downs come about has not yet been settled authoritatively.

"No, it is a following sea," said Frithiof, "and with a following sea you shall not get good steerage way."

The sea was as smooth as a duck-pond, except for a regular oily swell. As I looked over the side to see where it might be following us from, the sun rose in a perfectly clear sky and struck the water with its light so sharply that it seemed as though the sea should clang like a burnished gong. The wake of the screw and the little white streak cut by the log-line hanging over the stern were the only marks on the water as far as eye could reach.

Keller rolled out of his chair and went aft to get a pine-apple from the ripening stock that were hung inside the after awning.

"Frithiof, the log-line has got tired of swimming. It's coming home," he drawled.

"What?" said Frithiof, his voice jumping several octaves.

"Coming home," Keller repeated, leaning over the stern. I ran to his side and saw the log-line, which till then had been drawn tense over the stern railing, slacken loop, and come up off the port quarter. Frithiof called up the speaking-tube to the bridge, and the bridge answered, "Yes, nine knots." Then Frithiof spoke again, and the answer was, "What do you want of the skipper?" and Frithiof bellowed, "Call him up."

By this time Zuyland, Keller, and myself had caught something of Frithiof's excitement, for any emotion on shipboard is most contagious. The captain ran out of his cabin, spoke to Frithiof, looked at the log-line, jumped on the bridge, and in a minute we felt the steamer swing round as Frithiof turned her.

"Going back to Cape Town?" said Keller.

Frithiof did not answer, but tore away at the wheel. Then he beckoned us three to help, and we held the wheel down till the *Rathmines* answered it, and we found ourselves looking into the white of our own wake, with the still oily sea tearing past our bows, though we were not going more than half steam ahead.

The captain stretched out his arm from the bridge and shouted. A minute later I would have given a great deal to have shouted too, for one-half of the sea seemed to shoulder itself above the other half, and came on in the shape of a hill. There was neither crest, comb, nor curl-over to it; nothing but black water with little waves chasing each other about the flanks. I saw it stream past and on a level with the *Rathmines'* bow-plates before the steamer made up her mind to rise, and I argued that this would be the last of all earthly voyages for me. Then we rose for ever and ever and ever, till I heard Keller saying in my ear, "The bowels of the deep, good Lord!" and the *Rathmines* stood poised, her screw racing and drumming on the slope of a hollow that stretched downwards for a good half-mile.

We went down that hollow, nose under for the most part, and the air smelt wet and muddy, like that of an emptied aquarium. There was a second hill to climb; I saw that much: but the water came aboard and carried me aft till it jammed me against the smoking-room door, and before I could catch breath or clear my eyes again we were rolling to and fro in torn water, with the scuppers pouring like eaves in a thunderstorm.

"There were three waves," said Keller; "and the stoke-hold's flooded."

The firemen were on deck waiting, apparently, to be drowned. The engineer came and dragged them below, and the crew, gasping, began to work the clumsy Board of Trade pump. That showed nothing serious, and when I understood that the *Rathmines* was really on the water, and not beneath it, I asked what had happened.

"The captain says it was a blow-up under the sea—a volcano," said Keller.

"It hasn't warmed anything," I said. I was feeling bitterly cold, and cold was almost unknown in those waters. I went below to change my clothes, and when I came up everything was wiped out by clinging white fog.

"Are there going to be any more surprises?" said Keller to the captain.

"I don't know. Be thankful you're alive, gentlemen. That's a tidal wave thrown up by a volcano. Probably the bottom of the sea has been lifted a few feet somewhere or other. I can't quite understand this cold spell. Our sea-thermometer says the surface water is 44°, and it should be 68° at least."

"It's abominable," said Keller, shivering. "But hadn't you better attend to the fog-horn? It seems to me that I heard something."

"Heard! Good heavens!" said the captain from the bridge, "I should think you did." He pulled the string of our fog-horn, which was a weak one. It sputtered and choked, because the stoke-hold was full of water and the fires were half-drowned, and at last gave out a moan. It was answered from the fog by one of the most appalling steam-sirens I have ever heard. Keller turned as white as I did, for the fog, the cold fog, was upon us, and any man may be forgiven for fearing the death he cannot see.

"Give her steam there!" said the captain to the engine-room. "Steam for the whistle, if we have to go dead slow."

We bellowed again, and the damp dripped off the awnings to the deck as we listened for the reply. It seemed to be astern this time, but much nearer than before.

"The *Pembroke Castle*, by gum!" said Keller, and then, viciously, "Well, thank God, we shall sink her too."

"It's a side-wheel steamer," I whispered. "Can't you hear the paddles?"

This time we whistled and roared till the steam gave out, and the answer nearly deafened us. There was a sound of frantic threshing in the water, apparently about fifty yards away, and something shot past in the whiteness that looked as though it were gray and red.

"The *Pembroke Castle* bottom up," said Keller, who, being a journalist, always sought for explanations. "That's the colours of a Castle liner. We're in for a big thing."

"The sea is bewitched," said Frithiof from the wheel-house. "There are two steamers."

Another siren sounded on our bow, and the little steamer rolled in the wash of something that had passed unseen.

"We're evidently in the middle of a fleet," said Keller quietly. "If one doesn't run us down, the other will. Phew! What in creation is that?"

I sniffed for there was a poisonous rank smell in the cold air—a smell that I had smelt before.

"If I was on land I should say that it was an alligator. It smells like musk," I answered.

"Not ten thousand alligators could make that smell," said Zuyland; "I have smelt them."

"Bewitched! Bewitched!" said Frithiof. "The sea she is turned upside down, and we are walking along the bottom."

Again the *Rathmines* rolled in the wash of some unseen ship, and a silver-gray wave broke over the bow, leaving on the deck a sheet of sediment—the gray broth that has its place in the fathomless deeps of the sea. A sprinkling of the wave fell on my face, and it was so cold that it stung as boiling water stings. The dead and most untouched deep water of the sea had been heaved to the top by the submarine volcano—the chill, still water that kills all life and smells of desolation and emptiness. We did not need either the blinding fog or that indescribable smell of musk to make us unhappy—we were shivering with cold and wretchedness where we stood.

"The hot air on the cold water makes this fog," said the captain. "It ought to clear in a little time."

"Whistle, oh! whistle, and let's get out of it," said Keller.

The captain whistled again, and far and far astern the invisible twin steam-sirens answered us. Their blasting shriek grew louder, till at last it seemed to tear out of the fog just above our quarter, and I cowered while the *Rathmines* plunged bows-under on a double swell that crossed.

"No more," said Frithiof, "it is not good any more. Let us get away, in the name of God."

"Now if a torpedo-boat with a City of Paris siren went mad and broke her moorings and hired a friend to help her, it's just conceivable that we might be carried as we are now. Otherwise this thing is—"

The last words died on Keller's lips, his eyes began to start from his head, and his jaw fell. Some six or seven feet above the port bulwarks, framed in fog, and as utterly unsupported as the full moon, hung a FACE. It was not human, and it certainly was not animal, for it did not belong to this earth as known to man. The mouth was open, revealing a ridiculously tiny tongue—as absurd as the tongue of an elephant; there were tense wrinkles of white skin at the angles of the drawn lips; white feelers like those of a barbel sprang from the lower jaw, and there was no sign of teeth within the mouth. But the horror of the face lay in the eyes, for those were sightless—white, in sockets as white as scraped bone, and blind. Yet for all this the face, wrinkled as the mask of a lion is drawn in Assyrian sculpture, was alive with rage and terror. One long white feeler touched our bulwarks. Then the face disappeared with the swiftness of a blind worm popping into its burrow, and the next thing that I remember is my own voice in my own ears, saying gravely to the mainmast, "But the air-bladder ought to have been forced out of its mouth, you know."

Keller came up to me, ashy white. He put his hand into his pocket, took a cigar, bit it, dropped it, thrust his shaking thumb into his mouth and mumbled, "The giant gooseberry and the raining frogs! Gimme a light—gimme a light! I say, gimme a light." A little bead of blood dropped from his thumbnail.

I respected the motive, though the manifestation was absurd. "Stop, you'll bite your thumb off," I said, and Keller laughed brokenly as he picked up his cigar. Only Zuyland, leaning over the port bulwarks, seemed self-possessed. He declared later that he was very sick.

"We've seen it," he said, turning round. "That is it."

"What?" said Keller, chewing the unlighted cigar.

As he spoke the fog was blown into shreds, and we saw the sea, gray with mud, rolling on every side of us and empty of all life. Then in one spot it bubbled and became like the pot of ointment that the Bible speaks of. From that wide-ringed trouble a THING came up—a gray and red Thing with a neck—a Thing that bellowed and writhed in pain. Frithiof drew in his breath and held it till the red letters of the ship's name, woven across his jersey, straggled and opened out as though they had been type badly set. Then he said with a little cluck in his throat, "Ah, me! It is blind. *Hur illa!* That thing is blind," and a murmur of pity went through us all, for we could see that the thing on the water was blind and in pain. Something had gashed and cut the great sides cruelly and the blood was spurting out. The gray ooze of the undermost sea lay in the monstrous wrinkles of the back and poured away in sluices. The blind white head hung back and battered the wounds, and the body in its torment rose clear of the red and gray waves till we saw a pair of quivering shoulders streaked with weed and rough with shells, but as white in the clear spaces as the hairless, nameless, blind, toothless head. Afterwards came a dot on the horizon and the sound of a shrill scream, and it was as though a shuttle shot all across the sea in one breath, and a second head and neck tore through the levels, driving a whispering wall of water to right and left. The two Things met—the one untouched and the other in its death throe—male and female, we said, the female coming to the male. She circled round him bellowing, and laid her neck across the curve of his great turtle-back, and he disappeared under water for an instant, but flung up again, grunting in agony while the blood ran. Once the entire head and neck shot clear of the water and stiffened, and I heard Keller saying, as though he was watching a street accident, "Give him air. For God's sake give him air!" Then the death struggle began, with crampings and twistings and jerkings of the white bulk to and fro, till our little steamer rolled again, and each gray wave coated her plates with the gray slime. The sun was clear, there was no wind, and we watched, the whole crew, stokers and all, in wonder and pity, but chiefly pity. The Thing was so helpless,

and, save for his mate, so alone. No human eye should have beheld him; it was monstrous and indecent to exhibit him there in
trade waters between atlas degrees of latitude. He had been spewed
up, mangled and dying from his rest on the sea-floor, where he
might have lived till the Judgment Day, and we saw the tides of his
life go from him as an angry tide goes out across rocks in the teeth
of a landward gale. The mate lay rocking on the water a little distance off, bellowing continually, and the smell of musk came down
upon the ship making us cough.

At last the battle for life ended, in a batter of coloured seas. We
saw the writhing neck fall like a flail, the carcase turn sideways,
showing the glint of a white belly and the inset of a gigantic hind-
leg or flapper. Then all sank, and sea boiled over it, while the mate
swam round and round, darting her blind head in every direction.
Though we might have feared that she would attack the steamer,
no power on earth could have drawn any one of us from our places
that hour. We watched, holding our breaths. The mate paused in
her search; we could hear the wash beating along her sides; reared
her neck as high as she could reach, blind and lonely in all that
loneliness of the sea, and sent one desperate bellow booming across
the swells, as an oyster shell skips across a pond. Then she made
off to the westward, the sun shining on the white head and the
wake behind it, till nothing was left to see but a little pin point of
silver on the horizon. We stood on our course again, and the
Rathmines, coated with the sea-sediment, from bow to stern,
looked like a ship made gray with terror.

"We must pool our notes," was the first coherent remark from
Keller. "We're three trained journalists—we hold absolutely the biggest scoop on record. Start fair."

I objected to this. Nothing is gained by collaboration in journalism when all deal with the same facts, so we went to work each
according to his own lights. Keller triple-headed his account, talked
about our "gallant captain," and wound up with an allusion to
American enterprise in that it was a citizen of Dayton, Ohio, that
had seen the sea-serpent. This sort of thing would have discred-
ited the Creation, much more a mere sea tale, but as a specimen of

the picture-writing of a half-civilised people it was very interesting. Zuyland took a heavy column and a half, giving approximate lengths and breadths and the whole list of the crew whom he had sworn on oath to testify to his facts. There was nothing fantastic or flamboyant in Zuyland. I wrote three-quarters of a leaded bourgeois column, roughly speaking, and refrained from putting any journalese into it for reasons that had begun to appear to me.

Keller was insolent with joy. He was going to cable from Southampton to the *New York World*, mail his account to America on the same day, paralyse London with his three columns of loosely knitted headlines, and generally efface the earth. "You'll see how I work a big scoop when I get it," he said.

"Is this your first visit to England?" I asked.

"Yes," said he. "You don't seem to appreciate the beauty of our scoop. It's pyramidal—the death of the sea-serpent! Good heavens alive man, it's the biggest thing ever vouchsafed to a paper!"

"Curious to think that it will never appear in any paper, isn't it?" I said.

Zuyland was near me, and he nodded quickly.

"What do you mean?" said Keller. "If you're enough of a Britisher to throw this thing away, I sha'n't. I thought you were a newspaper man."

"I am. That's why I know. Don't be an ass, Keller. Remember, I'm seven hundred years your senior, and what your grandchildren may learn five hundred years hence, I learned from my grandfathers about five hundred years ago. You won't do it, because you can't."

This conversation was held in open sea, where everything seems possible, some hundred miles from Southampton. We passed the Needles Light at dawn, and the lifting day showed the stucco villas on the green and the awful orderliness of England—line upon line, wall upon wall, solid stone dock and monolithic pier. We waited an hour in the Customs shed, and there was ample time for the effect to soak in.

"Now, Keller, you face the music. The *Havel* goes out to-day. Mail by her, and I'll take you to the telegraph office," I said.

I heard Keller gasp as the influence of the land closed about him, cowing him as they say Newmarket Heath cows a young horse unused to open country.

"I want to retouch my stuff. Suppose we wait till we get to London?" he said.

Zuyland, by the way, had torn up his account and thrown it overboard that morning early. His reasons were my reasons.

In the train Keller began to revise his copy, and every time that he looked at the trim little fields, the red villas, and the embankments of the line, the blue pencil plunged remorselessly through the slips. He appeared to have dredged the dictionary for adjectives. I could think of none that he had not used. Yet he was a perfectly sound poker player and never showed more cards than were sufficient to take the pool.

"Aren't you going to leave him a single bellow?" I asked sympathetically. "Remember, everything goes in the States, from a trouser-button to a double eagle."

"That's just the curse of it," said Keller below his breath. "We've played 'em for suckers so often that when it comes to the golden truth—I'd like to try this on a London paper. You have first call there, though."

"Not in the least. I'm not touching the thing in the papers. I shall be happy to leave 'em all to you; but surely you'll cable it home?"

"No. Not if I can make the scoop here and see the Britishers sit up."

"You won't do it with three column of slushy headline, believe me. They don't sit up as quickly as some people."

"I'm beginning to think that too. Does nothing make any difference in this country?" he said, looking out of the window. "How old is that farmhouse?"

"New. It can't be more than two hundred years at the most."

"Um. Fields, too?"

"That hedge there must have been clipped for about eighty years."

"Labour cheap—eh?"

"Pretty much. Well, I suppose you'd like to try the *Times*, wouldn't you?"

"No," said Keller, looking at Winchester Cathedral. "Might as well try to electrify a hay-rick. And to think that the *World* would take three columns and ask for more—with illustrations too! It's sickening."

"But the *Times* might," I began.

Keller flung his paper across the carriage, and it opened in its austere majesty of solid type—opened with the crackle of an encyclopædia.

"Might! You might work your way through the bow-plates of a cruiser. Look at that first page!"

"It strikes you that way, does it?" I said. "Then I'd recommend you to try a light and frivolous journal."

"With a thing like this of mine—of ours? It's sacred history!"

I showed him a paper which I conceived would be after his own heart, in that it was modelled on American lines.

"That's homey," he said, "but it's not the real thing. Now, I should like one of these fat old *Times'* columns. Probably there'd be a bishop in the office, though."

When we reached London Keller disappeared in the direction of the *Strand*. What his experiences may have been I cannot tell, but it seems that he invaded the office of an evening paper at 11.45 a.m. (I told him English editors were most idle at that hour), and mentioned my name as that of a witness to the truth of his story.

"I was nearly fired out," he said furiously at lunch. "As soon as I mentioned you, the old man said that I was to tell you that they didn't want any more of your practical jokes, and that you knew the hours to call if you had anything to sell, and that they'd see you condemned before they helped to puff one of your infernal yarns in advance. Say, what record do you hold for truth in this city, anyway?"

"A beauty. You ran up against it, that's all. Why don't you leave the English papers alone and cable to New York? Everything goes over there."

"Can't you see that's just why?" he repeated.

"I saw it a long time ago. You don't intend to cable, then?"

"Yes, I do," he answered, in the over-emphatic voice of one who does not know his own mind.

That afternoon I walked him abroad and about, over the streets that run between the pavements like channels of grooved and tongued lava, over the bridges that are made of enduring stone, through subways floored and sided with yard-thick concrete, between houses that are never rebuilt, and by river steps hewn to the eye from the living rock. A black fog chased us into Westminster Abbey, and, standing there in the darkness, I could hear the wings of the dead centuries circling round the head of Litchfield A. Keller, journalist, of Dayton, Ohio, U. S. A., whose mission it was to make the Britishers sit up.

He stumbled gasping into the thick gloom, and the roar of the traffic came to his bewildered ears.

"Let's go to the telegraph office and cable," I said. "Can't you hear the New York World crying for news of the great sea-serpent, blind, white, and smelling of musk, stricken to death by a submarine volcano, assisted by his loving wife to die in midocean, as visualised by an independent American citizen, a breezy, newsy, brainy newspaper man of Dayton, Ohio? 'Rah for the Buckeye State. Step lively! Both gates! Szz! Boom—ah!'" Keller was a Princeton man, and he seemed to need encouragement.

"You've got me on your own ground," said he, tugging at his overcoat pocket. He pulled out his copy, with the cable forms—for he had written out his telegram—and put them all into my hand, groaning, "I pass. If I hadn't come to your cursed country—if I'd sent it off at Southampton—if I ever get you west of the Alleghanies, if—"

"Never mind, Keller. It isn't your fault. It's the fault of your country. If you had been seven hundred years older you'd have done what I'm going to do."

"What are you going to do?"

"Tell it as a lie."

"Fiction?" This with the full-blooded disgust of a journalist for the illegitimate branch of the profession.

"You can call it that if you like. I shall call it a lie."

And a lie it has become, for Truth is a naked lady, and if by accident she is drawn up from the bottom of the sea, it behoves a gentleman either to give her a print petticoat or to turn his face to the wall, and vow that he did not see.

THE RIVAL BEAUTIES
W. W. Jacobs

"If you hadn't asked me," said the night watchman, "I should never have told you; but, seeing as you've put the question point blank, I will tell you my experience of it. You're the first person I've ever opened my lips to upon the subject, for it was so eggstraordinary that all our chaps swore as they'd keep it to theirselves for fear of being disbelieved and jeered at.

"It happened in '84, on board the steamer George Washington, bound from Liverpool to New York. The first eight days passed without anything unusual happening, but on the ninth I was standing aft with the first mate, hauling in the log, when we hears a yell from aloft, an' a chap what we called Stuttering Sam come down as if he was possessed, and rushed up to the mate with his eyes nearly starting out of his 'ed.

"'There's the s-s-s-s-s-s-sis-sis-sip!' ses he.

"'The what?' ses the mate.

"'The s-s-sea-sea-sssssip!'

"'Look here, my lad,' ses the mate, taking out a pocket-hankerchief an' wiping his face, 'you just tarn your 'ed away till you get your breath. It's like opening a bottle o' soda water to stand talking to you. Now, what is it?'

"'It's the sssssssis-sea-sea-sea-sarpint!' ses Sam, with a bust.

"'Rather a long un by your account of it,' ses the mate, with a grin.

"'What's the matter?' ses the skipper, who just came up.

"'This man has seen the sea-sarpint, sir, that's all,' ses the mate.

"'Y-y-yes,' said Sam, with a sort o' sob.

"'Well, there ain't much doing just now,' ses the skipper, 'so you'd better get a slice o' bread and feed it.'

54

"The mate bust out larfing, an' I could see by the way the skipper smiled he was rather tickled at it himself.

"The skipper an' the mate was still larfing very hearty when we heard a dreadful 'owl from the bridge, an' one o' the chaps suddenly leaves the wheel, jumps on to the deck, and bolts below as though he was mad. T'other one follows 'm a'most d'reckly, and the second mate caught hold o' the wheel as he left it, and called out something we couldn't catch to the skipper.

"'What the d—'s the matter?' yells the skipper.

"The mate pointed to starboard, but as 'is 'and was shaking so that one minute it was pointing to the sky an' the next to the bottom o' the sea, it wasn't much of a guide to us. Even when he got it steady we couldn't see anything, till all of a sudden, about two miles off, something like a telegraph pole stuck up out of the water for a few seconds, and then ducked down again and made straight for the ship.

"Sam was the fust to speak, and, without wasting time stuttering or stammering, he said he'd go down and see about that bit o' bread, an' he went afore the skipper or the mate could stop 'im.

"In less than 'arf a minute there was only the three officers an' me on deck. The second mate was holding the wheel, the skipper was holding his breath, and the first mate was holding me. It was one o' the most exciting times I ever had.

"'Better fire the gun at it,' ses the skipper, in a trembling voice, looking at the little brass cannon we had for signalling.

"'Better not give him any cause for offence,' ses the mate, shaking his head.

"'I wonder whether it eats men,' ses the skipper. 'Perhaps it'll come for some of us.'

"'There ain't many on deck for it to choose from,' ses the mate, looking at 'im significant like.

"'That's true,' ses the skipper, very thoughtful; 'I'll go an' send all hands on deck. As captain, it's my duty not to leave the ship till the *last*, if I can anyways help it.'

"How he got them on deck has always been a wonder to me, but he did it. He was a brutal sort o' a man at the best o' times, an' he carried on so much that I s'pose they thought even the sarpint couldn't be worse. Anyway, up they came, an' we all stood in a crowd watching the sarpint as it came closer and closer.

"We reckoned it to be about a hundred yards long, an' it was about the most awful-looking creetur you could ever imagine. If you took all the ugliest things in the earth and mixed 'em up—gorillas an' the like—you'd only make a hangel compared to what that was. It just hung off our quarter, keeping up with us, and every now and then it would open its mouth and let us see about four yards down its throat.

"'It seems peaceable,' whispers the fust mate, arter awhile.

"'P'raps it ain't hungry,' ses the skipper. 'We'd better not let it get peckish. Try it with a loaf o' bread.'

"The cook went below and fetched up half-a-dozen, an' one o' the chaps, plucking up courage, slung it over the side, an' afore you could say 'Jack Robinson' the sarpint had woffled it up an' was looking for more. It stuck its head up and came close to the side just like the swans in Victoria Park, an' it kept that game up until it had 'ad ten loaves an' a hunk o' pork.

"'I'm afraid we're encouraging it,' ses the skipper, looking at it as it swam alongside with an eye as big as a saucer cocked on the ship.

"'P'raps it'll go away soon if we don't take no more notice of it,' ses the mate. 'Just pretend it isn't here.'

"Well, we did pretend as well as we could; but everybody hugged the port side o' the ship, and was ready to bolt down below at the shortest notice; and at last, when the beast got craning its neck up over the side as though it was looking for something, we gave it some more grub. We thought if we didn't give it he might take it, and take it off the wrong shelf, so to speak. But, as the mate said, it was encouraging it, and long arter it was dark we could hear it snorting and splashing behind us, until at last it 'ad such an effect on us the mate sent one o' the chaps down to rouse the skipper.

"'I don't think it'll do no 'arm,' ses the skipper, peering over the side, and speaking as though he knew all about sea-sarpints and their ways.

"'S'pose it puts its 'ead over the side and takes one o' the men,' ses the mate.

"'Let me know at once,' ses the skipper firmly; an' he went below agin and left us.

"Well, I was jolly glad when eight bells struck, an' I went below; an' if ever I hoped anything I hoped that when I got up that ugly brute would have gone, but, instead o' that, when I went on deck it was playing alongside like a kitten a'most, an' one o' the chaps told me as the skipper had been feeding it agin.

"'It's a wonderful animal,' ses the skipper, 'an' there's none of you now but has seen the sea-sarpint; but I forbid any man here to say a word about it when we get ashore.'

"'Why not, sir?' ses the second mate.

"'Becos you wouldn't be believed,' said the skipper sternly. 'You might all go ashore and kiss the Book an' make affidavits an' not a soul 'ud believe you. The comic papers 'ud make fun of it, and the respectable papers 'ud say it was seaweed or gulls.'

"Why not take it to New York with us?' ses the fust mate suddenly.

"'What?' ses the skipper.

"'Feed it every day,' ses the mate, getting excited, 'and bait a couple of shark hooks and keep 'em ready, together with some wire rope. Git 'im to foller us as far as he will, and then hook him. We might git him in alive and show him at a sovereign a head. Anyway, we can take in his carcase if we manage it properly.'

"'By Jove! if we only could,' ses the skipper, getting excited too.

"'We can try,' ses the mate. 'Why, we could have noosed it this mornin' if we had liked; and if it breaks the lines we must blow its head to pieces with the gun.'

"It seemed a most eggstraordinary thing to try and catch it that way; but the beast was so tame, and stuck so close to us, that it wasn't quite so ridikilous as it seemed at fust.

"Arter a couple o' days nobody minded the animal a bit, for it was about the most nervous thing of its size you ever saw. It hadn't got the soul of a mouse; and one day when the second mate, just for a lark, took the line of the foghorn in his hand and tooted it a bit, it flung up its 'ead in a scared sort o' way, and, after backing a bit, turned clean round and bolted.

"I thought the skipper 'ud have gone mad. He chucked over loaves o' bread, bits o' beef and pork, an' scores o' biskits, and by-

and-bye, when the brute plucked up heart an' came arter us again, he fairly beamed with joy. Then he gave orders that nobody was to touch the horn for any reason whatever, not even if there was a fog, or chance of collision, or anything of the kind; an' he also gave orders that the bells wasn't to be struck, but that the bosen was just to shove 'is 'ead in the fo'c's'le and call 'em out instead.

"Arter three days had passed, and the thing was still follering us, everybody made certain of taking it to New York, an' I b'leeve if it hadn't been for Joe Cooper the question about the sea-sarpint would ha' been settled long ago. He was a most eggstraordinary ugly chap was Joe. He had a perfic cartoon of a face, an' he was so delikit-minded and sensitive about it that if a chap only stopped in the street and whistled as he passed him, or pointed him out to a friend, he didn't like it. He told me once when I was symperthizing with him, that the only time a woman ever spoke civilly to him was one night down Poplar way in a fog, an' he was so 'appy about it that they both walked into the canal afore he knew where they was.

"On the fourth morning, when we was only about three days from Sandy Hook, the skipper got out o' bed wrong side, an' when he went on deck he was ready to snap at anybody, an' as luck would have it, as he walked a bit forrard, he sees Joe a-sticking his phiz over the side looking at the sarpint.

"'What the d— are you doing?' shouts the skipper, 'What do you mean by it?'

"'Mean by what, sir?' asks Joe.

"'Putting your ugly face over the side o' the ship an' frightening my sea-sarpint!' bellows the skipper, 'You know how easy it's skeered.'

"'Frightening the sea-sarpint?' ses Joe, trembling all over, an' turning very white.

"'If I see that face o' yours over the side agin, my lad,' ses the skipper very fierce, 'I'll give it a black eye. Now cut!'

"Joe cut, an' the skipper, having worked off some of his ill-temper, went aft again and began to chat with the mate quite pleasant like. I was down below at the time, an' didn't know anything about it for hours arter, and then I heard it from one o' the firemen. He comes up to me very mysterious like, an' ses, 'Bill,' he ses, 'you're a pal o' Joe's; come down here an' see what you can make of 'im.'

"Not knowing what he meant, I follered 'im below to the engine-room, an' there was Joe sitting on a bucket staring wildly in front of 'im, and two or three of 'em standing round looking at 'im with their 'eads on one side.

"'He's been like that for three hours,' ses the second engineer in a whisper, 'dazed like.'

"As he spoke Joe gave a little shudder; 'Frighten the sea-sarpint!' ses he, 'O Lord!'

"'It's turned his brain,' ses one o' the firemen, 'he keeps saying nothing but that.'

"'If we could only make 'im cry,' ses the second engineer, who had a brother what was a medical student, 'it might save his reason. But how to do it, that's the question.'

"'Speak kind to 'im, sir,' ses the fireman. 'I'll have a try if you don't mind.' He cleared his throat first, an' then he walks over to Joe and puts his hand on his shoulder an' ses very soft an' pitiful like:

"'Don't take on, Joe, don't take on, there's many a ugly mug 'ides a good 'art.'

"Afore he could think o' anything else to say, Joe ups with his fist an' gives 'im one in the ribs as nearly broke 'em. Then he turns away 'is 'ead an' shivers again, an' the old dazed look come back.

"'Joe,' I ses, shaking him, 'Joe!'

"'Frightened the sea-sarpint!' whispers Joe, staring.

"'Joe,' I ses, 'Joe. You know me, I'm your pal, Bill.'

"'Ay, ay,' ses Joe, coming round a bit.

"'Come away,' I ses, 'come an' git to bed, that's the best place for you.'

"I took 'im by the sleeve, and he gets up quiet an' obedient and follers me like a little child. I got 'im straight into 'is bunk, an' arter a time he fell into a soft slumber, an' I thought the worst had passed, but I was mistaken. He got up in three hours' time an' seemed all right, 'cept that he walked about as though he was thinking very hard about something, an' before I could make out what it was he had a fit.

"He was in that fit ten minutes, an' he was no sooner out o' that one than he was in another. In twenty-four hours he had six

full-sized fits, and I'll allow I was fairly puzzled. What pleasure he
could find in tumbling down hard and stiff an' kicking at everybody an' everything I couldn't see. He'd be standing quiet and
peaceable like one minute, and the next he'd catch hold o' the nearest thing to him and have a bad fit, and lie on his back and kick us
while we was trying to force open his hands to pat 'em.

"The other chaps said the skipper's insult had turned his brain,
but I wasn't quite so soft, an' one time when he was alone I put it
to him.

"'Joe, old man,' I ses, 'you an' me's been very good pals.'

"'Ay, ay,' ses he, suspicious like.

"'Joe,' I whispers, 'what's yer little game?'

"'Wodyermean?' ses he, very short.

"'I mean the fits,' ses I, looking at 'im very steady, 'It's no good
looking hinnercent like that, 'cos I see yer chewing soap with my
own eyes.'

"'Soap,' ses Joe, in a nasty sneering way, 'you wouldn't recker-
nise a piece if you saw it.'

"Arter that I could see there was nothing to be got out of 'im,
an' I just kept my eyes open and watched. The skipper didn't worry
about his fits, 'cept that he said he wasn't to let the sarpint see his
face when he was in 'em for fear of scaring it; an' when the mate
wanted to leave him out o' the watch, he ses, 'No, he might as well
have fits while at work as well as anywhere else.'

"We were about twenty-four hours from port, an' the sarpint
was still following us; and at six o'clock in the evening the officers
puffected all their arrangements for ketching the creetur at eight
o'clock next morning. To make quite sure of it an extra watch was
kept on deck all night to chuck it food every half-hour; an' when I
turned in at ten o'clock that night it was so close I could have
reached it with a clothes-prop.

"I think I'd been abed about 'arf-an-hour when I was awoke by
the most infernal row I ever heard. The foghorn was going inces-
santly, an' there was a lot o' shouting and running about on deck.
It struck us all as 'ow the sarpint was gitting tired o' bread, and
was misbehaving himself, consequently we just shoved our 'eds out
o' the fore-scuttle and listened. All the hullaballoo seemed to be

on the bridge, an' as we didn't see the sarpint there we plucked up courage and went on deck.

"Then we saw what had happened. Joe had 'ad another fit while at the wheel, and, *not knowing what he was doing*, had clutched the line of the foghorn, and was holding on to it like grim death, and kicking right and left. The skipper was in his bedclothes, raving worse than Joe; and just as we got there Joe came round a bit, and, letting go o' the line, asked in a faint voice what the foghorn was blowing for. I thought the skipper 'ud have killed him; but the second mate held him back, an', of course, when things quieted down a bit, an' we went to the side, we found the sea-sarpint had vanished.

"We stayed there all that night, but it warn't no use. When day broke there wasn't the slightest trace of it, an' I think the men was as sorry to lose it as the officers. All 'cept Joe, that is, which shows how people should never be rude, even to the humblest; for I'm sartin that if the skipper hadn't hurt his feelings the way he did we should now know as much about the sea-sarpint as we do about our own brothers."

THE SEA RAIDERS
H. G. Wells

I

Until the extraordinary affair at Sidmouth, the peculiar species *Haploteuthis ferox* was known to science only generically, on the strength of a half-digested tentacle obtained near the Azores, and a decaying body pecked by birds and nibbled by fish, found early in 1896 by Mr. Jennings, near Land's End.

In no department of zoological science, indeed, are we quite so much in the dark as with regard to the deep-sea cephalopods. A mere accident, for instance, it was that led to the Prince of Monaco's discovery of nearly a dozen new forms in the summer of 1895, a discovery in which the before-mentioned tentacle was included. It chanced that a cachalot was killed off Terceira by some sperm-whalers, and in its last struggles charged almost to the Prince's yacht, missed it, rolled under, and died within twenty yards of his rudder. And in its agony it threw up a number of large objects, which the Prince, dimly perceiving they were strange and important, was, by a happy expedient, able to secure before they sank. He set his screws in motion, and kept them circling in the vortices thus created until a boat could be lowered. And these specimens were whole cephalopods and fragments of cephalopods, some of gigantic proportions, and almost all of them unknown to science!

It would seem, indeed, that these large and agile creatures, living in the middle depths of the sea, must, to a large extent, for ever remain unknown to us, since under water they are too nimble for nets, and it is only by such rare unlooked-for accidents that specimens can be obtained. In the case of *Haploteuthis ferox*, for instance, we are still altogether ignorant of its habitat, as ignorant as we are of the breeding-ground of the herring or the sea-ways of the salmon. And zoologists are altogether at a loss to account for its sudden appearance on our coast. Possibly it was the stress of a hunger migration that drove it hither out of the deep. But it will be, perhaps, better to avoid necessarily inconclusive discussion, and to proceed at once with our narrative.

The first human being to set eyes upon a living *Haploteuthis*— the first human being to survive, that is, for there can be little doubt now that the wave of bathing fatalities and boating accidents that travelled along the coast of Cornwall and Devon in early May was due to this cause—was a retired tea-dealer of the name of Fison, who was stopping at a Sidmouth boarding-house. It was in the afternoon, and he was walking along the cliff path between Sidmouth and Ladram Bay. The cliffs in this direction are very high, but down the red face of them in one place a kind of ladder staircase has been made. He was near this when his attention was attracted by what at first he thought to be a cluster of birds struggling over a fragment of food that caught the sunlight, and glistened pinkish-white. The tide was right out, and this object was not only far below him, but remote across a broad waste of rock reefs covered with dark seaweed and interspersed with silvery, shining, tidal pools. And he was, moreover, dazzled by the brightness of the further water.

In a minute, regarding this again, he perceived that his judgment was in fault, for over this struggle circled a number of birds, jackdaws and gulls for the most part, the latter gleaming blindingly when the sunlight smote their wings, and they seemed minute in comparison with it. And his curiosity was, perhaps, aroused all the more strongly because of his first insufficient explanations.

As he had nothing better to do than amuse himself, he decided to make this object, whatever it was the goal of his afternoon walk, instead of Ladram Bay, conceiving it might perhaps be a great fish of some sort, stranded by some chance, and flapping about in its distress. And so he hurried down the long steep ladder, stopping at intervals of thirty feet or so to take breath and scan the mysterious movement.

At the foot of the cliff he was, of course, nearer his object than he had been; but, on the other hand, it now came up against the incandescent sky, beneath the sun, so as to seem dark and indistinct. Whatever was pinkish of it was now hidden by a skerry of weedy boulders. But he perceived that it was made up of seven rounded bodies, distinct or connected, and that the birds kept up a constant croaking and screaming, but seemed afraid to approach it too closely.

Mr. Fison, torn by curiosity, began picking his way across the wave-worn rocks, and, finding the wet seaweed that covered them thickly rendered them extremely slippery, he stopped, removed his shoes and socks, and coiled his trousers above his knees. His object was, of course, merely to avoid stumbling into the rocky pools about him, and perhaps he was rather glad, as all men are, of an excuse to resume, even for a moment, the sensations of his boyhood. At any rate, it is to this, no doubt, that he owes his life.

He approached his mark with all the assurance which the absolute security of this country against all forms of animal life gives its inhabitants. The round bodies moved to and fro, but it was only when he surmounted the skerry of boulders I have mentioned that he realised the horrible nature of the discovery. It came upon him with some suddenness.

The rounded bodies fell apart as he came into sight over the ridge, and displayed the pinkish object to be the partially devoured body of a human being, but whether of a man or woman he was unable to say. And the rounded bodies were new and ghastly-looking creatures, in shape somewhat resembling an octopus, and with huge and very long and flexible tentacles, coiled copiously on the ground. The skin had a glistening texture, unpleasant to see, like shiny leather. The downward bend of the tentacle-surrounded mouth, the curious excrescence at the bend, the tentacles, and the large, intelligent eyes, gave the creatures a grotesque suggestion of a face. They were the size of a fair-sized swine about the body, and the tentacles seemed to him to be many feet in length. There were, he thinks, seven or eight at least of the creatures. Twenty yards beyond them, amid the surf of the now returning tide, two others were emerging from the sea.

Their bodies lay flatly on the rocks, and their eyes regarded him with evil interest; but it does not appear that Mr. Fison was afraid, or that he realised that he was in any danger. Possibly his confidence is to be ascribed to the limpness of their attitudes. But he was horrified, of course, and intensely excited and indignant at such revolting creatures preying upon human flesh. He thought they had chanced upon a drowned body. He shouted to them, with the idea of driving them off, and, finding they did not budge, cast about him, picked up a big rounded lump of rock, and flung it at one.

And then, slowly uncoiling their tentacles, they all began moving towards him—creeping at first deliberately, and making a soft, purring sound to each other.

In a moment Mr. Fison realised that he was in danger. He shouted again, threw both his boots, and started off, with a leap, forthwith. Twenty yards off he stopped and faced about, judging them slow, and, behold! the tentacles of their leader were already pouring over the rocky ridge on which he had just been standing!

At that he shouted again, but this time not threatening, but a cry of dismay, and began jumping, striding, slipping, wading across the uneven expanse between him and the beach. The tall red cliffs seemed suddenly at a vast distance, and he saw, as though they were creatures in another world, two minute workmen engaged in the repair of the ladder-way, and little suspecting the race for life that was beginning below them. At one time he could hear the creatures splashing in the pools not a dozen feet behind him, and once he slipped and almost fell.

They chased him to the very foot of the cliffs, and desisted only when he had been joined by the workmen at the foot of the ladder-way up the cliff. All three of the men pelted them with stones for a time, and then hurried to the cliff top and along the path towards Sidmouth, to secure assistance and a boat, and to rescue the desecrated body from the clutches of these abominable creatures.

II

And, as if he had not already been in sufficient peril that day, Mr. Fison went with the boat to point out the exact spot of his adventure.

As the tide was down, it required a considerable detour to reach the spot, and when at last they came off the ladder-way, the mangled body had disappeared. The water was now running in, submerging first one slab of slimy rock and then another, and the four men in the boat—the workmen, that is, the boatman, and Mr. Fison—now turned their attention from the bearings off shore to the water beneath the keel.

At first they could see little below them, save a dark jungle of laminaria, with an occasional darting fish. Their minds were set on adventure, and they expressed their disappointment freely. But presently they saw one of the monsters swimming through the water seaward, with a curious rolling motion that suggested to Mr. Fison the spinning roll of a captive balloon. Almost immediately after, the waving streamers of laminaria were extraordinarily perturbed, parted for a moment, and three of these beasts became darkly visible, struggling for what was probably some fragment of the drowned man. In a moment the copious olive-green ribbons had poured again over this writhing group.

At that all four men, greatly excited, began beating the water with oars and shouting, and immediately they saw a tumultuous movement among the weeds. They desisted, to see more clearly, and as soon as the water was smooth, they saw, as it seemed to them, the whole sea bottom among the weeds set with eyes.

"Ugly swine!" cried one of the men. "Why, there's dozens!"

And forthwith the things began to rise through the water about them. Mr. Fison has since described to the writer this startling eruption out of the waving laminaria meadows. To him it seemed to occupy a considerable time, but it is probable that really it was an affair of a few seconds only. For a time nothing but eyes, and then he speaks of tentacles streaming out and parting the weed fronds this way and that. Then these things, growing larger, until at last the bottom was hidden by their intercoiling forms, and the tips of tentacles rose darkly here and there into the air above the swell of the waters.

One came up boldly to the side of the boat, and, clinging to this with three of its sucker-set tentacles, threw four others over the gunwale, as if with an intention either of oversetting the boat or of clambering into it. Mr. Fison at once caught up the boathook, and, jabbing furiously at the soft tentacles, forced it to desist. He was struck in the back and almost pitched overboard by the boatman, who was using his oar to resist a similar attack on the other side of the boat. But the tentacles on either side at once relaxed their hold at this, slid out of sight, and splashed into the water.

"We'd better get out of this," said Mr. Fison, who was trembling violently. He went to the tiller, while the boatman and one of the workmen seated themselves and began rowing. The other workman stood up in the fore part of the boat, with the boathook, ready to strike any more tentacles that might appear. Nothing else seems to have been said. Mr. Fison had expressed the common feeling beyond amendment. In a hushed, scared mood, with faces white and drawn, they set about escaping from the position into which they had so recklessly blundered.

But the oars had scarcely dropped into the water before dark, tapering, serpentine ropes had bound them, and were about the rudder; and creeping up the sides of the boat with a looping motion came the suckers again. The men gripped their oars and pulled, but it was like trying to move a boat in a floating raft of weeds. "Help here!" cried the boatman, and Mr. Fison and the second workman rushed to help lug at the oar.

Then the man with the boathook—his name was Ewan, or Ewen—sprang up with a curse, and began striking downward over the side, as far as he could reach, at the bank of tentacles that now clustered along the boat's bottom. And, at the same time, the two rowers stood up to get a better purchase for the recovery of their oars. The boatman handed his to Mr. Fison, who lugged desperately, and, meanwhile, the boatman opened a big clasp-knife, and, leaning over the side of the boat, began hacking at the spiring arms upon the oar shaft.

Mr. Fison, staggering with the quivering rocking of the boat, his teeth set, his breath coming short, and the veins starting on his hands as he pulled at his oar, suddenly cast his eyes seaward. And there, not fifty yards off, across the long rollers of the incoming tide, was a large boat standing in towards them, with three women and a little child in it. A boatman was rowing, and a little man in a pink-ribboned straw hat and whites stood in the stern, hailing them. For a moment, of course, Mr. Fison thought of help, and then he thought of the child. He abandoned his oar forthwith, threw up his arms in a frantic gesture, and screamed to the party in the boat to keep away "for God's sake!" It says much for the modesty and courage of Mr. Fison that he does not seem to be aware that there was any quality of heroism in his action at this juncture. The oar he had abandoned was at once drawn under, and presently reappeared floating about twenty yards away.

At the same moment Mr. Fison felt the boat under him lurch violently, and a hoarse scream, a prolonged cry of terror from Hill, the boatman, caused him to forget the party of excursionists altogether. He turned, and saw Hill crouching by the forward rowlock, his face convulsed with terror, and his right arm over the side and drawn tightly down. He gave now a succession of short, sharp cries, "Oh! oh! oh!—oh!" Mr. Fison believes that he must have been hacking at the tentacles below the water-line, and have been grasped by them, but, of course, it is quite impossible to say now certainly what had happened. The boat was heeling over, so that the gunwale was within ten inches of the water, and both Ewan and the other labourer were striking down into the water, with oar and boathook, on either side of Hill's arm. Mr. Fison instinctively placed himself to counterpoise them.

Then Hill, who was a burly, powerful man, made a strenuous effort, and rose almost to a standing position. He lifted his arm, indeed, clean out of the water. Hanging to it was a complicated tangle of brown ropes; and the eyes of one of the brutes that had hold of him, glaring straight and resolute, showed momentarily above the surface. The boat heeled more and more, and the green-brown water came pouring in a cascade over the side.

Then Hill slipped and fell with his ribs across the side, and his arm and the mass of tentacles about it splashed back into the water. He rolled over; his boot kicked Mr. Fison's knee as that gentleman rushed forward to seize him, and in another moment fresh tentacles had whipped about his waist and neck, and after a brief, convulsive struggle, in which the boat was nearly capsized, Hill was lugged overboard. The boat righted with a violent jerk that all but sent Mr. Fison over the other side, and hid the struggle in the water from his eyes.

He stood staggering to recover his balance for a moment, and as he did so, he became aware that the struggle and the inflowing tide had carried them close upon the weedy rocks again. Not four yards off a table of rock still rose in rhythmic movements above the in-wash of the tide. In a moment Mr. Fison seized the oar from Ewan, gave one vigorous stroke, then, dropping it, ran to the bows and leapt. He felt his feet slide over the rock, and, by a frantic effort, leapt again towards a further mass. He stumbled over this, came to his knees, and rose again.

"Look out!" cried some one, and a large drab body struck him. He was knocked flat into a tidal pool by one of the workmen, and as he went down he heard smothered, choking cries, that he believed at the time came from Hill. Then he found himself marvelling at the shrillness and variety of Hill's voice. Some one jumped over him, and a curving rush of foamy water poured over him, and passed. He scrambled to his feet, dripping, and, without looking seaward, ran as fast as his terror would let him shoreward. Before him, over the flat space of scattered rocks, stumbled the two workmen—one a dozen yards in front of the other.

He looked over his shoulder at last, and, seeing that he was not pursued, faced about. He was astonished. From the moment of the rising of the cephalopods out of the water, he had been acting too swiftly to fully comprehend his actions. Now it seemed to him as if he had suddenly jumped out of an evil dream.

For there were the sky, cloudless and blazing with the afternoon sun, the sea, weltering under its pitiless brightness, the soft creamy foam of the breaking water, and the low, long, dark ridges of rock. The righted boat floated, rising and falling gently on the swell about a dozen yards from shore. Hill and the monsters, all the stress and tumult of that fierce fight for life, had vanished as though they had never been.

Mr. Fison's heart was beating violently; he was throbbing to the finger-tips, and his breath came deep.

There was something missing. For some seconds he could not think clearly enough what this might be. Sun, sky, sea, rocks—what was it? Then he remembered the boatload of excursionists. It had vanished. He wondered whether he had imagined it. He turned,

and saw the two workmen standing side by side under the projecting masses of the tall pink cliffs. He hesitated whether he should
make one last attempt to save the man Hill. His physical excitement seemed to desert him suddenly, and leave him aimless and
helpless. He turned shoreward, stumbling and wading towards his
two companions.

He looked back again, and there were now two boats floating,
and the one farthest out at sea pitched clumsily, bottom upward.

III

So it was *Haploteuthis ferox* made its appearance upon the
Devonshire coast. So far, this has been its most serious aggression.
Mr. Fison's account, taken together with the wave of boating and
bathing casualties to which I have already alluded, and the absence
of fish from the Cornish coasts that year, points clearly to a shoal
of these voracious deep-sea monsters prowling slowly along the
sub-tidal coast-line. Hunger migration has, I know, been suggested
as the force that drove them hither; but, for my own part, I prefer
to believe the alternative theory of Hemsley. Hemsley holds that a
pack or shoal of these creatures may have become enamoured of
human flesh by the accident of a foundered ship sinking among
them, and have wandered in search of it out of their accustomed
zone; first waylaying and following ships, and so coming to our
shores in the wake of the Atlantic traffic. But to discuss Hemsley's
cogent and admirably-stated arguments would be out of place here.

It would seem that the appetites of the shoal were satisfied by
the catch of eleven people—for so far as can be ascertained, there
were ten people in the second boat, and certainly these creatures
gave no further signs of their presence off Sidmouth that day. The
coast between Seaton and Budleigh Salterton was patrolled all that
evening and night by four Preventive Service boats, the men in
which were armed with harpoons and cutlasses, and as the evening
advanced, a number of more or less similarly equipped expeditions,
organised by private individuals, joined them. Mr. Fison took no
part in any of these expeditions.

About midnight excited hails were heard from a boat about a
couple of miles out at sea to the south-east of Sidmouth, and a

lantern was seen waving in a strange manner to and fro and up and down. The nearer boats at once hurried towards the alarm. The venturesome occupants of the boat, a seaman, a curate, and two schoolboys, had actually seen the monsters passing under their boat. The creatures, it seems, like most deep-sea organisms, were phosphorescent, and they had been floating, five fathoms deep or so, like creatures of moonshine through the blackness of the water, their tentacles retracted and as if asleep, rolling over and over, and moving slowly in a wedge-like formation towards the southeast.

These people told their story in gesticulated fragments, as first one boat drew alongside and then another. At last there was a little fleet of eight or nine boats collected together, and from them a tumult, like the chatter of a marketplace, rose into the stillness of the night. There was little or no disposition to pursue the shoal, the people had neither weapons nor experience for such a dubious chase, and presently—even with a certain relief, it may be—the boats turned shoreward.

And now to tell what is perhaps the most astonishing fact in this whole astonishing raid. We have not the slightest knowledge of the subsequent movements of the shoal, although the whole southwest coast was now alert for it. But it may, perhaps, be significant that a cachalot was stranded off Sark on June 3. Two weeks and three days after this Sidmouth affair, a living *Haploteuthis* came ashore on Calais sands. It was alive, because several witnesses saw its tentacles moving in a convulsive way. But it is probable that it was dying. A gentleman named Pouchet obtained a rifle and shot it.

That was the last appearance of a living *Haploteuthis*. No others were seen on the French coast. On the 15th of June a dead body, almost complete, was washed ashore near Torquay, and a few days later a boat from the Marine Biological station, engaged in dredging off Plymouth, picked up a rotting specimen, slashed deeply with a cutlass wound. How the former specimen had come by its death it is impossible to say. And on the last day of June, Mr. Egbert Caine, an artist, bathing near Newlyn, threw up his arms, shrieked, and was drawn under. A friend bathing with him made no attempt to save him, but swam at once for the shore. This is the last fact to tell of this extraordinary raid from the deeper sea. Whether it is really the last of these horrible creatures it is, as yet, premature to say. But it is believed, and certainly it is to be hoped, that they have returned now, and returned for good, to the sunless depths of the middle seas, out of which they have so strangely and so mysteriously arisen.

In the Abyss
H. G. Wells

The Lieutenant stood in front of the steel sphere and gnawed a piece of pine splinter. "What do you think of it, Steevens?" he said.

"It's an idea," said Steevens, in the tone of one who keeps an open mind.

"I believe it will smash—flat," said the lieutenant.

"He seems to have calculated it all out pretty well," said Steevens, still impartial.

"But think of the pressure," said the lieutenant. "At the surface of the water it's fourteen pounds to the inch, thirty feet down it's double that; sixty, treble; ninety, four times; nine hundred, forty times; five thousand, three hundred—that's a mile—it's two hundred and forty times fourteen pounds; that's—let's see—thirty hundredweight—a ton and a half, Steevens; a ton and a half to the square inch. And the ocean where he's going is five miles deep. That's seven and a half—"

"Sounds a lot," said Steevens, "but it's jolly thick steel."

The lieutenant made no answer, but resumed his pine splinter. The object of their conversation was a huge ball of steel, having an exterior diameter of perhaps nine feet. It looked like the shot for some titanic piece of artillery. It was elaborately nested in a monstrous scaffolding built into the framework of the vessel, and the gigantic spars that were presently to sling it overboard gave the stern of the ship an appearance that had raised the curiosity of every decent sailor who had sighted it, from the Pool of London to the Tropic of Capricorn. In two places, one above the other, the steel gave place to a couple of circular windows of enormously thick glass, and one of these, set in steel frame of great solidity, was

73

now partially unscrewed. Both the men had seen the interior of this globe for the first time that morning. It was elaborately padded with air cushions, with little studs sunk between bulging pillows to work the simple mechanism of the affair. Everything was elaborately padded, even the Myers apparatus which was to absorb carbonic acid and replace the oxygen inspired by its tenant, when he had crept in by the glass manhole, and had been screwed in. It was so elaborately padded that a man might have been fired from a gun in it with perfect safety. And it had need to be, for presently a man was to crawl in through that glass manhole, to be screwed up tightly, and to be flung overboard, and to sink down—down—down, for five miles, even as the lieutenant said. It had taken the strongest hold of his imagination; it made him a bore at mess; and he found Steevens the new arrival aboard, a godsend to talk to about it, over and over again.

"It's my opinion," said the lieutenant, "that, that glass will simply bend in and bulge and smash, under a pressure of that sort. Daubrée has made rocks run like water under big pressures—and you mark my words—"

"If the glass did break in," said Steevens, "what then?"

"The water would shoot in like a jet of iron. Have you ever felt a straight jet of high pressure water? It would hit as hard as a bullet. It would simply smash him and flatten him. It would tear down his throat, and into his lungs; it would blow in his ears—"

"What a detailed imagination you have!" protested Steevens, who saw things vividly.

"It's a simple statement of the inevitable," said the lieutenant.

"And the globe?"

"Would just give out a few little bubbles, and it would settle down comfortably against the Day of Judgment, among the oozes and the bottom clay—with poor Elstead spread over his own smashed cushions like butter over bread."

He repeated this sentence as though he liked it very much. "Like butter over bread," he said.

"Having a look at the jigger?" said a voice, and Elstead stood behind them, spick and span in white, with a cigarette between his teeth, and his eyes smiling out of the shadow of his ample hat-brim.

"What's that about bread and butter, Weybridge? Grumbling as usual about the insufficient pay of naval officers? It won't be more than a day now before I start. We are to get the slings ready to-day. This clean sky and gentle swell is just the kind of thing for swinging off a dozen tons of lead and iron, isn't it?"

"It won't affect you much," said Weybridge.

"No. Seventy or eighty feet down, and I shall be there in a dozen seconds, there's not a particle moving, though the wind shriek itself hoarse up above, and the water lifts halfway to the clouds. No. Down there—" He moved to the side of the ship and the other two followed him. All three leant forward on their elbows and stared down into the yellow-green water.

"Peace," said Elstead, finishing his thought aloud.

"Are you dead certain that clockwork will act?" asked Weybridge presently.

"It has worked thirty-five times," said Elstead. "It's bound to work."

"But if it doesn't?"

"Why shouldn't it?"

"I wouldn't go down in that confounded thing," said Weybridge, "for twenty thousand pounds."

"Cheerful chap you are," said Elstead, and spat sociably at a bubble below.

"I don't understand yet how you mean to work the thing," said Steevens.

"In the first place, I'm screwed into the sphere," said Elstead, "and when I've turned the electric light off on three times to show I'm cheerful, I'm swung out over the stern by that crane, with all those big lead sinkers slung below me. The top lead weight has a roller carrying a hundred fathoms of strong cord rolled up, and that's all that joins the sinkers to the sphere, except the slings that will be cut when the affair is dropped. We use cord rather than wire rope because it's easier to cut and more buoyant—necessary points, as you will see.

"Through each of these lead weights you notice there is a hole, and an iron rod will be run through that and will project six feet on the lower side. If that rod is rammed up from below, it knocks up a lever and sets the clockwork in motion at the side of the cylinder on which the cord winds.

"Very well. The whole affair is lowered gently into the water, and the slings are cut. The sphere floats—, with the air in it, it's lighter than water—, but the lead weights go down straight and the cord runs out. When the cord is all paid out, the sphere will go down too, pulled down by the cord."

"But why the cord?" asked Steevens. "Why not fasten the weights directly to the sphere?"

"Because of the smash down below. The whole affair will go rushing down, mile after mile, at a headlong pace at last. It would be knocked to pieces on the bottom if it wasn't for that cord. But the weights will hit the bottom, and directly they do, the buoyancy of the sphere will come into play. It will go on sinking slower and slower; come to stop at last, and then begin to float upward again.

"That's where the clockwork comes in. Directly the weights smash against the sea bottom, the rod will be knocked through and will kick up the clockwork, and the cord will be rewound on the reel. I shall be lugged down to the sea bottom. There I shall stay for half an hour, with the electric light on, looking about me. Then the clockwork will release a spring knife, the cord will be cut, and up I shall rush again, like a soda-water bubble. The cord itself will help the flotation."

"And if you should chance to hit a ship?" said Weybridge.

"I should come up at such a pace, I should go clean through it," said Elstead, "like a cannon ball. You needn't worry about that."

"And suppose some nimble crustacean should wriggle into your clockwork—"

"It would be a pressing sort of invitation for me to stop," said Elstead, turning his back on the water and staring at the sphere.

They had swung Elstead overboard by eleven o'clock. The day was serenely bright and calm, with the horizon lost in haze. The electric glare in the little upper compartment beamed cheerfully three times. Then they let him down slowly to the surface of the water, and a sailor in the stern chains hung ready to cut the tackle that held the lead weights and the sphere together. The globe, which had looked so large on deck, looked the smallest thing conceivable under the stern of the ship. It rolled a little, and its two dark windows, which floated uppermost, seemed like eyes turned up in round wonderment at the people who crowded the rail. A voice wondered how Elstead liked the rolling. "Are you ready?" sang out the commander. "Ay, ay, sir!" "Then let her go!"

The rope of the tackle tightened against the blade and was cut, and an eddy rolled over the globe in a grotesquely helpless fashion. Someone waved a handkerchief, someone else tried an ineffectual cheer, a middy was counting slowly, "Eight, nine, ten!" Another roll, then a jerk and a splash the thing righted itself.

It seemed to be stationary for a moment, to grow rapidly smaller, and then the water closed over it, and it became visible, enlarged by refraction and dimmer, below the surface. Before one could count three it had disappeared. There was a flicker of white light far down in the water, that diminished to a speck and vanished. Then there was nothing but a depth of water going down into blackness, through which a shark was swimming.

Then suddenly the screw of the cruiser began to rotate, the water was crickled, the shark disappeared in a wrinkled confusion, and a torrent of foam rushed across the crystalline clearness that had swallowed up Elstead. "What's the idea?" said one A. B. to another.

"We're going to lay off about a couple of miles, 'fear he should hit us when he comes up," said his mate.

The ship steamed slowly to her new position. Aboard her almost everyone who was unoccupied remained watching the breathing swell into which the sphere had sunk. For the next half-hour it is doubtful if a word was spoken that did not bear directly or indirectly on Elstead. The December sun was now high in the sky, and the heat very considerable.

"He'll be cold enough down there," said Weybridge. "They say that below a certain depth sea water's always just about freezing."

"Where'll he come up?" asked Steevens. "I've lost my bearings."

"That's the spot," said the commander, who prided himself on his omniscience. He extended a precise finger south-eastward. "And this, I reckon, is pretty nearly the moment," he said. "He's been thirty-five minutes."

"How long dose it take to reach the bottom of the ocean?" asked Steevens.

"For a depth of five miles, and reckoning—as we did—an acceleration of two feet per second, both ways, is just about three-quarters of a minute."

"Then he's overdue," said Weybridge.

"Pretty nearly," said the commander. "I suppose it takes a few minutes for that cord of his to wind in."

"I forgot that," said Weybridge, evidently relieved.

And then began the suspense. A minute slowly dragged itself out, and no sphere shot out of the water. Another followed, and nothing broke the low oily swell. The sailors explained to one another that little point about the winding-in of the cord. The rigging was dotted with expectant faces. "Come up, Elstead!" called one hairy-chested salt impatiently, and the others caught it up, and shouted as though they were waiting for the curtain of a theatre to rise.

The commander glanced irritably at them.

"Of course, if the acceleration's less than two," he said, "he'll be all the longer. We aren't absolutely certain that was the proper figure. I'm no slavish believer in calculations."

Steevens agreed concisely. No one on the quarter-deck spoke for a couple of minutes. Then Steevens' watchcase clicked.

When, twenty-one minutes after the sun reached the zenith, they were still waiting for the globe to reappear, and not a man aboard had dared to whisper that hope was dead. It was Weybridge who first gave expression to that realisation. He spoke while the sound of eight bells still hung in the air. "I always distrusted that window," he said quite suddenly to Steevens.

"Good God!" said Steevens; "you don't think—?"

"Well!" said Weybridge, and left the rest to his imagination.

"I'm no great believer in calculations myself," said the commander dubiously, "so that I'm not altogether hopeless yet." And at midnight the gunboat was steaming slowly in a spiral round the spot where the globe had sunk, and the white beam of the electric light fled and halted and swept discontentedly onward again over the waste of phosphorescent waters under the little stars.

"If his window hasn't burst and smashed him," said Weybridge, "then it's a cursed sight worse, for his clockwork has gone wrong, and he's alive now, five miles under our feet, down there in the cold and dark, anchored in that little bubble of his, where never a ray of light has shone or a human being lived, since the waters were gathered together. He's there without food, feeling hungry and thirsty and scared, wondering whether he'll starve or stifle. Which will it be? The Myers apparatus is running out, I suppose. How long do they last?"

"Good heavens!" he exclaimed; "What little things we are! What daring little devils! Down there, miles and miles of water—all water, and all this empty water about us and this sky. Gulfs!" He threw his hands out, and as he did so, a little white streak swept noiselessly up the sky, travelled more slowly, stopped, became a motionless dot, as though a new star had fallen up into the sky. Then it went sliding back again and lost itself amidst the reflections of the stars and the white haze of the sea's phosphorescence.

At the sight he stopped, arm extended and mouth open. He shut his mouth, opened it again, and waved his arms with an impatient gesture. Then he turned, shouted "*El*-stead ahoy!" to the first watch, and went at a run to Lindley and the search-light. "I saw him," he said "Starboard there! His light's on, and he's just shot out of the water. Bring the light round. We ought to see him drifting, when he lifts on the swell."

But they never picked up the explorer until dawn. Then they almost ran him down. The crane was swung out and a boat's crew hooked the chain to the sphere. When they had shipped the sphere, they unscrewed the manhole and peered into the darkness of the interior (for the electric light chamber was intended to illuminate the water about the sphere, and was shut off entirely from its general cavity).

The air was very hot within the cavity, and the india-rubber at the lip of the manhole was soft. There was no answer to their eager questions and no sound of movement within. Elstead seemed to be lying motionless, crumpled in the bottom of the globe. The ship's doctor crawled in and lifted him out to the men outside. For a moment or so they did not know whether Elstead was alive or dead.

His face, in the yellow light of the ship's lamps, glistened with perspiration. They carried him down to his own cabin.

He was not dead, they found, but in a state of absolute nervous collapse, and besides cruelly bruised. For some days he had to lie perfectly still. It was a week before he could tell his experiences.

Almost his first words were that he was going down again. The sphere would have to be altered, he said, in order to allow him to throw off the cord if need be, and that was all. He had had the most marvellous experience. "You thought I should find nothing but ooze," he said. "You laughed at my explorations, and I've discovered a new world!" He told his story in disconnected fragments, and chiefly from the wrong end, so that it is impossible to re-tell it in his words. But what follows is the narrative of his experience.

It began atrociously, he said. Before the cord ran out, the thing kept rolling over. He felt like a frog in a football. He could see nothing but the crane and the sky overhead, with an occasional glimpse of people on the ships rail. He couldn't tell a bit which way the thing would roll next. Suddenly he would find his footing going up, and try to step, and over he went rolling, head over heels, and just anyhow, on the padding. Any other shape would have been more comfortable, but no other shape was to be relied upon under the huge pressure of the nethermost abyss.

Suddenly the swaying ceased; the globe righted, and when he had picked himself up, he saw the water all about him greeny-blue, with an attenuated light filtering down from above, and a shoal of little floating things went rushing up past him, as it seemed to him, towards the light. And even as he looked, it grew darker and darker, until the water above was as dark as the midnight sky, albeit of greener shade, and the water below black. And little transparent things in the water developed a faint glint of luminosity, and shot past him in faint greenish streaks.

And the feeling of falling! It was just like the start of a lift, he said, only it kept on. One has to imagine what that means, that keeping on. It was then of all times that Elstead repented of his adventure. He saw the chances against him in an altogether new light. He thought of the big cuttle-fish people knew to exist in the middle waters, the kind of things they find half digested in whales at times, or floating dead and rotten and half eaten by fish. Suppose one caught hold and wouldn't let go. And had the clockwork really been sufficiently tested? But whether he wanted to go on or go back mattered not the slightest now.

In fifty seconds everything was as black as night outside, except where the beam from his light struck through the waters, and picked out every now and then some fish or scrap of sinking matter. They flashed by too fast for him to see what they were. Once he thinks he passed a shark. And then the sphere began to get hot by friction against the water. They had underestimated this, it seems.

The first thing he noticed was that he was perspiring, and then he heard a hissing growing louder under his feet, and saw a lot of little bubbles—very little bubbles they were—rushing upward like a fan through the water outside. Steam! He felt the window, and it was hot. He turned on the minute glow-lamp that lit his own cavity, looked at the padded watch by the studs, and saw he had been travelling now for two minutes. It came into his head that the window would crack through the conflict of temperatures, for he knew the bottom water is very near freezing.

Then suddenly the floor of the sphere seemed to press against his feet, the rush of bubbles outside grew slower and slower, and the hissing diminished. The sphere rolled a little. The window had not cracked, nothing had given, and he knew that the dangers of sinking, at any rate, were over.

In another minute or so he would be on the floor of the abyss. He thought, he said, of Steevens and Weybridge and the rest of them five miles overhead, higher to him than the highest clouds that ever floated over land are to us, steaming slowly and staring down and wondering what had happened to him.

He peered out of the window. There were no more bubbles now, and the hissing had stopped. Outside there was a heavy blackness—as black as black velvet—except where the electric light pierced the empty water and showed the colour of it—a yellow-green. Then three things like shapes of fire swam into sight, following each other through the water. Whether they were little and near or big and far off he could not tell.

Each was outlined in a bluish light almost as bright as the lights of a fishing smack, a light which seemed to be smoking greatly, and all along the sides of them were specks of this, like the lighter portholes of a ship. Their phosphorescence seemed to go out as they came into the radiance of his lamp, and he saw then that they were little fish of some strange sort, with huge heads, vast eyes, and dwindling bodies and tails. Their eyes were turned towards him, and he judged they were following him down. He supposed they were attracted by his glare.

Presently others of the same sort joined them. As he went on down, he noticed that the water became of a pallid colour, and that little specks twinkled in his ray like motes in a sunbeam. This was probably due to the clouds of ooze and mud that the impact of his leaden sinkers had disturbed.

By the time he was drawn down to the lead weights he was in a dense fog of white that his electric light failed altogether to pierce for more than a few yards, and many minutes elapsed before the hanging sheets of sediment subsided to any extent. Then, lit by his light and by the transient phosphorescence of a distant shoal of fishes, he was able to see under the huge blackness of the super-incumbent water an undulating expanse of greyish-white ooze, broken here and there by tangled thickets of a growth of sea lilies, waving hungry tentacles in the air.

Farther away were the graceful, translucent outlines of a group of gigantic sponges. About this floor there were scattered a number of bristling flattish tufts of rich purple and black, which he decided must be some sort of sea-urchin, and small, large-eyed or blind things having a curious resemblance, some to woodlice, and others to lobsters, crawled sluggishly across the track of the light and vanished into the obscurity again, leaving furrowed trails behind them.

Then suddenly the hovering swarm of little fishes veered about and came towards him as a flight of starlings might do. They passed over him like a phosphorescent snow, and then he saw behind them some larger creature advancing towards the sphere.

At first he could see it only dimly, a faintly moving figure remotely suggestive of a walking man, and then it came into the spray of light that the lamp shot out. As the glare struck it, it shut its eyes, dazzled. He stared in rigid astonishment.

It was a strange vertebrated animal. Its dark purple head was dimly suggestive of a chameleon, but it had such a high forehead and such a braincase as no reptile ever displayed before; the vertical pitch of its face gave it a most extraordinary resemblance to a human being.

Two large and protruding eyes projected from sockets in chameleon fashion, and it had a broad reptilian mouth with horny lips beneath its little nostrils. In the position of the ears were two huge gill-covers, and out of these floated a branching tree of coralline filaments, almost like the tree-like gills that very young rays and sharks possess.

But the humanity of the face was not the most extraordinary thing about the creature. It was a biped; its almost globular body was poised on a tripod of two frog-like legs and a long thick tail, and its fore limbs, which grotesquely caricatured the human hand, much as a frog's do, carried a long shaft of bone, tipped with copper. The colour of the creature was variegated; its head, hands and legs were purple; but its skin, which hung loosely upon it, even as clothes might do, was a phosphorescent grey. And it stood there blinded by the light.

At last this unknown creature of the abyss blinked its eyes open, and shading them with its disengaged hand, opened its mouth and gave vent to a shouting noise, articulate almost as speech might be, that penetrated even the steel case and padded jacket of the sphere. How a shouting may be accomplished without lungs Elstead does not profess to explain. It then moved sideways out of the glare into the mystery of shadow that bordered it on either side, and Elstead felt rather than saw that it was coming towards him. Fancying the light had attracted it, he turned the switch that cut off the current. In another moment something soft dabbed upon the steel, and the globe swayed.

Then the shouting was repeated, and it seemed to him that a distant echo answered it. The dabbing recurred, and the whole globe swayed and ground against the spindle over which the wire was rolled. He stood in the blackness and peered out into the everlasting night of the abyss. And presently he saw, very faint and remote, other phosphorescent quasi-human forms hurrying towards him.

Hardly knowing what he did, he felt about in his swaying prison for the stud of the exterior electric light, and came by accident against his own small glow-lamp in its padded recess. The sphere twisted, and then threw him down; he heard shouts like shouts of surprise, and when he rose to his feet, he saw two pairs of stalked eyes peering into the lower window and reflecting his light.

In another moment hands were dabbing vigorously at his steel casing, and there was a sound, horrible enough in his position, of the metal protection of the clockwork being vigorously hammered. That indeed sent his heart into his mouth, for if these strange creatures succeeded in stopping that, his release would never occur. Scarcely had he thought as much when he felt the sphere sway violently, and the floor of it press hard against his feet. He turned off the small glow-lamp that lit the interior, and sent the ray of the large light in the separate compartment, out into the water. The sea-floor and the man-like creatures had disappeared, and a couple of fish chasing each other dropped suddenly by the window.

He thought at once that these strange denizens of the deep sea had broke the rope, and that he had escaped. He drove up faster and faster, and then stopped with a jerk that sent him flying against the padded roof of his prison. For half a minute perhaps, he was too astonished to think.

Then he felt that the sphere was spinning slowly, and rocking, and it seemed to him that it was also being drawn through the water. By crouching close to the window, he managed to make his weight effective and roll that part of the sphere downward, but he could see nothing save the pale ray of his light striking down ineffectively into the darkness. It occurred to him that he would see more if he turned the lamp off, and allowed his eyes to grow accustomed to the profound obscurity.

In this he was wise. After some minutes the velvety blackness became a translucent blackness, and then, far away, and as faint as zodiacal light of an English summer evening, he saw shapes moving below. He judged these creatures had detached his cable, and were towing him along the sea bottom.

And then he saw something faint and remote across the undulations of the submarine plain, a broad horizon of pale luminosity that extended this way and that way as far as the range of his little window permitted him to see. To this he was being towed, as a balloon might be towed by men out of the open country into a town. He approached it very slowly, and very slowly the dim irradiation was gathered together into more definite shapes.

It was nearly five o'clock before he came over this luminous area, and by that time he could make out an arrangement suggestive of streets and houses grouped about a vast roofless erection that was grotesquely suggestive of a ruined abbey. It was spread out like a map below him. The houses were all roofless enclosures of walls, and their substance being, as he afterwards saw, of phosphorescent bones, gave the place an appearance as if it were built of drowned moonshine.

Among the inner caves of the place waving trees of crinoid stretched their tentacles, and tall, slender, glassy sponges shot like shining minarets and lilies of filmy light out of the general glow of the city. In the open spaces of the place he could see a stirring movement as of crowds of people, but he was too many fathoms above them to distinguish the individuals in those crowds.

Then slowly they pulled him down, and as they did so, the details of the place crept slowly upon his apprehension. He saw that the courses of the cloudy buildings were marked out with beaded lines of round objects, and then he perceived that at several points below him, in broad open spaces, were forms like the encrusted shapes of ships.

Slowly and surely he was drawn down, and the forms below him became brighter, clearer, more distinct. He was being pulled down, he perceived, towards the large building in the centre of the town, and he could catch a glimpse ever and again of the multitudinous forms that were lugging at his cord. He was astonished to see that the rigging of one of the ships, which formed such a prominent feature of the place, was crowded with a host of gesticulating figures regarding him, and then the walls of the great building rose about him silently, and hid the city from his eyes.

And such walls they were, of water-logged wood, and twisted wire-rope, and iron spars, and copper, and the bones and skulls of dead men. The skulls ran in zigzag lines and spirals and fantastic curves over the building; and in and out of their eye-sockets, and over the whole surface of the place, lurked and played a multitude of silvery little fishes.

Suddenly his ears were filled with a low shouting and a noise like the violent blowing of horns, and this gave place to a fantastic chant. Down the sphere sank, past the huge pointed windows, through which he saw vaguely a great number of these strange, ghostlike people regarding him, and at last he came to rest, as it seemed, on a kind of altar that stood in the centre of the place.

And now he was at such a level that he could see these strange people of the abyss plainly once more. To his astonishment, he perceived that they were prostrating themselves before him, all save one, dressed as it seemed in a robe of placoid scales, and crowned with a luminous diadem, who stood with his reptilian mouth opening and shutting, as though he led the chanting of the worshippers.

A curious impulse made Elstead turn on his small glow-lamp again, so that he became visible to these creatures of the abyss, albeit the glare made them disappear forthwith into night. At this sudden sight of him, the chanting gave place to a tumult of exultant shouts; and Elstead, being anxious to watch them, turned his light off again, and vanished from before their eyes. But for a time he was too blind to make out what they were doing, and when at last he could distinguish them, they were kneeling again. And thus they continued worshipping him, without rest or intermission, for a space of three hours.

Most circumstantial was Elstead's account of this astounding city and its people, these people of perpetual night, who have never seen sun or moon or stars, green vegetation, nor any living, air-breathing creatures, who know nothing of fire, nor any light but the phosphorescent light of living things.

Startling as is his story, it is yet more startling to find that scientific men, of such eminence as Adams and Jenkins, find nothing incredible in it. They tell me they see no reason why intelligent, water-breathing, vertebrated creatures, inured to a low temperature and enormous pressure, and of such a heavy structure, that neither alive nor dead would they float, might not live upon the bottom of the deep sea, and quite unsuspected by us, descendants like ourselves of the great Theriomorpha of the New Red Sandstone age.

We should be known to them however, as strange, meteoric creatures, wont to fall catastrophically dead out of the mysterious blackness of their watery sky. And not only we ourselves, but our ships, our metals, our appliances, would come raining down out of the night. Sometimes sinking things would smite down and crush them, as if it were the judgment of some unseen power above, and sometimes would come things of utmost rarity or utility, or shapes of inspiring suggestion. One can understand, perhaps, something of their behaviour at the descent of a living man, if one thinks what a barbaric people might do, to whom an enhaloed, shining creature came suddenly out of the sky.

At one time or another Elstead probably told the officers of the *Ptarmigan* every detail of his strange twelve hours in the abyss. That he also intended to write them down is certain, but he never did, and so unhappily we have to piece together the discrepant fragments of his story from the reminiscences of Commander Simmons, Weybridge, Steevens, Lindley, and the others.

We see the thing darkly in fragmentary glimpses—the huge ghostly building, the bowing, chanting people, with their dark chameleon-like heads and faintly luminous clothing, and Elstead, with his light turned on again, vainly trying to convey to their minds that the cord by which the sphere was held was to be severed. Minute after minute slipped away, and Elstead, looking at his watch, was horrified to find that he had oxygen only for four hours more. But the chant in his honour kept on as remorselessly as if it was the marching song of his approaching death.

The manner of his release he does not understand, but to judge by the end of cord that hung from the sphere, it had been cut through by rubbing against the edge of the altar. Abruptly the sphere rolled over, and he swept up, out of their world, as an ethereal creature clothed in a vacuum would sweep through our own atmosphere back to its native ether again. He must have torn out of their sight as a hydrogen bubble hastens upwards from our air. A strange ascension it must have seemed to them.

The sphere rushed up with even greater velocity than, when weighted with the lead sinkers, it had rushed down. It became exceedingly hot. It drove up with the windows uppermost, and he remembers the torrent of bubbles frothing against the glass. Every moment he expected this to fly. Then suddenly something like a huge wheel seemed to be released in his head, the padded compartment began spinning about him, and he fainted. His next recollection was of his cabin, and of the doctor's voice.

But that is the substance of the extraordinary story that Elstead related in fragments to the officers of the *Ptarmigan*. He promised to write it all down at a later date. His mind was chiefly occupied with the improvement of his apparatus, which was effected at Rio.

It remains only to tell that on February 2, 1896, he made his second descent into the ocean abyss, with the improvements his first experience suggested. What happened we shall probably never know. He never returned. The *Ptarmigan* beat about over the point of his submersion, seeking him in vain for thirteen days. Then she returned to Rio, and the news was telegraphed to his friends. So the matter remains for the present. But it is hardly probable that no further attempt will be made to verify his strange story of these hitherto unsuspected cities of the deep sea.

THE LAST STAND OF THE DECAPODS
Frank T. Bullen

Probably few of the thinking inhabitants of dry land, with all
their craving for tales of the marvellous, the gloomy, and the gigantic, have in these later centuries of the world's history given much
thought to the conditions of constant warfare existing beneath the
surface of the ocean. As readers of ancient classics well know, the
fathers of literature gave much attention to the vast, awe-inspiring
inhabitants of the sea, investing and embellishing the few fragments of fact concerning them which were available with a thousand fantastic inventions of their own naïve imaginations, until
there emerged, chief and ruler of them all, the Kraken, Leviathan,
or whatever other local name was considered to best convey in one
word their accumulated ideas of terror. In lesser degree, but still
worthy compeers of the fire-breathing dragon and sky-darkening
"Rukh" of earth and sky, a worthy host of attendant sea-monsters
were conjured up, until, apart from the terror of loneliness, of irresistible fury and instability that the sea presented to primitive
peoples, the awful nature of its supposed inhabitants made the
contemplation of an ocean journey sufficient to appall the stoutest
heart. A better understanding of this aspect of the sea to early voy-
agers may be obtained from some of the artistic efforts of those
days than anything else. There you shall see gigantic creatures with
human faces, teeth like foot-long wedges, armour-plated bodies,
and massive feet fitted with claws like scythe-blades, calmly issuing from the waves to prey upon the dwellers on the margin, or
devouring with much apparent enjoyment ships with their crews,
as a child crunches a stick of barley-sugar. Even such innocent-
looking animals as the seals were distorted and decorated until

the contemplation of their counterfeit presentment is sufficient to give a healthy man the nightmare, while such monsters as really were so terrible of aspect that they could hardly be "improved" upon were increased in size until they resembled islands whereon whole tribes might live. To these chimaeras were credited all natural phenomena such as waterspouts, whirlpools, and the upheaval of submarine volcanoes. Some imaginative people went even farther than that by attributing the support of the whole earth to a vast sea-monster; while others, like the ancient Jews, fondly pictured Leviathan awaiting in the solitude and gloom of ocean's depths the glad day of Israel's reunion, when the mountain ranges of his flesh would be ready to furnish forth the family feast for all the myriads of Abraham's children.

Surely we may pause awhile to contemplate the overmastering courage of the earliest seafarers, who, in spite of all these terrors, unappalled by the comparison between their tiny shallops and the mighty waves that towered above them, set boldly out from shore into the unknown, obeying that deeply rooted instinct of migration which has peopled every habitable part of the earth's surface. Those who remember their childhood's dread of the dark, with its possible population of bogeys, who have ever been lost in early youth in some lonely place, can have some dim conception, though only a dim one, after all, of the inward battle these ancients fought and won, until it became possible for the epigram to be written in utmost truth—

"The seas but join the nations they divide,"

But, after all, we are not now concerned with the warlike doings of men. It is with the actualities of submarine struggle we wish to deal—those wars without an armistice, where to be defeated is to be devoured, and from the sea-shouldering whale down to the smallest sea-insect every living thing is carnivorous, dependent directly upon the flesh of its neighbours for its own life, and incapable of altruism in any form whatever, except among certain of the mammalia and the sharks. In dealing with the more heroic phases of this unending warfare, then, it must be said, once for all, that the ancient writers had a great deal of reason on their side. They distorted and exaggerated, of course, as all children do, but

they did not disbelieve. But moderns, rushing to the opposite extreme, have neglected the marvels of the sea by the simple process
of disbelieving in them, except in the case of the sea-serpent, that
myth which seems bound to persist for ever, and ever. Only of late
years have the savants of the world allowed themselves to be convinced of the existence of a far more wondrous monster than the
sea-serpent (if that "loathly worm" were a reality), the original
Kraken of old-world legends. Hugest of all the mollusca, whose
prevailing characteristics are ugliness, ferocity, and unappeasable
hunger, he has lately assorted himself so firmly that current imaginative literature bristles with allusions to him, albeit oftentimes
in situations where he could by no possibility be found. No matter,
he has supplied a long-felt want; but the curious fact remains that
he is not a discovery, but a re-appearance. The gigantic cuttle-fish
of actual, indisputable fact is, in all respects except size, the Kraken;
and any faithful representation of him will justify the assertion
that no imagination could add anything to the terror-breeding potentialities of his aspect. That is so, even when he is viewed by the
light of day in the helplessness of death or disabling sickness, or
in the invincible grip of his only conqueror. In his proper realm,
crouching far below the surface of the sea in some coral cave or
labyrinth of rocks, he must present a sight so awful that the imagination recoils before it. For consider him but a little. He possesses
a cylindrical body reaching in the largest specimens yet recorded
as having been seen, a length of between sixty and seventy feet,
with an average girth of half that amount. That is to say, considerably larger than a Pullman railway-car. Now, this immense mass
is of boneless gelatinous matter, capable of much greater disten-
sion than a snake; so that in the improbable event of his obtaining
an extra-abundant supply of food, it is competent to swell to the
occasion and still give the flood of digestive juices that it secretes
full opportunity to dispose of the burden with almost incredible
rapidity. Now, the apex of this mighty cylinder—I had almost said
"tail," but remembered that it would give a wrong impression, since
it is the part of the monster that always comes first when he is
moving from place to place, is conical, that is to say, it tapers off
to a blunt point something like a whitehead torpedo. Near this apex

there is a broad fin-like arrangement looking much like the body of a skate without its tail, which, however, is used strictly for steering purposes only. So far there is nothing particularly striking about the appearance of this mighty cylinder except in colour. This characteristic varies in different individuals, but is always reminiscent of the hues of a very light-coloured leopard; that is to say, the ground is of a livid greenish white, while the detail is in splashes and spots of lurid red and yellow, with an occasional nimbus of pale blue around these deeper markings. But it is the head of the monster that appalls. Nature would seem in the construction of this greatest of all molluscs to have combined every weapon of offence possessed by the rest of the animal kingdom in one amazing arsenal, disposing them in such a manner that not only are they capable of terrific destruction, but their appearance defies adequate description.

The trunk at the head end is sheath-like, its terminating edges forming a sort of collar around the vast cable of muscles without a fragment of bone which connects it with the head. Through a large opening within this collar is pumped a jet of water, the pressure of which upon the surrounding sea is sufficiently great to drive the whole bulk of the creature, weighing perhaps sixty or seventy tons, backwards through the water, at the rate of sixteen to twenty miles per hour, not in steady progression, of course, but by successive leaps. At will, this propelling jet is deeply stained with sepia, a dark-brown inky fluid, which, mingling with the encompassing sea, fills all the neighbourhood of the monster with a gloom so deep that nothing, save one of its own species, can see either to fight or whither to fly. The head itself is of proportionate size; it is rounded underneath, and of much lighter hue than the trunk. On either side of it is set an eye, of such dimensions that the mere statement of them sounds like the efforts of one of those grand old medieval romancers, whose sole object was to make their reader's flesh creep. It is perfectly safe to say that even in proportion to size, no other known creature has such organs of vision as the cuttle-fish, for the pupils of such an one as I am now describing are fully two feet in diameter. They are perfectly black, with a dead white rim, and cannot be closed. No doubt their enormous size is for the purpose of enabling their possessor to discern what is going on amidst the thick darkness that he himself has raised, so that while all other organisms are groping blindly in the gloom, he may work his will among them. Then come the weapons which give the cuttle-fish its power of destruction, the arms or tentacles. These are not eight in number, as in the octopus, an ugly beast enough and spiteful withal, but a babe of innocence compared with our present subject. Every schoolboy should know that *octopus* signifies an eight-armed or eight-footed creature, and yet in nine cases out of ten where writers of fiction and would-be teachers of fact are describing the deadly doings of the gigantic cuttle-fish they call *him* an octopus; whereas he is nothing of the kind, for, in addition to the eight arms which the octopus possesses, the cuttle-fish flaunts two, each of which is double the length of the eight, making him a *decapod*. This confusion is the more unpardonable, because even the most ancient of scribes always spoke of this mollusc as the "ten-armed one," while a reference to any standard work on Natural History will show even the humbler cuttle-fish with their full complement of arms—that is, ten. But this is digression.

Our friend has, then, ten arms springing from the crown of his head, of which eight are forty feet in length, and two are seventy to eighty. The eight each taper outward from the head, from the thickness of a stout man's body at the base to the slenderness of a whip-lash at the end. On their inner sides they are studded with saucer-like hollows, each of which has a fringe of curving claws set just within its rim. So that in addition to their power of holding on to anything they touch by a suction so severe that it would strip flesh from bone, these cruel claws, large as those of a full-grown tiger's, get to work upon the subject being held, lacerating and tearing until the quivering body yields up its innermost secrets. Each of these destroying, serpent-like arms is also gifted with an almost independent power of volition. Whatever it touches it holds with an unreleasable grip, but with wonderful celerity it brings its prey inwards to where, in the centre of all those infernal purveyors, lies a black chasm, whose edges are shaped like the upper and lower mandibles of a parrot, and these complete the work so well begun. The outliers, those two far-reaching tentacles, unlike the busy eight, are comparatively slender from their bases to near (within two feet or so of) their ends. There they expand into broad paddle-like masses, thickly studded with *acetabulae*, those holding sucking-discs that garnish the inner arms for their entire length. So, thus armed, this nightmare monstrosity crouches in the darkling depths of ocean, like some unimaginable web, whereof every line is alive to hold and tear. Its digestion is like a furnace of dissolution, needing a continual inflow of flesh, and nothing living that inhabits the sea comes amiss to its never-satisfied cravings. It is very near the apex of the pyramid of interdependence into which sea-life is built, but not quite. For at the summit is the sperm whale, the monarch of all seas, whom man alone is capable of meeting in fair fight and overcoming.

The head of the sperm whale is of heroic size, being in bulk quite one-third of the entire body, but in addition to its size it has characteristics that fit it peculiarly to compete with such a dangerous monster as the gigantic decapod. Imagine a solid block of crude indiarubber, between twenty and thirty feet in length, and eight feet through, in shape not at all unlike a railway-carriage, but perfectly smooth in surface. Fit this mass beneath with a movable shaft of solid bone, twenty feet in length, studded with teeth, each protruding nine inches, and resembling the points of an elephant's tusks. You will then have a fairly complete notion of the equipment with which the ocean monarch goes into battle against the Kraken. And behind it lies the warm blood of the mammal, the massive framework of bone belonging to the highly developed vertebrate animal, governed by a brain impelled by irresistible instinct to seek its sustenance where alone it can be found in sufficiently satisfying bulk. And there for you are the outlines of the highest form of animal warfare existing within our ken, a conflict of Titans, to which a combat between elephants and rhinoceri in the jungle is but as the play of schoolboys compared with the gladiatorial combats of Ancient Rome.

This somewhat lengthy preamble is necessary in order to clear the way for an account of the proceedings leading up to the final subjugation of the huge molluscs of the elder slime to the needs of the great vertebrates like the whales, who were gradually emerging into a higher development, and, finding new wants oppressing them, had to obey the universal law, and fight for the satisfaction of their urgent needs. Fortunately, the period with which we have to deal was before chronology, so that we are not hampered by dates; and, as the disposition of sea and land, except in its main features, was altogether different to what we have long been accustomed to regard as the always existing geographical order of things, we need not be greatly troubled by place considerations either. What must be considered as the first beginning of the long struggle occurred when some predecessors of the present sperm whales, wandering through the vast morasses and among the sombre forests of that earlier world, were compelled to recognize that the conditions of shore life were rapidly becoming too onerous for them. Their immensely weighty bodies, lumbering slowly as a seal over the rugged land surface, handicapped them more and more in the universal business of life, the procuring of food. Not only so, but as by reason of their slowness they were confined for hunting-grounds to a very limited area, the slower organism upon which their vast appetites were fed grew scarcer and scarcer, in spite of the fecundity of that prolific time. And in proportion as they found it more and more difficult to get a living, so did their enemies grow more numerous and bolder. Vast dragon-like shapes, clad in complete armour that clanged as the wide-spreading bat-wings bore them swiftly through the air, descended upon the sluggish whales, and with horrid rending by awful shear-shaped jaws, plentifully furnished with foot-long teeth, speedily stripped from their gigantic bodies the masses of succulent flesh. Other enemies, weird of shape and swift of motion, although confined to the earth, fastened also upon the easily attainable prey that provided flesh in such bountiful abundance, and was unable to fight or flee.

Well was it, then, for the whales that, living always near the sea, they had formed aquatic habits, finding in the limpid element a medium wherein their huge bulk was rather a help than a hindrance to them. Gradually they grew to use the land less and less as they became more and more accustomed to the food provided in plenty by the inexhaustible ocean. Continual practice enabled them to husband the supplies of air which they took in on the surface for use beneath the waves; and, better still, they found that whereas they had been victims to many a monster on land whose proportions and potentialities seemed far inferior to their own, here in their new element they were supreme, nothing living but fled from before them. But presently a strange thing befell them. As they grew less and less inclined to use the dry land, they found that their powers of locomotion thereon gradually became less and less also, until at last their hind legs dwindled away and disappeared. Their vast and far-reaching tails lost their length, and their bones spread out laterally into flexible fans of toughest gristle, with which they could propel themselves through the waves at speeds to which their swiftest progress upon land had been but a snail's crawl. Also their fore legs grew shorter and wider, and the separation of the toes disappeared, until all that was left of these once ponderous supports were elegant fan-like flippers of gristle, of not the slightest use for propulsion, but merely acting as steadying-vanes to keep the whole great structure in its proper position according to the will of the owner. All these radical physical changes, however, had not affected the real classification of the whales. They were still mammals, still retained in the element which was now entirely their habitat the high organization belonging to the great carnivora of the land. Therefore it took them no long period of time to realize that in the ocean they would be paramount, that with the tremendous facilities for rapid movement afforded them by their new habitat they were able to maintain that supremacy against all comers, unless their formidable armed jaws should also become modified by degeneration into some such harmless cavities for absorbing food as are possessed by their distant relatives, the mysticetae, or toothless whales.

With a view to avoiding any such disaster, they made good use of their jaws, having been taught by experience that the simple but effectual penalty for the neglect of any function, whether physical or mental, was the disappearance of the organs where such functions had been performed. But their energetic use of teeth and jaws had a result entirely unforeseen by them. Gradually the prey they sought, the larger fish and smaller sea-mammals, disappeared from the shallow seas adjacent to the land, from whence the whales had

been driven; and in order to satisfy the demands of their huge stom-
achs, they were fain to follow their prey into deeper and deeper
waters, meeting as they went with other and stranger denizens of
those mysterious depths, until at last the sperm whale met the
Kraken. There in his native gloom, vast, formless, and insatiable,
brooded the awful Thing. Spread like a living net whereof every
mesh was armed, sensitive and lethal, this fantastic complication
of horrors took toll of all the sea-folk, needing not to pursue its
prey, needing only to lie still, devour, and grow. Sometimes, moved
by mysterious impulses, one of these chimaeras would rise to the
sea-surface and bask in the beams of the offended sun, poisoning
the surrounding air with its charnel-house odours, and occasionally finding within the never-resting nervous clutching of its tentacles some specimens of the highest, latest product of creation,
man himself. Ages of such experiences as these had left the Kraken
defenceless as to his body. The absence of any necessity for exertion had arrested the development of a backbone; the inability of
any of the sea-people to retaliate upon their sateless foe had made
him neglect any of those precautions that weaker organisms had
provided themselves with, and even the cloud of sepia with which
all the race were provided, and which often assisted the innocent
and weaker members of the same great family to escape, was only
used by these masters of the sea to hide their monstrous lures from
their prey.

Thus on a momentous day a ravenous sperm whale, hunting
eagerly for wherewithal to satisfy his craving, suddenly found himself encircled by many long, cable-like arms. They clung, they tore,
they sucked. But whenever a stray end of them flung itself across
the bristling parapet of the whale's lower jaw it was promptly bitten off, and a portion having found its way down into the craving
stomach of the big mammal, it was welcomed as good beyond all
other food yet encountered. Once this had been realized, what had
originally been an accidental entrapping changed itself into a vigorous onslaught and banquet. True, the darkness fought for the
mollusc, but that advantage was small compared with the feeling
of incompetence, of inability to make any impression upon this
mighty impervious mass that was moving as freely amid the clinging

embarrassments of those hitherto invincible arms as if they were
only fronds of sea-weed. And then the foul mass of the Kraken
found itself, contrary to all previous experience, rising involun-
tarily, being compelled to leave its infernal shades, and, without
any previous preparation for such a change of pressure, to visit
the upper air. The fact was that the whale, finding its stock of air
exhausted, had put forth a supreme effort to rise, and found that,
although unable to free himself from those enormous cables, he
was actually competent to raise the whole mass. What an upheaval!
Even the birds that, allured by the strong carrion scent, were as-
sembling in their thousands, fled away from that appalling vision,
their wild screams of affright filling the air with lamentation. The
tormented sea foamed and boiled in wide-spreading whirls, its deep
sweet blue changed into an unhealthy nondescript tint of muddy
yellow as the wide expanse of the Kraken's body yielded up its cor-
rupt fluids, and the healthful breeze did its best to disperse the
bad smells that rose from the ugly mass. Then the whale, having
renewed his store of air, settled down seriously to the demolition
of his prize. Length after length of tentacle was torn away from
the central crown and swallowed, gliding down the abysmal throat
of the gratified mammal in snaky convolutions until even that great
store-room would contain no more. The vanquished Kraken lay
helplessly rolling upon the wave while its conqueror in satisfied
ease lolled near, watching with good-humoured complacency the
puny assault made upon that island of gelatinous flesh by the multitude of smaller hungry things. The birds returned, reassured, and
added by their clamour to the strangeness of the scene, where the
tribes of air and sea, self-bidden to the enormous banquet, were
making full use of their exceptional privilege. So the great feast
continued while the red sun went down and the white moon rose
in placid beauty. Yet for all the combined assaults of those hungry
multitudes the tenacious life of that largest of living things lay so
deeply seated that when the rested whale resumed his attentions
he found the body of his late antagonist still quivering under the
attack of his tremendous jaws. But its proportions were so immense
that his utmost efforts left store sufficient for at least a dozen of his
companions, had they been there, to have satisfied their hunger

upon. And, satisfied at last, he turned away, allowing the smaller fry, who had waited his pleasure most respectfully, to close in again and finish the work he had so well begun.

Now, this was a momentous discovery indeed, for the sperm whales had experienced, even when fish and seals were plentiful, great difficulty in procuring sufficient food at one time for a full meal, and the problem of how to provide for themselves as they grew and multiplied had become increasingly hard to solve. Therefore this discovery filled the fortunate pioneer with triumph, for his high instincts told him that he had struck a new source of supply that promised to be inexhaustible. So, in the manner common to his people, he wasted no time in convening a gathering of them as large as could be collected. Far over the placid surface of that quiet sea lay gently rocking a multitude of vast black bodies, all expectant, all awaiting the momentous declaration presently to be made. The epoch-making news circulated among them in perfect silence, for to them has from the earliest times been known the secret that is only just beginning to glimmer upon the verge of human intelligence, the ability to communicate with one another without the aid of speech, sight, or touch—a kind of thought transference, if such an idea as animal thought may be held allowable. And having thus learned of the treasures held in trust for them by the deep waters, they separated and went, some alone and some in compact parties of a dozen or so, upon their rejoicing way.

But among the slimy hosts of the gigantic Molluscs there was raging a sensation unknown before—a feeling of terror, of insecurity born of the knowledge that at last there had appeared among them a being proof against the utmost pressure of their awful arms, who was too great to be devoured, who, on the other hand, had evinced a greedy partiality for devouring them. How this information became common property among them it is impossible to say, since they dwelt alone, each in his own particular lair, rigidly respected by one another, because any intrusion upon another's domains was invariably followed by the absorption of either the intruder or the intruded upon by the stronger of the two. This, although not intended by them, had the effect of vastly heightening the fear with which they were regarded by the smaller sea-folk, for they took to a restless prowling along the sea-bed, enwreathing themselves about the mighty bases of the islands, and invading cool coral caverns where their baleful presence had been till then unknown. Never before had there been such a panic among the multitudinous sea-populations. What could this new portent signify? Were the foundations of the great deep again about to be broken up, and the sea-bed heaved upward to replace the tops of the towering mountains on dry land? There was no reply, for there were none that could answer questions like these.

Still the fear-smitten decapods wandered, seeking seclusion from the coming enemy, and finding none to their mind. Still the crowds of their victims rushed blindly from shoal to shoal, plunging into depths unfitted for them, or rising into shallows where their natural food was not. And the whole sea was troubled, until at last there appeared, grim and vast, the advance-guard of the sperm whales, and hurled itself with joyful anticipation upon the shrinking convolutions of those hideous monsters that had so long dominated the dark places of the sea. For the whales it was a time of feasting hitherto without parallel. Without any fear, uncaring to take even the most elementary precautions against a defeat which they felt to be an impossible contingency, they sought out and devoured one after another of these vast uglinesses, already looked upon by them as their natural provision, their store of food accumulated of purpose against their coming. Occasionally, it is true, some rash youngster, full of pride, and rejoicing in his pre-eminence over all life in the depths, would hurl himself into a smoky network of far-spreading tentacles which would wrap him round so completely that his jaws were fast bound together, his flukes would vainly essay to propel him any whither, and he would presently perish miserably, his cable-like sinews falling slackly and his lungs suffused with crimson brine. Even then, the advantage gained by the triumphant Kraken was a barren one, for in every case the bulk of the victim was too great, his body too firm in its build, for the victor, despite his utmost efforts, to succeed in devouring his prize. So that the disappointed Kraken had perforce to witness the gradual disappearance of his lawful prize beneath the united efforts of myriads of tiny sea-scavengers, secure in their insignificance against any attack from him, and await with tremor extending to the remotest extremity of every tentacle, the retribution that he felt sure would speedily follow.

This desultory warfare was waged for long, until, driven by despair to a community of interest unknown before, the Krakens gradually sought one another out with but a single idea—that of combining against the new enemy; for, knowing to what an immense size their kind could attain in the remoter fastnesses of ocean, they could not yet bring themselves to believe that they were to become the helpless prey of these new-corners, visitors of yesterday, coming from the cramped acreage of the land into the limitless fields of ocean, and invading the immemorial freeholds of its hitherto unassailable sovereigns. From the remotest recesses of ocean they came, that grisly gathering—came in ever-increasing hosts, their silent progress spreading unprecedented dismay among the fairer inhabitants of the sea. Figure to yourselves, if you can, the advance of this terrible host. But the effort is vain. Not even Martin, that frenzied delineator of the frightful halls of hell, the scenes of the Apocalypse, and the agonies of the Deluge, could have done justice to the terrors of such a scene. Only dimly can we imagine what must have been the appearance of those vast masses of writhing flesh, as through the palely gleaming phosphorescence of the depths they sped backwards in leaps of a hundred fathoms each, their terrible arms, close-clustered together, streaming behind like Medusa's hair magnified ten thousand times in size, and with each snaky tress bearing a thousand mouths instead of one.

So they converged upon the place of meeting, an area of the sea-bed nowhere more than 500 fathoms in depth, from whose rugged floor rose irregularly stupendous columnar masses of lava hurled upwards by the cosmic forces below in a state of incandescence and solidified as they rose, assuming many fantastic shapes, and affording perfect harbourage to such dire scourges of the sea as were now making the place their rendezvous. For, strangely enough, this marvellous portion of the submarine world was more densely peopled with an infinite variety of sea-folk than any other; its tepid waters seemed to bring forth abundantly of all kinds of fish, crustacea, and creeping things. Sharks in all their fearsome

varieties prowled greasily about, scenting for dead things whereon
to gorge, shell-fish from the infinitesimal globigerina up to the gigantic clam whose shells were a yard each in diameter; crabs, lobsters,
and other freakish varieties of crustacea of a size and ugliness unknown to-day lurked in every crevice, while about and among all
these scavengers flitted the happy, lovely fish in myriads of glorious hues, matching the tender shades of the coral groves that
sprang from the summits of those sombre lava columns beneath.
Hitherto this happy hunting-ground had not been invaded by the
sea-mammals. None of the air-breathing inhabitants of the ocean
had ventured into its gloomy depths, or sought their prey among
the blazing shallows of the surface-reefs, although no more
favourable place for their exertions could possibly have been se-
lected over all the wide sea. It had long been a favourite haunt of
the Kraken, for whom it was, as aforesaid, an ideal spot, but now it
was to witness a sight unparalleled in ocean history. Heralded by
an amazing series of under-waves, the gathering of monsters drew
near. They numbered many thousands, and no one in all their hosts
was of lesser magnitude than sixty feet long by thirty in girth of
body alone. From that size they increased until some—the acknowl-
edged leaders—discovered themselves like islands, their cylindrical
carcases huge as that of an ocean liner, and their tentacles capable
of overspreading an entire village.

In concentric rings they assembled, all heads pointing outward,
the mightiest within, and four clear avenues through the circles
left for coming and going. Contrary to custom, but by mutual con-
sent, all the tentacles lay closely arranged in parallel lines, not
outspread to every quarter of the compass, and all a-work. They
looked, indeed, in their inertia and silence, like nothing so much
as an incalculable number of dead squid of enormous size neatly
laid out at the whim of some giant's fancy. Yet communication between them was active; a subtle interchange of experiences and
plans went briskly on through the medium of the mobile element
around them. The elder and mightier were full of disdain at the
reports they were furnished with, utterly incredulous as to the ability of any created thing to injure them, and, as the time wore on,
an occasional tremor was distinctly noticeable through the whole

length of their tentacles, which boded no good to their smaller brethren. Doubtless but little longer was needed for the development of a great absorption of the weaker by the stronger, only that, darting into their midst like, a lightning streak, came a messenger squid, bearing the news that a school of sperm whales, numbering at least ten thousand, were coming at top-speed direct for their place of meeting. Instantly to the farthest confines of that mighty gathering the message radiated, and as if by one movement there uprose from the sea-bed so dense a cloud of sepia that for many miles around the clear blue of the ocean became turbid, stagnant, and foul. Even the birds that hovered over those dark-brown waves took fright at this terrible phenomenon, to them utterly incomprehensible, and with discordant shrieks they fled in search of sweeter air and cleaner sea. But below the surface under cover of this thickest darkness there was the silence of death.

Twenty miles away, under the bright sunshine, an advance-guard of about a hundred sperm whales came rushing on. Line abreast, their bushy breath rising like the regular steam-jets from a row of engines, they dashed aside the welcoming wavelets, every sense alert, and full of eagerness for the consummation of their desires. Such had been their despatch that throughout the long journey of 500 leagues they had not once stayed for food, so that they were ravenous with hunger as well as full of fight. They passed, and before the foaming of their swift passage had ceased, the main body, spread over a space of thirty miles, came following on, the roar of their multitudinous march sounding like the voice of many waters. Suddenly the advance-guard, with stately elevation of the broad fans of their flukes, disappeared, and by one impulse the main body followed them. Down into the depths they bore, noting with dignified wonder the absence of all the usual inhabitants of the deep, until, with a thrill of joyful anticipation which set all their masses of muscle a-quiver, they recognized the scent of the prey. No thought of organized resistance presented itself; without a halt, or even the faintest slackening of their great rush, they plunged forward into the abysmal gloom; down, down withal into that wilderness of waiting devils. And so, in darkness and silence like that of the beginning of things, this great battle was joined. Whale after whale

succumbed, anchored to the bottom by such bewildering entangle-
ments, such enlacement of tentacles, that their vast strength was
helpless to free them; their jaws were bound hard together, and
even the wide sweep of their flukes gat no hold upon the slimy
water. But the Decapods were in evil case. Assailed from above
while their groping arms writhed about below, they found themselves more often locked in unreleasable hold of their fellows than
they did of their enemies. And the quick-shearing jaws of those
enemies shredded them into fragments, made nought of their bulk,
revelled and frolicked among them, slaying, devouring, exulting.
Again and again the triumphant mammals drew off for air and from
satiety, went and bled upon the sleek oily surface, in water now so
thick that the fiercest hurricane that ever blew would have failed
to raise a wave thereon.

So through a day and a night the slaying ceased not, except for
these brief interludes, until those of the Decapods left alive had
disentangled themselves from the debris of their late associates
and returned with what speed they might to depths and crannies,
where they fondly hoped their ravenous enemies could never come.
They bore with them the certain knowledge that from henceforth
they were no longer lords of the sea, that instead of being, as hitherto, devourers of all things living that crossed the radius of their
outspread toils, they were now and for all time to be the prey of a
nobler race of creatures, a higher order of being, and that at last
they had taken their rightful position as creatures of usefulness in
the vast economy of Creation.

THE VOYAGE OF THE "MARY SIMPSON"
Arthur Colton

Captain David Brett was an ex-whaler, and spun yarns that smelt of the sea, not fishy, but salty. When he got on a chair and cried, "There she blows!" it was a remarkable thing.

The captain had a horse named Borneo, an iron gray, whose gait was like unto that of a storm-tossed ship. I never could understand how an inland-born horse like Borneo came to achieve so nautical a manner. The captain taught him to chew tobacco. We would have liked it if Borneo could have hitched up his trousers, but this was beyond him.

Northeast of Hagar lies Cumming's alder swamp. It is a nucleus into which gather numerous little threads of shining water, from the Cattle Ridge, from the meadows farther east, and even from the gentle slopes of the Salem hills. And all these dribble somehow through the gentle swamp, and come out in the Mill Stream marvellously clear.

The Muck Hole is on the south side of the swamp, so that when you fish for eels you do not mind that it looks dark and cold, because the comfortable meadows are behind you, with only a few rods of alders between. Otherwise it would be a doubtful place, for it is a bit uncanny, anyway. The banks are steep and slippery, of grayish clay, and ten feet high. The water is inky black. We called it forty feet deep in order to be moderate. Beyond is the swamp, where no one goes, except herons sometimes and kingfishers. Bullfrogs live there, for you can hear them gulp and bellow in the twilight, and a great number of silent and creeping things.

We sat on the bank of the Muck Hole, with our feet dangling over the smooth, inky water. Borneo, with the deacon's buckboard.

105

was hitched in the alders behind. Moses Durfey had a bamboo rod. Chub Leroy and I had no bamboos; we despised snobbishness. The captain had a massive black pole and a thick line. The eels that summer afternoon paid us very little attention. Being so cool in the Muck Hole, they did not understand how hot it was sitting on the bank and waiting for them. And here Captain David told us the manner of the voyage of the *Mary Simpson*.

"It don't amount to much," he said, indifferently. "Some cur'us—one o' those things that happens without no point to 'em, as you might say;" and he yawned, with a fine air of wearied experience.

The *Mary Simpson*, it appeared, as the captain's tale progressed, was a stanch ship. She was, in fact, "a buster in a gale." But so many things happened to her connected with different kinds of wind, her tackle and sails were so hauled about with strange language, that she must have been tired of busting, and glad enough to be becalmed in the Pacific, even if "sou'east o' the Austral Islands, bearing away from Lan'ster Reef."

There were no whales in sight, and not a ripple on the flat sea. The crew of the *Mary Simpson* amused themselves by hooking sharks and sword-fish over the side of the ship, but it was dull and difficult to keep awake doing this, for even the sharks were seldom over thirty feet long. Sometimes, when the sharks and sword-fish took to fighting, it was more interesting, for the sharks would swallow the sword-fish, and the sword-fish would thrash around inside, and make an exit for themselves, and come out: and the expression on the faces of the sharks at this point was always worth seeing.

But, on the whole—Captain David said—it was dull; so that when he hooked a sea-serpent every one was delighted, even the sea-serpent; and it had the best reason, in the way that when two people are hooked together the joke is on the smaller. In this way the joke was on the *Mary Simpson*.

The sea-serpent put its head up a little way out of the water, fifty or sixty feet, and grinned at the *Mary Simpson*, and began to back off, nearly dragging the rope out of the captain's hands: but he held on, so that the *Mary Simpson* followed, of course. Presently the serpent grew tired of hauling the *Mary Simpson*, and tried to shake the hook out of its mouth. Then it pulled the other end of itself from the bottom of the ocean and slapped the *Mary Simpson* in a disgusted kind of way, as much as to say, "Aw, let up there, will you!" It is no joke to be slapped by anything as broad as a house. The *Mary Simpson* did not like it. It threw tons of mud on her deck, so that every one said the sea-serpent had better mind what it was about before somebody got angry.

It came nearer to look into the matter, and the trouble seemed to be mostly the captain, who was holding the line, and wondering how much half a mile of sea-serpent would bring if sold to a museum by the yard; so the sea-serpent pulled in its tail again and slapped Captain David. It was done in an impertinent way, and Captain David went overboard in a very bad temper.

The sea-serpent swam, and Captain David hung on to the line, partly on account of his great anger, and partly because when he cleared the mud from his eyes the *Mary Simpson* was far away on the horizon and quite out of the question. He found himself swishing along, with the great coils going up and down close beside him in a way that would have frightened another man.

After a time the serpent felt something twitching at its lip, eased up, and looked around. First it seemed surprised, and then disgusted: and if one ever meets a surprised and disgusted sea-serpent, he should take particular notice. Captain David remarked it at the time.

"I can't make it out at all. Blow me!" said the sea-serpent, or seemed to say, "it's ridiculous." Then it flung its tail in the air like a skyrocket and started for the bottom of the ocean. The captain let it go, but he was angry, and showed it.

"I give you fair warning!" he shouted. "You an' me parts. I don't have nothin' more to do with you."

"An' I didn't," he added to us. "I never saw him again."

Now this happened on a Saturday night, and Captain David swam from then till Monday morning. It is very bad luck to be swimming on Sunday, and that was the reason that on Monday morning he landed on a cannibal island. The cannibals had all been converted and were dead, and the missionaries had gone away. Still it was bad luck: the next worse thing to being eaten is not to eat, and there was little on the island to eat but a musty kind of clam.

On Wednesday the wind blew a gale, and on Thursday who should come along but the *Mary Simpson*, busting! She poked her nose into the island looking for the captain, who was angry with her for thinking that he could not look after himself; and the *Mary Simpson* was angry with the captain for losing the sea-serpent: so that they all sailed toward the south pole, very grumpy and looking for whales, whales being fish of a fair size, and yet not so long but that you can account for both ends of them.

"An' now," said the captain, "would you believe it—Ho! I got a bite. It's a buster!"

This was not the end of the voyage of the *Mary Simpson*, but at this point the captain had a bite.

"It's an eel!" he cried. "It's a buster!"

Then we knew what busting was like, and wished we could have seen the *Mary Simpson* busting. The great eel went round in circles, did itself up into knots and shot out again, plunged to the bottom, and flashed over the surface.

"Get him!" yelled Moses.

"Play him!" cried Chub.

"Hrrrnp! Hi! Hold on to me!" said the captain, and he went over the bank, coasting down the soft clay, with his stout legs in the air kicking vehemently, till he splashed in the water. We three overhead performed a cannibal dance that was neither decorative nor useful.

The captain got on his feet with a deal of tumult and looked himself over, dripping with muddy water and plastered with sticky clay. "Now ain't that disgustin'!" he said.

He could not climb the bank, and it was undignified to have rolled down it. There were no cannibal islands to swim to between Saturday and Monday. Things were a deal more convenient in the Pacific. The eel kept perfectly quiet, and did not offer to tow the captain anywhere. There seemed to be something for us to do, and we were not satisfied that a cannibal dance was the right thing. We felt that even as cannibals we ought to consider the captain's rheumatism.

"Here!" howled Captain David. "You git me out o' this."

"It's the sea-serpent's business," said Moses, who was very literal. "Poke it up."

"Can't, it's gone to the bottom," I said.

"Borneo!" said Chub, and dove into the alders and brought Borneo.

We tied the lines to the traces; the captain wound them around his hands and came up the bank as if there were nothing in gravitation, and gripping his pole.

"Hi!" said Moses. "Go it, Borneo! Here comes the eel."

Captain David gathered himself and looked at the squirming thing on the grass.

"Hitched himself to the wrong man that time, didn't he? Can't fool me!"

He stumped through the alders, leading Borneo and dragging the eel.

"Cap'n David," said Chub, thoughtfully, "if you'd had Borneo 'stead of the *Mary Simpson*, you'd have landed the sea-serpent, wouldn't you?"

"Ay," said Captain David. "Yes. You're right. Borneo's a good hoss."

Out of the Deep
Owen Oliver

The *Adolf Karl* brought the first news of the evil that had come upon the earth. She was a Norwegian timber-ship, and a coal-brig running from Newcastle found her waterlogged in the North Sea, and towed her to port. There were only two tall, light-haired sailors left alive. The older man said one phrase over and over again, and nothing else. "Fishes—fishes! O Lord, the devils of fishes!" The younger sailor kept laughing and sobbing, and clasping and unclasping his hands for hours after he came ashore; but by degrees they got a rambling narrative from him.

He said that a great company of big fishes had come out of the sea in flying machines, and taken and eaten the rest of the crew; but he and the other man had hidden under an old sail. The sea-devils, as he called them, had pulled up the decks and torn open the storehouses, and eaten all the food aboard except a few fragments of biscuit. He and the other mad had lived on these for two days till they were rescued. He shivered and clung to those around him whenever he saw a bird flying in the air, thinking it was a sea-devil afar.

The old-fashioned papers ignored the wild story, and merely said that the men had lost their reason through privations; but the halfpenny papers happened to be short of news. So they expanded it into two or three columns, with glaring headlines. They pointed out, also, that three other ships reported having seen afar "enormous flocks of enormous birds," and that nearly twenty vessels were overdue at East Coast ports. This was on Thursday, 26th July, 1906.

On Friday, the P. & O. *Alamanzar* drove ashore near Plymouth, with the furnaces just burnt out. There was no one aboard, and no feed except in the refrigerators. Her decks, upper and lower, were burst open. It was noticed that all the planks were broken upwards.

A question upon the subject was put to the Home Secretary in the House of Commons that night; but the Home Secretary considered that the matter came within the province of his Rt. Hon. friend the First Lord of the Admiralty, and his Rt. Hon. friend had "no official knowledge of the matter."

On Saturday morning the *Maplin Castle* came in at Southampton with only a third of her passengers and a fifth of her crew remaining. They told a plainer tale.

They were nearly two days out from Madeira, they said, and two from home, when what appeared to be a cloud of remarkable blackness and size was observed ahead. The captain, who had been forty years at sea, had never seen anything like it, and feared a hurricane. In about half-an-hour, it was close upon them, and looked more like an incredibly great swarm of large black birds.

At this time a multitude of huge fishes, with six wings, three on each side, began to show themselves upon the surface of the sea. The cloud proved to be composed of similar monsters flying by machinery, and with a paddle-wheel arrangement, revolving with enormous velocity, on each side of their heads. Professor Thorne, who was aboard but did not survive, surmised that these were contrivances for supplying their gills with oxygen from the air to enable them to breathe in our thin atmosphere.

As they bore upon the ship, the fishes in the water rose and joined them. The crew and a few of the male passengers prepared to resist them with hatchets and revolvers. The rest rushed to their companions. While they blocked one another in their struggles to get down, the fishes angled for them with lines which seemed to adhere to whatever they touched. The majority of the passengers were borne shrieking into the air and devoured, before the remainder succeeded in closing the entrances. The crew, and the bolder passengers who had joined them, suffered still more severely. Meanwhile the captain had ordered full speed ahead; and as the pace proved too great for the monsters, the vessel ultimately escaped. The third officer brought a piece of one of the "fishing-rods," which was broken in a door when it was closed. Major Dunne shot its owner in several places, and the beastly creature fell upon the deck, but two other "fish-devils" had carried it away. The rod was made of a curious, flexible metal unknown to science, but akin to iron. It was apparently used to transmit some attractive force, for it had no adhesiveness in itself.

A dozen torpedo-boat-destroyers were at once sent out to scour the seas. Two only returned. The *Leopard* reported having put a head of some five thousand sea-devils to flight with its quick-firing guns as they were rising from the sea. The *Myra* had been attacked by a multitude flying overhead, and half the crew, including the commander, seized and devoured; but ultimately escaped by its speed. Portions of the deck and bulwarks had been torn away by the fishing-rods.

The *Myra* returned on Monday, 30th July. On the next day cablegrams reached England that several villages on the Bay of Biscay had been attacked by the sea-devils, and nearly all the inhabitants carried off. The following morning Lisbon, and several other Portuguese and French ports were reported devastated. The evening papers had huge placards:

BRIGHTON, HASTINGS, AND PLYMOUTH
ATTACKED BY SEA-DEVILS.
CHANNEL FLEET DESTROYED.
INDIA AND CHINA INVADED.

After that there were no newspapers.

A continuous service of trains was run night and day from the Southern Coast to London; and trains left London every few minutes for the Midlands, with every carriage and truck carrying double its proper number. Seats were booked for a week ahead. It was understood that millions of monsters were making their way slowly to London, clearing out every town and village as they came. People who could not get in the trains left in carts or on foot.

The Government sent officers down to the coast to report, but none returned; and telegraphic communications was rare. Wires came, however, to say that the monsters were approaching from Hythe, Chatham, and Ashford. It was pretty well established that all the towns on the South Coast were destroyed, and some on the East, and in the North of Scotland; and there was an authenticated statement that a cargo of refugees had arrived from Holland, and stated that the country was completely wiped out. We knew these things from "town criers" sent round by the Home Office. They ceased to come round on August 8th.

The next morning, I walked along the Strand, and saw two shops open, and counted eighteen people. The buses and cabs had long since departed with passengers inland. I stayed in town myself because I had no money, and could live gratis at the deserted restaurants. In one of them I met a slight, ladylike girl. She had no money either, she said, and no friends in town, and she was very frightened. We kept together afterwards. Her name was Elsie, and she was twenty-two. She had been a typewriter before business stopped. We joined company with a man and his wife for two days. They had three children, they told us, and had sent them to Derby in a County Council train. The Council ran forty a day for children only, before the train service ceased. They could not get in the trains themselves, and the woman was weak and could not walk far. On the third day the man found a wheelbarrow and took her off in it. We never thought to ask their names.

On the 10th August we met a wild-eyed man running in the Mall. He would hardly stop to speak to us. He had come from Wimbledon, he said, and the air was thick with the sea-devils there. A woman who came on a horse told him that they were breaking open every house systematically, and gathering up the people and cattle. They seized her father just as he had placed her on the horse. Elsie and I decided to go inland on foot the next morning. We had found money in some of the empty houses, and we thought that with that and a bag of provisions we could live on the road.

We slept at the Army and Navy Club that night, as we had done for two days previously. There were five old officers there, but they were hospitable, and placed two rooms at our disposal. They'd never run away from anything yet, they said, and they were too old to learn sense. Four of them played Bridge all day, while the fifth, in turn, kept guard at the front door with a revolver to stop the three club servants who remained from flight.

Elsie woke me by banging at my door at about seven o'clock.

"They're coming," she cried. "They're coming, Fred!"

"Run!" I shouted. "Don't wait for me. Go up Shaftesbury Avenue. I'll catch you!"

When I had dressed, however, I found her waiting outside the door; and when I reproached her, she smiled and tucked her arm in mine.

"I thought we'd make a better dish together," she said with a little laugh—and a little shudder.

The veterans were growling in the front hall because the cook had escaped out of a window. We advised them to fly, but they said they might as well be eaten if they would get nothing decent to eat; and they were going to stop and have a final hand of Bridge. So we left them.

We had intended going North, but there were black objects in the sky in that direction. So we made for Charing Cross. The morning was exceedingly dull. It was probably raining; but I do not remember.

When we came to Trafalgar Square we found that the black things were converging upon it from every point of the compass, and driving in the remnants of humanity from the outskirts of London. There were more left than I thought, perhaps five thousand in all. A shrieking mob was rushing up Whitehall, and another along Northumberland Avenue, and another down the Strand, and another down St. Martin's Lane. In the air behind each crowd, and from every other direction, came troops of the sea-devils. The foremost were so near that we could hear their breathing-wheels and distinguish a white line of teeth in their heads. We stood still and gazed helplessly at them.

"It is the end," Elsie said. "You—you have been good to me, Fred." She touched my shoulder softly with the side of her head. It is strange, the power of little things—an old phrase—a glance—the breath of a woman's hair. If she had not done that I should have stood rooted there till we were taken. As it was I caught her by the hand and pulled her along.

"The National Gallery!" I cried, "They may want to preserve it as it memorial of our art—who knows?" I chuckled a metallic chuckle. "Run!"

We knew that a lower door was open, as we had been in there the day before. We reached it just as the forerunners of the crowds came to the square. There was a dark shadow over the doorway; the shadow of an overhanging monster. Its wings were making a slow, clapping clatter as it descended, and the whirr of its breathing-wheels was loud in our ears. Elsie gasped, and staggered. I seized her in one arm, and carried her to the door and fumbled at it. It was perhaps two seconds before I turned the handle the right way. It seemed hours. My teeth chattered, and my hands trembled so that I could scarcely fasten the door.

We wandered aimlessly through the galleries and tried to talk about the pictures, but our words broke all in the middle. At last we stood still, holding one another's hands. Elsie's face was ashy white; and I felt cold and moist and sick.

"We'd better hide in a cellar," I suggested. "They mightn't find us there."

"Anything is better than waiting like this," she said suddenly. "Let's look out and see what they are doing."

We found a room, at the end of the water-colours, looking into the Square, and stood in the corner behind a screen, and peered round it. Sometimes when I am in the middle of a jest the scene comes back to me and I am struck dumb. Sometimes Elsie will pause in her laughter, as she plays with her baby, and put her face in her hands; and it is years ago now.

The crowd had huddled together in the Square and the empty basins of the fountains—a sea of white upturned faces, with the statues in between. A few—very few—were screaming. A few were laughing insanely. Others were contorting their faces horribly. Some had fainted, but still kept their feet, wedged in by the crowd. Most of the women had their heads on men's shoulders. Some held children in their arms.

A guard of the sea-devils had settled on the roadways round the Square. A countless multitude were poised in the air overhead. It was proved afterwards that there were some twenty varieties, but they all looked of one devilish pattern—fishes, about ninety feet long, with disproportionately large heads and disproportion-ately short, broad tails. They were covered with blackish-green scales that looked like armour. They had light-green, phosphorescent eyes, about twice the bigness of a liner's port-hole, and terrible mouths, ten or twelve feet wide, shaped like a shark's, and showing immense jagged teeth. Their scales crackled and rustled as they moved.

The front half of their body was girt with a framework of black-grey metal, since called *marium*. It extended along their backs towards the tail, like a skeleton deck. This deck carried three pairs of wings with marium ribs, and an inky-black membrane stretched between. The front of the framework supported the breathing-wheels, or artificial gills, as they are accepted to have been. These were composed of concentric circles of a substance now termed *pelagium*, which scientists say is neither metal nor nonmetal, but a new class of element. Each circle revolved upon that within it, so that the velocity of the outer circle was enormous. The outermost layer was a soft leathery material, which has been named *philoxon*, from its extraordinary powers of drawing the oxygen from the air. The few remains of this, however, were so charred by combustion that nothing definite can be said about it. The "fishing-line" was a thin, flexible, marium rod, which operated from the front of the "deck," and was coiled there when not in use. It was about two hundred feet long, and the thickness of a very stout clothes-line.

How this machinery was controlled, or how it had been made by these creatures, who had no members, like our hands, capable of graduated pressure and contact, remains unknown. Most people, however, accept the conjecture of the learned Von Raben, that they manipulated matter by means of what he termed "piscian magnetism" —a force generated by the fishes themselves, and which they were able to graduate and control, to the finest degree. The experiments upon the scales of the monsters (which ended with his unfortunate death) proved that when electrically stimulated in a certain manner, some portions of a scale would attract, and others repel, and so work a wire, or a thin plate of metal into various shapes— portions being held firmly, while the neighbouring parts were driven away. So that each scale was virtually a many-fingered hand.

As we watched the monsters, the long fishing-rods came slowly forth, wavered in the air, dipped among the crowd, that ceased to sway, as if fascinated. There was a shriek—shriek upon shriek—

men, women, and children were lifted up in the air as if they were bound to the fishing-lines, though there was no visible means of attachment. Some of them hung limply; others beat at it with their hands—and could not draw them away again. Then it carried them to the shark-like mouth.

Elsie buried her face under my jacket, and we shrank behind the screen. The shrieks grew fewer and fewer. Presently they ceased. Then a series of crashes began. I laid Elsie down (she had fainted) and peeped round the screen again. The long metallic lines were tearing out the windows and sides of the houses across the Square, by adhering to them and pulling them outwards, and searching the premises. Now and then one brought out a man or a woman. They would fish for us, I thought, next.

I lifted Elsie up and staggered away to the galleries, till I came to the end room of the Dutch-Flemish school. I pulled a big screen covered with small pictures close to the wall, and sat huddled on the floor behind it, with her head on my knee. We were just under a man's portrait by Rembrandt, with a painting of a fish and poultry shop beside it. I have forgotten the name of the painter, and I would not, for worlds, go there again to look. I listened with my ear against the wall for the approach of a clinging line; but I heard nothing. Possibly they wished to preserve some specimens of our art, for throughout the country they did very little damage to churches, museums, or galleries.

A lean, half-starved cat came round the screen and mewed piteously. I screamed aloud at the sound. Then I held my breath, wondering if *they* had heard. A spider made its way slowly down a cobweb, and dropped on the floor. I could hear it drop, everything was so still. I shook Elsie to try and rouse her, to hear her voice. I half rose to fetch some water to restore her, but sat down again. Her unconsciousness was so merciful! I stroked her face gently. She had been so cheerful, and so contented, and so kind. Poor little Elsie! There was a sound of distant thunder outside, and a flash of light invaded the darkness. I saw the cat standing there with its back arched. I called to it, "Puss, puss." There was another flash and rumble. Elsie sighed, turned her face a little closer against my hand, and looked up.

"Are—we—dead?" she asked in an awed, halting whisper. "Dead?"

I told her briefly what had happened. She was silent till another flash startled her.

"I thought they were coming," she whispered. "If they took us it would be over. I must see what they are doing. I *must!*"

"Very well," I agreed dully. It did not much matter, I thought. Nothing mattered. I lifted her on her feet and half carried her to the stairs that led down to the Turner water-colours. There was a good view of the Square from there, and we stood some way back, a few steps down the stairs.

It was thundering heavily now, and jagged streaks of lightning were darting across the yellow sky. The rain was pouring down in streams. The sea-devils were bellowing to one another. I could not tell whether in pleasure or fright. Some were marshalling the rest, and those on the ground were rising into the air. One stared in at our window as he passed, but he did not pause. His eyes looked like great green lamps. The bellowing grew louder and more urgent, and the rain became so heavy that one could scarcely see through it. Then a sea of light covered the place, and a hurricane of thunder. The windows shivered in fragments, and the wet air rushed in. Nelson's Column tottered. I was blinded and deafened for a few moments. When I could see again the Column was down and the monsters were falling headlong on the Square and the houses. In a few seconds the place was heaped with their mangled remains. I thought I was mad or dreaming, because I heard no sound as they fell; but when I did not hear my own laugh, I knew that I was still deaf. We stood staring at the ruins—staring—staring!

"God has delivered us!" Elsie said at last—her voice sounded faint and a long way off. "God!"

"God!" I echoed—He had been only a name to me—before.

We stood looking out of the window in silence for a long time. The yellow fog melted away and the sun came out and the sky was blue. Then Elsie borrowed my handkerchief and wiped her eyes. "'If only we could forget," she said. "If only we could forget!"

We went back to the galleries. A dozen dead and mutilated monsters lay in them. The glass roofs were broken where they fell in, and most of them had crashed partially through the flooring. It shook as we walked over it; but we had been too frightened to fear any more. We found some biscuits and tinned meat and brandy and water in a room below, and ate and drank and washed. Then we slept for it couple of hours; till Elsie woke and woke me.

"They are all dead everywhere," she said confidently. "Let us go."

She tidied her hair with a brush and comb that she always carried, and put her hat straight before a glass. There was a pink bow at her neck, and she retied it carefully. I laughed suddenly—a jarring, unmirthful laugh.

"I thought the whole world was altered," I said; "but you are still a woman."

She drew a slow, deep breath.

"I suppose it *is* foolish," she said, "but I don't like you to see me look as if—as if I didn't care how I looked to you."

I took her hand and we went out. We found every way blocked with the corpses of the sea-devils. After several attempts to find a passage through, we decided to climb over them. It was then that we learnt that the scales were not armour, but tough hide, like that of a hippopotamus. We climbed by holding on to the metal framework, and finding footholds in the crinkly hides. I mounted first and pulled Elsie after me, and lowered her down before me.

The air was full of a fishy odour, and we felt faint. We thought at the time that this was due to the smell; but now I believe it was owing to the partial exhaustion of the oxygen of the air by the breathing-wheels. A few that were not broken or hampered still revolved slowly, and one or two of the monsters were breathing feebly. Their hides rose and fell a foot or so as we walked over them. Some of the "fishing-lines" were dangling in the air. One of them touched Elsie's dress, and I had to cut a piece with my penknife to get her away. She pinned the skirt carefully together to hide the rent. The green eyes were all open, and some blinked at us helplessly, malevolently. The journey across the Square was a waking nightmare of three hours, from one till four. In Pall Mall East we had to climb over several more dead monsters that lay across the road.

Dozens of the monsters were lying in St. James's Square. So many had fallen on the War Office that it was crushed like an eggshell.

The front of the club was broken out and none of our friends were left. The cards were scattered over the card-table, and on the floor there were a couple of cigar-cases. One of them bore the silver monogram—C. V.—of General Vine, the courteous, bent old warrior, who had invited us in as we wandered by.

We found food and drink in the basement, and laid down and slept. We did not wake till early in the morning. I put on some clean clothes that were lying in a dressing room, and Elsie found a new dress in a house in Pall Mall. Her hat did not match it, she said with a sigh. We took some money, in case there was still use for money in any part of the world. Also we took a big bag of food. We could get water anywhere.

Then we wandered to St. James's Park. Dead monsters lay all over it. Their breathing-wheels were all still now, and smoking as if they burnt. The oxygen had doubtless set up combustion, when the creatures no longer assimilated it.

Buckingham Palace was a heap of bricks, and most of the houses down Buckingham Palace Road were ruins. We reached Victoria Station without meeting a soul. Elsie gripped my arm suddenly with both hands.

"Suppose," she cried, "there is no one left, but you and me? It is the end of the world!"

"The end of the world!" I echoed with a groan.

"There *must* be someone left," she said after a pause of frenzied silence. "There *must!* We will find them. Come!"

We went into the S. E. & C. Station. The roof was smashed in, and the whole station badly damaged. There was a heap of luggage on the platform, and a guard's cap. A little further on there was a child's ball and doll. Elsie picked up the doll and kissed it. I did not look at her, but walked away down the long, main-line platform.

About, fifty yards beyond the platform there stood a solitary engine and tender. I walked out to them and inspected them while I waited for Elsie. The boiler, I saw from the gauge, was full of water, and the furnace was laid. I lit it, and we stood on the platform till there was enough pressure to start. Then I turned the steam on cautiously and we went forward at six or eight miles an hour. Luckily the points were set to a clear road out of the station.

We passed slowly over the bridge (the river was full of the bodies of the sea-devils), through Battersea, Clapham, and Brixton. There was no sign of life anywhere, not even a dog, or a cat, or a bird.

"There is no one left," Elsie said. "No one. I used to think people uninteresting, and now—and now—"

"We shall find them presently," I assured her; but I doubted it.

We passed Herne Hill and came to the long-gardened houses of Dulwich. There was a tent and a table laid with an unfinished meal in one. In another a bicycle was turned upside down for cleaning.

"That is Thurlow Park Road," I said, "where the station is. I used to know the man that lived there."

"Call to him," she suggested. "The people may be only hiding."

I stopped the train and shouted. Elsie cried out at the sound of my voice. We had spoken under breath for the last two days. There was no answer.

"Call again," she implored.

I shouted wildly; but there was only the echo in reply. The she called in her clear, high voice:

"People! Dear people! The monsters are dead—dead! We are friends—friends to everybody in the world—. They are all gone. And they live; and loved. Fred, we are all alone!"

"Perhaps—" I began; but she looked at me, and the hopeful words died on my lips. "If there is only me," I said, "I shall be good to you, Elsie."

"Oh, *yes!*" she cried. "It isn't *that!* I am glad it is you. Only let us go on."

We went slowly on till the houses grew fewer and the country more open; and still we saw no one—nothing—alive; only the dead monsters lying here and there.

Then we saw the Medway like a silver snake afar. At about three we came to Rochester Bridge Station. The water was getting low in the boiler and we were tired of standing on the platform. So we got out and walked on to the public bridge, and looked up and down the river. There was no smoke from the tall chimneys, or from the dockyard at Chatham below; no sound or movement anywhere. There were boats at the pier and boat raft, barges at anchor or run ashore; but no crew to any one. Great black bodies were floating on the tide. A number of them had jammed and blocked up two spans of the bridge.

We wandered along the banks of the river, and up into the Borstal Road. We found a house that had a couple of bed rooms undamaged, and stayed there for the night. The stillness was terrible—terrible! There was a half packed portmanteau in one room, and a litter of children's playthings in another. Some leaden soldiers were set out for a mimic battle. Elsie told me she should never smile again.

In the morning, however, she found a hat that matched her costume, and came down to the dining-room to show me.

"We *must* find people," she said with a gay little laugh, "if it is only to admire my hat. Oh! but she who wore it—she who wore it!"

She flung it suddenly on the ground and buried her face in her hands. I picked it up and put it on her.

"It makes you look nice," I said. "You are all I have to look at now, you know."

She put on the hat silently, and we went out together. As she passed the hall mirror she glanced at it and took my arm.

"It *does* suit me," she said, "and—you'll like me to look nice, won't you, Fred?"

"You always look nice," I told her.

We tramped out into the country and saw two birds. They were ungainly, flapping rooks, but we watched them lovingly. The air was sweet, and the sky was blue, and the sun was shining.

Presently we tramped back to the town by way of Watts's Avenue. The rents in the houses, and a long row of water-carts—some of the shafts had been broken evidently in tearing out the horses—made us depressed again. We went down the Maidstone Road, into the High Street, and turned to the right. We went as far as Luton Road, and found no one. Then we turned back to Rochester. We raided a few shops, and I offered Elsie some jewelry; but she would not have it. It did not matter what she were now, she said.

"We shall find people further down the line," I declared.

"But they will be changed," she said. "Life will be different—everything will be different—no one will laugh or sing or smile—no one will care how anyone looks. But if only we could find a few people to cry with. Hark!" She clutched my arm.

We listened, and heard the sound of a man's voice afar. We took a hasty step forward. Then we stopped and looked at one another. It was a man's voice—and we feared!

"We must be careful," I warned her. "We do not know what manner of men they are. There is no law, no order, no police. We are in it state of nature."

"Yes, yes!" She clung to me. "We must be careful. But their 'nature' may be good."

I shook my head.

"In the state of nature," I told her, "life is solitary, hasty, brutish, and poor. Everyone takes what he wants, and keeps what he can."

"Fred," she whispered. "You won't let them take me!"

I smiled grimly and drew a revolver from my pocket. I had taken it from a shop in town some days before.

"Not while I live," I vowed fiercely. "What I have is mine!"

"Yes," she said quietly. "I am yours."

That was our love-making and our betrothal.

We walked stealthily down the street, keeping close under the houses, till we came in view of the courtyard outside the town hall. About two dozen people—men, women and children—were standing there. They looked hungry and travel-worn and fierce. A tall, gaunt clergyman was preaching.

"The Lord," he said, "has taken much; but He has left us one another. The Lord has swept away the past; but He gives us the future. The Lord has given us sorrow; but He gives us work. Dear friends, our work is to comfort and help one another. Let us begin. And now to God the Father—"

We came out from the shadow and stood with the others for the benediction. When it was finished, the clergyman held out his hand to us.

"Dear friends," he asked, "what can I do for you?"

"Marry us," I said.

And we knelt down in the square, and were married there and then; and when we rose and would have joined in the day's labours, the others pushed us laughingly away. We should not work on our wedding day, they vowed, and they would make ready a house for us. And we went and stood on the bridge, and looked up the river and down the river—on the ruins and the black monsters turning in the tide. And we smiled—and smiled.

To-day, though there are so few of us on earth—handfuls of men and women and children (and our children among them)—toiling in the ruins of town and country we have still a smile. For here on earth we have one another; and afterwards there is God!

The Sea Serpent Syndicate
Everard Jack Appleton

If it wasn't for Jimmy Raines, I wouldn't try to write this story out. It ain't the kind of thing I like to think about, any more than I like to remember the name of a horse through which I have lost money; but Jimmy is a good fellow, and he asked me to do it—and what Jimmy Raines wants me to do, I do.

The reason he wants this story printed is because the people he tells it to don't believe him, and I don't know as I blame 'em; but he thinks if they see it in print they will.

The Sea Serpent Syndicate was a stroke of luck—bad or good, I don't know which. It started in a little summer garden, not far from Latonia, and it ended on an island somewhere south of Cuba. If it hadn't been for the earthquake—But I'm getting away before the flag drops.

To start right, it was a day that was hot enough to warp you— and Jimmy and I decided to absent ourselves from the Latonia races and take it easy.

We had dropped into John Porter's summer garden for a glass of beer and a cigar, and both of us tilted back in the shade, when the swing door from the street opened, and a chap that looked like the survivor of a North Pole expedition slouched in and dropped into a chair a few feet away from us.

The thermometer was somewhere at the hundred mark; but Mr. Coldfeet had on an overcoat with the collar turned up, and a muffler round his neck. Jimmy stared at him a moment, and then gave me the wink.

"I hope you ain't got your ears frosted, William," says he to me, as old John came out to get the stranger's order.

The guy had a big round package with him, and when John leant over the table to get his good ear near enough to catch the order, the stranger jerked the package away as if it had been a bunch of diamonds.

"Gimme a lemonade," said he, "and make it long and sour."

I was trying to make up my mind where I had seen him before when he looked up and straight into my eyes. The change that come over him was something remarkable. In a minute he had cleared the distance between us, and had hold of my hand, pumping it up and down like a steam engine, and saying: "Billy Martin, Billy Martin! Where did you come from?"

"I didn't come at all," says I, "I was here first. Where did you come from, Alphonse Doolan? That's the question!"

"From a mighty hot place," he answers, "and I ain't used to white man's weather yet. That's the reason I feel sorter chilly."

"We thought there must be something wrong," said I, waving my hand at Jimmy. "Mr. Doolan, shake hands with my side partner, Mr. Raines. Mr. Doolan is just back from a vacation in the middle of Africa, Jimmy."

Doolan shook his head.

"No, Billy," says he, "I left there five years ago. And I've been putting in my time in a hotter place than Africa. I've been surrounded by the equator, and glued to an island down in the Carib. And I'm nigh dead with the heat of it!"

"Won't you take off your overcoat, then?" I says. "The last I heard of you, you was sending daily reports about the temperature and barometer readings from some hole in the great American desert for the wise guys at Washington."

Alphonse dragged up his chair and the bundle with it.

"I was," he says, "but they transferred me. I had a joke one day, and sent a lot of dispatches to them about the ice forming and the snowstorm freezing my instruments. As it was August, they thought I needed a rest for a couple of months, and after that they shipped me to my island, where for four years I have been hanging on, broiling to death. Four years of heat and thirst, and nobody to talk to! Nothing to look at but scrub and sand—Lord, the sand there is on that island! It's a wonder it don't sink with the weight of it!"

"Working for the government still, Alphonse?" I asks.

"Sure," he answers. "Taking the readings every day, and sending them back to Havana whenever they happen to think of me and scow down with grub for me. I'm nigh crazy, Billy—but I'll soon be better, because—"

He stopped a minute, looking very foxy.

"Because I've got him!"

"Him?" says I. "Who's him?"

"Billy. I named him after you, Billy Martin, and you've got cause to be proud."

"Baby?" says I, yawning. I'd expected something more exciting from the way Alphonse had started out.

"Baby?" says he, scornful-like. "Naw! Sea serpent!" Jimmy kicked me under the table, and I sat up. Alphonse was madder than I had thought after all.

"Oh, I am proud," I says. "I am, Alphonse. Where do you keep him?"

"On the island," he answers, sucking his lemonade through the straw, and watching me closely. "In the middle of the lake the earthquake made. He come in with the quake, and I've tamed him. He eats out of my hand, and he's a good snake, I tell you—but I can't afford him. It takes all my supplies to keep him good-tempered—and sardines, his favourite, come high."

"Yes," I says, "it must be a kind of a luxury to have a pet sea serpent, Alphonse, following you round the house and eating out of your hand. And as for sleeping with one—"

"Cut it out, cut it out, Billy," says Alphonse, as sensible as could be. "You and I worked together long enough for you to know that I ain't a liar. This is straight goods, and here's the evidence," and he commenced to unwrap the package. He took out something that looked like an overgrown soup plate and put it down on the table. It smelt fearful fishy, I noticed, and it appeared to be made of horn, half an inch thick, and as big as a scale from the fish you didn't catch.

"Well," I says, "don't be silly, Alphonse. Go ahead with your fairy tale. I'll listen to it if Mr. Raines will."

"There ain't going to be no fairy tale," says Alphonse bristling up. "That's a scale from my sea serpent—come off him two weeks ago, when he got upset at something and throwed it at me."

He took a letter from his pocket.

"This here letter," says he, opening it and tossing it across the table, "is from the Natural History Society secretary across the river, and you can see what he says— 'The article in the possession of Mr. Alphonse Doolan appears to be, and probably is, a scale from an ocean reptile, popularly known as a sea serpent.'"

I looked at the letter, and sure enough that is what it said, and a lot more about the value of the discovery, and wishing the authorities at Washington would take the matter up with Mr. Doolan. I read it aloud, and Jimmy's eyes got bigger and bigger. When I finished and handed it back to Doolan, Jimmy spoke for the first time.

"Mr. Doolan," says he, "how much would it cost to go after that animal of yours, and bring him to the States for exhibition purposes?"

"Well," replied Alphonse, "I don't know. As soon as I get to Washington, I'm going to get the Smithsonian Institute to work it out."

"Smithsonian nothing," says Jimmy. "Can't you see something better ahead than that? If you bring that animal here, and if he is as big as that hunk of horn would seem to indicate, there's a fortune in it for three men."

Alphonse nodded his head slowly. "But it would cost all of five thousand dollars," he says, "and I'm broke."

Then Jimmy showed for the first time how sharp he had got all in a minute.

"Mr. Doolan," says he, leaning over the soup plate thing, "when I am a sport I try to be a game one. Billy Martin and I cleaned up a little more than the figure you name last month. That's why we are taking the afternoon off here in place of beating the bookies out of other people's money. Now, Mr. Martin seems interested in this story of yours, fishy as it looks to be, and I am, too. I am willing to make you a proposition. We will go back to your island, every fellow paying his own way. If that snake of yours is the real thing we'll pay for bringing him here, and split the profits on showing him. Is that fair?"

It was a long speech for Jimmy, and plain as an old shoe. Alphonse couldn't help seeing it was straight, too.

He thought a minute, looked at me, and then held out his hand to Jimmy.

"Shake," he says. I did the same, and the Doolan-Raines-Martin Sea Serpent Syndicate was formed.

Six days later we were aboard a little fruit boat on the Caribbean Sea, looking for Alphonse's island. It was my first experience on the raging deep, and I think it will be my last, unless I am chloroformed and dragged aboard another ship. The fourth day out, about ten o'clock in the morning, Alphonse let out a yell like an Indian, and grabbed a chart from the captain's hand.

"That's my island, cap," he says, pointing to a little black spot on the edge of the ocean. "Steer for her, and dump us off. I'm hungry to see that bunch of sand again."

In less than an hour we had drawn up alongside the hump of sand and scrub palm trees, and half an hour later we were sitting on our traps watching the fruit boat get smaller and smaller in the distance. It was hot enough to roast a pig, but Alphonse seemed really happy. He messed round and got something for us to eat out of his pack, and then we all lighted our pipes and waited for the sun to go down a bit.

"Alphonse," says I, as we stretched out under the biggest tree we could find, "I haven't asked you for any particulars since we started on this expedition. Now I want you to tell us how you came to round up that snake of yours."

Alphonse took a long draw at his pipe and clasped his hands behind his head.

"It ain't much of a story," says he, "but you've got a right to know it. My station ain't anything but a shanty, and a soapbox for furniture. It stands at the head of what was a ravine. One night there come a 'quake, and I got up to see where I was. The moon was shining bright, and when I looked for my ravine I made sure I was off my head. There wasn't none left.

"In place of the valley was a lake, half-a-mile wide and two long, boiling and churning. And in it was the curiousest creature you ever see. He's three hundred feet long—I made him lie still once while I measured him so you can bet on the figures—and has a head on him like a skinned cow. He was bellering and flapping his fins,

and smelt something fearful. That was Billy, and I soon figured
out what had happened. The 'quake had opened my island from
the bottom, let Billy and a lot of water in, closed up again—and
left the snake and me to get acquainted.

"I didn't get much sleep the rest of the night, with his thrashing around and bawling for his folks, but by morning he'd worn
himself out and was sleeping as peacefully as a lamb on top of the
water. I took a fancy to him right then. I don't know what made me
think of you just then, Bill Martin, but I did; and I named him after
you before he could wake up and object.

"When he opened his eyes and seen me observing him, he got
upset. He raised about ten feet of his neck out of the water, and
cut loose, with a twist of his head and a grunt, and this very scale
that brought us three together come sailing straight for me. I side-
stepped and it buried itself in the sand.

"'Look a-here, Bill,' I says, 'that's no way to treat the owner of
this island. I didn't invite you here, in the first place; you're unexpected company, and you oughter behave yourself polite. I'm willing for you to stay, but you've got to be good-natured.'

"I don't say he understood me, but he looked as if he might.
Then he opened his mouth and yawned like he was embarrassed,
so I throwed him a piece of meat. He caught it and swung around,
and started for the other side of the lake. From that on he acted
right, and I didn't have no cause to complain. I never realised what
company a sea-serpent could be; I'm right lonesome for him now.
He's an affectionate reptile, and it won't take him no time to get
broke in, once we git him to the States. A few more weeks of kind
treatment will make him as gentle as a kitten, and he will swim
after any boat I happen to be on. You hear me?"

"But suppose he does object?" asks Jimmy.

"Mr. Raines," says Alphonse, "I ain't teaching my snake polite-
ness through a correspondence school. If he is impertinent ain't I
there to administer the proper chastisement—and stop giving him fish?
You leave that to me. And now, as the sun is subsiding, let's be off."

At the end of two hours' hard walking over sand heaps we came
to a low hill, from which we could see a little lake with a few scrub
trees on the banks and a shanty at one end.

"There," says Alphonse, proud as a peacock, "there is Doolanville. Pleasant prospect, ain't it? I am thinking of cutting it up into lots and selling it to desirable parties only.

"Welcome to the Hotel de Doolan," says he, opening the door and peering into the shanty. "But mebbe you'd rather have the lizards out before you go in. They ain't very partial to strangers."

He steps inside, and raises a racket, and a menagerie of half-a-dozen scaly critters, not counting the land crabs and house snakes, ran out. "Now," says he, appearing once more, "your apartments are ready, gentlemen. Step inside and register. Sorry all our rooms with baths attached are took; but the lake is convenient and free."

By the time we had packed our things away and fixed our bunks the sun had almost set, and Alphonse was rustling around with his pots and pans on the outside, singing to himself. Jimmy and I watched him for a few minutes, and then Jimmy says to me, sorter quiet-like: "Is this real or am I dreaming?"

"Don't ask me," says I. "Feels like I ought to wake up myself before long."

Jimmy shook his head. "The worst of it is that we are here, and we can't get our money back at the gate. Looks to me as if we'd have to see it through. But where's the snake?"

Just as he spoke, I looked out across the lake, and my hat raised two inches off my head. Of course, I had some faith in all that Alphonse had told us, but I wasn't prepared to have it all come true so sudden and unexpected.

Before I could kick myself to see if I really was awake, the snake was almost on us. He come sailing across that lake looking very wicked. He was as big as a water-tower, and I could have sworn that he was long enough to go round Latonia race-track twice, and a lap or so over. He slid across the water, a giant, greased fishing-worm, the last rays of the sun shining on his scales and turning them as white as silver.

When he caught sight of us, I held my breath. He raised his head out of the water twenty feet or more and back-pedaled, churning up the lake till it frothed. His eyes was bigger than a barrel, and when he opened his mouth, showing a row of teeth resembling a white-washed fence, it was too much for Jimmy. He gave a sort of grunt, and went off into a dead faint.

As for me, I was fast getting seasick myself and wondering how I could hit the trail back to the coast again, leaving Jimmy and his faint to themselves, when Alphonse stuck his head out of the shanty.

"Ah, ha!" he cries, stepping out with his frying-pan in one hand and a box of sardines in the other. "Billy has come! Now, I guess you fellows know whether your Uncle Alphonse was toying with the truth or not. Ain't he a beaut, William—and ain't you proud he's your namesake?"

I was trying to get enough breath back to express my thoughts on that and other subjects, when the snake struck the beach, stopped short, and let out a roar that blowed me over against Jimmy. Alphonse seemed to think it a good joke, and snapped his fingers at the critter.

"Here, Billy; here, Billy boy!" he calls. "Come and say howdy to your proud old boss and his friends. You mustn't forgit your manners."

The snake ducked down for a foot or two, looked us over suspiciously for a minute, and then brought his head to a level with Alphonse. It wasn't a head that you'd want a picture of in the parlour, with his big eyes, one green, and the other blue, and long white whiskers. But Alphonse seemed tickled to have him so close, and shoved the open box of sardines at him; and Billy smiled.

You have never seen a sea-serpent smile, of course, so you can't imagine what it is. You haven't missed very much, though, so don't lose any sleep over it. The inside of a mammoth cave, painted red— that was Billy's smile. I was glad when he closed it up again, on the box of sardines, for he seemed so tickled with them that he kept his mouth shut and laid his head down on the sand beside Alphonse, like a sick kitten waiting to be petted. Alphonse scratched him with the frying-pan, and the snake lay there purring his gratitude and pleasure for five minutes.

It was the noise he made—you'd 'a' thought an engine was getting up steam—that brought Jimmy round. He came to, facing the snake, and when he clapped eyes on him, Jimmy let out a terrific yell. The snake didn't like it, and before Alphonse could speak to him, he had reared up, the scales standing out on his neck like bristles on a bulldog. The next minute he gave his head a short, sharp bob, and one of those horn wash basins broke loose from its moorings, and shot by Jimmy's ear, close enough to cut his hair.

"Wow! Take him away, take him away!" howls Jimmy, making for the shanty, followed by another little sea serpent souvenir. Alphonse waved his frying-pan at Billy, and called: "Behave yourself, Bill! Shame on you!"

But Billy was scared, too, and he kept firing scales at Jimmy until he reached the shanty and got hid under the boxes and barrels inside. Then the snake's short ears laid back, showing he didn't mean anything vicious; he lowered his head again, crawled up a few feet on the beach and butted his nose in the sand at Alphonse's feet, asking forgiveness for his behaviour as plain as any dog ever did.

Alphonse sat down and began to talk to his pet, and, not wishing to disturb a little family conversation like that, I sneaked away to find Jimmy, who was having a bunch of assorted fits in the furthest corner of the Hotel de Doolan.

And that was our introduction to Doolan's sea serpent.

It is hard to believe, I know, but inside a week I got so used to have that snake about that I didn't pay any more attention to him that I would to a big dog. We got to be good friends, too, although I never could find much enjoyment in his sea breath, which was strong and noticeable, him being so affectionate. Every morning when I went for a swim in the lake, he'd see me coming, and he'd cavort and do water gymnastics until I got out. He'd come to my call, just as he did to Alphonse's, and seemed to try his best to make me feet at home.

But he never did like Jimmy, I'm sorry to say. That yell he heard Jimmy give sort of prejudiced him, I guess. He didn't shy any more soup plates, but he just didn't take any more interest in him, and Jimmy seemed to rather enjoy the slight. It was a mutual dislike, too. If Jimmy could have handed Billy a dynamite sandwich, he'd have done it I reckon; but he never let on to Alphonse that the snake's vagaries hurt his feelings.

Even the night that Billy took Alphonse for a ride, Jimmy didn't look jealous. The snake was laying up on the beach, as usual, and

Alphonse was scraping his head with a piece of board, when Billy seemed took with an idea. He slipped his head under Alphonse, raised his back, and started for the lake again, with Alphonse sitting astride his neck, same as a bareback rider in the circus. Billy took him fast across the lake and back, and Alphonse was so tickled with the experience that he made me try it the next night.

Every night after that Alphonse and I would have a ride or two, and all Billy asked was a box of sardines and a three-minutes' scratch of the head. I don't believe there ever lived a kinder-hearted sea serpent than Billy.

But, of course, this couldn't last. The end was bound to come, and it came sudden enough when it did. Alphonse had just announced to us, about two weeks after we had landed, that he thought Billy was ready for his trip.

"He won't try to play hookey," said he, answering my question on that subject. "When we get him to the coast, he'll be afraid to leave me. I think we'll start tomorrow, and then—across the water for us, and, fortune waiting on the other side! We'll have Billy the talk of the world inside of—"

And that was as far as Alphonse got. Something broke loose under the island just then, and the lake commenced to tear about as if there were a cyclone at the bottom of it.

Billy looked back at his happy home, slid up on the bank, shoved his head between Alphonse's legs, and whirled out into the middle of that boiling, roaring sheet of water like he had been sent for. Alphonse at once grabbed him by the ears and yelled for him to go back, but it wasn't any use.

As they reached the middle of the lake, there come a noise like Niagara and a dynamite factory let loose at once, and the ground under Jimmy and me began to buckle and crawl.

I closed my eyes a minute and hung on to Jimmy, trying to think of something fitting to say, and when I opened them again, the lake was gone! In its place was the long ravine Alphonse had told us about, and a big, ugly-looking crack, into which the last of the lake was pouring. Out of the crack stuck a few yards of poor old Billy's tail. Before I could say a word, that had disappeared, and Jimmy and I were alone!

The lake was gone, the snake was gone, the earthquake had come and gone, and Alphonse—

"Come on!" I yelled. "That snake has kidnapped Alphonse, Jimmy Raines!"

Jimmy made some sort of answer, but I didn't hear him. I was running down the wet, slippery bed of the lake towards the hole Billy had gone into. It never come to me that Alphonse couldn't live in the water like Billy could; they had been so friendly and together so much I had forgotten they were different. But when I stumbled over a big boulder and fell flat, the jar brought me to my senses.

"You are right," I says, when Jimmy came panting up; "it ain't no use to hunt Alphonse. He's gone, and nothing left to show it."

Jimmy buried his face in his hands. "Ain't it terrible?" says he. "Not even a thing to bury!"

"He bragged too much," says I, "and he didn't have his fingers crossed!"

"But he ain't dead yet," says a weak voice from the other side of the boulder, and there was Alphonse, sound and well, though wet and weak.

"When I'd seen what was happening," he explained, "I knowed Billy was trying to take me with him back to his home. When we got here I jumped, and hung on to this rock, while the water whirled around me and sucked him down. I skun my knees and knuckles, but I ain't lost nothing but my snake."

We all looked at the little crack that had swallowed our fortunes, but we felt too bad to talk much.

"I reckon," says Jimmy, after a while, "that it won't pay to cry over spilt sea serpents. Let's make the best of it. We played Billy off the boards, and we lost. It's back to the States for me!"

"I guess you are right," says Alphonse, "and the 'quake seems to have wound up the affairs of the Sea Serpent Syndicate. Well, gentlemen, I'm sorry, but I hope you'll hold me blameless. I could tame a sea serpent, but I ain't much on taming earthquakes."

The next day we drilled back to the coast. Alphonse wouldn't hear of us taking him along, though. "My work is here," says he, "and here I stay." Then he added very wistful, and the tears pretty close, I tell you: "And if Billy ever should come back, I wouldn't want him to think I had deserted him."

As luck would have it, we sighted a vessel two hours after we reached the coast, and the captain sent a small boat to take us aboard. Jimmy and I shook hands hard with Alphonse, and when we had got aboard the steamer, we watched him until we couldn't see no more.

That was five years ago—and we have never heard from Alphonse. So I guess the Sea Serpent Syndicate was dissolved for good and all the day Billy went out with the earthquake.

A Tropical Horror
William Hope Hodgson

We are a hundred and thirty days out from Melbourne, and for three weeks we have lain in this sweltering calm.

It is midnight, and our watch on deck until four a.m. I go out and sit on the hatch. A minute later, Joky, our youngest 'prentice, joins me for a chatter. Many are the hours we have sat thus and talked in the night watches; though, to be sure, it is Joky who does the talking. I am content to smoke and listen, giving an occasional grunt at seasons to show that I am attentive.

Joky has been silent for some time, his head bent in meditation. Suddenly he looks up, evidently with the intention of making some remark. As he does so, I see his face stiffen with a nameless horror. He crouches back, his eyes staring past me at some unseen fear. Then his mouth opens. He gives forth a strangulated cry and topples backward off the hatch, striking his head against the deck. Fearing I know not what, I turn to look.

Great Heavens! Rising above the bulwarks, seen plainly in the bright moonlight, is a vast slobbering mouth a fathom across. From the huge dripping lips hang great tentacles. As I look the Thing comes further over the rail. It is rising, rising, higher and higher. There are no eyes visible; only that fearful slobbering mouth set on the tremendous trunk-like neck; which, even as I watch, is curling inboard with the stealthy celerity of an enormous eel. Over it comes in vast heaving folds. Will it never end? The ship gives a slow, sullen roll to starboard as she feels the weight. Then the tail, a broad, flat-shaped mass, slips over the teak rail and falls with a loud slump on to the deck.

For a few seconds the hideous creature lies heaped in writhing, slimy coils. Then, with quick, darting movements, the monstrous

137

head travels along the deck. Close by the mainmast stand the harness casks, and alongside of these a freshly opened cask of salt beef with the top loosely replaced. The smell of the meat seems to attract the monster, and I can hear it sniffing with a vast indrawing breath. Then those lips open, displaying four huge fangs; there is a quick forward motion of the head, a sudden crashing, crunching sound, and beef and barrel have disappeared. The noise brings one of the ordinary seamen out of the fo'cas'le. Coming into the night, he can see nothing for a moment. Then, as he gets further aft, he sees, and with horrified cries rushes forward. Too late! From the mouth of the Thing there flashes forth a long, broad blade of glistening white, set with fierce teeth. I avert my eyes, but cannot shut out the sickening "Glut! Glut!" that follows.

The man on the "look-out," attracted by the disturbance, has witnessed the tragedy, and flies for refuge into the fo'cas'le, flinging to the heavy iron door after him.

The carpenter and sailmaker come running out from the half-deck in their drawers. Seeing the awful Thing, they rush aft to the cabin with shouts of fear. The second mate, after one glance over the break of the poop, runs down the companion-way with the helmsman after him. I can hear them barring the scuttle, and abruptly I realise that I am on the main deck alone.

So far I have forgotten my own danger. The past few minutes seem like a portion of an awful dream. Now, however, I comprehend my position and, shaking off the horror that has held me, turn to seek safety. As I do so my eyes fall upon Joky, lying huddled and senseless with fright where he has fallen. I cannot leave him there. Close by stands the empty half-deck—a little steel-built house with iron doors. The lee one is hooked open. Once inside I am safe.

Up to the present the Thing has seemed to be unconscious of my presence. Now, however, the huge barrel-like head sways in my direction; then comes a muffled bellow, and the great tongue flickers in and out as the brute turns and swirls aft to meet me. I know there is not a moment to lose, and, picking up the helpless lad, I make a run for the open door. It is only distant a few yards, but that awful shape is coming down the deck to me in great wreathing coils. I reach the house and tumble in with my burden; then out on deck again to unhook and close the door. Even as I do so something white curls round the end of the house. With a bound I am inside and the door is shut and bolted. Through the thick glass of the ports I see the Thing sweep round the house, in vain search for me.

Joky has not moved yet; so, kneeling down, I loosen his shirt collar and sprinkle some water from the breaker over his face. While I am doing this I hear Morgan shout something; then comes a great shriek of terror, and again that sickening "Glut! Glut!"

Joky stirs uneasily, rubs his eyes, and sits up suddenly.

"Was that Morgan shouting—?" He breaks off with a cry. "Where are we? I have had such awful dreams!"

At this instant there is a sound of running footsteps on the deck and I hear Morgan's voice at the door.

"Tom, open—!"

He stops abruptly and gives an awful cry of despair. Then I hear him rush forward. Through the porthole, I see him spring into the fore rigging and scramble madly aloft. Something steals up after him. It shows white in the moonlight. It wraps itself around his right ankle. Morgan stops dead, plucks out his sheath-knife, and hacks fiercely at the fiendish thing. It lets go, and in a second he is over the top and running for dear life up the t'gallant rigging.

A time of quietness follows, and presently I see that the day is breaking. Not a sound can be heard save the heavy gasping breathing of the Thing. As the sun rises higher the creature stretches itself out along the deck and seems to enjoy the warmth. Still no sound, either from the men forward or the officers aft. I can only suppose that they are afraid of attracting its attention. Yet, a little later, I hear the report of a pistol away aft, and looking out I see the serpent raise its huge head as though listening. As it does so I get a good view of the fore part, and in the daylight see what the night has hidden.

There, right about the mouth, is a pair of little pig-eyes, that seem to twinkle with a diabolical intelligence. It is swaying its head slowly from side to side; then, without warning, it turns quickly and looks right in through the port. I dodge out of sight; but not soon enough. It has seen me, and brings its great mouth up against the glass.

I hold my breath. My God! If it breaks the glass! I cower, horrified. From the direction of the port there comes a loud, harsh, scraping sound. I shiver. Then I remember that there are little iron doors to shut over the ports in bad weather. Without a moment's waste of time I rise to my feet and slam to the door over the port. Then I go round to the others and do the same. We are now in darkness, and I tell Joky in a whisper to light the lamp, which, after some fumbling, he does.

About an hour before midnight I fall asleep. I am awakened suddenly some hours later by a scream of agony and the rattle of a water-dipper. There is a slight scuffling sound; then that soul-revolting "Glut! Glut!"

I guess what has happened. One of the men forrad has slipped out of the fo'cas'le to try and get a little water. Evidently he has trusted to the darkness to hide his movements. Poor beggar! He has paid for his attempt with his life!

After this I cannot sleep, though the rest of the night passes quietly enough. Towards morning I doze a bit, but wake every few minutes with a start. Joky is sleeping peacefully; indeed, he seems worn out with the terrible strain of the past twenty-four hours. About eight a.m. I call him, and we make a light breakfast off the dry ship's biscuit and water. Of the latter happily we have a good supply. Joky seems more himself, and starts to talk a little—possibly somewhat louder than is safe; for, as he chatters on, wondering how it will end, there comes a tremendous blow against the side of the house, making it ring again. After this Joky is very silent. As we sit there I cannot but wonder what all the rest are doing, and how the poor beggars forrad are faring, cooped up without water, as the tragedy of the night has proved.

Towards noon, I hear a loud bang, followed by a terrific bellowing. Then comes a great smashing of woodwork, and the cries of men in pain. Vainly I ask myself what has happened. I begin to reason. By the sound of the report it was evidently something much heavier than a rifle or pistol, and judging from the mad roaring of the Thing, the shot must have done some execution. On thinking it over further, I become convinced that, by some means, those aft have got hold of the small signal cannon we carry, and though I know that some have been hurt, perhaps killed, yet a feeling of exultation seizes me as I listen to the roars of the Thing, and realise that it is badly wounded, perhaps mortally. After a while, however, the bellowing dies away, and only an occasional roar, denoting more of anger than aught else, is heard.

Presently I become aware, by the ship's canting over to starboard, that the creature has gone over to that side, and a great hope springs up within me that possibly it has had enough of us and is going over the rail into the sea. For a time all is silent and my hope grows stronger. I lean across and nudge Joky, who is sleeping with his head on the table. He starts up sharply with a loud cry.

"Hush!" I whisper hoarsely. "I'm not certain, but I do believe it's gone."

Joky's face brightens wonderfully, and he questions me eagerly. We wait another hour or so, with hope ever rising. Our confidence is returning fast. Not a sound can we hear, not even the breathing of the Beast. I get out some biscuits, and Joky, after rummaging in the locker, produces a small piece of pork and a bottle of ship's vinegar. We fall to with a relish. After our long abstinence from food the meal acts on us like wine, and what must Joky do but insist on opening the door, to make sure the Thing has gone. This I will not allow, telling him that at least it will be safer to open the iron port-covers first and have a look out. Joky argues, but I am immovable. He becomes excited. I believe the youngster is light-headed. Then, as I turn to unscrew one of the after-covers, Joky makes a dash at the door. Before he can undo the bolts I have him, and after a short struggle lead him back to the table. Even as I endeavour to quieten him there comes at the starboard door—the door that Joky has tried to open—a sharp, loud sniff, sniff, followed immediately by a thunderous grunting howl and a foul stench of putrid breath sweeps in under the door. A great trembling takes me, and were it not for the carpenter's tool-chest I should fall. Joky turns very white and is violently sick, after which he is seized by a hopeless fit of sobbing.

Hour after hour passes, and, weary to death, I lie down on the chest upon which I have been sitting, and try to rest.

It must be about half-past two in the morning, after a somewhat longer doze, that I am suddenly awakened by a most tremendous uproar away forrad—men's voices shrieking, cursing, praying; but in spite of the terror expressed, so weak and feeble; while in the midst, and at times broken off short with that hellishly suggestive "Glut! Glut!" is the unearthly bellowing of the Thing. Fear incarnate seizes me, and I can only fall on my knees and pray. Too well I know what is happening.

Joky has slept through it all, and I am thankful.

Presently, under the door there steals a narrow ribbon of light, and I know that the day has broken on the second morning of our imprisonment. I let Joky sleep on. I will let him have peace while he may. Time passes, but I take little notice. The Thing is quiet, probably sleeping. About midday I eat a little biscuit and drink some of the water. Joky still sleeps. It is best so.

A sound breaks the stillness. The ship gives a slight heave, and I know that once more the Thing is awake. Round the deck it moves, causing the ship to roll perceptibly. Once it goes forrad—I fancy to again explore the fo'cas'le. Evidently it finds nothing, for it returns almost immediately. It pauses a moment at the house, then goes on further aft. Up aloft, somewhere in the fore-rigging, there rings out a peal of wild laughter, though sounding very faint and far away. The Horror stops suddenly. I listen intently, but hear nothing save a sharp creaking beyond the after end of the house, as though a strain had come upon the rigging.

A minute later I hear a cry aloft, followed almost instantly by a loud crash on deck that seems to shake the ship. I wait in anxious fear. What is happening? The minutes pass slowly. Then comes another frightened shout. It ceases suddenly. The suspense has become terrible, and I am no longer able to bear it. Very cautiously I open one of the after port-covers, and peep out to see a fearful sight. There, with its tail upon the deck and its vast body curled round the mainmast, is the monster, its head above the topsail yard, and its great claw-armed tentacle waving in the air. It is the first proper sight that I have had of the Thing. Good Heavens! It must weigh a hundred tons! Knowing that I shall have time, I open the port itself, then crane my head out and look up. There on the extreme end of the lower topsail yard I see one of the able seamen. Even down here I note the staring horror of his face. At this moment he sees me and gives a weak, hoarse cry for help. I can do nothing for him. As I look the great tongue shoots out and licks him off the yard, much as might a dog a fly off the window-pane.

Higher still, but happily out of reach, are two more of the men. As far as I can judge they are lashed to the mast above the royal yard. The Thing attempts to reach them, but after a futile effort it ceases, and starts to slide down, coil on coil, to the deck. While doing this I notice a great gaping wound on its body some twenty feet above the tail.

I drop my gaze from aloft and look aft. The cabin door is torn from its hinges, and the bulkhead—which, unlike the half-deck, is of teak wood—is partly broken down. With a shudder I realise the cause of those cries after the cannon-shot. Turning I screw my head round and try to see the foremast, but cannot. The sun, I notice, is low, and the night is near. Then I draw in my head and fasten up both port and cover.

How will it end? Oh! how will it end?

After a while Joky wakes up. He is very restless, yet though he has eaten nothing during the day I cannot get him to touch anything.

Night draws on. We are too weary—too dispirited to talk. I lie down, but not to sleep... Time passes.

A ventilator rattles violently somewhere on the main deck, and there sounds constantly that slurring, gritty noise. Later I hear a cat's agonised howl, and then again all is quiet. Some time after comes a great splash alongside. Then, for some hours all is silent as the grave. Occasionally I sit up on the chest and listen, yet never a whisper of noise comes to me. There is an absolute silence, even the monotonous creak of the gear has died away entirely, and at last a real hope is springing up within me. That splash, this silence—surely I am justified in hoping. I do not wake Joky this time. I will prove first for myself that all is safe. Still I wait. I will run no unnecessary risks. After a time I creep to the after-port and will listen; but there is no sound. I put up my hand and feel at the screw, then again I hesitate, yet not for long. Noiselessly I begin to unscrew the fastening of the heavy shield. It swings loose on its hinge, and I pull it back and peer out. My heart is beating madly. Everything seems strangely dark outside. Perhaps the moon has gone behind a cloud. Suddenly a beam of moonlight enters through the port, and goes as quickly. I stare out. Something moves. Again the light streams in, and now I seem to be looking into a great cavern, at the bottom of which quivers and curls something palely white.

My heart seems to stand still! It is the Horror! I start back and seize the iron port-flap to slam it to. As I do so, something strikes the glass like a steam ram, shatters it to atoms, and flicks past me into the berth. I scream and spring away. The port is quite filled with it. The lamp shows it dimly. It is curling and twisting here and there. It is as thick as a tree, and covered with a smooth slimy skin. At the end is a great claw, like a lobster's, only a thousand times larger. I cower down into the farthest corner... It has broken the tool-chest to pieces with one click of those frightful mandibles. Joky has crawled under a bunk. The Thing sweeps round in my direction. I feel a drop of sweat trickle slowly down my face—it tastes salty. Nearer comes that awful death... Crash! I roll over backwards. It has crushed the water breaker against which I leant, and I am rolling in the water across the floor. The claw drives up, then down, with a quick uncertain movement, striking the deck a dull, heavy blow, a foot from my head. Joky gives a little gasp of horror. Slowly the Thing rises and starts feeling its way round the berth. It plunges into a bunk and pulls out a bolster, nips it in half and drops it, then moves on. It is feeling along the deck. As it does so it comes across a half of the bolster. It seems to toy with it, then picks it up and takes it out through the port...

A wave of putrid air fills the berth. There is a grating sound, and something enters the port again—something white and tapering and set with teeth. Hither and thither it curls, rasping over the bunks, ceiling, and deck, with a noise like that of a great saw at work. Twice it flickers above my head, and I close my eyes. Then off it goes again. It sounds now on the opposite side of the berth and nearer to Joky. Suddenly the harsh, raspy noise becomes muffled, as though the teeth were passing across some soft substance. Joky gives a horrid little scream, that breaks off into a bubbling, whistling sound. I open my eyes. The tip of the vast tongue is curled tightly round something that drips, then is quickly withdrawn, allowing the moonbeams to steal again into the berth. I rise to my feet. Looking round, I note in a mechanical sort of way the wrecked state of the berth—the shattered chests, dismantled bunks, and something else—

"Joky!" I cry, and tingle all over.

There is that awful Thing again at the port. I glance round for a weapon. I will revenge Joky. Ah! there, right under the lamp, where the wreck of the carpenter's chest strews the floor, lies a small hatchet. I spring forward and seize it. It is small, but so keen—so keen! I feel its razor edge lovingly. Then I am back at the port. I stand to one side and raise my weapon. The great tongue is feeling its way to those fearsome remains. It reaches them. As it does so, with a scream of "Joky! Joky!" I strike savagely again and again and again, gasping as I strike; once more, and the monstrous mass falls to the deck, writhing like a hideous eel. A vast, warm flood rushes in through the porthole. There is a sound of breaking steel and an enormous bellowing. A singing comes in my ears and grows louder—louder. Then the berth grows indistinct and suddenly dark.

EXTRACT FROM THE LOG OF THE STEAMSHIP *HISPANIOLA*.

June 24.—Lat.—N. Long.—W. 11 a.m.—Sighted four-masted barque about four points on the port bow, flying signal of distress. Ran down to her and sent a boat aboard. She proved to be the *Glen Doon*, homeward bound from Melbourne to London. Found things in a terrible state. Decks covered with blood and slime. Steel deckhouse stove in. Broke open door, and discovered youth of about nineteen in last stage of inanition, also part remains of boy about fourteen years of age. There was a great quantity of blood in the place, and a huge curled-up mass of whitish flesh, weighing about half a ton, one end of which appeared to have been hacked through with a sharp instrument. Found forecastle door open and hanging from one hinge. Doorway bulged, as though something had been

forced through. Went inside. Terrible state of affairs, blood everywhere, broken chests, smashed bunks, but no men nor remains.
Went aft again and found youth showing signs of recovery. When
he came round, gave the name of Thompson. Said they had been
attacked by a huge serpent—thought it must have been sea-serpent.
He was too weak to say much, but told us there were some men up the
mainmast. Sent a hand aloft, who reported them lashed to the royal
mast, and quite dead. Went aft to the cabin. Here we found the
bulkhead smashed to pieces, and the cabin-door lying on the deck
near the after-hatch. Found body of captain down lazarette, but
no officers. Noticed amongst the wreckage part of the carriage of a
small cannon. Came aboard again.

Have sent the second mate with six men to work her into port.
Thompson is with us. He has written out his version of the affair.
We certainly consider that the state of the ship, as we found her,
bears out in every respect his story. (Signed)

William Norton (Master).

Tom Briggs (1st Mate).

From the Tideless Sea
William Hope Hodgson

I

The Captain of the schooner leant over the rail, and stared for a moment, intently.

"Pass us them glasses, Jock," he said, reaching a hand behind him.

Jock left the wheel for an instant, and ran into the little companionway. He emerged immediately with a pair of marine-glasses, which he pushed into the waiting hand.

For a little, the Captain inspected the object through the binoculars. Then he lowered them, and polished the object glasses.

"Seems like er water-logged barr'l as sumone's doin' fancy paintin' on," he remarked after a further stare. "Shove ther 'elm down er bit, Jock, we'll 'ave er closer look at it."

Jock obeyed, and soon the schooner bore almost straight for the object which held the Captain's attention. Presently, it was within some fifty feet, and the Captain sung out to the boy in the caboose to pass along the boathook.

Very slowly, the schooner drew nearer, for the wind was no more than breathing gently. At last the cask was within reach, and the Captain grappled at it with the boathook. It bobbed in the calm water, under his ministrations; and, for a moment, the thing seemed likely to elude him. Then he had the hook fast in a bit of rotten-looking rope which was attached to it. He did not attempt to lift it by the rope; but sung out to the boy to get a bowline round it. This was done, and the two of them hove it up on to the deck.

The Captain could see now, that the thing was a small water-breaker, the upper part of which was ornamented with the remains of a painted name.

"H—M—E—B—" spelt out the Captain with difficulty, and scratched his head. "'ave or look at this 'ere, Jock. See wot you makes of it."

Jock bent over from the wheel, expectorated, and then stared at the breaker. For nearly a minute he looked at it in silence.

"I'm thinkin' some of the letterin's washed awa'," he said at last, with considerable deliberation. "I have ma doots if he'll be able to read it."

"Hadn't ye no better, knock in the end?" he suggested, after a further period of pondering. "I'm thinkin' ye'll be lang comin' at them contents otherwise."

"It's been in ther water er thunderin' long time," remarked the Captain, turning the bottom side upwards. "Look at them barnacles!"

Then, to the boy:—

"Pass erlong ther 'atchet outer ther locker."

Whilst the boy was away, the Captain stood the little barrel on end, and kicked away some of the barnacles from the underside. With them, came away a great shell of pitch. He bent, and inspected it.

"Blest if thor thing ain't been pitched!" he said. "This 'ere's been put afloat er purpose, an' they've been mighty anxious as ther stuff in it shouldn't be 'armed."

He kicked away another mass of the barnacle-studded pitch. Then, with a sudden impulse, he picked up the whole thing and shook it violently. It gave out a light, dull, thudding sound, as though something soft and small were within. Then the boy came with the hatchet.

"Stan' clear!" said the Captain, and raised the implement. The next instant, he had driven in one end of the barrel. Eagerly, he stooped forward. He dived his hand down and brought out a little bundle stitched up in oilskin.

"I don' spect as it's anythin' of valley," he remarked. "But I guess as there's sumthin' 'ere as 'll be worth tellin' 'bout w'en we gets 'ome."

He slit up the oilskin as be spoke. Underneath, there was another covering of the same material, and under that a third. Then a longish bundle done up in tarred canvas. This was removed, and a black, cylindrical shaped case disclosed to view. It proved to be a tin canister, pitched over. Inside of it, neatly wrapped within a last strip of oilskin, was a roll of papers, which, on opening, the Captain found to be covered with writing. The Captain shook out the various wrappings; but found nothing further. He handed the MS. across to Jock.

"More 'n your line 'n mine, I guess," he remarked. "Jest you read it up, an' I'll listen." He turned to the boy.

"Fetch ther dinner erlong 'ere. Me an' thor Mate 'll 'ave it comfortable up 'ere, an' you can take ther vheel. . . . Now then, Jock!"

And, presently, Jock began to read:

"The Losing of the *Homebird*."

"The 'Omebird!" exclaimed the Captain. "Why, she were lost w'en I wer' quite a young feller. Let me see—seventy-three. That were it. Tail end er seventy-three w'en she left 'ome, an never 'eard of since; not as I knows. Go a'ead with ther yarn, Jock."

"It is Christmas eve. Two years ago to-day, we became lost to the world. Two years! It seems like twenty since I had my last Christmas in England. Now, I suppose, we are already forgotten— and this ship is but one more among the missing! My God! to think upon our loneliness gives me a choking feeling, a tightness across the chest!

"I am writing this in the saloon of the sailing ship, *Homebird*, and writing with but little hope of human eye ever seeing that which I write; for we are in the heart of the dread Sargasso Sea—the Tideless Sea of the North Atlantic. From the stump of our mizzen mast, one may see, spread out to the far horizon, an interminable waste of weed—a treacherous, silent vastitude of slime and hideousness!

"On our port side, distant some seven or eight miles, there is a great, shapeless, discoloured mass. No one, seeing it for the first time, would suppose it to be the hull of a long lost vessel. It bears but little resemblance to a sea-going craft, because of a strange superstructure which has been built upon it. An examination of the vessel herself, through a telescope, tells one that she is unmistakably ancient. Probably a hundred, possibly two hundred, years.

Think of it! Two hundred years in the midst of this desolation! It is an eternity.

"At first we wondered at that extraordinary superstructure. Later, we were to learn its use—and profit by the teaching of hands long withered. It is inordinately strange that we should have come upon this sight for the dead! Yet, thought suggests, that there may be many such, which have lain here through the centuries in this World of Desolation. I had not imagined that the earth contained so much loneliness, as is held within the circle, seen from the stump of our shattered mast. Then comes the thought that I might wander a hundred miles in any direction—and still be lost.

"And that craft yonder, that one break in the monotony, that monument of a few men's misery, serves only to make the solitude the more atrocious; for she is a very effigy of terror, telling of tragedies the past, and to come!

"And now to get back to the beginnings of it. I joined the *Homebird*, as a passenger, in the early part of November. My health was not quite the thing, and I hoped the voyage would help to set me up. We had a lot of dirty weather for the first couple of weeks out, the wind dead ahead. Then we got a Southerly slant, that carried us down through the forties; but a good deal more to the Westward than we desired. Here we ran right into a tremendous cyclonic storm. All hands were called to shorten sail and so urgent seemed our need, that the very officers went aloft to help make up the sails, leaving only the Captain (who had taken the wheel) and myself upon the poop. On the maindeck, the cook was busy letting go such ropes as the Mates desired.

"Abruptly, some distance ahead, through the vague sea-mist, but rather on the port bow, I saw loom up a great black wall of cloud.

"'Look, Captain!' I exclaimed; but it had vanished before I had finished speaking. A minute later it came again, and this time the Captain saw it.

"'O, my God!' he cried, and dropped his hands from the wheel. He leapt into the companionway, and seized a speaking trumpet. Then out on deck. He put it to his lips.

"'Come down from aloft! Come down! Come down!' he shouted. And suddenly I lost his voice in a terrific mutter of sound from somewhere to port. It was the voice of the storm—shouting. My God! I had never heard anything like it! It ceased as suddenly as it had begun, and, in the succeeding quietness, I heard the whining of the kicking-tackles through the blocks. Then came a quick clang of brass upon the deck, and I turned quickly. The Captain had thrown down the trumpet, and sprung back to the wheel. I glanced aloft, and saw that many of the men were already in the rigging, and racing down like cats.

"I heard the Captain draw his breath with a quick gasp. 'Hold on for your lives!' he shouted, in a hoarse, unnatural voice.

"I looked at him. He was staring to windward with a fixed stare of painful intentness, and my gaze followed his. I saw, not four hundred yards distant, an enormous mass of foam and water coming down upon us. In the same instant, I caught the hiss of it, and immediately it was a shriek, so intense and awful, that I cringed impotently with sheer terror.

"The smother of water and foam took the ship, a little foreside of the beam, and the wind was with it. Immediately, the vessel rolled over on to her side, the sea-froth flying over her in tremendous cataracts.

"It seemed as though nothing could save us. Over, over we went, until I was swinging against the deck, almost as against the side of a house; for I had grasped the weather rail at the Captain's warning. As I swung there, I saw a strange thing. Before me was the port quarter boat. Abruptly, the canvas cover was flipped clean off it, as though by a vast, invisible hand.

"The next instant, a flurry of oars, boats' masts and odd gear flittered up into the air, like so many feathers, and blew to leeward and was lost in the roaring chaos of foam. The boat, herself, lifted in her chocks, and suddenly was blown clean down on to the main-deck, where she lay all in a ruin of white-painted timbers.

"A minute of the most intense suspense passed; then, suddenly, the ship righted, and I saw that the three masts had carried away. Yet, so hugely loud was the crying of the storm, that no sound of their breaking had reached me.

"I looked towards the wheel; but no one was there. Then I made out something crumpled up against the lee rail. I struggled across to it, and found that it was the Captain. He was insensible, and queerly limp in his right arm and leg. I looked round. Several of the men were crawling aft along the poop. I beckoned to them, and pointed to the wheel, and then to the Captain. A couple of them came towards me, and one went to the wheel. Then I made out through the spray the form of the Second Mate. He had several more of the men with him, and they had a coil of rope, which they took forrard. I learnt afterwards that they were hastening to get out a sea-anchor, so as to keep the ship's head towards the wind.

"We got the Captain below, and into his bunk. There, I left him in the hands of his daughter and the steward, and returned on deck.

"Presently, the Second Mate came back, and with him the remainder of the men. I found then that only seven had been saved in all. The rest had gone.

"The day passed terribly—the wind getting stronger hourly; though, at its worst, it was nothing like so tremendous as that first burst.

"The night came—a night of terror, with the thunder and hiss of the giant seas in the air above us, and the wind bellowing like some vast Elemental beast.

"Then, just before the dawn, the wind lulled, almost in a moment; the ship rolling and wallowing fearfully, and the water coming aboard—hundreds of tons at a time. Immediately afterwards it caught us again; but more on the beam, and bearing the vessel over on to her side, and this only by the pressure of the element upon the stark hull. As we came head to wind again, we righted, and rode, as we had for hours, amid a thousand fantastic hills of phosphorescent flame.

"Again the wind died—coming again after a longer pause, and then, all at once, leaving us. And so, for the space of a terrible half hour, the ship lived through the most awful, windless sea that can be imagined. There was no doubting but that we had driven right into the calm centre of the cyclone—calm only so far as lack of wind, and yet more dangerous a thousand times than the most furious hurricane that ever blew.

"For now we were beset by the stupendous Pyramidal Sea; a sea once witnessed, never forgotten; a sea in which the whole bosom of the ocean is projected towards heaven in monstrous hills of water; not leaping forward, as would be the case if there were wind; but hurling upwards in jets and peaks of living brine, and falling back in a continuous thunder of foam.

"Imagine this, if you can, and then have the clouds break away suddenly overhead, and the moon shine down upon that hellish turmoil, and you will have such a sight as has been given to mortals but seldom, save with death. And this is what we saw, and to my mind there is nothing within the knowledge of man to which I can liken it.

"Yet we lived through it, and through the wind that came later. But two more complete days and nights had passed, before the storm ceased to be a terror to us, and then, only because it had carried us into the seaweed laden waters of the vast Sargasso Sea.

"Here, the great billows first became foamless; and dwindled gradually in size as we drifted further among the floating masses of weed. Yet the wind was still furious, so that the ship drove on steadily, sometimes between banks, and other times over them.

"For a day and a night we drifted thus; and then astern I made out a great bank of weed, vastly greater than any which hitherto we had encountered. Upon this, the wind drove us stern foremost, so that we over-rode it. We had been forced some distance across it, when it occurred to me that our speed was slackening. I guessed presently that the sea-anchor, ahead, had caught in the weed, and was holding. Even as I surmised this, I heard from beyond the bows a faint, droning, twanging sound, blending with the roar of the wind. There came an indistinct report, and the ship lurched backwards through the weed. The hawser, connecting us with the sea-anchor, had parted.

"I saw the Second Mate run forrard with several men. They hauled in upon the hawser, until the broken end was aboard. In the meantime, the ship, having nothing ahead to keep her 'bows on,' began to slew broadside towards the wind. I saw the men attach a chain to the end of the broken hawser; then they paid it out again, and the ship's head came back to the gale.

"When the Second Mate came aft, I asked him why this had been done, and he explained that so long as the vessel was end-on, she would travel over the weed. I inquired why he wished her to go over the weed, and he told me that one of the men had made out what appeared to be clear water astern, and that—could we gain it—we might win free.

"Through the whole of that day, we moved rear-wards across the great bank; yet, so far from the weed appearing to show signs of thinning, it grew steadily thicker, and, as it became denser, so did our speed slacken, until the ship was barely moving. And so the night found us.

"The following morning discovered to us that we were within a quarter of a mile of a great expanse of clear water—apparently the open sea; but unfortunately the wind had dropped to a moderate breeze, and the vessel was motionless, deep sunk in the weed; great tufts of which rose up on all sides, to within a few feet of the level of our main-deck.

"A man was sent up the stump of the mizzen, to take a look round. From there, he reported that he could see something, that might be weed, across the water; but it was too far distant for him to be in any way certain. Immediately afterwards, he called out that there was something, away on our port beam; but what it was, he could not say, and it was not until a telescope was brought to bear, that we made it out to be the hull of the ancient vessel I have previously mentioned.

"And now, the Second Mate began to cast about for some means by which he could bring the ship to the clear water astern. The first thing which he did, was to bend a sail to a spaze yard, and hoist it to the top of the mizzen stump. By this means, he was able to dispense with the cable towing over the bows, which, of course, helped to prevent the ship from moving. In addition, the sail would prove helpful to force the vessel across the weed. Then he routed out a couple of kedges. These, he bent on to the ends of a short piece of cable, and, to the bight of this, the end of a long coil of strong rope.

"After that, he had the starboard quarter boat lowered into the weed, and in it he placed the two kedge anchors. The end of an-other length of rope, he made fast to the boat's painter. This done, he took four of the men with him, telling them to bring chain-hooks, in addition to the oars—his intention being to force the boat through the weed, until he reached the clear water. There, in the marge of the weed, he would plant the two anchors in the thickest clumps of the growth; after which we were to haul the boat back to the ship, by means of the rope attached to the painter.

"'Then,' as he put it, 'we'll take the kedge-rope to the capstan, and heave her out of this blessed cabbage heap!'

"The weed proved a greater obstacle to the progress of the boat, than, I think, he had anticipated. After half an hour's work, they had gone scarcely more than some two hundred feet from the vessel; yet, so thick was the stuff, that no sign could we see of them, save the movement they made among the weed, as they forced the boat along.

"Another quarter of an hour passed away, during which the three men left upon the poop, paid out the ropes as the boat forged slowly ahead. All at once, I heard my name called. Turning, I saw the Captain's daughter in the companionway, beckoning to me. I walked across to her.

"'My father has sent me up to know, Mr. Philips, how they are getting on?'

"'Very slowly, Miss Knowles,' I replied. 'Very slowly indeed. The weed is so extraordinarily thick.'

"She nodded intelligently, and turned to descend; but I detained her a moment.

"'Your father, how is he?' I asked.

"She drew her breath swiftly.

"'Quite himself,' she said; 'but so dreadfully weak. He—'

"An outcry from one of the men, broke across her speech:—

"'Lord 'elp us, mates! wot were that!'

"I turned sharply. The three of them were staring over the taffrail. I ran towards them, and Miss Knowles followed.

"'Hush!' she said, abruptly. 'Listen!'

"I stared astern to where I knew the boat to be. The weed all about it was quaking queerly—the movement extending far beyond the radius of their hooks and oars. Suddenly, I heard the Second Mate's voice:—

"'Look out, lads! My God, look out!'

"And close upon this, blending almost with it, came the hoarse scream of a man in sudden agony.

"I saw an oar come up into view, and descend violently, as though someone struck at something with it. Then the Second Mate's voice, shouting:—

"'Aboard there! Aboard there! Haul in on the rope! Haul in on the rope—!' It broke off into a sharp cry.

"As we seized hold of the rope, I saw the weed hurled in all directions, and a great crying and choking swept to us over the brown hideousness around.

"'Pull!' I yelled, and we pulled. The rope tautened; but the boat never moved.

"'Tek it ter ther capsting!' gasped one of the men.

"Even as he spoke, the rope slackened.

"'It's coming!' cried Miss Knowles. 'Pull! Oh! Pull!'

"She had hold of the rope along with us, and together we hauled, the boat yielding to our strength with surprising ease.

"'There it is!' I shouted, and then I let go of the rope. There was no one in the boat.

"For the half of a minute, we stared, dumfoundered. Then my gaze wandered astern to the place from which we had plucked it. There was a heaving movement among the great weed masses. I saw something waver up aimlessly against the sky; it was sinuous, and it flickered once or twice from side to side; then sank back among the growth, before I could concentrate my attention upon it.

"I was recalled to myself by a sound of dry sobbing. Miss Knowles was kneeling upon the deck, her hands clasped round one of the iron uprights of the rail. She seemed momentarily all to pieces.

"'Come! Miss Knowles,' I said, gently. 'You must be brave. We cannot let your father know of this in his present state.'

"She allowed me to help her to her feet. I could feel that she was trembling badly. Then, even as I sought for words with which to reassure her, there came a dull thud from the direction of the companionway. We looked round. On the deck, face downward, lying half in and half out of the scuttle, was the Captain. Evidently, he had witnessed everything. Miss Knowles gave out a wild cry, and ran to her father. I beckoned to one of the men to help me, and, together, we carried him back to his bunk. An hour later, he recovered from his swoon. He was quite calm, though very weak, and evidently in considerable pain.

"Through his daughter, he made known to me that he wished me to take the reins of authority in his place. This, after a slight demur, I decided to do; for, as I reassured myself, there were no duties required of me, needing any special knowledge of ship-craft. The vessel was fast; so far as I could see, irrevocably fast. It would be time to talk of freeing her, when the Captain was well enough to take charge once more.

"I returned on deck, and made known to the men the Captain's wishes. Then I chose one to act as a sort of bo'sun over the other two, and to him I gave orders that everything should be put to rights before the night came. I had sufficient sense to leave him to manage matters in his own way; for, whereas my knowledge of what was needful, was fragmentary, his was complete.

"By this time, it was near to sunsetting, and it was with melancholy feelings that I watched the great hull of the sun plunge lower. For awhile, I paced the poop, stopping ever and anon to stare over the dreary waste by which we were surrounded. The more I looked about, the more a sense of lonesomeness and depression and fear assailed me. I had pondered much upon the dread happening of the day, and all my ponderings led to a vital questioning:—What was there among all that quiet weed, which had come upon the crew of the boat, and destroyed them? And I could not make answer, and the weed was silent—dreadly silent!

"The sun had drawn very near to the dim horizon, and I watched it, moodily, as it splashed great clots of red fire across the water that lay stretched into the distance across our storm. Abruptly, as I gazed, its perfect lower edge was marred by an irregular shape. For a moment, I stared, puzzled. Then I fetched a pair of glasses from the holdfast in the companion. A glance through these, and I knew the extent of our fate. That line, blotching the round of the sun, was the conformation of another enormous weed bank.

"I remembered that the man had reported something as showing across the water, when he was sent up to the top of the mizzet stump in the morning; but, what it was, he had been unable to say. The thought flashed into my mind that it had been only just visible from aloft in the morning, and now it was in sight from the deck. It occurred to me that the wind might be compacting the weed, and driving the bank which surrounded the ship, down upon a larger portion. Possibly, the clear stretch of water had been but a temporary rift within the heart of the Sargasso Sea. It seemed only too probable.

"Thus it was that I meditated, and so, presently, the night found me. For some hours further, I paced the deck in the darkness, striving to understand the incomprehensible; yet with no better result than to weary myself to death. Then, somewhere about midnight, I went below to sleep.

"The following morning, on going on deck, I found that the stretch of clear water had disappeared entirely, during the night, and now, so far as the eye could reach, there was nothing but a stupendous desolation of weed.

"The wind had dropped completely, and no sound came from all that weed-ridden immensity. We had, in truth, reached the Cemetery of the Ocean!

"The day passed uneventfully enough. It was only when I served out some food to the men, and one of them asked whether they could have a few raisins, that I remembered, with a pang of sudden misery, that it was Christmas day. I gave them the fruit, as they desired, and they spent the morning in the galley, cooking their dinner. Their stolid indifference to the late terrible happenings, appalled me somewhat, until I remembered what their lives were, and had been. Poor fellows! One of them ventured aft at dinner time, and offered me a slice of what he called 'plum duff.' He brought it on a plate which he had found in the galley and scoured thoroughly with sand and water. He tendered it shyly enough, and I took it, so graciously as I could, for I would not hurt his feelings; though the very smell of the stuff was an abomination.

"During the afternoon, I brought out the Captain's telescope, and made a thorough examination of the ancient hulk on our port beam. Particularly did I study the extraordinary superstructure around her sides; but could not, as I have said before, conceive of its use.

"The evening, I spent upon the poop, my eyes searching wearily across that vile quietness, and so, in a little, the night came—Christmas night, sacred to a thousand happy memories. I found myself dreaming of the night a year previous, and, for a little while, I forgot what was before me. I was recalled suddenly—terribly. A voice rose out of the dark which hid the maindeck. For the fraction of an instant, it expressed surprise; then pain and terror leapt into it. Abruptly, it seemed to come from above, and then from somewhere beyond the ship, and so in a moment there was silence, save for a rush of feet and the bang of a door forrard.

"I leapt down the poop ladder, and ran along the maindeck, towards the fo'cas'le. As I ran, something knocked off my cap. I scarcely noticed it then. I reached the fo'cas'le, and caught at the latch of the port door. I lifted it and pushed; but the door was fastened.

"'Inside there!' I cried, and banged upon the panels with my clenched fist.

"A man's voice came, incoherently.

"'Open the door!' I shouted. 'Open the door!'

"'Yes, Sir—I'm com—ming, Sir,' said one of them, jerkily.

"I heard footsteps stumble across the planking. Then a hand fumbled at the fastening, and the door flew open under my weight.

"The man who had opened to me, started back. He held a flaring slush-lamp above his head, and, as I entered, he thrust it forward. His hand was trembling visibly, and, behind him, I made out the face of one of his mates, the brow and dirty, clean-shaven upper lip drenched with sweat. The man who held the lamp, opened his mouth, and gabbered at me; but, for a moment, no sound came.

"'Wot—wot were it? Wot we-ere it?' he brought out at last, with a gasp.

"The man behind, came to his side, and gesticulated.

"'What was what?' I asked sharply, and looking from one to the other. 'Where's the other man? What was that screaming?'

"The second man drew the palm of his hand across his brow; then flirted his fingers deckwards.

"'We don't know, Sir! We don't know! It were Jessop! Somethin's took 'im just as we was comin' forrid! We—we—He—he—HARK!'

"His head came forward with a jerk as he spoke, and then, for a space, no one stirred. A minute passed, and I was about to speak, when, suddenly, from somewhere out upon the deserted maindeck, there came a queer, subdued noise, as though something moved stealthily hither and thither. The man with the lamp caught me by the sleeve, and then, with an abrupt movement, slammed the door and fastened it.

"'That's *it*, Sir!' he exclaimed, with a note of terror and conviction in his voice.

"I bade him be silent, while I listened; but no sound came to us through the door, and so I turned to the men and told them to let me have all they knew.

"It was little enough. They had been sitting in the galley, yarning, until, feeling tired, they had decided to go forrard and turn-in. They extinguished the light, and came out upon the deck, closing the door behind them. Then, just as they turned to go forrard, Jessop gave out a yell. The next instant they heard him screaming in the air above their heads, and, realising that some terrible thing was upon them, they took forthwith to their heels, and ran for the security of the fo'cas'le.

"Then I had come.

"As the men made an end of telling me, I thought I heard something outside, and held up my hand for silence. I caught the sound again. Someone was calling my name. It was Miss Knowles. Likely enough she was calling me to supper—and she had no knowledge of the dread thing which had happened. I sprang to the door. She might be coming along the maindeck in search of me And there was Something out, there, of which I had no conception—something unseen, but deadly tangible!

"'Stop, Sir!' shouted the men, together; but I had the door open.

"'Mr. Philips!' came the girl's voice at no great distance. 'Mr. Philips!'

"'Coming, Miss Knowles!' I shouted, and snatched the lamp from the man's hand.

"The next instant, I was running aft, holding the lamp high, and glancing fearfully from side to side. I reached the place where the mainmast had been, and spied the girl coming towards me.

"'Go back!' I shouted. 'Go back!'

"She turned at my shout, and ran for the poop ladder. I came up with her, and followed close at her heels. On the poop, she turned and faced me.

"'What is it, Mr. Philips?'

"I hesitated. Then:—

"'I don't know!' I said.

"'My father heard something,' she began. 'He sent me. He—'

"I put up my hand. It seemed to me that I had caught again the sound of something stirring on the maindeck.

"'Quick!' I said sharply. 'Down into the cabin!' And she, being a sensible girl, turned and ran down without waste of time. I followed, closing and fastening the companion-doors behind me.

"In the saloon, we had a whispered talk, and I told her everything. She bore up bravely, and said nothing; though her eyes were very wide, and her face pale. Then the Captains's voice came to us from the adjoining cabin.

"'Is Mr. Philips there, Mary?'

"'Yes, father.'

"'Bring him in.'

"I went in.

"'What was it, Mr. Philips?' he asked, collectedly.

"I hesitated; for I was willing to spare him the ill news; but he looked at me with calm eyes for a moment, and I knew that it was useless attempting to deceive him.

"'Something has happened, Mr. Philips,' he said, quietly. 'You need not be afraid to tell me.'

"At that, I told him so much as I knew, he listening, and nodding his comprehension of the story.

"'It must be something big,' he remarked, when I had made an end. 'And yet you saw nothing when you came aft?'

"'No,' I replied.

"'It is something in the weed,' he went on. 'You will have to keep off the deck at night.'

"After a little further talk, in which he displayed a calmness that amazed me, I left him, and went presently to my berth. The following day, I took the two men, and, together, we made a thorough search through the ship; but found nothing. It was evident to me that the Captain was right. There was some dread Thing hidden within the weed. I went to the side and looked down. The two men followed me. Suddenly, one of them pointed.

"'Look, Sir!' he exclaimed, 'Right below you, Sir! Two eyes like blessed great saucers! Look!'

"I stared; but could see nothing. The man left my side, and ran into the galley. In a moment, he was back with a great lump of coal.

"'Just there, Sir,' he said, and hove it down into the weed immediately beneath where we stood.

"Too late, I saw the thing at which he aimed—two immense eyes, some little distance below the surface of the weed. I knew instantly to what they belonged; for I had seen large specimens of the octopus some years previously, during a cruise in Australasian waters.

"'Look out, man!' I shouted, and caught him by the arm. 'It's an octopus! Jump back!' I sprang down on to the deck. In the same instant, huge masses of weed were hurled in all directions, and half a dozen immense tentacles whirled up into the air. One lapped itself about his neck. I caught his leg; but he was torn from my grasp, and I tumbled backwards on to the deck. I heard a scream from the other man as I scrambled to my feet. I looked to where he had been; but of him there was no sign. Regardless of the danger, in my great agitation, I leapt upon the rail, and gazed down with frightened eyes. Yet, neither of him nor his mate, nor the monster, could I perceive a vestige.

"How long I stood there staring down bewilderedly, I cannot say; certainly some minutes. I was so bemazed that I seemed incapable of movement. Then, all at once, I became aware that a light quiver ran across the weed, and the next instant, something stole up out of the depths with a deadly celerity. Well it was for me that I had seen it in time, else should I have shared the fate of those two— and the others. As it was, I saved myself only by leaping backwards on to the deck. For a moment, I saw the feeler wave above the rail with a certain apparent aimlessness; then it sank out of sight, and I was alone.

"An hour passed before I could summon a sufficiency of courage to break the news of this last tragedy to the Captain and his daughter, and when I had made an end, I returned to the solitude of the poop; there to brood upon the hopelessness of our position.

"As I paced up and down, I caught myself glancing continuously at the nearer weed tufts. The happenings of the past two days had shattered my nerves, and I feared every moment to see some slender death-grapple searching over the rail for me. Yet, the poop, being very much higher out of the weed than the maindeck, was comparatively safe; though only comparatively.

"Presently, as I meandered up and down, my gaze fell upon the hulk of the ancient ship, and, in a flash, the reason for that great superstructure was borne upon me. It was intended as a protection against the dread creatures which inhabited the weed. The thought came to me that I would attempt some similar means of protection; for the feeling that, at any moment, I might be caught and lifted out into that slimy wilderness, was not to be borne. In addition, the work would serve to occupy my mind, and help me to bear up against the intolerable sense of loneliness which assailed me.

"I resolved that I would lose no time, and so, after some thought as to the manner in which I should proceed, I routed out some coils of rope and several sails. Then I went down on to the maindeck and brought up an armful of capstan bars. These I lashed vertically to the rail all round the poop. Then I knotted the rope to each, stretching it tightly between them, and over this framework stretched the sails, sewing the stout canvas to the rope, by means of twine and some great needles which I found in the Mate's room.

"It is not to be supposed that this piece of work was accomplished immediately. Indeed, it was only after three days of hard labour that I got the poop completed. Then I commenced work upon the maindeck. This was a tremendous undertaking, and a whole fortnight passed before I had the entire length of it enclosed; for I had to be continually on the watch against the hidden enemy. Once, I was very nearly surprised, and saved myself only by a quick leap. Thereafter, for the rest of that day, I did no more work; being too greatly shaken in spirit. Yet, on the following morning, I recommenced, and from thence, until the end, I was not molested.

"Once the work was roughly completed, I felt at ease to begin and perfect it. This I did, by tarring the whole of the sails with

Stockholm tar; thereby making them stiff, and capable of resisting the weather. After that, I added many fresh uprights, and much strengthening ropework, and finally doubled the sailcloth with additional sails, liberally smeared with the tar.

"In this manner, the whole of January passed away, and a part of February. Then, it would be on the last day of the month, the Captain sent for me, and told me, without any preliminary talk, that he was dying. I looked at him; but said nothing; for I had known long that it was so, In return, he stared back with a strange intentness, as though he would read my inmost thoughts, and this for the space of perhaps two minutes.

"'Mr. Philips,' he said at last, 'I may be dead by this time to-morrow. Has it ever occurred to you that my daughter will be alone with you?'

"'Yes, Captain Knowles,' I replied, quietly, and waited.

"For a few seconds, he remained silent; though, from the changing expressions of his face, I knew that he was pondering how best to bring forward the thing which it was in his mind to say.

"'You are a gentleman—' he began, at last.

"'I will marry her,' I said, ending the sentence for him.

"A slight flush of surprise crept into his face.

"'You—you have thought seriously about it?'

"'I have thought very seriously,' I explained.

"'Ah!' he said, as one who comprehends. And then, for a little, he lay there quietly. It was plain to me that memories of past days were with him. Presently, he came out of his dreams, and spoke, evidently referring to my marriage with his daughter.

"'It is the only thing,' he said, in a level voice.

"I bowed, and after that, he was silent again for a space. In a little, however, he turned once more to me:—

"'Do you—do you love her?'

"His tone was keenly wistful, and a sense of trouble lurked in his eyes.

"'She will be my wife,' I said, simply; and he nodded.

"'God has dealt strangely with us,' he murmured presently, as though to himself.

"Abruptly, he bade me tell her to come in.

"And then he married us.

"Three days later, he was dead, and we were alone.

"For a while, my wife was a sad woman; but gradually time eased her of the bitterness of her grief.

"Then, some eight months after our marriage, a new interest stole into her life. She whispered it to me, and we, who had borne our loneliness uncomplainingly, had now this new thing to which to look forward. It became a bond between us, and bore promise of some companionship as we grew old. Old! At the idea of age, a sudden flash of thought darted like lightning across the sky of my mind:—*Food!* Hitherto, I had thought of myself, almost as of one already dead, and had cared naught for anything beyond the immediate troubles which each day forced upon me. The loneliness of the vast Weed World had become an assurance of doom to me which had clouded and dulled my faculties, so that I had grown apathetic. Yet, immediately, as it seemed, at the shy whispering of my wife, was all this changed.

"That very hour, I began a systematic search through the ship. Among the cargo, which was of a 'general' nature, I discovered large quantities of preserved and tinned provisions, all of which I put carefully on one side. I continued my examination until I had ransacked the whole vessel. The business took me near upon six months to complete, and when it was finished, I seized paper, and made calculations, which led me to the conclusion that we had sufficient food in the ship to preserve life in three people for some fifteen to seventeen years. I could not come nearer to it than this; for I had no means of computing the quantity the child would need year by year. Yet it is sufficient to show me that seventeen years must be the limit. Seventeen years! And then—

"Concerning water, I am not troubled; for I have rigged a great sailcloth tun-dish, with a canvas pipe into the tanks; and from every rain, I draw a supply, which has never run short.

"The child was born nearly five months ago. She is a fine little girl, and her mother seems perfectly happy. I believe I could be quietly happy with them, were it not that I have ever in mind the end of those seventeen years. True! we may be dead long before then; but, if not, our little girl will be in her teens—and it is a hungry age.

"If one of us died—but no! Much may happen in seventeen years. I will wait.

"My method of sending this clear of the weed is likely to succeed. I have constructed a small fire-balloon, and this missive, safely enclosed in a little barrel, will be attached. The wind will carry it swiftly hence.

"Should this ever reach civilised beings, will they see that it is forwarded to:—" (Here followed an address, which, for some reason, had been roughly obliterated. Then came the signature of the writer)

"Arthur Samuel Philips."

The captain of the schooner looked over at Jock, as the man made an end of his reading.

"Seventeen years pervisions," he muttered thoughtfully. "An' this 'ere were written sumthin' like twenty-nine years ago!" He nodded his head several times. "Poor creatures!" he exclaimed. "It'd be er long while, Jock—a long while!"

II

In the August of 1902, Captain Bateman, of the schooner *Agnes*, picked up a small barrel, upon which was painted a half obliterated word; which, finally, he succeeded in deciphering as "Homebird," the name of a full-rigged ship, which left London in the November of 1873, and from thenceforth was heard of no more by any man.

Captain Bate man opened the barrel, and discovered a packet of Manuscript, wrapped in oilskin. This, on examination, proved to be an account of the losing of the *Homebird* amid the desolate wastes of the Sargasso Sea. The papers were written by one, Arthur Samuel Philips, a passenger in the ship; and, from them, Captain Bateman was enabled to gather that the ship, mastless, lay in the very heart of the dreaded Sargasso; and that all of the crew had been lost— some on the storm which drove them thither, and some on attempts to free the ship from the weed, which locked them in on all sides.

Only Mr. Philips and the Captain's daughter had been left alive, and they two, the dying Captain had married. To them had been born a daughter, and the papers ended with a brief but touching allusion to their fear that, eventually, they must run short of food.

There is need to say but little more. The account was copied into most of the papers of the day, and caused widespread comment. There was even some talk of fitting out a rescue expedition; but this fell through, owing chiefly to lack of knowledge of the whereabouts of the ship in all the vastness of the immense Sargasso Sea. And so, gradually, the matter has slipped into the background of the Public's memory.

Now, however, interest will be once more excited in the lonesome fate of this lost trio; for a second barrel, identical, it would seem, with that found by Captain Bateman, has been picked up by a Mr. Bolton, of Baltimore, master of a small brig, engaged in the South American coast-trade. In this barrel was enclosed a further message from Mr. Philips—the fifth that he has sent abroad to the world; but the second, third and fourth, up to this time, have not been discovered.

This "fifth message" contains a vital and striking account of their lives during the year 1879, and stands unique as a document informed with human lonesomeness and longing. I have seen it, and read it through, with the most intense and painful interest. The writing, though faint, is very legible; and the whole manuscript bears the impress of the same hand and mind that wrote the piteous account of the losing of the *Homebird*, of which I have already made mention, and with which, no doubt, many are well acquainted.

In closing this little explanatory note, I am stimulated to wonder whether, somewhere, at some time, those three missing messages ever shall be found. And then there may be others. What stories of human, strenuous fighting with Fate may they not contain.

We can but wait and wonder. Nothing more may we ever learn; for what is this one little tragedy among the uncounted millions that the silence of the sea holds so remorselessly. And yet, again, news may come to us out of the Unknown—out of the lonesome silences of the dread Sargasso Sea—the loneliest and the most inaccessible place of all the lonesome and inaccessible places of this earth.

And so I say, let us wait. W. H. H.

THE FIFTH MESSAGE

"This is the fifth message that I have sent abroad over the loathsome surface of this vast Weed-World, praying that it may come to the open sea, ere the lifting power of my fire-balloon be gone, and yet, if it come there—the which I could now doubt—how shall I be the better for it! Yet write I must, or go mad, and so I choose to write, though feeling as I write that no living creature, save it be the giant octopi that live in the weed about me, will ever see the thing I write.

"My first message I sent cut on Christmas Eve, 1875, and since then, each eve of the birth of Christ has seen a message go skywards upon the winds, towards the open sea. It is as though this approaching time of festivity and the meeting of parted loved ones, overwhelms me, and drives away the half apathetic peace that has been mine through spaces of these years of lonesomeness; so that I seclude myself from my wife and the little one, and with ink, pen, and paper, try to ease my heart of the pent emotions that seem at times to threaten to burst it.

"It is now six completed years since the Weed-World claimed us from the World of the Living—six years away from our brothers and sisters of the human and living world—It has been six years of living in a grave! And there are all the years ahead! Oh! My God! My God! I dare not think upon them! I must control myself—

"And then there is the little one, she is nearly four and a half now, and growing wonderfully, out among these wilds. Four and a half years, and the little woman has never seen a human face besides ours—think of it! And yet, if she lives four and forty years, she will never see another... Four and forty years! It is foolishness to trouble about such a space of time; for the future, for us, ends in ten years—eleven at the utmost. Our food will last no longer than that... My wife does not know; for it seems to me a wicked thing to add unnecessarily to her punishment. She does but know that we must waste no ounce of food-stuff, and for the rest she imagines that the most of the cargo is of an edible nature. Perhaps, I have nurtured this belief. If anything happened to me, the food would last a few extra years; but my wife would have to imagine it an accident, else would each bite she took sicken her.

"I have thought often and long upon this matter, yet I fear to leave them; for who knows but that their very lives might at any time depend upon my strength, more pitifully, perhaps, than upon the food which they must come at last to lack. No, I must not bring upon them, and myself, a near and certain calamity, to defer one that, though it seems to have but little less certainty, is yet at a further distance.

"Until lately, nothing has happened to us in the past four years, if I except the adventures that attended my mad attempt to cut a way through the surrounding weed to freedom, and from which it pleased God that I and these with me should be preserved.[1] Yet, in the latter part of this year, an adventure, much touched with grimness, came to us most unexpectedly, in a fashion quite unthought of—an adventure that has brought into our lives a fresh and more active peril; for now I have learned that the weed holds other terrors besides that of the giant octopi.

"Indeed, I have grown to believe this world of desolation capable of holding any horror, as well it might. Think of it—an interminable stretch of dank, brown loneliness in all directions, to the distant horizon; a place where monsters of the deep and the weed have undisputed reign; where never an enemy may fall upon them; but from which they may strike with sudden deadliness! No human can ever bring an engine of destruction to bear upon them, and the humans whose fate it is to have sight of them, do so only from the decks of lonesome derelicts, whence they stare lonely with fear, and without ability to harm.

"I cannot describe it, nor can any hope ever to imagine it! When the wind falls, a vast silence holds us girt, from horizon to horizon, yet it is a silence through which one seems to feel the pulse of hidden things all about us, watching and waiting—waiting and watching; waiting but for the chance to reach forth a huge and sudden death-grapple... It is no use! I cannot bring it home to any; nor shall I be better able to convey the frightening sound of the wind, sweeping

---

[1] This is evidently a reference to something which Mr. Philips has set forth in an earlier message—one of the three lost messages.—W. H. H.

across these vast, quaking plains—the shrill whispering of the weed-fronds, under the stirring of the winds. To hear it from beyond our canvas screen, is like listening to the uncounted dead of the mighty Sargasso wailing their own requiems. Or again, my fancy, diseased with much loneliness and brooding, likens it to the advancing rustle of armies of the great monsters that are always about us—waiting.

"And so to the coming of this new terror:—

"It was in the latter end of October that we first had knowledge of it—a tapping in the night time against the side of the vessel, below the water-line; a noise that came distinct, yet with a ghostly strangeness in the quietness of the night. It was on a Monday night when first I heard it. I was down in the lazarette, overhauling our stores, and suddenly I heard it—tap—tap—tap—against the outside of the vessel upon the starboard side, and below the water line. I stood for awhile listening; but could not discover what it was that should come a-tapping against our side, away out here in this lonesome world of weed and slime. And then, as I stood there listening, the tapping ceased, and so I waited, wondering, and with a hateful sense of fear, weakening my manhood, and taking the courage out of any heart.

"Abruptly, it recommenced; but now upon the opposite side of the vessel, and as it continued, I fell into a little sweat; for it seemed to me that some foul thing out in the night was tapping for admittance. Tap—tap—tap—it went, and continued, and there I stood listening, and so gripped about with frightened thoughts, that I seemed without power to stir myself; for the spell of the Weed-World, and the fear bred of its hidden terrors and the weight and dreeness of its loneliness have entered into my marrow, so that I could, then and now, believe in the likelihood of matters which, ashore and in the midst of my fellows, I might laugh at in contempt. It is the dire lonesomeness of this strange world into which I have entered that serves so to take the heart out of a man.

"And so, as I have said, I stood there listening, and full of frightened, but undefined, thoughts; and all the while the tapping continued, sometimes with a regular insistence, and anon with a quick spasmodic tap, tap, tap-a-tap, as though some Thing, Thing Intelligence, signalled to me.

"Presently, however, I shook off something of the foolish fright that had taken me, and moved over to the place from which the tapping seemed to sound. Coming near to it, I bent my head down, close to the side of the vessel, and listened. Thus, I heard the noises with greater plainness, and could distinguish easily, now, that something knocked with a hard object upon the outside of the ship, as though someone had been striking her iron side with a small hammer.

"Then, even as I listened, came a thunderous blow close to my ear, so loud and astonishing, that I leaped sideways in sheer fright. Directly afterwards there came a second heavy blow, and then a third, as though someone had struck the ship's side with a heavy sledge-hammer, and after that, a space of silence, in which I heard my wife's voice at the trap of the lazarette, calling down to me to know what had happened to cause so great a noise.

"'Hush, My Dear!' I whispered; for it seemed to me that the thing outside might hear her; though this could not have been possible, and I do but mention it as showing how the noises had set me off my natural balance.

At my whispered command, my wife turned her about and came down the ladder into the semi-darkness of the place.

"'What is it, Arthur?' she asked, coming across to me, and slipping her hand between my arm and side.

"As though in reply to her query, there came against the outside of the ship, a fourth tremendous blow, filling the whole of the lazarette with a dull thunder.

"My wife gave out a frightened cry, and sprang away from me; but the next instant, she was back, and gripping hard at my arm.

"'What is it, Arthur? What is it?' she asked me; her voice, though no more than a frightened whisper, easily heard in the succeeding silence.

"'I don't know, Mary,' I replied, trying to speak in a level tone. 'It's—'

"'There's something again,' she interrupted, as the minor tapping noises recommenced.

"For about a minute, we stood silent, listening to those eerie taps. Then my wife turned to me:—

"'Is it anything dangerous, Arthur—tell me? I promise you I shall be brave."

"'I can't possibly say, Mary,' I answered. 'I can't say; but I'm going up on deck to listen... Perhaps,' I paused a moment to think; but a fifth tremendous blow against the ship's side, drove whatever I was going to say, clean from me, and I could do no more than stand there, frightened and bewildered, listening for further sounds. After a short pause, there came a sixth blow. Then my wife caught me by the arm, and commenced to drag me towards the ladder.

"'Come up out of this dark place, Arthur,' she said. 'I shall be ill if we stay here any longer. Perhaps the—the thing outside can hear us, and it may stop if we go upstairs.'

"By this, my wife was all of a shake, and I but little better, so that I was glad to follow her up the ladder. At the top, we paused for a while to listen, bending down over the open hatchway. A space of, maybe, some five minutes passed away in silence; then there commenced again the tapping noises, the sounds coming clearly up to us where we crouched. Presently, they ceased once more, and after that, though we listened for a further space of some ten minutes, they were not repeated. Neither were there any more of the great bangs.

"In a little, I led my wife away from the hatch, to a seat in the saloon; for the hatch is situated under the saloon table. After that, I returned to the opening, and replaced the cover. Then I went into our cabin—the one which had been the Captain's, her father,—and brought from there a revolver, of which we have several. This, I loaded with care, and afterwards placed in my side pocket.

"Having done this, I fetched from the pantry, where I have made it my use to keep such things at hand, a bull's-eye lantern, the same having been used on dark nights when clearing up the ropes from the decks. This, I lit, and afterwards turned the dark-slide to cover the light. Next, I slipped off my boots; and then, as an afterthought, I reached down one of the long-handled American axes from the rack about the mizzenmast—these being keen and very formidable weapons.

"After that, I had to calm my wife and assure her that I would run no unnecessary risks, if, indeed, there were any risks to run; though, as may be imagined, I could not say what new peril might not be upon us. And then, picking up the lantern, I made my way silently on stockinged feet, up the companionway. I had reached the top, and was just stepping out on to the deck, when something caught my arm. I turned swiftly, and perceived that my wife had followed me up the steps, and from the shaking of her hand upon my arm, I gathered that she was very much agitated.

"'Oh, My Dear, My Dear, don't go! don't go!' she whispered, eagerly. 'Wait until it is daylight. Stay below to-night. You don't know what may be about in this horrible place.'

"I put the lantern and the axe upon the deck beside the companion; then bent towards the opening, and took her into my arms, soothing her, and stroking her hair; yet with ever an alert glance to and fro along the indistinct decks. Presently, she was more like her usual self, and listened to my reasoning, that she would do better to stay below, and so, in a little, left me, having made me promise afresh that I would be very wary of danger.

"When she had gone, I picked up the lantern and the axe, and made my way cautiously to the side of the vessel. Here, I paused and listened very carefully, being just above that spot upon the port side where I had heard the greater part of the tapping, and all of the heavy bangs; yet, though I listened, as I have said, with much attention, there was no repetition of the sounds.

"Presently, I rose and made my way forrard to the break of the poop. Here, bending over the rail which ran across, I listened, peering along the dim maindecks; but could neither see nor hear anything; not that, indeed, I had any reason for expecting to see or hear ought unusual aboard of the vessel; for all of the noises had come from over the side, and, more than that, from beneath the water-line. Yet in the state of mind in which I was, I had less use for reason than fancy; for that strange thudding and tapping, out here in the midst of this world of loneliness, had set me vaguely imagining unknowable terrors, stealing upon me from every shadow that lay upon the dimly-seen decks.

"Then, as still I listened, hesitating to go down on to the maindeck, yet too dissatisfied with the result of my peerings, to cease from my search, I heard, faint yet clear in the stillness of the night, the tapping noises recommence.

"I took my weight from off the rail, and listened; but I could no longer hear them, and at that, I leant forward again over the rail, and peered down on to the maindeck. Immediately, the sounds came once more to me, and I knew now, that they were borne to me by the medium of the rail, which conducted them to me through the iron stanchions by which it is fixed to the vessel.

"At that, I turned and vent aft along the poop deck, moving very warily and with quietness. I stopped over the place where first I had heard the louder noises, and stooped, putting my ear against the rail. Here, the sounds came to me with great distinctness.

"For a little, I listened; then stood up, and slid away that part of the tarred canvas-screen which covers the port opening through which we dump our refuse; they being made here for convenience, one upon each side of the vessel. This, I did very silently; then, leaning forward through the opening, I peered down into the dimness of the weed. Even as I did so, I heard plainly below me a heavy thud, muffled and dull by reason of the intervening water, against the iron side of the ship. It seemed to me that there was some disturbance amid the dark, shadowy masses of the weed. Then I had opened the dark-slide of my lantern, and sent a clear beam of light down into the blackness. For a brief instant, I thought I perceived a multitude of things moving. Yet, beyond that they were oval in shape, and showed white through the weed fronds, I had no clear conception of anything; for with the flash of the light, they vanished, and there lay beneath me only the dark, brown masses of the weed—demurely quiet.

"But an impression they did leave upon my over excited imagination—an impression that might have been due to morbidity, bred of too much loneliness; but nevertheless it seemed to me that I had seen momentarily a multitude of dead white faces, upturned towards me among the meshes of the weed.

"For a little, I leant there, staring down at the circle of illumined weed; yet with my thoughts in such a turmoil of frightened doubts and conjectures, that my physical eyes did but poor work, compared with the orb that looks inward. And through all the chaos of my mind there rose up weird and creepy memories—ghouls, the un-dead. There seemed nothing improbable, in that moment, in associating the terms with the fears that were besetting me. For no man may dare to say what terrors this world holds, until he has become lost to his brother men, amid the unspeakable desolation of the vast and slimy weed-plains of the Sargasso Sea.

"And then, as I leaned there, so foolishly exposing myself to those dangers which I had learnt did truly exist, my eyes caught and subconsciously noted the strange and subtle undulation which always foretells approach of one of the giant octopi. Instantly, I leapt back, and whipped the tarred canvas-cover across the opening, and so stood alone there in the night, glancing frightenedly before and behind me, the beam from my lamp casting wavering splashes of light to and fro about the decks. And all the time, I was listening—listening; for it seemed to me that some Terror was brooding in the night, that might come upon us at any moment and in some unimagined form.

"Then, across the silence, stole a whisper, and I turned swiftly towards the companionway. My wife was there, and she reached out her arms to me, begging me to come below into safety. As the light from my lantern flashed upon her, I saw that she had a revolver in her right hand, and at that, I asked her what she had it for; whereupon she informed me that she had been watching over me, through the whole of the time that I had been on deck, save for the little while that it had taken her to get and load the weapon.

"At that, as may be imagined, I went and embraced her very heartily, kissing her for the love that had prompted her actions; and then, after that, we spoke a little together in low tones—she asking that I should come down and fasten up the companiondoors, and I demurring, telling her that I felt too unsettled to sleep; but would rather keep watch about the poop for a while longer.

"Then, even as we discussed the matter, I motioned to her for quietness. In the succeeding silence, she heard it, as well as I, a slow—tap! tap! tap! coming steadily along the dark maindecks. I felt a swift vile fear, and my wife's hold upon me became very tense, despite that she trembled a little. I released her grip from my arm, and made to go towards the break of the poop; but she was after me instantly, praying me at least to stay where I was, if I would not go below.

"Upon that, I bade her very sternly to release me, and go down into the cabin; though all the while I loved her for her very solicitude. But she disobeyed me, asserting very stoutly, though in a whisper, that if I went into danger, she would go with me; and at that I hesitated; but decided, after a moment, to go no further than the break of the poop, and not to venture on to the maindeck.

"I went very silently to the break, and my wife followed me. From the rail across the break, I shone the light of the lantern; but could neither see nor hear anything; for the tapping noise had ceased. Then it recommenced, seeming to have come near to the port side of the stump of the mainmast. I turned the lantern towards it, and, for one brief instant, it seemed to me that I saw something pale, just beyond the brightness of my light. At that, I raised my pistol and fired, and my wife did the same, though without any telling on my part. The noise of the double explosion went very loud and hollow sounding along the decks, and after the echoes had died away, we both of us thought we heard the tapping going away forrard again.

"After that, we stayed awhile, listening and watching; but all was quiet, and, presently, I consented to go below and bar up the companion, as my wife desired; for, indeed, there was much sense in her plea of the futility of my staying up upon the decks.

"The night passed quietly enough, and on the following morning, I made a very careful inspection of the vessel, examining the decks, the weed outside of the ship, and the sides of her. After that, I removed the hatches, and went down into the holds; but could nowhere find anything of an unusual nature.

"That night, just as we were making an end of our supper, we heard three tremendous blows given against the starboard side of the ship, whereat, I sprang to my feet, seized and lit the dark-lantern, which I had kept handy, and ran quickly and silently up on to the deck. My pistol, I had already in my pocket, and as I had soft slippers upon my feet, I needed not to pause to remove my footgear. In the companionway, I had left the axe, and this I seized as I went up the steps.

"Reaching the deck, I moved over quietly to the side, and slid back the canvas door; then I leant out and opened the slide of the lantern, letting its light play upon the weed in the direction from which the bangs had seemed to proceed; but nowhere could I perceive anything out of the ordinary, the weed seeming undisturbed. And so, after a little, I drew in my head, and slid-to the door in the canvas screen; for it was but wanton folly to stand long exposed to any of the giant octopi that might chance to be prowling near; beneath the curtain of the weed.

"From then, until midnight, I stayed upon the poop, talking much in a quiet voice to my wife, who had followed me up into the companion. At times, we could hear the knocking, sometimes against one side of the ship, and again upon the other. And, between the louder knocks, and accompanying them, would sound the minor tap, tap, tap-a-tap, that I had first heard.

"About midnight, feeling that I could do nothing, and no harm appearing to result to us from the unseen things that seemed to be encircling us, my wife and I made our way below to rest, securely barring the companion-doors behind us.

"It would be, I should imagine, about two o'clock in the morning, that I was aroused from a somewhat troubled sleep, by the agonised screaming of our great boar, away forrard. I leant up upon my elbow, and listened, and so grew speedily wide awake. I sat up, and slid from my bunk to the floor. My wife, as I could tell from her breathing, was sleeping peacefully, so that I was able to draw on a few clothes without disturbing her.

"Then, having lit the dark-lantern, and turned the slide over the light, I took the axe in my other hand, and hastened towards the door that gives out of the forrard end of the saloon, on to the. maindeck, beneath the shelter of the break of the poop. This door, I had locked before turning-in, and now, very noiselessly, I unlocked it, and turned the handle, opening the door with much caution. I peered out along the dim stretch of the maindeck; but could see nothing; then I turned on the slide of the lamp, and let the light play along the decks; but still nothing unusual was revealed to me.

"Away forrard, the shrieking of the pig had been succeeded by an absolute silence, and there was nowhere any noise, if I except an occasional odd tap-a-tap, which seemed to come from the side of the ship. And so, taking hold of my courage, I stepped out on to the maindeck, and proceeded slowly forrard, throwing the beam of light to and fro continuously, as I walked.

"Abruptly, I heard away in the bows of the ship a sudden multitudinous tapping and scraping and slithering; and so loud and near did it sound, that I was brought up all of a round-turn, as the saying is. For, perhaps, a whole minute, I stood there hesitating, and playing the light all about me, not knowing but that some hateful thing might leap upon me from out of the shadows.

"And then, suddenly, I remembered that I had left the door open behind me, that led into the saloon, so that, were there any deadly thing about the decks, it might chance to get in upon my wife and child as they slept. At the thought, I turned and ran swiftly aft again, and in through the door to my cabin. Here, I made sure that all was right with the two sleepers, and after that, I returned to the deck, shutting the door, and locking it behind me.

"And now, feeling very lonesome out there upon the dark decks, and cut off in a way from a retreat, I had need of all my manhood to aid me forrard to learn the wherefore of the pig's crying, and the cause of that manifold tapping. Yet go I did, and have some right to be proud of the act; for the dreeness and lonesomeness and the cold fear of the Weed-World, squeeze the pluck out of one in a very woeful manner.

"As I approached the empty fo'cas'le, I moved with all wariness, swinging the light to and fro, and holding my axe very handily, and the heart within my breast like a shape of water, so in fear was I. Yet, I came at last to the pig-sty, and so discovered a dreadful sight. The pig, a huge boar of twenty-score pounds, had been dragged out on to the deck, and lay before the sty with all his belly ripped up, and stone dead. The iron bars of the sty—great bars they are too—had been torn apart, as though they had been so many straws; and, for the rest, there was a deal of blood both within the sty and upon the decks.

"Yet, I did not stay then to see more; for, all of a sudden, the realisation was borne upon me that this was the work of some monstrous thing, which even at that moment might be stealing upon me; and, with the thought, an overwhelming fear leapt upon me, overbearing my courage; so that I turned and ran for the shelter of the saloon, and never stopped until the stout door was locked between me and that which had wrought such destruction upon the pig. And as I stood there, quivering a little with very fright, I kept questioning dumbly as to what manner of wild-beast thing it was that could burst asunder iron bars, and rip the life out of a great boar, as though it were of no more account than a kitten. And then more vital questions:—How did it get aboard, and where had it hidden? And again:—What was it? And so in this fashion for a good while, until I had grown something more calmed.

"But through all the remainder of that night, I slept not so much as a wink.

"Then in the morning when my wife awoke, I told her of the happenings of the night; whereat she turned very white, and fell to reproaching me for going out at all on to the deck, declaring that I had run needlessly into danger, and that, at least, I should not have left her alone, sleeping in ignorance of what was towards. And after that, she fell into a fit of crying, so that I had some to-do comforting her. Yet, when she had come back to calmness, she was all for accompanying me about the decks, to see by daylight what had indeed befallen in the night-time. And from this decision, I could not turn her; though I assured her I should have told her nothing, had it not been that I wished to warn her from going to and fro between the saloon and the galley, until I had made a thorough search about the decks. Yet, as I have remarked, I could not turn her from her purpose of accompanying me, and so was forced to let her come, though against my desire.

"We made our way on deck through the door that opens under the break of the poop, my wife carrying her loaded revolver half-clumsily in both hands, whilst I had mine held in my left, and the long-handled axe in my right—holding it very readily.

"On stepping out on to the deck, we closed the door behind us, locking it and removing the key; for we had in mind our sleeping child. Then we went slowly forrard along the decks, glancing about warily. As we came fore-side of the pig-sty, and my wife saw that which lay beyond it, she let out a little exclamation of horror, shuddering at the sight of the mutilated pig, as, indeed, well she might.

"For my part, I said nothing; but glanced with much apprehension about us; feeling a fresh access of fright; for it was very plain to me that the boar had been molested since I had seen it— the head having been torn, with awful might, from the body; and there were, besides, other new and ferocious wounds, one of which had come nigh to severing the poor brute's body in half. All of which was so much additional evidence of the formidable character of the monster, or Monstrosity, that had attacked the animal.

"I did not delay by the pig, nor attempt to touch it; but beckoned my wife to follow me up on to the fo'cas'le head. Here, I removed the canvas cover from the small skylight which lights the fo'cas'le beneath; and, after that, I lifted off the heavy top, letting a flood of light down into the gloomy place. Then I leant down into the opening, and peered about; but could discover no signs of any lurking thing, and so returned to the maindeck, and made an entrance into the fo'cas'le through the starboard doorway. And now I made a more minute search; but discovered nothing, beyond the mournful array of sea-chests that had belonged to our dead crew.

"My search concluded, I hastened out from the doleful place, into the daylight, and after that made fast the door again, and saw to it that the one upon the port side was also securely locked. Then I went up again on to the fo'cas'le head, and replaced the sky-light-top and the canvas cover, battening the whole down very thoroughly.

"And in this wise, and with an incredible care, did I make my search through the ship, fastening up each place behind me, so that I should be certain that no Thing was playing some dread game of hide and seek with me.

"Yet I found nothing, and had it not been for the grim evidence of the dead and mutilated boar, I had been like to have thought nothing more dreadful than an ever vivid Imagination had roamed the decks in the darkness of the past night.

"That I had reason to feel puzzled, may be the better understood, when I explain that I had examined the whole of the great, tarred-canvas screen, which I have built about the ship as a protection against the sudden tentacles of any of the roaming giant octopi, without discovering any torn place such as must have been made if any conceivable monster had climbed aboard out of the weed. Also, it must be borne in mind that the ship stands many feet out of the weed, presenting only her smooth iron sides to anything that desires to climb aboard.

"And yet there was the dead pig, lying brutally torn before its empty sty! An undeniable proof that, to go out upon the decks after dark, was to run the risk of meeting a horrible and mysterious death!

"Through all that day, I pondered over this new fear that had come upon us, and particularly upon the monstrous and unearthly power that had torn apart the stout iron bars of the sty, and so ferociously wrenched off the head of the boar. The result of my pondering was that I removed our sleeping belongings that evening from the cabin to the iron half-deck—a little, four-bunked house, standing fore-side of the stump of the main mast, and built entirely of iron, even to the single door, which opens out of the after end.

"Along with our sleeping matters, I carried forrard to our new lodgings, a lamp, and oil, also the dark-lantern, a couple of the axes, two rifles, and all of the revolvers, as well as a good supply of ammunition. Then I bade my wife forage out sufficient provisions to last us for a week, if need be, and whilst she was so busied, I cleaned out and filled the water breaker which belonged to the half-deck.

"At half-past six, I sent my wife forrard to the little iron house, with the baby, and then I locked up the saloon and all of the cabin doors, finally locking after me the heavy, teak door that opened out under the break of the poop.

"Then I went forrard to my wife and child, and shut and bolted the iron door of the half-deck for the night. After that, I went round and saw to it that all of the iron storm-doors, that shut over the eight ports of the house, were in good working order, and so we sat down, as it were, to await the night.

"By eight o'clock, the dusk was upon us, and before half-past, the night hid the decks from my sight. Then I shut down all the iron port-flaps, and screwed them up securely, and after that, I lit the lamp.

"And so a space of waiting ensued, during which I whispered reassuringly to my wife, from time to time, as she looked across at me from her seat beside the sleeping child, with frightened eyes, and a very white face; for somehow there had come upon us within the last hour, a sense of chilly fright, that went straight to one's heart, robbing one vilely of pluck.

"A little later, a sudden sound broke the impressive silence—a sudden dull thud against the side of the ship; and, after that, there came a succession of heavy blows, seeming to be struck all at once upon every side of the vessel; after which there was quietness for maybe a quarter of an hour.

"Then, suddenly, I heard, away forrard, a tap, tap, tap, and then a loud rattling, slurring noise, and a loud crash. After that, I heard many other sounds, and always that tap, tap, tap, repeated a hundred times, as though an army of wooden-legged men were busied all about the decks at the fore end of the ship.

"Presently, there came to me the sound of something coming down the deck, tap, tap, tap, it came. It drew near to the house, paused for nigh a minute; then continued away aft towards the saloon:—tap, tap, tap. I shivered a little, and then fell half consciously to thanking God that I had been given wisdom to bring my wife and child forrard to the security of the iron deck-house.

"About a minute later, I heard the sound of a heavy blow struck somewhere away aft; and after that a second, and then a third, and seeming by the sounds to have been against iron—the iron of the bulkshead that runs across the break of the poop. There came the noise of a fourth blow, and it blended into the crash of broken woodwork. And therewith, I had a little tense quivering inside me; for the little one and my wife might have been sleeping aft there at that very moment, had it not been for the Providential thought which had sent us forrard to the half-deck.

"With the crash of the broken door, away aft, there came, from forrard of us, a great tumult of noises; and, directly, it sounded as though a multitude of wooden-legged men were coming down the decks from forrard. Tap, tap, tap; tap-a-tap, the noises came, and drew abreast of where we sat in the house, crouched and holding our breaths, for fear that we should make some noise to attract THAT which was without. The sounds passed us, and went tapping away aft, and I let out a little breath of sheer easement. Then, as a sudden thought came to me, I rose and turned down the lamp, fearing that some ray from it might be seen from beneath the door. And so, for the space of an hour, we sat wordless, listening to the sounds which came from away aft, the thud of heavy blows, the occasional crash of wood, and, presently, the tap, tap, tap, again, coming forrard towards us.

"The sounds came to a stop, opposite the starboard side of the house, and, for a full minute, there was quietness. Then suddenly, 'Boom!' a tremendous blow had been struck against the side of the house. My wife gave out a little gasping cry, and there came a second blow; and, at that, the child awoke and began to wail, and my wife was put to it, with trying to soothe her into immediate silence.

"A third blow was struck, filling the little house with a dull thunder of sound, and then I heard the tap, tap, tap, move round to the after end of the house. There came a pause, and then a great blow right upon the door. I grasped the rifle, which I had leant against my chair, and stood up; for I did not know but that the thing might be upon us in a moment, so prodigious was the force of the blows it struck. Once again it struck the door, and after that went tap, tap, tap, round to the port side of the house, and there struck the house again; but now I had more ease of mind; for it was its direct attack upon the door, that had put such horrid dread into my heart.

"After the blows upon the port side of the house, there came a long spell of silence, as though the thing outside were listening; but, by the mercy of God, my wife had been able to soothe the child, so that no sound from us, told of our presence.

"Then, at last, there came again the sounds:—tap, tap, tap, as the voiceless thing moved away forrard. Presently, I heard the noises cease aft; and, after that, there came a multitudinous tap-a-tapping, coming along the decks. It passed the house without so much as a pause, and receded away forrard.

"For a space of over two hours, there was an absolute silence; so that I judged that we were now no longer in danger of being molested. An hour later, I whispered to my wife; but, getting no reply, knew that she had fallen into a doze, and so I sat on, listening tensely; yet making no sort of noise that might attract attention.

"Presently, by the thin line of light from beneath the door, I saw that the day was breaking; and, at that, I rose stiffly, and commenced to unscrew the iron port-covers. I unscrewed the forrard ones first, and looked out into the wan dawn; but could discover nothing unusual about so much of the decks as I could see from there.

"After that, I went round and opened each, as I came to it, in its turn; but it was not until I had uncovered the port which gave me a view of the port side of the after maindeck, that I discovered anything extraordinary. Then I saw, at first dimly, but more clearly as the day brightened, that the door, leading from beneath the break of the poop into the saloon, had been broken to flinders, some of which lay scattered upon the deck, and some of which still hung from the bent hinges; whilst more, no doubt, were strewed in the passage beyond my sight.

"Turning from the port, I glanced towards my wife, and saw that she lay half in and half out of the baby's bunk, sleeping with her head beside the child's, both upon one pillow. At the sight, a great wave of holy thankfulness took me, that we had been so wonderfully spared from the terrible and mysterious danger that had stalked the decks in the darkness of the preceding night. Feeling thus, I stole across the floor of the house, and kissed them both very gently, being full of tenderness, yet not minded to waken them. And, after that, I lay down in one of the bunks, and slept until the sun was high in the heaven.

"When I awoke, my wife was about and had tended to the child and prepared our breakfast, so that I had naught to do but tumble out and set to, the which I did with a certain keenness of appetite, induced, I doubt not, by the stress of the night. Whilst we ate, we discussed the peril through which we had just passed; but without coming any the nearer to a solution of the weird mystery of the Terror.

"Breakfast over, we took a long and final survey of the decks, from the various ports, and then prepared to sally out. This we did with instinctive caution and quietness, both of us armed as on the previous day. The door of the half-deck we closed and locked behind us, thereby ensuring that the child was open to no danger whilst we were in other parts of the ship.

"After a quick look about us, we proceeded aft towards the shattered door beneath the break of the poop. At the doorway, we stopped, not so much with the intent to examine the broken door, as because of an instinctive and natural hesitation to go forward into the saloon, which but a few hours previous had been visited by some incredible monster or monsters. Finally, we decided to go up upon the poop and peer down through the skylight. This we did, lifting the sides of the dome for that purpose; yet though we peered long and earnestly, we could perceive no signs of any lurking thing. But broken woodwork there appeared to be in plenty, to judge by the scattered pieces.

"After that, I unlocked the companion, and pushed back the big, over-arching slide. Then, silently, we stole down the steps and into the saloon. Here, being now able to see the big cabin through all its length, we discovered a most extraordinary scene; the whole place appeared to be wrecked from end to end; the six cabins that line each side had their bulks-heading driven into shards and slivers of broken wood in places. Here, a door would be standing untouched, whilst the bulkshead beside it was in a mass of flinders— There a door would be driven completely from its hinges, whilst the surrounding woodwork was untouched. And so it was, wherever we looked.

"My wife made to go towards our cabin; but I pulled her back, and went forward myself. Here the desolation was almost as great. My wife's bunk-board had been ripped out, whilst the supporting side-batten of mine had been plucked forth, so that all the bottom-boards of the bunk had descended to the floor in a cascade.

"But it was neither of these things that touched us so sharply, as the fact that the child's little swing cot had been wrenched from its standards, and flung in a tangled mass of white-painted iron-work across the cabin. At the sight of that, I glanced across at my wife, and she at me, her face grown very white. Then down she slid to her knees, and fell to crying and thanking God together, so that I found myself beside her in a moment, with a very humble and thankful heart.

"Presently, when we were more controlled, we left the cabin, and finished our search. The pantry, we discovered to be entirely untouched, which, somehow, I do not think was then a matter of great surprise to me; for I had ever a feeling that the things which had broken a way into our sleeping cabin, had been looking for us.

"In a little while, we left the wrecked saloon and cabins, and made our way forrard to the pigsty; I for was anxious to see whether the carcass of the pig had been touched. As we came round the corner of the sty, I uttered a great cry; for there, lying upon the deck, on its back, was a gigantic crab, so vast size that I had not conceived so huge a monster existed. Brown it was in colour, save for the belly part, which was of a light yellow.

"One of its pincer-claws, or mandibles, had been torn off in the fight in which it must have been slain (for it was all disembowelled), And this one claw weighed so heavy that I had some to-do to lift it from the deck; and by this you may have some idea of the size and formidableness of the creature itself.

"Around the great crab, lay half a dozen smaller ones, no more than from seven or eight to twenty inches across, and all white in colour, save for an occasional mottling of brown. These had all been killed by a single nip of an enormous mandible, which had in every case smashed them almost into two halves. Of the carcass of the great boar, not a fragment remained.

"And so was the mystery solved; and, with the solution, departed the superstitious terror which had suffocated me through those three nights, since the tapping had commenced. We had been attacked by a wandering shoal of giant crabs, which, it is quite possible, roam across the weed from place to place, devouring aught that comes in their path.

"Whether they had ever boarded a ship before, and so, perhaps, developed a monstrous lust for human flesh, or whether their attack had been prompted by curiosity, I cannot possibly say. It may be that, at first, they mistook the hull of the vessel for the body of some dead marine monster, and hence their blows upon her sides, by which, possibly, they were endeavouring to pierce through our somewhat unusually tough hide!

"Or, again, it may be that they have some power of scent, by means of which they were able to smell our presence aboard the ship; but this (as they made no general attack upon us in the deck-house) I feel disinclined to regard as probable. And yet—I do not know. Why their attack upon the saloon, and our sleeping-cabin? As I say, I cannot tell, and so must leave it there.

"The way in which they came aboard, I discovered that same day; for, having learned what manner of creature it was that had attacked us, I made a more intelligent survey of the sides of the ship; but it was not until I came to the extreme bows, that I saw how they had managed. Here, I found that some of the gear of the broken bowsprit and jibboom, trailed down on to the weed, and as I had not extended the canvas-screen across the heel of the bow-sprit, the monsters had been able to climb up the gear, and thence aboard, without the least obstruction being opposed to their progress.

"This state of affairs, I very speedily remedied; for, with a few strokes of my axe, I cut through the gear, allowing it to drop down among the weed; and after that, I built a temporary breastwork of wood across the gap, between the two ends of the screen; later on making it more permanent.

"Since that time, we have been no more molested by the giant crabs; though for several nights afterwards, we heard them knocking strangely against our sides. Maybe, they are attracted by such refuse as we are forced to dump overboard, and this would explain their first tappings being aft, opposite to the lazarette; for it is from the openings in this part of the canvas-screen that we cast our rubbish.

"Yet, it is weeks now since we heard aught of them, so that I have reason to believe that they have betaken themselves else-where, maybe to attack some other lonely humans, living out their short span of life aboard some lone derelict, lost even to memory in the depth of this vast sea of weed and deadly creatures.

"I shall send this message forth on its journey, as I have sent the other four, within a well-pitched barrel, attached to a small fire balloon. The shell of the severed claw of the monster crab, I shall enclose,[2] as evidence of the terrors that beset us in this dread-ful place. Should this message, and the claw, ever fall into human

---

[2] Captain Bolton makes no mention of the claw, in the cov-ering letter which he has enclosed with the MS.—W. H. H.

hands, let them, contemplating this vast mandible, try to imagine the size of the other crab or crabs that could destroy so formidable a creature as the one to which this claw belonged.

"What other terrors does this hideous world hold for us?

"I had thought of inclosing, along with the claw, the shell of one of the white smaller crabs. It must have been some of these moving in the weed that night, that set my disordered fancy to imagining of ghouls and the Un-Dead. But, on thinking it over, I shall not; for to do so would be to illustrate nothing that needs illustration, and it would but increase needlessly the weight which the balloon will have to lift.

"And so I grow wearied of writing. The night is drawing near, and I have little more to tell. I am writing this in the saloon, and, though I have mended and carpentered so well as I am able, nothing I can do will hide the traces of that night when the vast crabs raided through these cabins, searching for—WHAT?

"There is nothing more to say. In health, I am well, and so is my wife and the little one, but...

"I must have myself under control, and be patient. We are beyond all help, and must bear that which is before us, with such bravery as we are able. And with this, I end; for my last word shall not be one of complaint.

"Arthur Samuel Philips.

"Christmas Eve, 1879."

The Terror of the Sea Caves
Charles G. D. Roberts

I

It was in Singapore that big Jan Laurvik, the diver, heard about the lost pearls.

As he was passing the head of a mean-looking alley near the waterside, late one sweltering afternoon, he was halted by a sudden uproar of cries and curses. The noise came from a courtyard about twenty paces up the alley. It was a fight evidently, and Jan's blood responded with a sympathetic thrill. But the curses which he caught were all in Malay or Chinese, and he curbed his natural desire to rush in and help somebody. Though he knew both languages very well, he knew that he did not know, and never could know, the people who spoke those languages. Interference on the part of a stranger might be resented by both parties to the quarrel. He shrugged his great shoulders and walked on reluctantly.

Hardly three steps had he taken, however, when above the shrill cries a great voice shouted.

"Take that, you—" it began, in English. And at that it ended, with a kind of choking.

Jan Laurvik wheeled round in a flash and ran furiously for the door of the courtyard, which stood half open. He was a Norwegian, but English was as a native tongue to him; and amid the jumble of races in the East he counted all of European speech his brothers. An Englishman was being killed in there. The quarrel was clearly his.

Six feet two in height, swift, and of huge strength, with yellow hair, so light as to be almost white, waving thickly over a face that was sunburnt to a high red, his blue eyes flaming with the delight

189

of battle, Jan burst in upon the mob of fighters. Several bodies lay
on the floor. One dark-faced, low-browed fellow, a Lascar apparently, with his back to the wall and a bloody kreese in his hand,
was putting up a savage fight against five or six assailants, who
seemed to be Chinamen and Malays. The body of the Englishman
whose voice Jan had heard lay in an ugly heap against the wall, its
head far back and almost severed.

Jan's practised eye took in everything at a glance. The heavy
stick he carried was, for a melee like this, a better weapon than
knife or gun. With a great bellowing roar he sprang upon the knot
of fighters.

The result was almost instantaneous. The two nearest rascals
went down at his first two strokes. At the sound of that huge roar
of his all had turned their eyes; and the man at bay, seizing his
opportunity, had cut down two more of his foes with lightning
slashes of his blade. The remaining two, scattering and ducking,
had leaped for the door like rabbits. Jan wheeled, and sprang after
them. But they were too quick for him. As he reached the head of
the alley they darted into a narrow doorway across the street which
led into a regular warren of low structures. Knowing it would be
madness to follow, Jan turned back to the courtyard, curious to
find out what it had all been about.

The silence was now startling. As he entered, there was no
sound but the painful breathing of the Lascar, whom he found sitting with his back against the wall, close beside the body of the
Englishman. He was desperately slashed. His eyes were half closed;
and Jan saw that there was little chance of his recovery. Besides
that of the Englishman, there were six bodies lying on the floor,
all apparently quite lifeless. Jan saw that the place was a kind of
drinking den. The proprietor, a brutal-looking Chinaman, lay dead
beside his jugs and bottles. Jan reached for a jug of familiar appearance, poured out a cup of arrack, and held it to the lips of the dying
Lascar. At the first gulp of the potent spirit his eyes opened again.
He swallowed it all eagerly, then straightened himself up, held out his
hand in European fashion to Jan, and thanked him in Malayan.

"Who's that?" enquired Jan in the same tongue, pointing to the
dead white man.

Grief and rage convulsed the fierce face of the wounded Lascar.

"He was my friend," he answered. "The sons of filthy mothers, they killed him!"

"Too bad!" said Jan sympathetically. "But you gave a pretty good account of yourselves, you two. I like a man that can fight like you were fighting when I came in. What can I do for you?"

"I'm dead, pretty soon now!" said the fellow indifferently. And from the blood that was soaking down his shirt and spreading on the floor about him, Jan saw that the words were true. Anxious, however, to do something to show his goodwill, he pulled out his big red handkerchief, and knelt to bandage a gaping slash straight across the man's left forearm, from which the bright arterial blood was jumping hotly. As he bent, the fellow's eyes lifted and looked over his shoulder.

"Look out!" he screamed. Before the words were fairly out of his mouth Jan had thrown himself violently to one side and sprung to his feet. He was just in time. The knife of one of the Chinamen whom he had supposed to be dead was sticking in the wall beside the Lascar's arm.

Jan stared at the bodies—all, apparently, lifeless.

"That's the one did it," cried the Lascar excitedly, pointing to one whom Jan had struck on the head with his stick. "Put your knife into the son of a dog!"

But that was not the big Norseman's way. He wanted to assure himself. He went and bent over the limp-looking, sprawling shape, to examine it. As he did so, the slant eyes opened upon his with a flash of such maniacal hate that he started back. He was just in time to save his eyes, for the Chinaman had clutched at them like lightning with his long nails.

Startled and furious at this novel attack, Jan reached for his knife. But before he could get his hand on it the Chinaman had leaped into the air like a wild-cat, wound arms and legs about his body, and was struggling like a mad beast to set teeth into his throat. The attack was so miraculously swift, so disconcerting in its beast-like ferocity, that Jan felt a strange qualm that was almost akin to panic. Then a black rage swelled his muscles; and tearing the creature from him he dashed him down upon the floor, on the back of his neck, with a violence which left no need of pursuing the question further. Not till he had examined each of the bodies carefully, and tried them with his knife, did he turn again to the wounded Lascar leaning against the wall.

"Thank you, my friend!" he said simply.

"You're a good fighting man. You're—like him", answered the Lascar feebly, nodding toward the dead Englishman. "Give me more arrack. I will tell you something. Hurry, for I go soon."

Jan brought him the liquor, and he gulped it. Then from a pouch within his knotted silk waistband he hurriedly produced a bit of paper which he unfolded with trembling fingers. Jan saw that it was a rough map sketched with India ink and marked with Malayan characters. The Lascar peered about him with fierce eyes already growing dim.

"Are you sure they are all gone?" he demanded.

"Certain!" answered Jan, highly interested.

"They'll try their best to kill you," went on the dying man. "Don't let them. If you let them get the pearls, I'll come back and haunt you."

"I won't let them kill me, and I won't let them get the pearls, if that's what it is that's made all the trouble. Don't worry about that," responded Jan confidently, reaching out his great hand for the paper, which was evidently so precious that men were giving up their lives for it.

The man handed it over with a groping gesture, though his savage black eyes were wide open.

"That'll show you where the wreck of the junk lies, in seven or eight fathoms of water, close inshore. The pearls are in the deckhouse. *He* kept them. The steamer was on a reef, going to pieces, and we came up just as the boats were putting off. We sunk them all, and got the pearls. And next night, in a storm, the junk was carried on to the rocks by a current we didn't know about. Only five of us got ashore—for the sharks were around, and the 'killers', that night. *Him* and me, we were the only ones knew enough to make that map."

Here the dying pirate—for such he had declared himself—sank forward with his face upon his knees. But with a mighty effort he sat up again and fixed Jan Laurvik with terrible eyes.

"Don't let the sons of a dog get them, or I will come back and choke you in your sleep," he gasped, suddenly pointing a lean finger straight at the Norseman's face. Then his black eyes opened wide, a strange red light blazed up in them for an instant and faded. With a sigh he toppled over, dead, his head resting on the dead Englishman's feet.

II

Jan Laurvik looked down upon the slack form with a sort of grim indulgence. "He was game, and he loved his comrade, though he was but a bloodthirsty pirate!" he muttered to himself.

With the paper folded small and hidden in his great palm, he glanced again from the door to see if any of the routed scoundrels were coming back. Satisfied on this point, he once more investigated the dead bodies on the floor, to assure himself that all were as dead as they appeared. Then he set himself to examine the precious paper, which held out to his imagination all sorts of fascinating possibilities. He knew that the swift boats carrying the proceeds of the pearl fisheries were always eagerly watched by the piratical junks infesting those waters, but carried an armament which secured them from all interference. In case of wreck, however, the pirates' opportunity would come. Jan knew that the story he had just heard was no improbable one.

The map proved to be rough, but very intelligible. It indicated a stretch of the eastern coast of Java, which Jan recognized; but the spot where the junk had gone down was one to which passing ships always gave a wide berth. It was a place of treacherous anchorage, of abrupt, forbidding, uninhabited shore, and of violent currents that shifted erratically. So much the better, thought Jan, for his investigations, if only the pirate junk should prove to have been considerate enough to sink in water not too deep for a diver to work in. There would be so much the less danger of interruption.

Jan was on the point of hurrying away from the gruesome scene, which might at any moment become a scene of excitement and annoying investigation, when a new idea flashed into his mind. It was over this precious paper that all the trouble had been. The scoundrels who had fled would undoubtedly return as soon as they dared and would search for it. Finding it gone, they would conclude that he had it; and they would be hot on his trail. He had no fancy for the sleepless vigilance that this would entail upon him. He had no fancy for the heavy armed expedition which it would force him to organize for the pearl hunt. He saw his airy palaces toppling ignominiously to earth. He saw that all he was likely to get was a slit throat.

As he glanced about him for a way out of his dilemma his eyes fell on a bottle of India ink containing the fine-tipped brush with which these Orientals did their writing. His resourcefulness awoke to this chance. The moments were becoming very pearls themselves for preciousness, but seizing the brush, he made a workable copy of the map on the back of a letter which he had in his pocket. Then he made a minute and very careful correction in the original, in such a manner as to indicate that the position of the wreck was in a deep fiord some fifty miles east of where it actually was. This done to his critical satisfaction, he returned the map to its hiding-place in the dead pirate's belt, and made all haste away. Not till he was back in the European quarter did he feel himself secure. Once among his fellow whites, where he was a man of known standing and reputed to be the best diver in the Archipelago, he knew that he would run no risk of being connected with a drinking brawl of Lascars and pirates. As for the dead Englishman, he knew the odds were that the Singapore police would know all about him.

Jan Laurvik had a little capital. But he needed a trusty partner with more. To his experienced wits his other needs were clear. There would have to be a very seaworthy little steamer, powerfully engined for service on that stormy coast, and armed to defend herself against prowling pirate junks. This small and fit craft would have to be manned by a crew equally fit, and at the same time as small as possible, for the reason that in a venture of this sort everyone concerned would of necessity come in for a share of the winnings. Moreover, the fewer there were to know, the fewer the chances of the secret leaking out; and Jan was even more in dread of the Dutch Government getting wind of it than he was of the pirates picking up his trail.

Up to a certain point, he had no difficulty in verifying the dead pirate's story. He had heard of the wreck of the Dutch steamer

Viecht on a reef off the Celebes, and of the massacre of all the crew and passengers, except one small boatload, by pirates. This had happened about eight months ago. Discreet enquiry developed the fact that the *Viecht* had carried about $300,000 worth of pearls. The evidence was sufficiently convincing, and the prize was sufficiently alluring to make it worth his while to risk the adventure.

It was with a certain amount of Northern deliberation that Jan Laurvik thought these points all out, and made up his mind what to do. Then he acted promptly. First he cabled to Calcutta, to one Captain Jerry Parsons, to join him in Singapore without fail by the very next steamer. Then he set himself unobtrusively to the task of finding the craft he wanted and looking up the equipment for her.

Captain Jerry Parsons was a New Englander, from Portland, Maine. He had been whaler, gold-hunter, filibuster, copra-trader, general-in-chief to a small Central American republic, and sheep-farmer in the Australian bush. At present he was conducting a more or less regular trade in precious stones among the lesser Indian potentates. He loved gain much, but he loved adventure more.

When he received the cable from his good friend Jan Laurvik, he knew that both were beckoning to him. With light-hearted zest he betook himself to the steamship offices, found a P. and O. boat sailing on the morrow, and booked his passage. Throughout the journey he amused himself with trying to guess what Jan Laurvik was after; and, as it happened, almost the only thing he failed to think of was pearls.

When Captain Jerry reached Singapore Jan Laurvik told him the story of the dead pirate's map.

"Let's see the map!" said he, chewing hard on the butt of his unlighted Manila.

Jan passed his copy over. The New Englander inspected it carefully, in silence, for several minutes.

"Tain't much of a map!" said he at length disparagingly. "You think the varmint was straight?"

"In his way, yes," answered Jan with conviction. "He had it in him to be straight in his way to a friend, which wouldn't hinder him cuttin' the throats of a thousand chaps he didn't take an interest in."

"When shall we start?" asked Captain Jerry. Now that his mind was quite made up he took out his matchbox and carefully lighted his cheroot.

The big Norseman's face lighted up with pleasure, and he reached out his hand. The grip was all, in the way of a bargain, that was needed between them.

"Why, tomorrow night!" he answered.

"Well," said the New Englander, "I'll draw some cash in the morning."

The boat which Jan had hired was a fast and sturdy sea-going tug, serviceable, but not designed for comfort. Jan had retained her engineer, a shrewd and close-mouthed Scotsman. Her sailing-master would be Captain Jerry. For crew he had chosen a wiry little Welshman and two lank leather-skinned Yankees. To these four, for whose honesty and loyalty he trusted to his own insight as a reader of men, he explained, partially, the nature of the undertaking, and agreed to give them, over and above their wages, a substantial percentage of whatever treasure he might succeed in recovering. He had made his selection wisely, and every man of the four laid hold of the opportunity with ardour.

The tug was swift enough to elude any of the junks infesting those waters, but the danger was that she might be taken by surprise at her anchorage while Laurvik was under water. He fitted her, therefore, with a Maxim gun on the roof of the deck-house, and armed the crew with repeating Winchesters.

Thus equipped, he felt ready for any perils that might confront him above the surface of the water. As to what might lurk below he felt somewhat less confident, as these he should have to face alone, and he remembered the ominous warning of his pirate friend, about the sharks and the "killers". For sharks Jan Laurvik had comparatively small concern; but for the "killers", those swift and implacable little whales who fear no living thing, he entertained the highest respect.

On the evening of the day after Captain Jerry's arrival, the tug *Sarawak* steamed quietly out of the harbour. As this was a customary thing for her to do, it excited no particular comment among the frequenters of the waterside. By the pirates' spies, who abounded in the city, it was not considered an event worth noting.

The journey, across the Straits, and down the treacherous Javan Sea, was so prosperous that Jan Laurvik, his blood steeped in Norse superstition, began to feel uneasy. The sea was like a millpond all the way, and they were sighted by no one likely to interfere or ask questions. Jan distrusted Fortune when she seemed to smile too blandly. But Captain Jerry comforted him with the assurance that there'd be trouble enough ahead; and strangely enough, this singular variety of comfort quite relieved Jan's depression.

The unusual calm made it easy to hold close inshore, when they reached that portion of the coast where they must keep watch for the landmarks indicated on the pirate's map. Every reef and surface-ledge boiled ceaselessly in the smooth swell, and by that clear green sea they were saved the trouble of tedious soundings. When they came exactly abreast of a low headland which they had been watching for some time, it suddenly opened out into the semblance of a two-humped camel crouching sidewise to the sea, exactly as it was represented in Jan's map. Just beyond was a narrow bay, and across the middle of its mouth, with a dangerous passage on either side, stretched the reef on which the pirate junk had gone down. At this hour of low water the reef was showing its teeth and snarling with surf. At high tide it would be hidden, and a perfect snare of ships. According to the map, the wreck lay in some eight fathoms of water, midway of the outer crescent of the reef. Behind the reef, where the latter might serve them as a partial shelter from the sweep of the seas if a north-easter should blow up, they found tolerable anchorage for the tug. For the preliminary soundings, and for the diving operations, of course, Jan planned to use the launch. And, in order to take utmost advantage of the phenomenal calm, which seemed determined to smooth away every obstacle for the adventurers, Jan got instantly to work. Within a half-hour of the *Sarawak*'s anchoring he had the launch outside the reef with all his diving apparatus aboard, with Captain Jerry to manage the air-pump, and the Scottish engineer to run the motor.

III

Along the outer face of the reef, at a depth varying from eight to twelve fathoms, ran an irregular rocky shelf which dipped gradually seaward for several hundred yards, then dropped sheer to the ocean depths. In the warm water along this shelf swarmed a teeming life, of gay-coloured gigantic weeds, and of strange fish that outdid the brightest weeds in brilliancy and unexpectedness of hue. Where the tropic sunlight filtered dimly down through the beryl tide it sank into a marvellous garden whose flowers, for the most part, were living and moving forms, some monstrous, many terrifying, and almost all as grotesque in shape as they were radiant in colour. But in that insufficient, glimmering light, which was rather, to a human eye, a vaguely translucent, greenish darkness, these colours were almost blotted out. It took eyes adapted to the depth and gloom to differentiate them clearly.

In the great deeps, also, beyond the edge of the shelf, thronged life in swimming, crawling, or moveless forms, of every imagined and many unimagined shapes, from creatures so tiny that a whole colony could dwell at ease in the eye of a cambric needle, to the titanic squid, or cuttlefish, with oval body fifty feet in length and arms like writhing constrictors reaching twenty or thirty feet further. It was a life of noiseless but terrific activity, of unrelenting and incessant death, in a darkness streaked fitfully with phosphorescent gleams from the bodies of the darting, writhing, or pouncing creatures that slew and were slain in the stupendous silence.

Down to these dwellers in the profound had come some mysterious message or exciting influence, no man knows what, from the prolonged calm on the surface. It affected individuals among various species, in such a way that they moved upward, into a twilight where they were aliens and intruders. Among those so stung with unrest were several of the gigantic, pallid cuttles. Far offshore, one of these monsters came up and sprawled upon the surface in the unfriendly sun, his dreadful arms curling and uncurling like snakes, till a great sperm-whale, of scarcely more than his own size, came by and fell upon him ravenously, and devoured him.

Another of the restless monsters, however, kept his restlessness within the bounds of discretion. Slowly rising, a vast and spectral horror as he came up into the green light, he reached the rim of the ledge. The growing light had already made him uneasy, and he wanted no more of it. Here on the ledge, where food, though novel in character, was unlimited in supply, was variety enough to content him. Gorging himself as he went with everything that swam within reach of his darting tentacles, he moved over the rocky floor till he came to the wreck of the junk.

To his huge unwinking eyes of crystal black, which caught every tiniest ray of light in their smooth, appalling deeps, the wreck looked strange enough to attract his attention at once. It was quite unlike any rock-form which he had ever seen. Rather cautiously he advanced a giant tentacle to investigate it. But at the touch of the unfamiliar and alien substance the tentacle recoiled in aversion. The pale monster backed away. But the wreck made no attempt to pounce upon him. It seemed to have no fight in it. Possibly, on closer investigation, it might prove to be good to eat; and he was hungry. In fact, he was always hungry, for the irresistible corrosives in his great stomach—and he was nearly all stomach—were so swift in their action that whatever he swallowed was digested almost in the swallowing. Since coming upon the ledge he had clutched and devoured two small basking sharks, from six to eight feet long, and a sawfish fully ten feet long, who had not been on their guard against the approach of such a peril. Besides these substantial victims, countless small fry, of every kind, had been drawn deftly to the insatiable vortex of his maw. Nevertheless, his appetite was again crying out. He tried the wreck again, first carefully, then boldly, till the writhing tentacles, with their sensitive tips and suckers, had enveloped it from stem to stern and searched it inside and out. A few lurking fish and molluscs were snatched from the dark interior by those insinuating and inexorable feelers; and a toothsome harvest of anchored crustaceans was gathered from the hidden surfaces along beside the keel. But of the bodies of the pirates that had gone down in the sudden foundering there was nothing left but bones, which the myriad scavengers of the sea had polished to the barren smoothness of ivory.

While the pallid monster was occupied in the investigation of the wreck those two great bulging black mirrors of his eyes were sleeplessly alert to everything that passed above or about them. Once a swordfish, about seven feet long, sailed carelessly though swiftly some ten feet overhead. Up darted a livid tentacle, and fixed upon it with the deadly sucking discs. In vain the splendid and ferocious fish lashed out in the effort to wrench itself free. In vain it strove to plunge downward and pierce the puffy monster with its sword. In a second or two more tentacles were wrapped about it. Then, all force crushed out of it, it was dragged down and crammed into the conqueror's horrible mouth.

While its mouth was yet working with the satisfaction of this meal, the monster saw a graceful but massive black shape, nearly half as long as himself, swimming slowly between his eyes and the shining surface. At the sight a shudder of fear passed over him. Every waving tentacle shrank back and lay moveless, as if suddenly paralysed, and he flattened himself down as best he could beside the dark hulk of the wreck. Well he knew that dark shape was a whale—and a whale was the one being he knew of which he had cause to fear. Against those rending jaws his cable-like tentacles and tearing beak were of no avail, his unarmoured body utterly defenceless.

The whale, however—not a sperm, but one of a much smaller, though more savage species, the "killer"—did not catch sight of the giant cuttlefish cringing below him. Intent on other game, he passed swiftly on. His presence, however, had for the moment destroyed the monster's appetite. Instead of continuing his search for food, he wanted a hiding-place. He could no longer be at ease for a moment there in the open.

Just behind the wreck the rock wall rose abruptly to the surface of the reef. Its base was hollowed into a series of low caves, where masses of softer rock had been eaten out from beneath a slanting stratum of more enduring material. The more spacious of these caves was immediately behind the wreck. It was exactly what the monster craved. He backed into it with alacrity, completely filling it with his spectral and swollen body. In the doorway the convex inky lenses of his eyes kept watch, moveless and all-seeing. And his ten pale-spotted tentacles, each thicker at the base than a man's thigh, lay outspread and hidden among the seaweeds, waiting for such victims as might come within reach of their lightning snap and coil.

The monster had no more than got himself fairly installed in his new quarters, when into the range of his awful eyes came a singular figure, descending slowly through the glimmering green directly over the wreck. It was not so long as the swordfish he had lately swallowed, but it was thick and massive-looking; and it was blunt at the ends, unlike any fish he had ever seen. Its eyes were enormous, round and bulging. From its head and from one of its curious round, thick fins, extended two slender antennae straight up towards the surface, and so long that their extremities were beyond the monster's vision. It was indeed a strange-looking creature, but he felt sure that it would be very good to eat. In their concealment among the many-coloured seaweeds his tentacles thrilled with expectancy, and he waited, like some stupendous nightmare of a spider, to spring the moment the prey came within reach.

It chanced, however, that just as the strange creature, descending without any movement of its fins, did come within reach, there also appeared again, in the distance, the black form of the "killer" whale, swimming far overhead. The monster changed his plans instantly. His interest in the newcomer died out. He became intent on nothing but keeping himself inconspicuous. The newcomer, unconscious of the terror lying in wait so near him and of the dark form patrolling the upper green, alighted upon the wreck and groped his way lumberingly into the cabin, dragging those two slim antennae behind him.

IV

When Jan Laurvik, in his up-to-date and well-tested diving-suit, went down through the green twilight of the sea, he was doing what it was his profession to do, and he had few misgivings. He had confidence in his equipment, in his skill, and in his mate at the rope and the air-pump, Captain Jerry. For defence against any obtrusive shark or sawfish he carried a heavy, long-bladed, two-edged knife, by far the most effective weapon in deep water. This knife he wore in a sheath at his waist, with a cord attached to the handle so that it could not get away from him. He carried also a tiny electric battery supplying a strong lamp on the front of his head-piece just above his eyes.

From his long experience in sounding and in locating wrecks, Jan Laurvik had acquired an accuracy that seemed almost like divination.

His soundings, in this instance, had been particularly thorough, because he did not wish to waste any more time than necessary at the depth in which he would have to work. He was not surprised, therefore, when he found himself descending upon the wreck of a junk. Moreover, as it was not an old wreck, he concluded that it was the junk which he was looking for. The wreck had settled almost on an even keel; and as he was familiar with craft of her type, he had no difficulty in finding his way about.

It was in the narrow, closet-like structure which served as the junk's cabin that the pirate had said the pearls would be found. The door was open. Turning on his light, which struggled with the water and diffused a ghostly glow, he found himself confronted by a hideous little joss of red-and-gilt lacquer. He knew it was lacquer, and of the best, for nothing else, except gold itself, would have withstood the months of soaking in sea-water. Jan grinned to himself, there within his rubber and copper shell, at this evidence of pirate piety. Then it occurred to him that a man like the pirate captain would probably have turned his piety to practical use. What better guardian of the treasure than a god? Dragging the gaudy deity from his altar, he found the altar hollow. In that secure receptacle lay a series of packages done up with careful precision in wrappings of oiled silk. He knew the style of wrapping very well. For all his coolness, his heart fell to thumping painfully at the sight of this vast wealth beneath his hand. Then he realized that the pressure of the water, and of the compressed air in his helmet, was beginning to tell upon him. In fierce but orderly haste he corded the packages about his middle and turned to leave the cabin. He would make another trip for the lacquer god, and for such other articles of value or *vertu* as the junk might contain.

Jan turned to leave the cabin. But in the doorway he started back with a shudder of dread and loathing. A slender, twisting thing, whitish in colour and minutely speckled with livid spots, reached in, and fastened upon his arm with soft-looking suckers which held like death.

Jan knew instantly what the pale, writhing thing was. Out flashed his knife. With a swift stroke he slashed off the detaining tip, where it had a thickness of perhaps two inches. The raw stump shrank back, like a severed worm, and Jan, leaping clear of the doorway, signalled furiously to be hauled up. But at the same instant two more of the curling white things came reaching over the bulwarks and fastened upon him—one upon his right arm, hampering him so that he was almost helpless, and the other upon his left leg just above the knee. He felt his signal promptly answered by a powerful tug on the rope. But he was anchored to the wreck as if he had grown to it.

Never before had Jan Laurvik felt the clutch of fear at his heart as he did at this moment. But not for an instant, in the horror, did he lose his presence of mind. He knew that in a pulling match with the giant devil-fish of the deeps his comrades in the boat far overhead would be nowhere. He had made a mistake in leaving the cabin. Frantically he signalled with his left hand, to "slack away" on the rope; and at the same time, though hampered by the grip on his right arm, he managed to slash off the end of the feeler that had fixed upon his leg. On the instant, whipping the knife over to his left, he cut his right arm clear, and sprang back into the doorway.

Jan's idea was that by keeping just inside the cabin door he could defend himself from being surrounded by the assault of the writhing things. He knew that in the open he would speedily be enfolded and crushed, and engulfed between the jaws of the monstrous squid. But in the narrow doorway the swift play of his blade would have some chance. He gained the doorway. He got fairly inside it, indeed. But as he entered he was horrified to see the thick stump, whose tip he had shorn off, dart in with him and fix itself, by its bigger and more irresistible suckers, upon the middle of his breast. With a shiver he sliced off the fatal discs, in one long sweep of his blade; then turned like a flash to sever a pallid tip which had fastened upon his helmet.

Jan was now thankful enough that he had got himself into the narrow doorway. Seemingly undisturbed by the slashings and slicings which some of them had received, the whole ten squirming horrors now darted at the doorway. Jan's knife swooped this way and that; but as fast as he severed one clutch two more would make good. The cut tentacles grew to be the more terrifying, because their suckers were so big; and they themselves were so thick and hard to cut. Presently no fewer than three of the diabolical things laid their loathsome hold upon his right leg, below the knee, and began to haul it out through the door. Jan slashed at them madly, but not altogether effectually, for at this moment another tentacle had laid grip upon his arm below the elbow. He had just time to shift the knife again to his left and catch the jamb of the door, when he felt his helmet almost jerked from his head. This grip he dared not interfere with, lest he should cut, at the same time, the air-tube that fed his lungs, and drown like a rat in a hole. All he could do was to hold on to the doorjamb, and carve away savagely at the tentacles which were within reach. If he could get free of those, he calculated that he could then reach the one which had fastened to his headpiece by throwing himself over on his back and so bringing it within range of his vision and his knife. At this moment, however, just as the pressure upon his neck was becoming intolerable, he felt his head suddenly released. One of the great sucking discs had crushed in the glass of the electric lamp and fastened upon the live wire. The sensation it experienced was evidently not pleasant, for it let go promptly, and secured a new hold upon Jan's left arm.

This hold left him almost helpless, because he could no longer wield the knife freely with either hand. He felt himself slowly being pulled out of the doorway by his right leg. Throwing himself partly backward, and partly behind the door, he gained a firmer brace and at the same time brought his knife again into better play. He would fight to the very last gasp, but he felt that the odds had now gone overwhelmingly against him. The fear of death itself was not heavy upon him. He had faced it too often, and too coolly, for that. But at the manner of this death that confronted him his very soul sickened with loathing. As he thought of it, his horror was not lessened by the sight which now greeted his view. A colossal, swollen, leprous-looking bulk, pallid and spotted, was mounting over the bulwark. Two great oval lenses of clear blackness, set close together, were in the front of the bulk, just over the spot where the tentacles started. These gigantic, appalling, expressionless eyes were fixed upon him. The monster was coming aboard to see what kind of creature it was that was giving him so much trouble.

Jan saw that the end of the fight was very near. The thought, however, did not unnerve him. Rather, it put new fire into his nerves and muscles. By a tremendous wrench he succeeded in reaching with the knife the tentacle that bound his right arm. This freedom was like a new lease of life to him. He made swift play with his blade, so savagely that he was able to drag himself back almost completely into the cabin before the writhing horrors again closed upon him. But meanwhile the monster's gigantic body had gained the deck. Those two awful eyes were slowly drawing nearer; and below them he saw the viscid mouth opening and shutting in anticipation.

At this a kind of madness began to surge up in Jan Laurvik's overtaxed brain. His veins seemed to surge with fresh power, as if there were nothing too tremendous for him to accomplish. He was on the very point of stopping his resistance, plunging straight in among the arms, and burying his big blade in those unspeakable eyes.

It would be a satisfaction, at least, to force them to change their expression. And then, well, something might happen!

Before he could put this desperate scheme into execution, however, something did happen. Jan was aware of a sudden darkness overhead. The monster was evidently aware of it too, for every one of the twisting horrors suddenly shrank away, leaving Jan to lean up against the doorway, free. The next moment, a huge black shape descended perpendicularly upon the fleshy mountain of the monster's back, and a rush of water drove Jan backward into the cabin.

As the electric lamp had gone out when the glass was broken, Jan could see but dimly the awful battle of giants now going on before him. So excited was he that he forgot his own new peril. The danger was now that in the struggle one or other of the battling bulks might well crush the cabin flat, or entangle the air-tube and life-line. In either case Jan's finish would be swift; but in comparison with the loathsome death from which he had just been so miraculously saved, such an end seemed no very dreadful thing. He was altogether absorbed in watching the prowess of his avenging rescuer.

Skilled in deep-sea lore as he was, he knew the dark fury which had swooped down upon the devil-fish. It was a "killer" whale, or grampus, the most redoubtable and implacable fighter of all the kindreds of the sea. Jan saw its wide jaws shear off three mighty tentacles at once, close at the base. The others writhed up hideously and fastened upon him, but under the surging of his resistless muscles their tissues tore apart like snapped cables. Huge masses of the monster's ghastly flesh were bitten off, and thrown aside. Then, gaining a grip that took in the monster's head and the roots of the tentacles, the killer shook his prey as a bulldog might shake a fat sheep. The tentacles straightened out sharply. Jan saw that the fight was over; and that it was high time for him to remove from that too strenuous neighbourhood. He gave the signal vehemently, and was drawn up, without attracting his dangerous rescuer's notice. When Captain Jerry hauled him in over the boatside, he fell in an unconscious heap.

When Jan came to himself he was in his bunk on the *Sarawak*. It was an utter physical and nervous exhaustion that had overcome him. His swoon had passed into a heavy sleep, and when he awoke he sat up with a start. Captain Jerry was at his side, bursting with suppressed curiosity; and the Scottish engineer was standing by the bunk.

"Waal, partner, you've delivered the goods all right!" drawled Captain Jerry. "They're the stuff, not a doubt of it. But kind o' seemed to us up here you were having high jinks of one kind or another down there. What was it?"

"It was hell!" responded Jan with a shudder. Then he took hold of Captain Jerry's hand, and felt it, as if to make sure it was real, or as if he needed the feel of honest human flesh again to bring him to his senses.

"Ugh!" he went on, swinging out of the bunk. "Let me get out into the sunlight again! Let me see the sky again! I'll tell you all about it by-an'-by, Jerry. But wait. Were all the packages on me, all right?"

"I reckon!" responded Captain Jerry. "There was six of 'em tied on to you. I reckon they're worth the three hundred an' fifty thousand all right!"

"Well, let's get away from this place quick as we can get steam up again!" said Jan. "There's more swag down there, I guess—lots of it. But I wouldn't go down again, nor send another man down, for all the millions we've all of us ever heard tell of. Mr. McWha, how soon can we be moving?"

"Ten meenutes, more or less!" replied the Scotsman.

"All right! When we're outside of this accursed bay, an' round the 'Camel' yonder, I'll tell you what it's like down there under that shiny green."

The Mystery of the Derelict
William Hope Hodgson

All the night had the four-masted ship, *Tarawak*, lain motion-less in the drift of the Gulf Stream; for she had run into a "calm pitch" —into a stark calm which had lasted now for two days and nights.

On every side, had it been light, might have been seen dense masses of floating gulf-weed, studding the ocean even to the dis-tant horizon. In places, so large were the weed-masses that they formed long, low banks, that by daylight, might have been mis-taken for low-lying land.

Upon the lee side of the poop, Duthie, one of the 'prentices, leaned with his elbows upon the rail, and stared out across the hid-den sea, to where in the Eastern horizon showed the first pink and lemon streamers of the dawn—faint, delicate streaks and washes of colour.

A period of time passed, and the surface of the leeward sea began to show—a great expanse of grey, touched with odd, wavering belts of silver. And everywhere the black specks and islets of the weed.

Presently, the red dome of the sun protruded itself into sight above the dark rim of the horizon; and, abruptly, the watching Duthie saw something—a great, shapeless bulk that lay some miles away to starboard, and showed black and distinct against the gloomy red mass of the rising sun.

"Something in sight to board, Sir," he informed the Mate, who was leaning, smoking, over the rail that ran across the break of the poop. "I can't just make out what it is."

The Mate rose from his easy position, stretched himself yawned, and came across to the boy.

"Whereabouts, Toby?" he asked, wearily, and yawning again.

"There, Sir," said Duthie—alias Toby— "broad away on the beam, and right in the track of the sun. It looks something like a big houseboat, or a haystack."

The Mate stared in the direction indicated, and saw the thing which puzzled the boy, and immediately the tiredness went out of his eyes and face.

"Pass me the glasses off the skylight, Toby," he commanded, and the youth obeyed.

After the Mate had examined the strange object through his binoculars for, maybe, a minute, he passed them to Toby, telling him to take a squint, and say what he made of it.

"Looks like an old powder-hulk, Sir," exclaimed the lad, after awhile, and to this description the Mate nodded agreement.

Later, when the sun had risen somewhat, they were able to study the derelict with more exactness. She appeared to be a vessel of an exceedingly old type, mastless, and upon the hull of which had been built a roof-like superstructure; the use of which they could not determine. She was lying just within the borders of one of the weed-banks, and all her side was splotched with a greenish growth.

It was her position, within the borders of the weed, that suggested to the puzzled Mate, how so strange and unseaworthy looking a craft had come so far abroad into the greatness of the ocean. For, suddenly, it occurred to him that she was neither more nor less than a derelict from the vast Sargasso Sea—a vessel that had, possibly, been lost to the world, scores and scores of years gone, perhaps hundreds. The suggestion touched the Mate's thoughts with solemnity, and he fell to examining the ancient hulk with an even greater interest, and pondering on all the lonesome and awful years that must have passed over her, as she had lain desolate and forgotten in that grim cemetery of the ocean.

Through all that day, the derelict was an object of the most intense interest to those aboard the *Tarawak*, every glass in the ship being brought into use to examine her. Yet, though within no more than some six or seven miles of her, the Captain refused to listen to the Mate's suggestions that they should put a boat into the water, and pay the stranger a visit; for he was a cautious man, and the glass warned him that a sudden change might be expected in the weather; so that he would have no one leave the ship on any unnecessary business. But, for all that he had caution, curiosity was by no means lacking in him, and his telescope, at intervals, was turned on the ancient hulk through all the day.

Then, it would be about six bells in the second dog watch, a sail was sighted astern, coming up steadily but slowly. By eight bells they were able to make out that a small barque was bringing the wind with her; her yards squared, and every stitch set. Yet the night had advanced apace, and it was nigh to eleven o'clock before the wind reached those aboard the *Tarawak*. When at last it arrived, there was a slight rustling and quaking of canvas, and odd creaks here and there in the darkness amid the gear, as each portion of the running and standing rigging took up the strain.

Beneath the bows, and alongside, there came gentle rippling noises, as the vessel gathered way; and so, for the better part of the next hour, they slid through the water at something less than a couple of knots in the sixty minutes.

To starboard of them, they could see the red light of the little barque, which had brought up the wind with her, and was now forging slowly ahead, being better able evidently than the big, heavy *Tarawak* to take advantage of so slight a breeze.

About a quarter to twelve, just after the relieving watch had been roused, lights were observed to be moving to and fro upon the small barque, and by midnight it was palpable that, through some cause or other, she was dropping astern.

When the Mate arrived on deck to relieve the Second, the latter officer informed him of the possibility that something unusual had occurred aboard the barque, telling of the lights about her decks,[1] and how that, in the last quarter of an hour, she had begun to drop astern.

---

[1] Unshaded lights are never allowed on the decks at night, as they are likely to blind the vision of the officer of the watch.—W. H. H.

On hearing the Second Mate's account, the First sent one of the 'prentices for his night-glasses, and, when they were brought, studied the other vessel intently, that is, so well as he was able through the darkness; for, even through the night-glasses, she showed only as a vague shape, surmounted by the three dim towers of her masts and sails.

Suddenly, the Mate gave out a sharp exclamation; for, beyond the barque, there was something else shown dimly in the field of vision. He studied it with great intentness, ignoring for the instant, the Second's queries as to what it was that had caused him to exclaim.

All at once, he said, with a little note of excitement in his voice:—

"The derelict! The barques run into the weed around that old hooker!"

The Second Mate gave a mutter of surprised assent, and slapped the rail.

"That's it!" he said. "That's why we're passing her. And that explains the lights. If they're not fast in the weed, they've probably run slap into the blessed derelict."

"One thing," said the Mate, lowering his glasses, and beginning to fumble for his pipe, "she won't have had enough way on her to do much damage."

The Second Mate, who was still peering through his binoculars, murmured an absent agreement, and continued to peer. The Mate, for his part, filled and lit his pipe, remarking meanwhile to the unhearing Second, that the light breeze was dropping.

Abruptly, the Second Mate called his superior's attention, and in the same instant, so it seemed, the failing wind died entirely away, the sails settling down into runkles, with little rustles and flutters of sagging canvas.

"What's up?" asked the Mate, and raised his glasses.

'There's something queer going on over yonder," said the Second. "Look at the lights moving about, and—Did you see *that*?"

The last portion of his remark came out swiftly, with a sharp accentuation of the last word.

"What?" asked the Mate, staring hard.

"They're shooting," replied the Second. "Look! There again!"

"Rubbish!" said the Mate, a mixture of unbelief and doubt in his voice.

With the falling of the wind, there had come a great silence upon the sea. And, abruptly, from far across the water, sounded the distant, dullish thud of a gun, followed almost instantly by several minute, but sharply defined, reports, like the cracking of a whip out in the darkness.

"Jove!" cried the Mate. "I believe you're right." He paused and stared. "There!" he said. "I saw the flashes then. They're firing from the poop. I believe... I must call the Old Man."

He turned and ran hastily down into the saloon, knocked on the door of the Captain's cabin, and entered. He turned up the lamp, and, shaking his superior into wakefulness, told him of the thing he believed to be happening aboard the barque.

"It's mutiny, Sir; they're shooting from the poop. We ought to do something—" The Mate said many things, breathlessly; for he was a young man; but the Captain stopped him, with a quietly lifted hand.

"I'll be up with you in a minute, Mr. Johnson," he said, and the Mate took the hint, and ran up on deck.

Before the minute had passed, the Skipper was on the poop, and staring through his night-glasses at the barque and the derelict. Yet now, aboard of the barque, the lights had vanished, and there showed no more the flashes of discharging weapons—only there remained the dull, steady red glow of the port sidelight; and, behind it, the night-glasses showed the shadowy outline of the vessel.

The Captain put questions to the Mates, asking for further details.

"It all stopped while the Mate was calling you, Sir," explained the Second. "We could hear the shots quite plainly."

"They seemed to be using a gun as well as their revolvers," interjected the Mate, without ceasing to stare into the darkness.

For awhile the three of them continued to discuss the matter, whilst down on the maindeck the two watches clustered along the starboard rail, and a low hum of talk rose fore and aft.

Presently, the Captain and the Mates came to a decision. If there had been a mutiny, it had been brought to its conclusion, whatever that conclusion might be, and no interference from those aboard the *Tarawak* at that period, would be likely to do good. They were utterly in the dark—in more ways than one—and, for all they knew, there might not even have been any mutiny. If there had been a mutiny, and the mutineers had won, then they had done their worst; whilst if the officers had won well and good. They had managed to do so without help. Of course, if the *Tarawak* had been a man-of-war with a large crew, capable of mastering any situation, it would have been a simple matter to send a powerful, armed boat's crew to inquire; but as she was merely a merchant vessel, under-manned, as is the modern fashion, they must go warily. They would wait for the morning, and signal. In a couple of hours it would be light. Then they would be guided by circumstances.

The Mate walked to the break of the poop, and sang out to the men:

"Now then, my lads, you'd better turn in, the watch below, and have a sleep; we may be wanting you by five bells."

There was a muttered chorus of "i, i, Sir," and some of the men began to go forrard to the fo'cas'le; but others of the watch below remained, their curiosity overmastering their desire for sleep.

On the poop, the three officers leaned over the starboard rail, chatting in a desultory fashion, as they waited for the dawn. At some little distance hovered Duthie, who, as eldest 'prentice just out of his time, had been given the post of acting Third Mate.

Presently, the sky to starboard began to lighten with the solemn coming of the dawn. The light grew and strengthened, and the eyes of those in the *Tarawak* scanned with growing intentness that portion of the horizon where showed the red and dwindling glow of the barque's sidelight.

Then, it was in that moment when all the world is full of the silence of the dawn, something passed over the quiet sea, coming out of the East—a very faint, long-drawn-out, screaming, piping noise. It might almost have been the cry of a little wind wandering out of the dawn across the sea—a ghostly, piping skirl, so attenuated and elusive was it; but there was in it a weird, almost threatening note, that told the three on the poop it was no wind that made so dree and inhuman a sound.

The noise ceased, dying out in an indefinite, mosquito-like shrilling, far and vague and minutely shrill. And so came the silence again.

"I heard that, last night, when they were shooting," said the Second Mate, speaking very slowly, and looking first at the Skipper and then at the Mate. "It was when you were below, calling the Captain," he added.

"Ssh!" said the Mate, and held up a warning hand; but though they listened, there came no further sound; and so they fell to disjointed questionings, and guessed their answers, as puzzled men will. And ever and anon, they examined the barque through their glasses; but without discovering anything of note, save that, when the light grew stronger, they perceived that her jibboom had struck through the superstructure of the derelict, tearing a considerable gap therein.

Presently, when the day had sufficiently advanced, the Mate sung out to the Third, to take a couple of the 'prentices, and pass up the signal flags and the code book. This was done, and a "hoist" made; but those in the barque took not the slightest heed; so that finally the Captain bade them make up the flags and return them to the locker.

After that, he went down to consult the glass; and when he reappeared, he and the Mates had a short discussion, after which, orders were given to hoist out the starboard life-boat. This, in the course of half an hour, they managed: and, after that, six of the men and two of the 'prentices were ordered into her.

Then half a dozen rifles were passed down, with ammunition, and the same number of cutlasses. These were all apportioned among the men, much to the disgust of the two apprentices, who were aggrieved that they should be passed over; but their feelings altered when the Mate descended into the boat, and handed them each a loaded revolver, warning them, however, to play no "monkey tricks" with the weapons.

Just as the boat was about to push off, Duthie, the eldest 'prentice, came scrambling down the side ladder, and jumped for the after thwart. He landed, and sat down, laying the rifle which he had brought, in the stern; and, after that, the boat put off for the barque.

There were now ten in the boat, and all well aimed, so that the Mate had a certain feeling of comfort that he would be able to meet any situation that was likely to arise.

After nearly an hour's hard pulling, the heavy boat had been brought within some two hundred yards of the barque, and the Mate sung out to the men to lie on their oars for a minute. Then he stood up and shouted to the people on the barque; but though he repeated his cry of "Ship ahoy!" several times, there came no reply.

He sat down, and motioned to the men to give way again, and so brought the boat nearer the barque by; another hundred yards. Here, he hailed again: but still receiving no reply, he stooped for his binoculars, and peered for awhile through them at the two vessels— the ancient derelict, and the modern sailing-vessel.

The latter had driven clean in over the weed, her stern being perhaps some two score yards from the edge of the bank. Her jibboom, as I have already mentioned, had pierced the green-blotched superstructure of the derelict, so that her cutwater had come very close to the grass-grown side of the hulk.

That the derelict was indeed a very ancient vessel, it was now easy to see; for at this distance the Mate could distinguish which was hull, and which superstructure. Her stern rose up to a height considerably above her bows, and possessed galleries, coming round the counter. In the window frames some of the glass still remained: but others were securely shuttered, and some missing, frames and all, leaving dark holes in the stern. And everywhere grew the dank, green growth, giving to the beholder a queer sense of repulsion. Indeed, there was that about the whole of the ancient craft, that repelled in a curious way—something elusive—a remoteness from humanity, that was vaguely abominable.

The Mate put down his binoculars, and drew his revolver, and, at the action, each one in the boat gave an instinctive glance to his own weapon. Then he sung out to them to give-way, and steered straight for the weed. The boat struck it, with something of a sog; and, after that, they advanced slowly, yard by yard, only with considerable labour.

They reached the counter of the barque, and the Mate held out his hand for an oar. This, he leaned up against the side of the vessel, and a moment later was swarming quickly up it. He grasped the rail, and swung himself aboard; then, after a swift glance fore and aft, gripped the blade of the oar, to steady it, and bade the rest follow as quickly as possible, which they did, the last man bringing up the painter with him, and making it fast to a cleat.

Then commenced a rapid search through the ship. In several places about the maindeck they found broken lamps, and aft on the poop, a shot-gun, three revolvers, and several capstan-bars lying about the poop-deck. But though they pried into every possible corner, lifting the hatches, and examining the lazarette, not a human creature was to be found—the barque was absolutely deserted.

After the first rapid search, the Mate called his men together; for there was an uncomfortable sense of danger in the air, and he felt that it would be better not to straggle. Then, he led the way forrard, and went up on to the t'gallant fo'cas'le head. Here, finding the port sidelight still burning, he bent over the screen, as it were mechanically, lifted the lamp, opened it, and blew out the flame; then replaced the affair on its socket.

After that, he climbed into the bows, and out along the jibboom, beckoning to the others to follow, which they did, no man saying a word, and all holding their weapons handily; for each felt the oppressiveness of the Incomprehensible about them.

The Mate reached the hole in the great superstructure, and passed inside, the rest following. Here they found themselves in what looked something like a great, gloomy barracks, the floor of which was the deck of the ancient craft. The superstructure, as seen from the inside, was a very wonderful piece of work, being beautifully shored and fixed; so that at one time it must have possessed immense strength; though now it was all rotted, and showed many a gape and rip. In one place, near the centre, or midships part, was a sort of platform, high up, which the Mate conjectured might have been used as a "look-out"; though the reason for the prodigious superstructure itself, he could not imagine.

Having searched the decks of this craft, he was preparing to go below, when, suddenly, Duthie caught him by the sleeve, and whispered to him, tensely, to listen. He did so, and heard the thing that had attracted the attention of the youth—it was a low, continuous shrill whining that was rising from out of the dark hull beneath their feet, and, abruptly, the Mate was aware that there was an intensely disagreeable animal-like smell in the air. He had noticed it, in a subconscious fashion, when entering through the broken superstructure: but now, suddenly, he was *aware* of it.

Then, as he stood there hesitating, the whining noise rose all at once into a piping, screaming squeal, that filled all the space in which they were inclosed, with an inhuman and threatening clamour. The Mate turned and shouted at the top of his voice to the rest, to retreat to the barque, and he, himself, after a further quick nervous glance round, hurried towards the place where the end of the barque's jibboom protruded in across the decks.

He waited, with strained impatience, glancing ever behind him, until all were off the derelict, and then sprang swiftly onto the spar that was their bridge to the other vessel. Even as he did so, the squealing died away into a tiny shrilling, twittering sound, that made him glance back; for the suddenness of the quiet was as effective as though it had been a loud noise. What he saw, seemed to him in that first instant so incredible and monstrous, that he was almost too shaken to cry out. Then he raised his voice in a shout of warning to the men, and a frenzy of haste shook him in every fibre, as he scrambled back to the barque, shouting ever to the men to get into the boat. For in that backward glance, he had seen the whole decks of the derelict a-move with living things—giant rats, thousands and tens of thousands of them; and so in a flash had come to an understanding of the disappearance of the crew of the barque.

He had reached the fo'cas'le head now, and was running for the steps, and behind him, making all the long slanting length of the jibboom black, were the rats, racing after him. He made one leap to the main-deck, and ran. Behind, sounded a queer, multitudinous pattering noise, swiftly surging upon him. He reached the poop steps, and as he sprang up them, felt a savage bite in his left calf. He was on the poop deck now, and running with a stagger. A score of great rats leapt around him, and half a dozen hung grimly to his back, whilst the one that had gripped his calf flogged madly from side to side as he raced on. He reached the rail, gripped it, and vaulted clean over and down into the weed.

The rest were already in the boat, and strong hands and arms hove him aboard, whilst the others of the crew sweated in getting their little craft round from the ship. The rats still clung to the Mate; but a few blows with a cutlass eased him of his murderous burden. Above them, making the rails and half-round of the poop black and alive, raced thousands of rats.

The boar was now about an oar's length from the barque, and, suddenly, Duthie screamed out that *they* were coming. In the same instant, nearly a hundred of the largest rats launched themselves at the boat. Most fell short, into the weed; but over a score reached the boat, and sprang savagely at the men, and there was a minute's hard slashing and smiting, before the brutes were destroyed.

Once more the men resumed their task of urging their way through the weed, and so in a minute or two, had come to within some fathoms of the edge, working desperately. Then a fresh terror broke upon them. Those rats which had missed their leap, were now all about the boat, and leaping in from the weed, running up the oars, and scrambling in over the sides, and, as each one got inboard, straight for one of the crew it went; so that they were all bitten and be-bled in a score of places.

There ensued a short but desperate fight, and then, when the last of the beasts had been hacked to death, the men lay once more to the task of heaving the boat clear of the weed.

A minute passed, and they had come almost to the edge, when Duthie cried out, to look; and at that, all turned to stare at the barque, and perceived the thing that had caused the 'prentice to cry out; for the rats were leaping down into the weed in black multitudes, making the great weed- fronds quiver, as they hurled themselves in the direction of the boat. In an incredibly short space of time, all the weed between the boat and the barque was alive with the little monsters, coming at breakneck speed.

The Mate let out a shout, and, snatching an oar from one of the men, leapt into the stern of the boat, and commenced to thrash the weed with it, whilst the rest laboured infernally to pluck the boat forth into the open sea. Yet, despite their mad efforts, and the death-dealing blows of the Mate's great fourteen-foot oar, the black, living mass were all about the boat, and scrambling aboard in scores, before she was free of the weed. As the boat shot into the clear water, the Mate gave out a great curse, and, dropping his oar, began to pluck the brutes from his body with his bare hands, casting them into the sea. Yet, fast almost as he freed himself, others sprang upon him, so that in another minute he was like to have been pulled down, for the boat was alive and swarming with the pests, but that some of the men got to work with their cutlasses, and literally slashed the brutes to pieces, sometimes killing several with a single blow. And thus, in a while, the boat was freed once more; though it was a sorely wounded and frightened lot of men that manned her.

The Mate himself took an oar, as did all those who were able. And so they rowed slowly and painfully away from that hateful derelict, whose crew of monsters even then made the weed all of a-heave with hideous life.

From the *Tarawak* came urgent signals for them to haste; by which the Mate knew that the storm, which the Captain had feared, must be coming down upon the ship, and so he spurred each one to greater endeavour, until, at last, they were under the shadow of their own vessel, with very thankful hearts, and bodies, bleeding, tired and faint.

Slowly and painfully, the boat's crew scrambled up the side-ladder, and the boat was hoisted aboard: but they had no time then to tell their tale; for the storm was upon them.

It came half an hour later, sweeping down in a cloud of white fury from the Eastward, and blotting out all vestiges of the mysterious derelict and the little barque which had proved her victim. And after that, for a weary day and night, they battled with the storm. When it passed, nothing was to be seen, either of the two vessels or of the weed which had studded the sea before the storm; for they had been blown many a score of leagues to the westward of the spot, and so had no further chance—nor, I ween, inclination—to investigate further the mystery of that strange old derelict of a past time, and her habitants of rats.

Yet, many a time, and in many fo'cas'les has this story been told; and many a conjecture has been passed as to how came that ancient craft abroad there in the ocean. Some have suggested—as indeed I have made bold to put forth as fact—that she must have drifted out of the lonesome Sargasso Sea. And, in truth, I cannot but think this the most reasonable supposition. Yet, of the rats that evidently dwelt in her, I have no reasonable explanation to offer. Whether they were true ship's rats, or a species that is to be found in the weed-haunted plains and islets of the Sargasso Sea, I cannot say. It may be that they are the descendants of rats that lived in ships long centuries lost in the Weed Sea, and which have learned to live among the weed, forming new characteristics, and developing fresh powers and instincts. Yet, I cannot say; for I speak entirely without authority, and do but tell this story as it is told in the fo'cas'le of many an old-time sailing ship—that dark, brine-tainted place where the young men learn somewhat of the mysteries of the all mysterious sea.

WINKLER ASHORE: THE SEA-SERPENT
Gouverneur Morris

"It makes me mad," said Winkler, "to think how sailors is given the lie. Of course there's sea-serpints. Dozens of 'em. Dozens of sober men has seed them, and told about them and bin called liars. Dozens of sober men has seed them, and not told about them. And that proves, sir, that it takes more than soberness to make a man wise. But do you think sailors that knows their business, that knows the sea, don't believe? There's not one sailor in a hundred that don't believe in sea-serpints. Look at me. I could tell anecdotes that would make the hair rise to its feet on the heads of able seamen. But you'd only laugh, sir—behind your hand. That's why I only tells you things that anybody could believe. Will I tell you about the sea-serpint I saw with my two eyes? What's the use? If I told you about a two-headed shark, you'd believe. If I told you about a blue gull, you'd believe. If I told you about pirates, you'd believe—"

"You've never tried me with a sea-serpent, Winkler," I said. "So it's not fair to judge me in advance. But I'll tell you this in confidence—Did you ever hear of a man named Kipling?"

"Seaman, sir?"

"He's that, too," I said, "but he's been and is other things. He's a jack of all trades—now he's a sailor, now a soldier. Then he'll take a turn at engineering and build a ship or a bridge; or turn farmer and breed horses, or turn musician and sing songs—and all those things he does better than anybody else."

"Puts me in mind of Farallone," said Winkler. "He'd bin all that. But you was saying?"

"I was saying," said I, "that this man once told me a story—me and some others—about a sea-serpent. It came up from the very

deepest part of the sea, thrown up by an earthquake, and it was
the color of the gray ooze on the bottom of the sea, and blind, and
had long white feelers, and barnacles and shells stuck over it, and
he made it seem so real that I've always believed in that kind of a
sea-serpent. Sometimes I dream of it, sticking its blind head out
of the fog, and it gives me the horrors."

"Did it come in a fog, sir?" asked Winkler anxiously.

"Yes," I said, "it was in the tropics, and when the earthquake
pushed the cold deep water up to the hot air a fog was formed."

"Mine came in a fog, too," said Winkler "But it were'n't white,
nor blind," he added, a little disappointedly. "It were more eel
color; but it had barnacles stuck to it, same as Kipling's. Did his
raise hell?"

"No," said I. "It was terribly frightened, and its mate was hurt
by the earthquake, and died, and the whole thing made you feel
more unhappy than frightened—perhaps a little of both."

"Mine," said Winkler, "raised all kinds of hell before, then, and
after—and it weren't in no tropic out-o'-the-way place, it were right
off Sandy Hook in the track of liners. We was hove to, by reason of
the fog, which were thick and smoky. There weren't no sea runnin',
only a big, quiet ground-swell. Near or far there was no noise except fog-horns, and there was whole minutes when you didn't hear
none o' them. There was whole minutes when you didn't hear
nothin'. In the midst o' one o' them quiet spells, me and Brainie
M'Gan and a feller named Hodge, who was leanin' over the rail
spittin' and conversin', hears a kind of long fizzin' noise, like steam
escapin', followed by a noise like little waves breakin' on a beach.

"'What do you make that out to be?' says Brainie.

"'Sounds like steam escapin',' says I, 'and a rock puttin' its nose
above water at the same time.'

"'There ain't no rocks hereabouts,' says Brainie.

"'Maybe it's the sea-serpint hissin',' says Hodge.

"'Young feller,' says I, 'don't you know no better than to invite
happenings? You leave sea-serpints alone and they'll leave you
alone,' says I.

"We didn't hear nothin' but fog-horns for some time, and then
a dory come out o' the fog and passed close to us. She were half

full of fish and a man were takin' his time rowin' her. He made slow way of it by reason o' the tide headin' him.

"'Hurry up there,' sings Brainie, 'or you'll get left.'

"The feller turns his head sideways and grins, but don't say nothin' by reason of needin' his breath to row with, and then he an' his dory slips off into the fog.

"'There's that damned noise again,' says Brainie. 'Listen—!'

"We listens, sir, and all of a sudden, sir, out o' the fog there comes a screetch like no man in his senses could make.

"We looks at each other, and shivers.

"'That weren't no pretty noise,' says Brainie.

"Then the captain pokes his head up the hatchway.

"'Who's yellin',' says he.

"'Right, sir,' says Brainie. 'Look boys.'

"We looks, and there were the dory driftin' down on us, empty. She drifted so close that Brainie made out to reach her with a boat-hook. There were a piece gone from her side, sir, as big as a straw hat. It looked like it had bin bit out. And you mind, sir, she'd bin half full o' fish? Well, there weren't a one left. The man were gone and the fishes was gone. We tells the captain.

"'H'm,' says he, lookin' scared, 'what the hell!'

"'The fish is gone,' says Brainie, 'but they left their smell.'

"'Ugh,' says the captain, holdin' his nose, 'they have that!'

"I tell you, sir, the stink o' fish about that dory most turned me sick, and it were the same with the others.

"'That dory must be hundreds o' years old," says the captain, 'and full o' rotten fish all the time. Sing out, all of you; maybe the man ain't drowned and we can save him.'

"Then we all sings out. And then we listens.

"The answer, sir, come from over our heads, and were like the burstin' of a steam pipe. We ducks, turns and looks up. And there, sir, forty foot in the air, dartin' between the masts, were a snake's head, stuck to a long, shinin' body that come with one curve out o' the sea. The snake's mouth were open and I seed rows of white teeth bent toward its throat, and a tongue that buzzed like a fly's wings. And I smelted the breath that come out o' that mouth, sir, and it were the smell of millions of fish, dead, buried and dug up.

Then, sir, the head drops in the middle of us. I fetches a screetch and falls backwards, shuttin' my eyes. I opens them in a second, and sees Hodge half mast high, crosswise in the snake's jaws, like a stick in a dog's mouth. Then him and the snake swings outboard and sinks into the sea.

"Me and Brainie and the captain picks ourselves up and clings together like drunken men, whimperin' and sobbin'. And after a minute we crawls below and begins to drink like fishes.

"Then we hears a voice hailin' for help.

"'Go and see what that is, M'Gan,' says the captain.

"Brainie takes two steps, and stops.

"'I can't,' says he.

"'I'll go,' says the captain. And he steps into his cabin and comes out with a revolver.

"'I'll go too,' says Brainie.

"We goes on deck, and there, sir, were Hodge climbin' inboard over the rail. His clothes was all in streamers, and he were drippin' brine, and he smelt like a dead fish.

"'Get me a drink,' says he.

"We goes below, and drinks more. We drinks for maybe an hour. Then the captain says:

"'What happened, Hodge?'

"'For the love of God,' says Hodge, 'don't ask me. I don't know.' And for a long time he wouldn't answer, though we plies him with questions. Then he says:

"'Captain,' he said, 'if I thought you'd believe me, I'd tell you what happened.'

"'My God,' says the captain, 'I'd believe anything—now.'

"'So would Brainie and me,' says I.

"'Well,' says Hodge, 'then I'll tell you. I were swallered and give up.'

"And that were all he'd ever say. He were a changed man after that day—never himself again. Pretty soon he quit the sea, and went to farmin' in Arizona, and the last I heard of him he were bit by a rattlesnake and died."

"Well, Winkler," I said, "did the captain write down about the sea-serpent in his log?"

"No, sir," said Winkler, "he'd of bin fired by the owners if he had."

"That's true," I said.

"Was that the only one you ever saw?" I asked.

"Yes, sir," said Winkler. "But they're common enough in some places."

CREW SAVED BY SEA SERPENT
Anonymous

The old-time battleship *Pensacola* lay in the Horse Latitudes becalmed. Not a breath of air stirred her canvas, which hung limp and flabby from the yards. The only motion was the long gradual sway of her masts as she rolled slowly to starboard, then back to port on the deep-sea swells. The blocks creaked dismally and the slack crew ropes flapped occasionally against the canvas with a loud report. The deck was dry as a bone, and the pitch boiled out from between the planks as if it were in a heated caldron.

The Captain was in his bath tub taking his customary long afternoon "siesta," absorbing fresh water cooled by vaporization, in an endeavor to keep from being shriveled with the sultry heat. The door which led into his stateroom was open, also the door leading on into the cabin. The windows of the large stern ports had been removed, so that there was nothing to obstruct his view out upon the slimy sea.

On deck the crew were in no such state of listless comfort. They had no water in which to soak themselves; indeed, there was scarcely enough to drink, and the terrible fear of weeks piled upon weeks becalmed in that idle ocean held their faces drawn and white. They stood about the bulwarks gazing anxiously skyward for the faint sign of a Mare's Tail.

The mate spoke up, "Hans Hansen, they tell me you were born at Hamerfest. Is that right?"

"Aye, sir," answered Hans weakly.

"Then you go and sit on the binnacle stand looking sou'west and whistle the best tune you've got in that square head of yours. If nothing shows up by the second dog watch get into the fore-peake with Skyjarsen."

"Aye, aye, sir," said Hans, as he climbed the binnacle stand. His tune was a bit strained and tremulous, for his heart was clutched in fear of the fore-peake. Since Skyjarsen had failed he entertained little hope. The merry air he tried to whistle sounded, amid the rasping of the blocks and flapping of slack ropes, more like a dirge to the dead than a bonny tune for a fair wind.

Of a sudden the eager faces on deck turned a ghastly gray; something huge and green rose from the water and sank again directly off the starboard quarter. Hans fell off the binnacle and landed on deck with a thud. The ship seemed to stop swaying, the blocks ceased to creak and all was as still as death. The mate went over and peered into the sea, but could see nothing. The water spread away to the horizon, thick, glassy, unbroken.

"That settles it!" said he, turning resignedly to the rest, "we are in the edge of the Saragossa Sea. A ship was never known to get out. That monster out there is the one the old skippers say is always found in these waters, waiting to crawl through the hatchways and chase the crew overboard."

"I've heard tell, sir, that the Saragossa Sea floats around and even the best of them can't tell how close they are until they're in it," said one of the men greatly agitated.

This conversation took place amidships in subdued tones; so enrapt were they that no one perceived what took place under the stern of the vessel, until they heard the Captain shrieking in an agonized voice for help. The stern of the vessel began to jump about as if it were a cork, and the timbers could be heard to strain, as if about to burst.

This aroused the crew to action. They were in danger of being cast into the sea. The mate ran to the stern and looking over the staff-rail saw a hundred feet of green scales beating the water into a maelstrom. The hair rose stiff upon his head and he sprang back in horror. Several of the sailors started down the cabin hatchway, intending to investigate the cause of the Captain's frenzied cries, but they were confronted with a convulsing mass of green scales and were scarcely able to get back on deck. All hands were in a panic.

The great scaly monster had peered in at the open stern ports, and seeing the Captain's head and shoulders protruding above the edge of the tub, jammed its huge head through the port into the cabin and stretched its carcass on through the stateroom to the very edge of the tub in a mighty effort to reach him. The great horny fin upon its back caught on the timber above the port hole and it could enter no farther, strive as it might. At least a hundred feet of it remained in the water astern of the ship, and in its efforts to reach the captain, the gigantic tail began to disturb the calm of the sea in a frightful manner.

At the first flop of the tail the Captain opened his eyes and stared into the gaping mouth all hung with bits of sea kelp and dripping slime. Two convulsing feelers reached for him and all but touched him as he reclined. His eyes nearly darted from their sockets, his blood froze in spite of the heat, a paroxysm seized his brain; with an agonized shriek he fell backward fainting into the water where he almost drowned before it revived him.

The serpent hissed and spewed salt water into his face, struggling desperately to stretch a few feet farther. It seemed of no mind to give up the cherished morsel and under the powerful propulsion of its tail in the water the ship began to move slowly ahead.

When the mate became aware of this he called out to Hans Hansen at the binnacle: "Mind your wheel now! Put her on nor'west a half west."

Then the mate acquainted himself with the situation. He ordered the crew to their stations, and told the quartermaster to heave the log and ascertain the speed of the ship. It was found to be ten knots per hour. Being satisfied that the serpent could get no further into the cabin, he stepped to the ventilator and called down to the Captain:

"Belay the screeching down there. You're safe enough. He can't eat you. Take it easy."

But all did not go on so smoothly. The snake began to lose its enthusiasm, or its appetite, and ceased to propel the ship fast enough to suit the mate.

"This will never do!" he observed. "We must shake more speed out of him than this or the Captain will have to stay in his tub a week." Accordingly he sent for a deck broom and passed it down to the Captain.

"Take that," he called, "and tickle him under the chin. Act like you're going to jump down his throat. Kick him on the nose. Lay hold of those side whiskers and give them a pull. Anything to make his tail go faster, or you'll never get out of that tub."

The poor Captain shuddered in abject horror at these directions, but as the day wore on he finally realized it would be better to do so, and with a supreme effort he gave the snake a vigorous punch in the nostril. At this, such quantities of water shot from the monster that the Captain was almost drowned. The hideous body again convulsed with rage and desperate determination, and the ship began to pick up speed rapidly from the working of the long tail out astern.

"That's the thing. Captain! Give it to him heavy! We'll be out of here quick," called the mate, joyously.

The old skipper renewed the application of the broom, sticking it in the eyes, nose and even down the slimy mouth to the palate. He began to feel master of the situation. The faster the broom went, the faster the tail drove the ship ahead, with a swish as powerful as a turbine engine. The speed increased to 16 knots, from thence it jumped to 20, simply by means of a new twist of the broom the Captain found in his endeavor to do his part well. The smooth sea rolled away from the bow in curling breakers. On they sped faster than ever they had gone before, until far on the horizon a faint white speck appeared.

"A cloud! A cloud!" The cry rang out alone the deck. The Captain heard it aft in his tub and uttered a groan of relief. The mate came running to the ventilator and told him to desist with the broom. A line was passed down, and he was drawn out on deck. All the fear and wrath had fled. They were all saved and he had been the cause of it through his heroic application of the broom—and it might be added, his appetizing complexion.

The serpent, seeing nothing in the shape of edibles in the cabin, allowed himself to slip back into the water where he disappeared to be seen no more.

During the turmoil Hans Hansen held her on her course and grinned, for he had escaped the Fore-peake. As the mate walked past him, he said in a tense voice, "Don't let me catch you whistling again as long as you are shipmates with me."

And he never did.

The Thing in the Weeds
William Hope Hodgson

I

This is an extraordinary tale. We had come up from the Cape, and owing to the Trades heading us more than usual, we had made some hundreds of miles more westing than I ever did before or since.

I remember the particular night of the happening perfectly. I suppose what occurred stamped it solid into my memory, with a thousand little details that, in the ordinary way, I should never have remembered an hour. And, of course, we talked it over so often among ourselves that this, no doubt, helped to fix it all past any forgetting.

I remember the mate and I had been pacing the weather side of the poop and discussing various old shellbacks' superstitions. I was third mate, and it was between four and five bells in the first watch, *i.e.* between ten and half-past. Suddenly he stopped in his walk and lifted his head and sniffed several times.

"My word, mister," he said, "there's a rum kind of stink somewhere about. Don't you smell it?"

I sniffed once or twice at the light airs that were coming in on the beam; then I walked to the rail and leaned over, smelling again at the slight breeze. And abruptly I got a whiff of it, faint and sickly, yet vaguely suggestive of something I had once smelt before.

"I can smell something, Mr. Lammart," I said. "I could almost give it name; and yet somehow I can't." I stared away into the dark to windward. "What do you seem to smell?" I asked him.

"I can't smell anything now," he replied, coming over and standing beside me. "It's gone again. No! By Jove! there it is again. My goodness! Phew!"

230

The smell was all about us now, filling the night air. It had still that indefinable familiarity about it, and yet it was curiously strange, and, more than anything else, it was certainly simply beastly.

The stench grew stronger, and presently the mate asked me to go for'ard and see whether the look-out man noticed anything. When I reached the break of the fo'c's'le head I called up to the man, to know whether he smelled anything.

"Smell anythin', sir?" he sang out. "Jumpin' larks! I sh'u'd think I do. I'm fair p'isoned with it."

I ran up the weather steps and stood beside him. The smell was certainly very plain up there, and after savouring it for a few moments I asked him whether he thought it might be a dead whale. But he was very emphatic that this could not be the case, for, as he said, he had been nearly fifteen years in whaling ships, and knew the smell of a dead whale, "like as you would the smell of bad whiskey, sir," as he put it. "'Tain't no whale yon, but the Lord He knows what 'tis. I'm thinking it's Davy Jones come up for a breather."

I stayed with him some minutes, staring out into the darkness, but could see nothing; for, even had there been something big close to us, I doubt whether I could have seen it, so black a night it was, without a visible star, and with a vague, dull haze breeding an indistinctness all about the ship.

I returned to the mate and reported that the look-out complained of the smell, but that neither he nor I had been able to see anything in the darkness to account for it.

By this time the queer, disgusting odour seemed to be in all the air about us, and the mate told me to go below and shut all the ports, so as to keep the beastly smell out of the cabins and the saloon.

When I returned he suggested that we should shut the companion doors, and after that we commenced to pace the poop again, discussing the extraordinary smell, and stopping from time to time to stare through our night-glasses out into the night about the ship.

"I'll tell you what it smells like, mister," the mate remarked once, "and that's like a mighty old derelict I once went aboard in the North Atlantic. She was a proper old-timer, an' she gave us all the creeps. There was just this funny, dank, rummy sort of century-old bilge-water and dead men an' seaweed. I can't stop thinkin' we're nigh some lonesome old packet out there; an' a good thing we've not much way on us!"

"Do you notice how almighty quiet everything's gone the last half-hour or so?" I said a little later. "It must be the mist thickening down."

"It is the mist," said the mate, going to the rail and staring out. "Good Lord, what's that?" he added.

Something had knocked his hat from his head, and it fell with a sharp rap at my feet. And suddenly, you know, I got a premonition of something horrid.

"Come away from the rail, sir!" I said sharply, and gave one jump and caught him by the shoulders and dragged him back. "Come away from the side!"

"What's up, mister?" he growled at me, an twisted his shoulders free. "What's wrong with you? Was it you knocked off my cap?" He stooped and felt around for it, and as he did so I heard something unmistakably fiddling away at the rail which the mate had just left.

"My God, sir!" I said "there's something there. Hark!"

The mate stiffened up, listening; then he heard it. It was for all the world as if something was feeling and rubbing the rail there in the darkness, not two fathoms away from us.

"Who's there?" said the mate quickly. Then, as there was no answer: "What the devil's this hanky-panky? Who's playing the goat there?" He made a swift step through the darkness towards he rail, but I caught him by the elbow.

"Don't go, mister!" I said, hardly above a whisper. "It's not one of the men. Let me get a light."

"Quick, then!" he said, and I turned and ran aft to the binnacle and snatched out the lighted lamp. As I did so I heard the mate shout something out of the darkness in a strange voice. There came a sharp, loud, rattling sound, and then a crash, and immediately the mate roaring to me to hasten with the light. His voice changed even whilst he shouted, and gave out somthing that was nearer a scream than anything else. There came two loud, dull blows and an extraordinary gasping sound; and then, as I raced along the poop, there was a tremendous smashing of glass and an immediate silence.

"Mr. Lammart!" I shouted. "Mr. Lammart!" And then I had reached the place where I had left the mate for forty seconds before; but he was not there.

"Mr. Lammart!" I shouted again, holding the light high over my head and turning quickly to look behind me. As I did so my foot glided on some slippery substance, and I went headlong to the deck with a tremendous thud, smashing the lamp and putting out the light.

I was on my feet again in an instant. I groped a moment for the lamp, and as I did so I heard the men singing out from the maindeck and the noise of their feet as they came running aft. I found the broken lamp and realised it was useless; then I jumped for the companion-way, and in half a minute I was back with the big saloon lamp glaring bright in my hands.

I ran for'ard again, shielding the upper edge of the glass chimney from the draught of my running, and the blaze of the big lamp seemed to make the weather side of the poop as bright as day, except for the mist, that gave something of a vagueness to things.

Where I had left the mate there was blood upon the deck, but nowhere any signs of the man himself. I ran to the weather rail and held the lamp to it. There was blood upon it, and the rail itself seemed to have been wrenched by some huge force. I put out my hand and found that I could shake it. Then I leaned out-board and held the lamp at arm's length, staring down over the ship's side.

"Mr. Lammart!" I shouted into the night and the thick mist. "Mr. Lammart! Mr. Lammart!" But my voice seemed to go, lost and muffled and infinitely small, away into the billowy darkness.

I heard the men snuffling and breathing, waiting to leeward of the poop. I whirled round to them, holding the lamp high,

"We heard somethin', sir," said Tarpley, the leading seaman in our watch. "Is anythin' wrong, sir?"

"The mate's gone," I said blankly. "We heard something, and I went for the binnacle lamp. Then he shouted, and I heard a sound of things smashing, and when I got back he'd gone clean." I turned and held the light out again over the unseen sea, and the men crowded round along the rail and stared, bewildered.

"Blood, sir," said Tarpley, pointing. "There's somethin' almighty queer out there." He waved a huge hand into the darkness. "That's what stinks—"

He never finished; for suddenly one of the men cried out something in a frightened voice: "Look out, sir! Look out, sir!"

I saw, in one brief flash of sight, something come in with an infernal flicker of movement; and then, before I could form any notion of what I had seen, the lamp was dashed to pieces across the poop deck. In that instant my perceptions cleared, and I saw the incredible folly of what we were doing; for there we were, standing up against the blank, unknowable night, and out there in the darkness there surely lurked some thing of monstrousness; and we were at its mercy. I seemed to feel it hovering—hovering over us, so that I felt the sickening creep of gooseflesh all over me.

"Stand back from the rail!" I shouted. "Stand back from the rail!" There was a rush of feet as the men obeyed, in sudden apprehension of their danger, and I gave back with them. Even as I did so I felt some invisible thing brush my shoulder, and an indescribable smell was in my nostrils from something that moved over me in the dark.

"Down into the saloon everyone!" I shouted. "Down with you all! Don't wait a moment!"

There was a rush along the dark weather deck, and then the men went helter-skelter down the companion steps into the saloon, falling and cursing over one another in the darkness. I sang out to the man at the wheel to join them, and then I followed.

I came upon the men huddled at the foot of the stairs and filling up the passage, all crowding each other in the darkness. The skipper's voice was filling the saloon, and he was demanding in violent adjectives the cause of so tremendous a noise. From the steward's berth there came also a voice and the splutter of a match, and then the glow of a lamp in the saloon itself.

I pushed my way through the men and found the captain in the saloon in his sleeping gear, looking both drowsy and angry, though perhaps bewilderment topped every other feeling. He held his cabin lamp in his hand, and shone the light over the huddle of men.

I hurried to explain, and told him of the incredible disappearance of the mate, and of my conviction that some extraordinary thing was lurking near the ship out in the mist and the darkness. I mentioned the curious smell, and told how the mate had suggested that we had drifted down near some old-time, sea-rotted derelict. And, you know, even as I put it into awkward words, my imagination began to awaken to horrible discomforts; a thousand dreadful impossibilities of the sea became suddenly possible.

The captain (Jeldy was his name) did not stop to dress, but ran back into his cabin, and came out in a few moments with a couple of revolvers and a handful of cartridges. The second mate had come running out of his cabin at the noise, and had listed intensely to what I had to say; and now he jumped back into his berth and brought out his own lamp and a large Smith and Wesson, which was evidently ready loaded.

Captain Jeldy pushed one of his revolvers into my hands, with some of the cartridges, and we began hastily to load the weapons. Then the captain caught up his lamp and made for the stairway, ordering the men into the saloon out of his way.

"Shall you want them, sir?" I asked.

"No," he said. "It's no use their running any unnecessary risks." He threw a word over his shoulder: "Stay quiet here, men; if I want you I'll give you a shout; then come spry!"

"Aye, aye, sir," said the watch in a chorus; and then I was following the captain up the stairs, with the second mate close behind.

We came up through the companion-way on to the silence of the deserted poop. The mist had thickened up, even during the brief time that I had been below, and there was not a breath of wind. The mist was so dense that it seemed to press in upon us, and the two lamps made a kind of luminous halo in the mist, which seemed to absorb their light in a most peculiar way.

"Where was he?" the captain asked me, almost in a whisper.

"On the port side, sir," I said, "a little foreside the charthouse and about a dozen feet in from the rail. I'll show you the exact place."

We went for'ard along what had been the weather side, going quietly and watchfully, though, indeed, it was little enough that we could see, because of the mist. Once, as I led the way, I thought I heard a vague sound somewhere in the mist, but was all unsure because of the slow creak, creak of the spars and gear as the vessel rolled slightly upon an odd, oily swell. Apart from this slight sound, and the far-up rustle of the canvas slatting gently against the masts, there was no sound of all throughout the ship. I assure you the silence seemed to me to be almost menacing, in the tense, nervous state in which I was.

"Hereabouts is where I left him," I whispered to the captain a few seconds later. "Hold your lamp low, sir. There's blood on the deck."

Captain Jeldy did so, and made a slight sound with his mouth at what he saw. Then, heedless of my hurried warning, he walked across to the rail, holding his lamp high up. I followed him, for I could not let him go alone; and the second mate came too, with his lamp. They leaned over the port rail and held their lamps out into the mist and the unknown darkness beyond the ship's side. I remember how the lamps made just two yellow glares in the mist, ineffectual, yet serving somehow to make extraordinarily plain the vastitude of the night and the possibilities of the dark. Perhaps that is a queer way to put it, but it gives you the effect of that moment upon my feelings. And all the time, you know, there was upon me the brutal, frightening expectancy of something reaching in at us from out of that everlasting darkness and mist that held all the sea and the night, so that we were just three mist-shrouded, hidden figures, peering nervously.

The mist was now so thick that we could not even see the surface of the water overside, and fore and aft of us the rail vanished away into the fog and the dark. And then, as we stood here staring, I heard something moving down on the maindeck. I caught Captain Jeldy by the elbow.

"Come away from the rail, sir," I said, hardly above a whisper; and he, with the swift premonition of danger, stepped back and allowed me to urge him well inboard. The second mate followed, and the three of us stood there in the mist, staring round about us and holding our revolvers handily, and the dull waves of the mist beating in slowly upon the lamps in vague wreathings and swirls of fog.

"What was it you heard, mister?" asked the captain after a few moments.

"Ssst!" I muttered. "There it is again. There's something moving down on the maindeck!"

Captain Jeldy heard it himself now, and the three of us stood listening intensely. Yet it was hard to know what to make of the sounds. And then suddenly there was the rattle of a deck ringbolt, and then again, as if something or someone were fumbling and playing with it.

"Down there on the maindeck!" shouted the captain abruptly, his voice seeming hoarse close to my ear, yet immediately smothered by the fog. "Down there on the maindeck! Who's there?"

But there came never an answering sound. And the three of us stood there, looking quickly this way and that, and listening. Abruptly the second mate muttered something:

"The look-out, sir! The look-out!"

Captain Jeldy took the hint on the instant.

"On the look-out there!" he shouted.

And then, far away and muffled-sounding, there came the answering cry of the look-out man from the fo'c'sle head:

"Sir-r-r?" A little voice, long drawn out through unknowable alleys of fog.

"Go below into the fo'c'sle and shut both doors, an' don't stir out till you're told!" sung out Captain Jeldy, his voice going lost into the mist. And then the man's answering "Aye, aye, sir!" coming to us faint and mournful. And directly afterwards the clang of a steel door, hollow-sounding and remote; and immediately the sound of another.

"That puts them safe for the present, anyway," said the second mate. And even as he spoke there came again that indefinite noise down upon the maindeck of something moving with an incredible and unnatural stealthiness.

"On the maindeck there!" shouted Captain Jeldy sternly. "If there is anyone there, answer, or I shall fire!"

The reply was both amazing and terrifying, for suddenly a tremendous blow was stricken upon the deck, and then there came the dull, rolling sound of some enormous weight going hollowly across the maindeck. And then an abominable silence.

"My God!' said Captain Jeldy in a low voice, "what was that?" And he raised his pistol, but I caught him by the wrist. "Don't shoot,

sir!" I whispered. "It'll be no good. That—that—whatever it is I—
mean it's something enormous, sir. I—I really wouldn't shoot." I
found it impossible to put my vague idea into words; but I felt there
was a force aboard, down on the maindeck, that it would be futile
to attack with so ineffectual a thing as a puny revolver bullet.

And then, as I held Captain Jeldy's wrist, and he hesitated,
irresolute, there came a sudden bleating of sheep and the sound of
lashings being burst and the cracking of wood; and the next instant a huge crash, followed by crash after crash, and the anguished
m-aa-a-a-ing of sheep.

"My God!" said the second mate, "the sheep-pen's being beaten
to pieces against the deck. Good God! What sort of thing could do
that?"

The tremendous beating ceased, and there was a splashing
overside; and after that a silence so profound that it seemed as if
the whole atmosphere of the night was full of an unbearable, tense
quietness. And then the damp slatting of a sail, far up in the night,
that made me start—a lonesome sound to break suddenly through
that infernal silence upon my raw nerves.

"Get below, both of you. Smartly now!" muttered Captain Jeldy.
"There's something run either aboard us or alongside; and we can't
do anything till daylight."

We went below and shut the doors of the companion-way, and
there we lay in the wide Atlantic, without wheel or look-out or officer
in charge, and something incredible down on the dark maindeck.

II

For some hours we sat in the captain's cabin talking the matter
over whilst the watch slept, sprawled in a dozen attitudes on the
floor of the saloon. Captain Jeldy and the second mate still wore
their pyjamas, and our loaded revolvers lay handy on the cabin
table. And so we watched anxiously through the hours for the dawn
to come in.

As the light strengthened we endeavoured to get some view of
the sea from the ports, but the mist was so thick about us that it
was exactly like looking out into a grey nothingness, that became
presently white as the day came.

"Now," said Captain Jeldy, "we're going to look into this."

He went out through the saloon to the companion stairs. At the top he opened the two doors, and the mist rolled in on us, white and impenetrable. For a little while we stood there, the three of us, absolutely silent and listening, with our revolvers handy; but never a sound came to us except the odd, vague slatting of a sail or the slight creaking of the gear as the ship lifted on some slow, invisible swell.

Presently the captain stepped cautiously out on to the deck; he was in his cabin slippers, and therefore made no sound. I was wearing gum-boots, and followed him silently, and the second mate after me in his bare feet. Captain Jeldy went a few paces along the deck, and the mist hid him utterly. "Phew!" I heard him mutter, "the stink's worse than ever!" His voice came odd and vague to me through the wreathing of the mist.

"The sun'll soon eat up all this fog," said the second mate at my elbow, in a voice little above a whisper.

We stepped after the captain, and found him a couple of fathoms away, standing shrouded in the mist in an attitude of tense listening.

"Can't hear a thing!" he whispered. "We'll go for'ard to the break, as quiet as you like. Don't make a sound."

We went forward, like three shadows, and suddenly Captain Jeldy kicked his shin against something and pitched headlong over it, making a tremendous noise. He got up quickly, swearing grimly, and the three of us stood there in silence, waiting lest any infernal thing should come upon us out of all that white invisibility. Once I felt sure I saw something coming towards me, and I raised my revolver, but saw in a moment that there was nothing. The tension of imminent, nervous expectancy eased from us, and Captain Jeldy stooped over the object on the deck.

"The port hencoop's been shifted out here!" he muttered. "It's all stove!"

"That must be what I heard last night when the mate went," I whispered. "There was a loud crash just before he sang out to me to hurry with the lamp."

Captain Jeldy left the smashed hencoop, and the three of us tiptoed silently to the rail across the break of the poop. Here we leaned over and stared down into the blank whiteness of the mist that hid everything.

"Can't see a thing," whispered the second mate; yet as he spoke I could fancy that I heard a slight, indefinite, slurring noise somewhere below us; and I caught them each by an arm to draw them back.

"There's something down there," I muttered. "For goodness' sake come back from the rail."

We gave back a step or two, and then stopped to listen; and even as we did so there came a slight air playing through the mist.

"The breeze is coming," said the second mate. "Look, the mist is clearing already."

He was right. Already the look of white impenetrability had gone, and suddenly we could see the corner of the after-hatch coamings through the thinning fog. Within a minute we could see as far for'ard as the mainmast, and then the stuff blew away from us, clear of the vessel, like a great wall of whiteness, that dissipated as it went.

"Look!" we all exclaimed together. The whole of the vessel was now clear to our sight; but it was not at the ship herself that we looked, for, after one quick glance along the empty maindeck, we had seen something beyond the ship's side. All around the vessel there lay a submerged spread of weed, for, maybe, a good quarter of a mile upon every side.

"Weed!" sang out Captain Jeldy in a voice of comprehension. "Weed! Look! By Jove, I guess I know now what got the mate!"

He turned and ran to the port side and looked over. And suddenly he stiffened and beckoned silently over his shoulder to us to come and see. We had followed, and now we stood, one on each side of him, staring.

"Look!" whispered the captain, pointing. "See the great brute! Do you see it? There! Look!"

At first I could see nothing except the submerged spread of the weed, into which we had evidently run after dark. Then, as I stared intently, my gaze began to separate from the surrounding weed a leathery-looking something that was somewhat darker in hue than the weed itself.

"My God!" said Captain Jeldy. "What a monster! What a monster! Just look at the brute! Look at the thing's eyes! That's what got the mate. What a creature out of hell itself!"

I saw it plainly now; three of the massive feelers lay twined in and out among the clumpings of the weed; and then, abruptly, I realised that the two extraordinary round disks, motionless and inscrutable, were the creature's eyes, just below the surface of the water. It appeared to be staring, expressionless, up at the steel side of the vessel. I traced, vaguely, the shapeless monstrosity of what must be termed its head. "My God!" I muttered. "It's an enormous squid of some kind! What an awful brute! What—"

The sharp report of the captain's revolver came at that moment. He had fired at the thing, and instantly there was a most awful commotion alongside. The weed was hove upward, literally in tons. An enormous quantity was thrown aboard us by the thrashing of the monster's great feelers. The sea seemed almost to boil, in one great cauldron of weed and water, all about the brute, and the steel side of the ship resounded with the dull, tremendous blows that the creature gave in its struggle. And into all that whirling boil of tentacles, weed, and seawater the three of us emptied our revolvers as fast as we could fire and reload. I remember the feeling of fierce satisfaction I had in thus aiding to avenge the death of the mate.

Suddenly the captain roared out to us to jump back, and we obeyed on the instant. As we did so the weed rose up into a great mound over twenty feet in height, and more than a ton of it slopped aboard. The next instant three of the monstrous tentacles came in over the side, and the vessel gave a slow, sullen roll to port as the weight came upon her, for the monster had literally hove itself almost free of the sea against our port side, in one vast, leathery shape, all wreathed with weed-fronds, and seeming drenched with blood and curious black liquid.

The feelers that had come inboard thrashed round here and there, and suddenly one of them curled in the most hideous, snake-like fashion around the base of the mainmast. This seemed to attract it, for immediately it curled the two others about the mast, and forthwith wrenched upon it with such hideous violence that the whole towering length of spars, through all their height of a hundred and fifty feet, were shaken visibly, whilst the vessel herself vibrated with the stupendous efforts of the brute.

"It'll have the mast down, sir!" said the second mate, with a gasp. "My God! It'll strain her side open! My—"

"One of those blasting cartridges!" I said to Jeldy almost in a shout, as the inspiration took me. "Blow the brute to pieces!"

"Get one, quick!" said the captain, jerking his thumb towards the companion. "You know where they are."

In thirty seconds I was back with the cartridge. Captain Jeldy took out his knife and cut the fuse dead short; then, with a steady hand, he lit the fuse, and calmly held it, until I backed away, shouting to him to throw it, for I knew it must explode in another couple of seconds.

Captain Jeldy threw the thing like one throws a quoit, so that it fell into the sea just on the outward side of the vast bulk of the monster. So well had he timed it that it burst, with a stunning report, just as it struck the water. The effect upon the squid was amazing. It seemed literally to collapse. The enormous tentacles released themselves from the mast and curled across the deck helplessly, and were drawn inertly over the rail, as the enormous bulk sank away from the ship's side, out of sight, into the weed. The ship rolled slowly to starboard, and then steadied. "Thank God!" I muttered, and looked at the two others. They were pallid and sweating, and I must have been the same.

"Here's the breeze again," said the second mate, a minute later. "We're moving." He turned, without another word, and raced aft to the wheel, whilst the vessel slid over and through the weedfield.

"Look where that brute broke up the sheep-pen!" cried Jeldy, pointing. "And here's the skylight of the sail-locker smashed to bits!"

He walked across to it, and glanced down. And suddenly he let out a tremendous shout of astonishment:

"Here's the mate down here!" he shouted. "He's not overboard at all! He's here!"

He dropped himself down through the skylight on to the sails, and I after him; and, surely, there was the mate, lying all huddled and insensible on a hummock of spare sails. In his right hand he held a drawn sheath-knife, which he was in the habit of carrying A. B. fashion, whilst his left hand was all caked with dried blood, where he had been badly cut. Afterwards, we concluded he had cut himself in slashing at one of the tentacles of the squid, which had caught him round the left wrist, the tip of the tentacle being still curled tight about his arm, just as it had been when he hacked it through. For the rest, he was not seriously damaged, the creature having obviously flung him violently away through the framework of the skylight, so that he had fallen in a stunned condition on to the pile of sails.

We got him on deck, and down into his bunk, where we left the steward to attend to him. When we returned to the poop the vessel had drawn clear of the weed-field, and the captain and I stopped for a few moments to stare astern over the taffrail.

As we stood and looked something wavered up out of the heart of the weed—a long, tapering, sinous thing, that curled and wavered against the dawn-light, and presently sank back again into the demure weed—a veritable spider of the deep, waiting in the great web that Dame Nature had spun for it in the eddy of her tides and currents.

And we sailed away northwards, with strengthening "trades," and left that patch of monstrousness to the loneliness of the sea.

THE FINDING OF THE *GRAIKEN*
William Hope Hodgson

I

When a year had passed, and still there was no news of the full-rigged ship *Graiken*, even the most sanguine of my old chum's friends had ceased to hope perchance, somewhere, she might be above water.

Yet Ned Barlow, in his inmost thoughts, I knew, still hugged to himself the hope that she would win home. Poor, dear old fellow, how my heart did go out towards him in his sorrow!

For it was in the *Graiken* that his sweetheart had sailed on that dull January day some twelve months previously.

The voyage had been taken for the sake of her health; yet since then—save for a distant signal recorded at the Azores—there had been from all the mystery of ocean no voice; the ship and they within her had vanished utterly.

And still Barlow hoped. He said nothing actually, but at times his deeper thoughts would float up and show through the sea of his usual talk, and thus I would know in an indirect way of the thing that his heart was thinking.

Nor was time a healer.

It was later that my present good fortune came to me. My uncle died, and I—hitherto poor— was now a rich man. In a breath, it seemed, I had become possessor of houses, lands, and money; also—in my eyes almost more important—a fine fore-and-aft-rigged yacht of some two hundred tons register.

It seemed scarcely believable that the thing was mine, and I was all in a scutter to run away down to Falmouth and get to sea.

In old times, when my uncle had been more than usually gracious, he had invited me to accompany him for a trip round the

244

coast or elsewhere, as the fit might take him; yet never, even in my most hopeful moments, had it occurred to me that ever she might be mine.

And now I was hurrying my preparations for a good long sea trip—for to me the sea is, and always has been, a comrade.

Still, with all the prospects before me, I was by no means completely satisfied, for I wanted Ned Barlow with me, and yet was afraid to ask him.

I had the feeling that, in view of his overwhelming loss, he must positively hate the sea; and yet I could not be happy at the thought of leaving him, and going alone.

He had not been well lately, and a sea voyage would be the very thing for him, if only it were not going to freshen painful memories.

Eventually I decided to suggest it, and this I did a couple of days before the date I had fixed for sailing.

"Ned," I said, "you need a change."

"Yes," he assented wearily.

"Come with me, old chap," I went on, growing bolder. "I'm taking a trip in the yacht. It would be splendid to have—"

To my dismay, he jumped to his feet and came towards me excitedly. "I've upset him now," was my thought. "I am a fool!"

"Go to sea!" he said. "My God! I'd give—" He broke off short, and stood suppressed opposite to me, his face all of a quiver with suppressed emotion. He was silent a few seconds, getting himself in hand; then he proceeded more quietly: "Where to?"

"Anywhere," I replied, watching him keenly, for I was greatly puzzled by his manner. "I'm not quite clear yet. Somewhere south of here—the West Indies, I have thought. It's all so new, you know— just fancy being able to go just where we like. I can hardly realise it yet."

I stopped; for he had turned from me and was staring out of the window. "You'll come, Ned?" I cried, fearful that he was going to refuse me.

He took a pace away, and came back. "I'll come," he said, and there was a look of strange excitement in his eyes that set me off on a tack of vague wonder; but I said nothing, just told him how he had pleased me.

II

We had been at sea a couple of weeks, and were alone upon the Atlantic—at least, so much of it as presented itself to our view.

I was leaning over the taffrail, staring down into the boil of the wake; yet I noticed nothing, for I was wrapped in a tissue of somewhat uncomfortable thought. It was about Ned Barlow.

He had been queer, decidedly queer, since leaving port. His whole attitude mentally had been that of a man under the influence of an all-pervading excitement. I had said that he was in need of a change, and had trusted that the splendid tonic of the sea breeze would serve to put him soon to rights mentally and physically; yet here was the poor old chap, acting in a manner calculated to cause me anxiety as to his balance.

Scarcely a word had been spoken since leaving the Channel. When I ventured to speak to him, often he would take not the least notice, other times he would answer only by a brief word; but talk—never.

In addition, his whole time was spent on deck among the men, and with some of them he seemed to converse both long and earnestly; yet to me, his churn and true friend, not a word.

Another thing came to me as a surprise—Barlow betrayed the greatest interest in the position of the vessel, and the courses set, all in such a manner as left me no room to doubt but that his knowledge of navigation was considerable.

Once I ventured to express my astonishment at this knowledge, and ask a question or two as to the way in which he had gathered it, but had been treated with such an absurdly stony silence that since then I had not spoken to him.

With all this it may be easily conceived that my thoughts, as I stared down into the wake, were troublesome. Suddenly I heard a voice at my elbow:

"I should like to have a word with you, sir."

I turned sharply. It was my skipper, and something in his face told me that all was not as it should be.

"Well, Jenkins, fare away."

He looked round, as if afraid of being overheard; then came closer to me. "Someone's been messing with the compasses, sir," he said in a low voice.

"What?" I asked sharply.

"They've been meddled with, sir. The magnets have been shifted, and by someone who's a good idea of what he's doing."

"What on earth do you mean?" I inquired. "Why should any-one mess about with them? What good would it do them? You must be mistaken."

"No, sir, I'm not. They've been touched within the last forty-eight hours, and by someone that understands what he's doing."

I stared at him. The man was so certain. I felt bewildered. "But why should they?"

"That's more than I can say, sir; but it's a serious matter, and I want to know what I'm to do. It looks to me as though there were something funny going on. I'd give a month's pay to know just who it was, for certain."

"Well," I said, "if they have been touched, it can only be by one of the officers. You say the chap who has done it must understand what he is doing."

He shook his head. "No sir—" he began, and then stopped abruptly. His gaze met mine. I think the same thought must have come to us simultaneously. I gave a little gasp of amazement.

He wagged his head at me. "I've had my suspicions for a bit, sir," he went on; "but seeing that he's—he's—" He was fairly struck for the moment.

I took my weight off the rail and stood upright.

"To whom are you referring?" I asked curtly.

"Why, sir, to him—Mr. Ned—"

He would have gone on, but I cut him short.

"That will do, Jenkins!" I cried. "Mr. Ned Barlow is my friend. You are forgetting yourself a little. You will accuse me of tamper-ing with the compasses next!"

I turned away, leaving little Captain Jenkins speechless. I had spoken with an almost vehement over-loyalty, to quiet my own sus-picions.

All the same, I was horribly bewildered, not knowing what to think or do or say, so that, eventually, I did just nothing.

III

It was early one morning, about a week later, that I opened my eyes abruptly. I was lying on my back in my bunk, and the daylight was beginning to creep wanly in through the ports.

I had a vague consciousness that all was not as it should be, and feeling thus, I made to grasp the edge of my bunk, and sit up, but failed, owing to the fact that my wrists were securely fastened by a pair of heavy steel handcuffs.

Utterly confounded, I let my head fall back upon the pillow; and then, in the midst of my bewilderment, there sounded the sharp report of a pistol-shot somewhere on the decks over my head. There came a second, and the sound of voices and footsteps, and then a long spell of silence.

Into my mind had rushed the single word—mutiny! My temples throbbed a little, but I struggled to keep calm and think, and then, all adrift, I fell to searching round for a reason. Who was it? and why?

Perhaps an hour passed, during which I asked myself ten thousand vain questions. All at once I heard a key inserted in the door. So I had been locked in! It turned, and the steward walked into the cabin. He did not look at me, but went to the arm-rack and began to remove the various weapons.

"What the devil is the meaning of all this, Jones?" I roared, getting up a bit on one elbow. "What's happening?"

But the fool answered not a word—just went to and fro carrying out the weapons from my cabin into the next, so that at last I ceased from questioning him, and lay silent, promising myself future vengeance.

When he had removed the arms, the steward began to go through my table drawers, emptying them, so it appeared to me, of everything that could be used as a weapon or tool.

Having completed his task, he vanished, locking the door after him. Some time passed, and at last, about seven bells, he reappeared, this time bringing a tray with my breakfast. Placing it upon the table, he came across to me and proceeded to unlock the cuffs from off my wrists. Then for the first time he spoke.

"Mr. Barlow desires me to say, sir, that you have the liberty of your cabin so long as you will agree not to cause any bother. Should you wish for anything, I am under his orders to supply you." He retreated hastily toward the door.

On my part, I was almost speechless with astonishment and rage.

"One minute, Jones!" I shouted, just as he was in the act of leaving the cabin. "Kindly explain what you mean. You said Mr. Barlow. Is it to him that I owe all this?" And I waved my hand towards the irons which the man still held.

"It is by his orders," replied he, and turned once more to leave the cabin.

"I don't understand!" I said, bewildered. "Mr. Barlow is my friend, and this is my yacht! By what right do you dare to take your orders from him? Let me out!"

As I shouted the last command, I leapt from my bunk, and made a dash for the door, but the steward, so far from attempting to bar it, flung it open and stepped quickly through, thus allowing me to see that a couple of the sailors were stationed in the alleyway.

"Get on deck at once!" I said angrily. "What are you doing down here?"

"Sorry sir," said one of the men. "We'd take it kindly if you'd make no trouble. But we ain't lettin' you out, sir. Don't make no bloomin' error."

I hesitated, then went to the table and sat down. I would, at least, do my best to preserve my dignity.

After an inquiry as to whether he could do anything further, the steward left me to breakfast and my thoughts. As may be imagined, the latter were by no means pleasant.

Here was I prisoner in my own yacht, and by the hand of the very man I had loved and befriended through many years. Oh, it was too incredible and mad!

For a while, leaving the table, I paced the deck of my room; then, growing calmer, I sat down again and attempted to make some sort of a meal.

As I breakfasted, my chief thought was as to why my one-time chum was treating me thus; and after that I fell to puzzling how he had managed to get the yacht into his own hands.

Many things came back to me—his familiarity with the men, his treatment of me—which I had put down to a temporary want of balance—the fooling with the compasses; for I was certain now that he had been the doer of that piece of mischief. But why? That was the great point.

As I turned the matter over in my brain, an incident that had occurred some six days back came to me. It had been on the very day after the captain's report to me of the tampering with the compasses.

Barlow had, for the first time, relinquished his brooding and silence, and had started to talk to me, but in such a wild strain that he had made me feel vaguely uncomfortable about his sanity for he told me some yarn of an idea which he had got into his head. And then, in an overbearing way, he demanded that the navigation of the yacht should be put into his hands.

He had been very incoherent, and was plainly in a state of considerable mental excitement. He had rambled on about some derelict, and then had talked man extraordinary fashion of a vast world of seaweed.

Once or twice in his bewilderingly disconnected speech he had mentioned the name of his sweetheart, and now it was the memory of her name that gave me the first inkling of what might possibly prove a solution of the whole affair.

I wished now that I had encouraged his incoherent ramble of speech, instead of heading him off; but I had done so because I could not bear to have him talk as he had.

Yet, with the little I remembered, I began to shape out a theory. It seemed to me that he might be nursing some idea that had formed—goodness knows how or when—that his sweetheart (still alive) was aboard some derelict in the midst of an enormous "world," he had termed it, of seaweed.

He might have grown more explicit had I not attempted to reason with him, and so lost the rest. Yet, remembering back, it seemed to me that he must undoubtedly have meant the enormous Sargasso Sea—that great seaweed-laden ocean, vast almost as Continental Europe, and the final resting-place of the Atlantic's wreckage.

Surely, if he proposed any attempt to search through that, then there could be no doubt but that he was temporarily unbalanced. And yet I could do nothing. I was a prisoner and helpless.

IV

Eight days of variable but strongish winds passed, and still I was a prisoner in my cabin. From the ports that opened out astern and on each side—for my cabin runs right across the whole width of the stern—I was able to command a good view of the surrounding ocean, which now had commenced to be laden with great floating patches of Gulf weed—many of them hundreds and hundreds of yards in length.

And still we held on, apparently towards the nucleus of the Sargasso Sea. This I was able to assume by means of a chart which I found in one of the lockers, and the course I had been able to gather from the "tell-tale" compass let into the cabin ceiling.

And so another and another day went by, and now we were among weed so thick that at times the vessel found difficulty in forcing her way through, while the surface of the sea had assumed a curious oily appearance, though the wind was still quite strong.

It was later in the day that we encountered a bank of weed so prodigious that we had to up helm and run round it, and after that the same experience was many times repeated; and so the night found us.

The following morning found me at the ports, eagerly peering out across the water. From one of those on the starboard side I could discern at a considerable distance a huge bank of weed that seemed to be unending, and to run parallel with our broadside. It appeared to rise in places a couple of feet above the level of the surrounding sea.

For a long while I stared, then went across to the port side. Here I found that a similar bank stretched away on our port beam. It was as though we were sailing up an immense river, the low banks of which were formed of seaweed instead of land.

And so that day passed hour by hour, the weed-banks growing more definite and seeming to be nearer. Towards evening something came into sight—a far, dim hulk, the masts gone, the whole hull covered with growth, an unwholesome green, blotched with brown in the light from the dying sun.

I saw this lonesome craft from a port on the starboard side, and the sight roused a multitude of questions and thoughts.

Evidently we had penetrated into the unknown central portion of the enormous Sargasso, the Great Eddy of the Atlantic, and this was some lonely derelict, lost ages ago perhaps to the outside world.

Just at the going down of the sun, I saw another; she was nearer, and still possessed two of her masts, which stuck up bare and desolate into the darkening sky. She could not have been more than a quarter of a mile in from the edge of the weed. As we passed her I craned out my head through the port to stare at her. As I stared the dusk grew out of the abyss of the air, and she faded presently from sight into the surrounding loneliness.

Through all that night I sat at the port and watched, listening and peering; for the tremendous mystery of that inhuman weed-world was upon me.

In the air there rose no sound; even the wind was scarcely more than a low hum aloft among the sails and gear, and under me the oily water gave no rippling noise. All was silence, supreme and unearthly.

About midnight the moon rose away on our starboard beam, and from then until the dawn I stared out upon a ghostly world of noiseless weed, fantastic, silent, and unbelievable, under the moonlight.

On four separate occasions my gaze lit on black hulks that rose above the surrounding weeds—the hulks of long-lost vessels. And once, just when the strangeness of dawn was in the sky, a faint, long-drawn wailing seemed to come floating to me across the immeasurable waste of weed.

It startled my strung nerves, and I assured myself that it was the cry of some lone sea bird. Yet, my imagination reached out for some stranger explanation.

The eastward sky began to flush with the dawn, and the morning light grew subtly over the breadth of the enormous ocean of weed until it seemed tome to reach away unbroken on each beam into the grey horizons. Only astern of us, like a broad road of oil, ran the strange river-like gulf up which we had sailed.

Now I noticed that the banks of weed were nearer, very much nearer, and a disagreeable thought came to me. This vast rift that had allowed us to penetrate into the very nucleus of the Sargasso Sea—suppose it should close!

It would mean inevitably that there would be one more among the missing—another unanswered mystery of the inscrutable ocean. I resisted the thought, and came back more directly into the present.

Evidently the wind was still dropping, for we were moving slowly, as a glance at the ever-nearing weed-banks told me. The hours passed on, and my breakfast, when the steward brought it, I took to one of the ports, and there ate; for I would lose nothing of the strange surroundings into which we were so steadily plunging.

And so the morning passed.

V

It was about an hour after dinner that I observed the open channel between the weedbanks to be narrowing almost minute by minute with uncomfortable speed. I could do nothing except watch and surmise.

At times I felt convinced that the immense masses of weed were closing in upon us, but I fought off the thought with the more hopeful one that we were surely approaching some narrowing outlet of the gulf that yawned so far across the seaweed.

By the time the afternoon was half-through, the weed-banks had approached so close that occasional out-jutting masses scraped the yacht's sides in passing. It was now with the stuff below my face, within a few feet of my eyes, that I discovered the immense amount of life that stirred among all the hideous waste.

Innumerable crabs crawled among the seaweed, and once, indistinctly, something stirred among the depths of a large outlying tuft of weed. What it was I could not tell, though afterwards I had an idea; but all I saw was something dark and glistening. We were past it before I could see more.

The steward was in the act of bringing in my tea, when from above there came a noise of shouting, and almost immediately a slight jolt. The man put down the tray he was carrying, and glanced at me, with startled expression.

"What is it, Jones?" I questioned.

"I don't know sir. I expect it's the weed," he replied. I ran to the port, craned out my head, and looked forward. Our bow seemed to be embedded in a mass of weeds, and as I watched it came further aft.

Within the next five minutes we had driven through it into a circle of sea that was free from the weed. Across this we seemed to drift, rather than sail, so slow was our speed.

Upon its opposite margin we brought up the vessel swinging broadside on to the weed, being secured thus with a couple of kedges cast from the bows and stern, though of this I was not aware until later. As we swung, and at last I was able from my port to see ahead, I saw a thing that amazed me.

There, not three hundred feet distant across the quaking weed, a vessel lay embedded. She had been a three-master; but of these only the mizzen was standing. For perhaps a minute I stared, scarcely breathing in my exceeding interest.

All around above her bulwarks to the height of apparently some ten feet, ran a sort of fencing formed, so far as I could make out, from canvas, rope, and spars. Even as I wondered at the use of such a thing, I heard my chum's voice overhead. He was hailing her:

"*Graiken*, ahoy!" he shouted. "*Graiken*, ahoy!"

At that I fairly jumped. *Graiken*! What could he mean! I stared out of the port. The blaze of the sinking sun flashed redly upon her stern, and showed the lettering of her name and port; yet the distance was too great for me to read.

I ran across to my table to see if there were a pair of binoculars in the drawers. I found one in the first! opened; then I ran back to the port, racking them out as I went. I reached it, and clapped them to my eyes. Yes; I saw it plainly, her name *Graiken* and her port London.

From her name my gaze moved to that strange fencing about her. There was a movement in the aft part. As I watched a portion of it slid to one side, and a man's head and shoulders appeared.

I nearly yelled with the excitement of that moment. I could scarcely believe the thing I saw. The man waved an arm, and a vague hail reached us across the weed, then he disappeared. A moment later a score of people crowded the opening, and among them I made out distinctly the face and figure of a girl.

"He was right, after all!" I heard myself saying out loud in a voice that was toneless through very amazement.

In a minute, I was at the door, beating it with my fists. "Let me out, Ned! Let me out!" I shouted.

I felt that I could forgive him all the indignity that I had suffered. Nay, more; in a queer way I had a feeling that it was I who needed to ask him for forgiveness. All my bitterness had gone, and I wanted only to be out and give a hand in the rescue.

Yet though I shouted, no one came, so that at last I returned quickly to the port, to see what further developments there were.

Across the weed I now saw that one man had his hands up to his mouth shouting. His voice reached me only as a faint, hoarse cry; the distance was too great for anyone aboard the yacht to distinguish its import.

From the derelict my attention was drawn abruptly to a scene alongside. A plank was thrown down on to the weed, and the next moment I saw my chum swing himself down the side and leap upon it.

I had opened my mouth to call out to him that I would forgive all were I but freed to lend a hand in this unbelievable rescue.

But even as the words formed they died, for though the weed appeared so dense, it was evidently incapable of bearing any considerable weight, and the plank, with Barlow upon it, sank down into the weed almost to his waist.

He turned and grabbed at the rope with both hands, and in the same moment he gave a loud cry of sheer terror, and commenced to scramble up the yacht's side.

As his feet drew clear of the weed I gave a short cry. Something was curled about his left ankle—something oily, supple and tapered. As I stared another rose up out from the weed and swayed through the air, made a grab at his leg, missed and appeared to wave aimlessly. Others came towards him as he struggled upwards.

Then I saw hands reach down from above and seize Barlow beneath the arms. They lifted him by main force, and with a mass of weed that enfolded something leathery, from which numbers of curling arms writhed.

A hand slashed down with a sheath-knife, and the next instant the hideous thing had fallen back among the weed.

For a couple of seconds longer I remained, my head twisted upwards; then faces appeared once more over our rail, and I saw the men extending arms and fingers, pointing. From above me there rose a hoarse chorus of fear and wonder, and I turned my head swiftly to glance down and across that treacherous extraordinary weed-world.

The whole of the hitherto silent surface was all of a move in one stupendous undulation—as though life had come to all that desolation.

The undulatory movement continued, and abruptly, in a hundred places, the seaweed was tossed up into sudden billowy hicks. From these burst mighty arms, and in an instant the evening air was full of them, hundreds and hundreds, coming toward the yacht.

"Devil-fishes!" shouted a man's voice from the deck. "Octopuses! My Gord!" Then I caught my chum shouting.

"Cut the mooring ropes!" he yelled.

This must have been done almost on the instant, for immediately there showed between us and the nearest weed a broadening gap of scummy water.

"Haul away, lads!" I heard Barlow shouting; and the same instant I caught the splash, splash of something in the water on our port side. I rushed across and looked out. I found that a rope had been carried across to the opposite seaweed, and that the men were now warping us rapidly from those invading horrors.

I raced back to the starboard port, and, lo! as though by magic, there stretched between us and the *Graiken* only the silent stretch of demure weed and some fifty feet of water. It seemed inconceivable that it was a covering to so much terror.

And then speedily the night was upon us, hiding all; but from the decks above there commenced a sound of hammering that continued long throughout the night—long after I, weary with my previous night's vigil, had passed into a fitful slumber, broken anon by that hammering above.

VI

"Your breakfast, sir," came respectfully enough in the steward's voice; and I woke with a start. Overhead, there still sounded that persistent hammering, and I turned to the steward for an explanation.

"I don't exactly know, sir," was his reply. "It's something the carpenter's doing to one of the lifeboats." And then he left me.

I ate my breakfast standing at the port, staring at the distant *Graiken*. The weed was perfectly quiet, and we were lying about the centre of the little lake.

As I watched the derelict, it seemed to me that I saw a movement about her side, and I reached for the glasses. Adjusting them, I made out that there were several of the cuttlefish attached to her in different parts, their arms spread out almost starwise across the lower portions of her hull.

Occasionally a feeler would detached itself and wave aimlessly. This it was that had drawn my attention. The sight of these creatures, in conjunction with that extraordinary scene the previous evening, enabled me to guess the use of the great screen running about the *Graiken*. It had obviously been erected as a protection against the vile inhabitants of that strange weed-world.

From that my thoughts passed to the problem of reaching and rescuing the crew of the derelict. I could by no means conceive how this was to be effected.

As I stood pondering, whilst I ate, I caught the voices of men chaunteying on deck. For a while this continued; then came Barlow's voice shouting orders, and almost immediately a splash in the water on the starboard side.

I poked my head out through the port, and stared. They had got one of the lifeboats into the water. To the gunnel of the boat they had added a superstructure ending in a roof, the whole somewhat resembling a gigantic dog-kennel.

From under the two sharp ends of the boat rose a couple of planks at an angle or thirty degrees. These appeared to be firmly bolted to the boat and the superstructure. I guessed that their purpose was to enable the boat to over-ride the seaweed, instead of ploughing into it and getting fast.

In the stern of the boat was fixed a strong ringbolt, into which was spliced the end of a coil of one-inch manilla rope. Along the sides of the boat, and high above the gunnel, the superstructure was pierced with holes for oars. In one side of the roof was placed a trapdoor. The idea struck me as wonderfully ingenious, and a very probable solution of the difficulty of rescuing the crew of the *Graiken*.

A few minutes later one of the men threw over a rope on to the roof of the boat. He opened the trap, and lowered himself into the interior. I noticed that he was armed with one of the yacht's cutlasses and a revolver.

It was evident that my chum fully appreciated the difficulties that were to be overcome. In a few seconds the man was followed by four others of the crew, similarly armed; and then Barlow.

Seeing him, I craned my head as far as possible, and sang out to him. "Ned! Ned, old man!" I shouted. "Let me come along with you!"

He appeared never to have heard me. I noticed his face, just before he shut down the trap above him. The expression was fixed and peculiar. It had the uncomfortable remoteness of a sleepwalker.

"Confound it!" I muttered, and after that I said nothing; for it hurt my dignity to supplicate before the men.

From the interior of the boat I heard Barlow's voice, muffled. Immediately four oars were passed out through the holes in the sides, while from slots in the front and rear of the superstructure were thrust a couple of oars with wooden chocks nailed to the blades.

These, I guessed, were intended to assist in steering the boat, that in the bow being primarily for pressing down the weed before the boat, so as to allow her to surmount it the more easily.

Another muffled order came from the interior of the queer-looking craft, and immediately the four oars dipped, and the boat shot towards the weed, the rope trailing out astern as it was paid out from the deck above me.

The board-assisted bow of the lifeboat took the weed with a sort of squashy surge, rose up, and the whole craft appeared to leap from the water down in among the quaking mass.

I saw now the reason why the oar-holes had been placed so high. For of the boat itself nothing could be seen, only the upper portion of the superstructure wallowing amid the weed. Had the holes been lower, there would have been no handling the oars.

I settled myself to watch. There was the probability of a prodigious spectacle, and as I could not help, I would, at least, use my eyes.

Five minutes passed, during which nothing happened, and the boat made slow progress towards the derelict. She had accomplished perhaps some twenty or thirty yards, when suddenly from the *Graiken* there reached my ears a hoarse shout.

My glance leapt from the boat to the derelict. I saw that the people aboard had the sliding part of the screen to one side, and were waving their arms frantically, as though motioning the boat back.

Amongst them I could see the girlish figure that had attracted my attention the previous evening. For a moment I stared, then my gaze travelled back to the boat. All was quiet.

The boat had now covered a quarter of the distance, and I began to persuade myself that she would get across without being attacked.

Then, as I gazed anxiously, from a point in the weed a little ahead of the boat there came a sudden quaking ripple that shivered through the weed in a sort of queer tremor. The next instant, like a shot from a gun, a huge mass drove up clear through the tangled weed, hurling it in all directions, and almost capsizing the boat.

The creature had driven up rear foremost. It fell back with a mighty splash, and in the same moment its monstrous arms were reached out to the boat. They grasped it, enfolding themselves about it horribly. It was apparently attempting to drag the boat under.

From the boat came a regular volley of revolver shots. Yet, though the brute writhed, it did not relinquish its hold. The shots closed, and I saw the dull flash of cutlass blades. The men were attempting to hack at the thing through the oar holes, but evidently with little effect.

All at once the enormous creature seemed to make an effort to overturn the boat. I saw the half-submerged boat go over to one side, until it seemed to me that nothing could right it, and at the sight I went mad with excitement to help them.

I pulled my head in from the port, and glanced round the cabin. I wanted to break down the door, but there was nothing with which to do this.

Then my sight fell on my bunkboard, which fitted into a sliding groove. It was made of teak wood, and very solid and heavy. I lifted it out, and charged the door with the end of it.

The panels split from top to bottom, for I am a heavy man. Again I struck, and drove the two portions of the door apart. I hove down the bunk-board, and rushed through.

There was no one on guard; evidently they had gone on deck to view the rescue. The gunroom door was to my right, and I had the key in my pocket.

In an instant, I had it open, and was lifting down from its rack a heavy elephant gun. Seizing a box of cartridges, I tore off the lid, and emptied the lot into my pocket; then I leapt up the companion-way on the deck.

The steward was standing near. He turned at my step; his face was white and he took a couple of paces towards me doubtfully.

"They're—they're—" he began; but I never let him finish.

"Get out of my way!" I roared, and swept him to one side. I ran forward. "Haul in on that rope!" I shouted. "Tail on to it! Are you going to stand there like a lot of owls and see them drown!"

The men only wanted a leader to show them what to do, and, without showing any thought of insubordination, they tacked on to the rope that was fastened to the stern of the boat, and hauled her back across the weed—cuttle-fish and all.

The strain on the rope had thrown her on an even keel again, so that she took the water safely, though that foul thing was straddled all across her.

"Vast hauling!" I shouted. "Get the doc's cleavers, some of you—anything that'll cut!"

"This is the sort, sir!" cried the bo'sun; from somewhere he had got hold of a formidable double-bladed whale lance.

The boat, still under the impetus given by our pull, struck the side of the yacht immediately beneath where I was waiting with the gun. Astern of it towed the body of the monster, its two eyes—monstrous orbs of the Profound—staring out vilely from behind its arms.

I leant my elbows on the rail, and aimed full at the right eye. As I pulled on the trigger one of the great arms detached itself from the boat, and swirled up towards me. There was a thunderous bang as the heavy charge drove its way through that vast eye, and at the same instant something swept over my head.

There came a cry from behind: "Lookout, sir!" A flame of steel before my eyes, and a truncated something fell upon my shoulder, and thence to the deck.

Down below, the water was being churned to a froth, and three more arms sprang into the air, and then down among us.

One grasped the bo'sun, lifting him like a child. Two cleavers gleamed, and he fell to the deck from a height of some twelve feet, along with the severed portion of the limb.

I had my weapons reloaded again by now, and ran forward along the deck somewhat, to be clear of the flying arms that flailed on the rails and deck.

I fired again into the hulk of the brute, and then again. At the second shot, the murderous din of the creature ceased, and, with an ineffectual flicker of its remaining tentacles, it sank out of sight beneath the water.

A minute later we had the hatch in the roof of the superstructure open, and the men out, my chum coming last. They had been mightily shaken, but otherwise were none the worse.

As Barlow came over the gangway, I stepped up to him and gripped his shoulder. I was strangely muddled in my feelings. I felt that I had no sure position aboard my own yacht. Yet all I said was:

"Thank God, you're safe, old man!" And I meant it from my heart. He looked at me in a doubtful, puzzled sort of manner, and passed his hand across his forehead.

"Yes," he replied; but his voice was strangely toneless, save that some puzzledness seemed to have crept into it. For a couple of moments he stared at me in an unseeing way, and once more I was struck by the immobile, tensed-up expression of his features.

Immediately afterwards he turned away—having shown neither friendliness nor enmity—and commenced to clamber back over the side into the boat.

"Come up, Ned!" I cried. "It's no good. You'll never manage it that way. Look!" and I stretched out my arm, pointing. Instead of looking, he passed his hand once more across his forehead, with that gesture of puzzled doubt. Then, to my relief, he caught at the rope ladder, and commenced to make his way slowly up the side.

Reaching the deck, he stood for nearly a minute without saying a word, his back turned to the derelict. Then, still wordless, he walked slowly across to the opposite side, and leant his elbows upon the rail, as though looking back along the way the yacht had come.

For my part, I said nothing, dividing my attention between him and the men, with occasional glances at the quaking weed and the—apparently—hopelessly surrounded *Graiken*.

The men were quiet, occasionally turning towards Barlow, as though for some further order. Of me they appeared to take little notice. In this wise, perhaps a quarter of an hour went by; then abruptly Barlow stood upright, waving his arms and shouting:

"It comes! It comes!" He turned towards us, and his face seemed transfigured, his eyes gleaming almost maniacally.

I ran across the deck to his side, and looked away to port, and now I saw what it was that had excited him. The weed-barrier through which we had come on our inward journey was divided, a slowly broadening river of oil water showing clean across it.

Even as I watched it grew broader, the immense masses of weed being moved by some unseen impulsion.

I was still staring, amazed, when a sudden cry went up from some of the men to starboard. Turning quickly, I saw that the yawning movement was being continued to the mass of weed that lay between us and the *Graiken*.

Slowly, the weed was divided, surely as though an invisible wedge were being driven through it. The gulf of weed-clear water reached the derelict, and passed beyond. And now there was no longer anything to stop our rescue of the crew of the derelict.

VII

It was Barlow's voice that gave the order for the mooring ropes to be castoff, and then, as the light wind was right against us, a boat was out ahead, and the yacht was towed towards the ship, whilst a dozen of the men stood ready with their rifles on the fo'c's'le head.

As we drew nearer, I began to distinguish the features of the crew, the men strangely grizzled and old looking. And among them, white-faced with emotion, was my chum's lost sweetheart. I never expect to know a more extraordinary moment.

I looked at Barlow; he was staring at the white-faced girl with an extraordinary fixidity of expression that was scarcely the look of a sane man.

The next minute we were alongside, crushing to a pulp between our steel sides one of those remaining monsters of the deep that had continued to cling steadfastly to the *Graiken.*

Yet of that I was scarcely aware, for I had turned again to look at Ned Barlow. He was swaying slowly to his feet, and just as the two vessels closed he reached up both hands to his head, and fell like a log.

Brandy was brought, and later Barlow carried to his cabin; yet we had won clear of that hideous weed-world before he recovered consciousness.

During his illness I learned from his sweetheart how, on a terrible night a long year previously, the *Graiken* had been caught in a tremendous storm and dismasted, and how, helpless and driven by the gale, they at last found themselves surrounded by the great banks of floating weed, and finally held fast in the remorseless grip of the dread Sargasso.

She told me of their attempts to free the ship from the weed, and of the attacks of the cuttlefish. And later of various other matters; for all of which I have no room in this story.

In return I told her of our voyage, and her lover's strange behaviour. How he had wanted to undertake the navigation of the yacht, and had talked of a great world of weed. How I had— believing him unhinged—refused to listen to him.

How he had taken matters into his own hands, without which she would most certainly have ended her days surrounded by the quaking weed and those great beasts of the deep waters.

She listened with an ever-growing seriousness, so that I had, time and again, to assure her that I bore my old chum no ill, but

CETUS INSOLITUS

rather held myself to be in the wrong. At which she shook her head, but seemed mightily relieved.

It was during Barlow's recovery that I made the astonishing discovery that he remembered no detail of his imprisoning of me.

I am convinced now that for days and weeks he must have lived in a sort of dream in a hyper state, in which I can only imagine that he had possibly been sensitive to more subtle understandings than normal bodily and mental health allows.

One other thing there is in closing. I found that the captain and the two mates had been confined to their cabins by Barlow. The captain was suffering from a pistol-shot in the arm, due to his having attempted to resist Barlow's assumption of authority.

When I released him he vowed vengeance. Yet Ned Barlow being my chum, I found means to slake both the captain's and the two mates' thirst for vengeance, and the slaking thereof is—well, another story.

FROM THE DARKNESS AND THE DEPTHS
Morgan Robertson

I had known him for a painter of renown—a master of his art, whose pictures, which sold for high prices, adorned museums, the parlors of the rich, and, when on exhibition, were hung low and conspicuous. Also, I knew him for an expert photographer—an "art photographer," as they say, one who dealt with this branch of industry as a fad, an amusement, and who produced pictures that in composition, lights, and shades rivaled his productions with the brush.

His cameras were the best that the market could supply, yet he was able, from his knowledge of optics and chemistry, to improve them for his own uses far beyond the ability of the makers. His studio was filled with examples of his work, and his mind was stocked with information and opinions on all subjects ranging from international policies to the servant-girl problem.

He was a man of the world, gentlemanly and successful, about sixty years old, kindly and gracious of manner, and out of this kindliness and graciousness had granted me the compliment of his friendship, and access to his studio whenever I felt like calling upon him.

Yet it never occurred to me that the wonderful and technically correct marines hanging on his walls were due to anything but the artist's conscientious study of his subject, and only his casual mispronounciation of the word "leeward," which landsmen pronounce as spelled, but which rolls off the tongue of a sailor, be he former dock rat or naval officer, as "looward," and his giving the long sounds to the vowels of the words "patent" and "tackle," that induced me to ask if he had ever been to sea.

265

3

66   CETUS INSOLITUS

"Why, yes," he answered. "Until I was thirty I had no higher
ambition than to become a skipper of some craft; but I never
achieved it. The best I did was to sign first mate for one voyage—
and that one was my last. It was on that voyage that I learned something of the mysterious properties of light, and it made me a photographer, then an artist. You are wrong when you say that a search-
light cannot penetrate fog."

"But it has been tried," I remonstrated.

"With ordinary light. Yes, of course, subject to refraction, reflection, and absorption by the millions of minute globules of water it
encounters."

We had been discussing the wreck of the *Titanic*, the most terrible marine disaster of history, the blunders of construction and
management, and the later proposed improvements as to the lowering of boats and the location of ice in a fog.

Among these considerations was also the plan of carrying a
powerful searchlight whose beam would illumine the path of a
twenty-knot liner and render objects visible in time to avoid them.
In regard to this I had contended that a searchlight could not penetrate fog, and if it could, would do as much harm as good by blinding and confusing the watch officers and lookouts on other craft.

"But what other kind of light can be used?" I asked, in answer
to his mention of ordinary light.

"Invisible light," he answered. "I do not mean the Röntgen ray,
nor the emanation from radium, both of which are invisible, but
neither of which is light, in that neither can be reflected nor re-
fracted. Both will penetrate many different kinds of matter, but it
needs reflection or refraction to make visible an object on which it
impinges. Understand?"

"Hardly," I answered dubiously. "What kind of visible light is
there, if not radium or the Röntgen ray? You can photograph with
either, can't you?"

"Yes, but to see what you have photographed you must develop
the film. And there is no time for that aboard a fast steamer running through the ice and the fog. No, it is mere theory, but I have
an idea that the ultraviolet light—the actinic rays beyond the vio-
let end of the spectrum, you know—will penetrate fog to a great

distance, and in spite of its higher refractive power, which would distort and magnify an object, it is better than nothing."

"But what makes you think that it will penetrate fog?" I queried. "And if it is invisible itself, how will it illumine an object?"

"As to your first question," he answered, with a smile, "it is well known to surgeons that ultraviolet light will penetrate the human body to the depth of an inch, while the visible rays are reflected at the surface. And it has been known to photographers for fifty years that this light—easily isolated by dispersion through prisms—will act on a sensitized plate in an utterly dark room."

"Granted," I said. "But how about the second question? How can you see by this light?"

"There you have me," he answered. "It will need a quicker development than any now known to photography—a traveling film, for instance, that will show the picture of an iceberg or a ship before it is too late to avoid it—a traveling film sensitized by a quicker acting chemical than any now used."

"Why not puzzle it out?" I asked. "It would be a wonderful invention."

"I am too old," he answered dreamily. "My life work is about done. But other and younger men will take it up. We have made great strides in optics. The moving picture is a fact. Colored photographs are possible. The ultraviolet microscope shows us objects hitherto invisible because smaller than the wave length of visible light. We shall ultimately use this light to see through opaque objects. We shall see colors never imagined by the human mind, but which have existed since the beginning of light.

"We shall see new hues in the sunset, in the rainbow, in the flowers and foliage of forest and field. We may possibly see creatures in the air above never seen before.

"We shall certainly see creatures from the depths of the sea, where visible light cannot reach—creatures whose substance is of such a nature that it will not respond to the light it has never been exposed to—a substance which is absolutely transparent because it will not absorb, and appear black; will not reflect, and show a color of some kind; and will not refract, and distort objects seen through it."

"What!" I exclaimed. "Do you think there are invisible creatures?"

He looked gravely at me for a moment, then said: "You know that there are sounds that are inaudible to the human ear because of their too rapid vibration, others that are audible to some, but not to all. There are men who cannot hear the chirp of a cricket, the tweet of a bird, or the creaking of a wagon wheel.

"You know that there are electric currents much stronger in voltage than is necessary to kill us, but of wave frequency so rapid that the human tissue will not respond, and we can receive such currents without a shock. And I know"—he spoke with vehemence—"that there are creatures in the deep sea of color invisible to the human eye, for I have not only felt such a creature, but seen its photograph taken by the ultraviolet light."

"Tell me," I asked breathlessly. "Creatures solid, but invisible?"

"Creatures solid, and invisible because absolutely transparent. It is long since I have told the yarn. People would not believe me, and it was so horrible an experience that I have tried to forget it. However, if you care for it, and are willing to lose your sleep tonight, I'll give it to you."

He reached for a pipe, filled it, and began to smoke; and as he smoked and talked, some of the glamor and polish of the successful artist and clubman left him. He was an old sailor, spinning a yarn.

"It was about thirty years ago," he began, "or, to be explicit, twenty-nine years this coming August, at the time of the great Java earthquake. You've heard of it—how it killed seventy thousand people, thirty thousand of whom were drowned by the tidal wave.

"It was a curious phenomenon; Krakatoa Island, a huge conical mountain rising from the bottom of Sunda Strait, went out of existence, while in Java a mountain chain was leveled, and up from the bowels of the earth came an iceberg—as you might call it—that floated a hundred miles on a stream of molten lava before melting.

"I was not there; I was two hundred miles to the sou'west, first mate of one of those old-fashioned, soft-pine, centerboard barkentines—three sticks the same length, you know—with the mainmast stepped on the port side of the keel to make room for the centerboard—a craft that would neither stay, nor wear, nor scud, nor heave to, like a decent vessel.

"But she had several advantages; she was new, and well painted, deck, top-sides, and bottom. Hence her light timbers and planking were not water-soaked. She was fastened with 'trunnels,' not spikes and bolts, and hemp rigged.

"Perhaps there was not a hundredweight of iron aboard of her, while her hemp rigging, though heavier than water, was lighter than wire rope, and so, when we were hit by the back wash of that tidal wave, we did not sink, even though butts were started from one end to the other of the flimsy hull, and all hatches were ripped off.

"I have called it the back wash, yet we may have had a tidal wave of our own; for, though we had no knowledge of the frightful catastrophe at Java, still there had been for days several submarine earthquakes all about us, sending fountains of water, steam bubbles, and mud from the sea bed into the air.

"As the soundings were over two thousand fathoms in that neighborhood, you can imagine the seismic forces at work beneath us. There had been no wind for days, and no sea, except the agitation caused by the upheavals. The sky was a dull mud color, and the sun looked like nothing but a dark, red ball, rising day by day in the east, to move overhead and set in the west. The air was hot, sultry, and stifling, and I had difficulty in keeping the men—a big crew—at work.

"The conditions would try anybody's temper, and I had my own troubles. There was a passenger on board, a big, fat, highly educated German—a scientist and explorer—whom we had taken aboard at some little town on the West Australian coast, and who was to leave us at Batavia, where he could catch a steamer for Germany.

"He had a whole laboratory with him, with scientific instruments that I didn't know the names of, with maps he had made, stuffed beasts and birds he had killed, and a few live ones which he kept in cages and attended to himself in the empty hold; for we were flying light, you know, without even ballast aboard, and bound to Batavia for a cargo.

"It was after a few eruptions from the bottom of the sea that he got to be a nuisance; he was keenly interested in the strange dead fish and nondescript creatures that had been thrown up. He declared them new, unknown to science, and wore out my patience with entreaties to haul them aboard for examination and classification.

"I obliged him for a time, until the decks stank with dead fish, and the men got mutinous. Then I refused to advance the interests of science any farther, and, in spite of his excitement and pleadings, refused to litter the decks any more. But he got all he wanted of the unclassified and unknown before long.

"Tidal wave, you know, is a name we give to any big wave, and it has no necessary connection with the tides. It may be the big third wave of a series—just a little bigger than usual; it may be the ninth, tenth, and eleventh waves merged into one huge comber by uneven wind pressure; it may be the back wash from an earthquake that depresses the nearest coast, and it may be—as I think it was in our case—a wave sent out by an upheaval from the sea bed. At any rate, we got it, and we got it just after a tremendous spouting of water and mud, and a thick cloud of steam on the northern horizon.

"We saw a seeming rise to the horizon, as though caused by refraction, but which soon eliminated refraction as a cause by its becoming visible in its details—its streaks of water and mud, its irregular upper edge, the occasional combers that appeared on this edge, and the terrific speed of its approach. It was a wave, nothing else, and coming at forty knots at least.

"There was little that we could do; there was no wind, and we headed about west, showing our broadside; yet I got the men at the downhauls, clewlines, and stripping lines of the lighter kites; but before a man could leave the deck to furl, that moving mountain hit us, and buried us on our beam ends just as I had time to sing out: 'Lash yourselves, every man.'

"Then I needed to think of my own safety and passed a turn of the mizzen gaff-topsail downhaul about me, belaying to a pin as the cataclysm hit us. For the next two minutes—although it seemed an hour, I did not speak, nor breathe, nor think, unless my instinctive grip on the turns of the downhaul on the pin may have been an index of thought. I was under water; there was roaring in my ears, pain in my lungs, and terror in my heart.

"Then there came a lessening of the turmoil, a momentary quiet, and I roused up, to find the craft floating on her side, about a third out of water, but apt to turn bottom up at any moment from the weight of the water-soaked gear and canvas, which will sink, you know, when wet.

"I was hanging in my bight of rope from a belaying pin, my feet clear of the perpendicular deck, and my ears tortured by the sound of men overboard crying for help—men who had not lashed themselves. Among them I knew was the skipper, a mild-mannered little fellow, and the second mate, an incompetent tough from Portsmouth, who had caused me lots of trouble by his abuse of the men and his depending upon me to stand by him.

"Nothing could be done for them; they were adrift on the back wall of a moving mountain that towered thirty degrees above the horizon to port; and another moving mountain, as big as the first, was coming on from starboard—caused by the tumble into the sea of the uplifted water.

"Did you ever fall overboard in a full suit of clothes? If you did, you know the mighty exercise of strength required to climb out. I was a strong, healthy man at the time, but never in my life was I so tested. I finally got a grip on the belaying pin and rested; then, with an effort that caused me physical pain, I got my right foot up to the pinrail and rested again; then, perhaps more by mental strength than physical—for I loved life and wanted to live—I hooked my right foot over the rail, reached higher on the rope, rested again, and finally hove myself up to the mizzen rigging, where I sat for a few moments to get my breath, and think, and look around.

"Forward, I saw men who had lashed themselves to the starboard rail, and they were struggling, as I had struggled, to get up to the horizontal side of the vessel. They succeeded, but at the time I had no use for them. Sailors will obey orders, if they understand the orders, but this was an exigency outside the realm of mere seamanship.

"Men were drowning off to port; men, like myself, were climbing up to temporary safety afforded by the topsides of a craft on

her beam ends; and aft, in the alleyway, was the German professor, unlashed, but safe and secure in his narrow confines, one leg
through a cabin window, and both hands gripping the rail, while
he bellowed like a bull, not for himself, however—but for his menagerie in the empty hold.

"There was small chance for the brutes—smaller than for ourselves, left on the upper rail of an over-turned craft, and still
smaller than the chance of the poor devils off to port, some of whom
had gripped the half-submerged top-hamper, and were calling for
help.

"We could not help them; she was a Yankee craft, and there
was not a life buoy or belt on board; and who, with another big
wave coming, would swim down to looward with a line?

"Landsmen, especially women and boys, have often asked me
why a wooden ship, filled with water, sinks, even though not
weighted with cargo. Some sailors have pondered over it, too,
knowing that a small boat, built of wood, and fastened with nails,
will float if water-logged.

"But the answer is simple. Most big craft are built of oak or
hard pine, and fastened together with iron spikes and bolts—sixty
tons at least to a three-hundred-ton schooner. After a year or two
this hard, heavy wood becomes water-soaked, and, with the iron
bolts and spikes, is heavier than water, and will sink when the hold
is flooded.

"This craft of ours was like a small boat—built of soft light wood,
with trunnels instead of bolts, and no iron on board except the
anchors and one capstan. As a result, though ripped, twisted, broken, and disintegrated, she still floated even on her beam ends.

"But the soaked hemp rigging and canvas might be enough to
drag the craft down, and with this fear in my mind I acted quickly.
Singing out to the men to hang on, I made my way aft to where we had
an ax, lodged in its beckets on the after house. With this I attacked
the mizzen lanyards, cutting everything clear, then climbed forward to the main.

"Hard as I worked I had barely cut the last lanyard when that
second wave loomed up and crashed down on us. I just had time to
slip into the bight of a rope, and save myself; but I had to give up

the ax; it slipped from my hands and slid down to the port scuppers.

"That second wave, in its effect, was about the same as the first, except that it righted the craft. We were buried, choked, and half drowned; but when the wave had passed on, the main and mizzen-masts, unsupported by the rigging that I had cut away, snapped cleanly about three feet above the deck, and the broad, flat-bottomed craft straightened up, lifting the weight of the foremast and its gear, and lay on an even keel, with foresail, staysail, and jib set, the fore gaff-topsail, flying jib, and jib-topsail clewed down and the wreck of the masts bumping against the port side.

"We floated, but with the hold full of water, and four feet of it on deck amidships that surged from one rail to the other as the craft rolled, pouring over and coming back. All hatches were ripped off, and our three boats were carried away from their chocks on the house.

"Six men were clearing themselves from their lashings at the fore rigging, and three more, who had gone overboard with the first sea, and had caught the upper gear to be lifted as the craft righted, were coming down, while the professor still declaimed from the alley.

"'Hang on all,' I yelled; 'there's another sea coming.'

"It came, but passed over us without doing any more damage, and though a fourth, fifth, and sixth followed, each was of lesser force than the last, and finally it was safe to leave the rail and wade about, though we still rolled rails under in what was left of the turmoil.

"Luckily, there was no wind, though I never understood why, for earthquakes are usually accompanied by squalls. However, even with wind, our canvas would have been no use to us; for, water-logged as we were, we couldn't have made a knot an hour, nor could we have steered, even with all sail set. All we could hope for was the appearance of some craft that would tow the ripped and shivered hull to port, or at least take us off.

"So, while I searched for the ax, and the professor searched into the depths under the main hatch for signs of his menagerie—all drowned, surely—the remnant of the crew lowered the foresail and jibs, stowing them as best they could.

"I found the ax, and found it just in time; for I was attacked by what could have been nothing but a small-sized sea serpent, that had been hove up to the surface and washed aboard us. It was only about six feet long, but it had a mouth like a bulldog, and a row of spikes along its back that could have sawed a man's leg off.

"I managed to kill it before it harmed me, and chucked it overboard against the protests of the professor, who averred that I took no interest in science.

"'No, I don't,' I said to him. 'I've other things to think of. And you, too. You'd better go below and clean up your instruments, or you'll find them ruined by salt water.'

"He looked sorrowfully and reproachfully at me, and started to wade aft; but he halted at the forward companion, and turned, for a scream of agony rang out from the forecastle deck, where the men were coming in from the jibs, and I saw one of them writhing on his back, apparently in a fit, while the others stood wonderingly around.

"The forecastle deck was just out of water, and there was no wash; but in spite of this, the wriggling, screaming man slid headfirst along the break and plunged into the water on the main deck.

"I scrambled forward, still carrying the ax, and the men tumbled down into the water after the man; but we could not get near him. We could see him under water, feebly moving, but not swimming; and yet he shot this way and that faster than a man ever swam; and once, as he passed near me, I noticed a gaping wound in his neck, from which the blood was flowing in a stream—a stream like a current, which did not mix with the water and discolor it.

"Soon his movements ceased, and I waded toward him; but he shot swiftly away from me, and I did not follow, for something cold, slimy, and firm touched my hand—something in the water, but which I could not see.

"I floundered back, still holding the ax, and sang out to the men to keep away from the dead man; for he was surely dead by now. He lay close to the break of the topgallant forecastle, on the starboard side; and as the men mustered around me I gave one my ax, told the rest to secure others, and to chop away the useless wreck pounding our port side—useless because it was past all seamanship to patch up that basketlike hull, pump it out, and raise jury rigging.

"While they were doing it, I secured a long pike pole from its beckets, and, joined by the professor, cautiously approached the body prodding ahead of me.

"As I neared the dead man, the pike pole was suddenly torn from my grasp, one end sank to the deck, while the other raised above the water; then it slid upward, fell, and floated close to me. I seized it again and turned to the professor.

"'What do you make of this, Herr Smidt?' I asked. 'There is something down there that we cannot see—something that killed that man. See the blood?'

"He peered closely at the dead man, who looked curiously distorted and shrunken, four feet under water. But the blood no longer was a thin stream issuing from his neck; it was gathered into a misshapen mass about two feet away from his neck.

"'Nonsense,' he answered. 'Something alive which we cannot see is contrary to all laws of physics. Der man must have fallen und hurt himself, which accounts for der bleeding. Den he drowned in der water. Do you see?—mine Gott! What iss?'

"He suddenly went under water himself, and dropping the pike pole, I grabbed him by the collar and braced myself. Something was pulling him away from me, but I managed to get his head out, and he spluttered:

"'Help! Holdt on to me. Something haf my right foot.'

"'Lend a hand here,' I yelled to the men, and a few joined me, grabbing him by his clothing. Together we pulled against the invisible force, and finally all of us went backward, professor and all, nearly to drown ourselves before regaining our feet. Then, as the agitated water smoothed, I distinctly saw the mass of red move slowly forward and disappear in the darkness under the forecastle deck.

"'You were right, mine friend,' said the professor, who, in spite of his experience, held his nerve. 'Dere is something invisible in der water—something dangerous, something which violates all laws of physics und optics. Oh, mine foot, how it hurts!'

"'Get aft,' I answered, 'and find out what ails it. And you fellows,' I added to the men, 'keep away from the forecastle deck. Whatever it is, it has gone under it.'

"Then I grabbed the pike pole again, cautiously hooked the barb into the dead man's clothing, and, assisted by the men, pulled him aft to the poop, where the professor had preceded, and was examining his ankle. There was a big, red wale around it, in the middle of which was a huge blood blister. He pricked it with his knife, then rearranged his stocking and joined us as we lifted the body.

"'Great God, sir!' exclaimed big Bill, the bosun. 'Is that Frank? I wouldn't know him.'

"Frank, the dead man, had been strong, robust, and full-blooded. But he bore no resemblance to his living self. He lay there, shrunken, shortened, and changed, a look of agony on his emaciated face, and his hands clenched—not extended like those of one drowned.

"'I thought drowned men swelled up,' ventured one of the men.

"'He was not drowned,' said Herr Smidt. 'He was sucked dry, like a lemon. Perhaps in his whole body there is not an ounce of blood, nor lymph, nor fluid of any kind.'

"I secured an iron belaying pin, tucked it inside his shirt, and we hove him overboard at once; for, in the presence of this horror, we were not in the mood for a burial service. There we were, eleven men on a water-logged hulk, adrift on a heaving, greasy sea, with a dark-red sun showing through a muddy sky above, and an invisible thing forward that might seize any of us at any moment it chose, in the water or out; for Frank had been caught and dragged down.

"Still, I ordered the men, cook, steward, and all, to remain on the poop and—the galley being forward—to expect no hot meals, as we could subsist for a time on the cold, canned food in the storeroom and lazaret.

"Because of an early friction between the men and the second mate, the mild-mannered and peace-loving skipper had forbidden the crew to wear sheath knives; but in this exigency I overruled the edict. While the professor went down into his flooded room to doctor his ankle and attend to his instruments, I raided the slop chest, and armed every man of us with a sheath knife and belt; for while we could not see the creature, we could feel it—and a knife is better than a gun in a hand-to-hand fight.

"Then we sat around, waiting, while the sky grew muddier, the sun darker, and the northern horizon lighter with a reddish glow that was better than the sun. It was the Java earthquake, but we did not know it for a long time.

"Soon the professor appeared and announced that his instruments were in good condition, and stowed high on shelves above the water.

"'I must resensitize my plates, however,' he said. 'Der salt water has spoiled them; but mine camera merely needs to dry out; und mine telescope, und mine static machine und Leyden jars—why, der water did not touch them.'

"'Well,' I answered. 'That's all right. But what good are they in the face of this emergency? Are you thinking of photographing anything now?'

"'Perhaps. I haf been thinking some.'

"'Have you thought out what that creature is—forward, there?'

"'Partly. It is some creature thrown up from der bottom of der sea, und washed on board by der wave. Light, like wave motion, ends at a certain depth, you know; und we have over twelve thousand feet beneath us. At that depth dere is absolute darkness, but we know that creatures live down dere, und fight, und eat, und die.'

"'But what of it? Why can't we see that thing?'

"'Because, in der ages that haf passed in its evolution from der original moneron, it has never been exposed to light—I mean visible light, der light that contains der seven colors of der spectrum. Hence it may not respond to der three properties of visible light—reflection, which would give it a color of some kind; absorption, which would make it appear black; or refraction, which, in der absence of der other two, would distort things seen through it. For it would be transparent, you know.'

"'But what can be done?' I asked helplessly, for I could not understand at the time what he meant.

"'Nothing, except that der next man attacked must use his knife. If he cannot see der creature, he can feel it. Und perhaps—I do not know yet—perhaps, in a way, we may see it—its photograph.'

"I looked blankly at him, thinking he might have gone crazy, but he continued.

"'You know,' he said, 'that objects too small to be seen by the microscope, because smaller than der amplitude of der shortest wave of visible light, can be seen when exposed to der ultraviolet light—der dark light beyond der spectrum? Und you know that this light is what acts der most in photography? That it exposes on a sensitized plate new stars in der heavens invisible to der eye through the strongest telescope?'

"'Don't know anything about it,' I answered. 'But if you can find a way out of this scrape we're in, go ahead.'

"'I must think,' he said dreamily. 'I haf a rock-crystal lens which is permeable to this light, und which I can place in mine camera. I must have a concave mirror, not of glass, which is opaque to this light, but of metal.'

"'What for?' I asked.

"'To throw der ultraviolet light on der beast. I can generate it with mine static machine.'

"'How will one of our lantern reflectors do? They are of polished tin, I think.'

"'Good! I can repolish one.'

"We had one deck lantern larger than usual, with a metallic reflector that concentrated the light into a beam, much as do the present day searchlights. This I procured from the lazaret, and he pronounced it available. Then he disappeared, to tinker up his apparatus.

"Night came down, and I lighted three masthead lights, to hoist at the fore to inform any passing craft that we were not under command; but, as I would not send a man forward on that job, I went myself, carefully feeling my way with the pike pole. Luckily, I escaped contact with the creature, and returned to the poop, where we had a cold supper of canned cabin stores.

"The top of the house was dry, but it was cold, especially so as we were all drenched to the skin. The steward brought up all the blankets there were in the cabin—for even a wet blanket is better than none at all—but there were not enough to go around, and one man volunteered, against my advice, to go forward and bring aft bedding from the forecastle.

"He did not come back; we heard his yell, that finished with a gurgle; but in that pitch black darkness, relieved only by the red glow from the north, not one of us dared to venture to his rescue. We knew that he would be dead, anyhow, before we could get to him; so we stood watch, sharing the blankets we had when our time came to sleep.

"It was a wretched night that we spent on the top of that after house. It began to rain before midnight, the heavy drops coming down almost in solid waves; then came wind, out of the south, cold and biting, with real waves, that rolled even over the house, forcing us to lash ourselves. The red glow to the north was hidden by the rain and spume, and, to add to our discomfort, we were showered with ashes, which, even though the surface wind was from the south, must have been brought from the north by an upper air current.

"We did not find the dead man when the faint daylight came; and so could not tell whether or not he had used his knife. His body must have washed over the rail with a sea, and we hoped the invisible killer had gone, too. But we hoped too much. With courage born of this hope a man went forward to lower the masthead lights, prodding his way with the pike pole.

"We watched him closely, the pole in one hand, his knife in the other. But he went under at the fore rigging without even a yell, and the pole went with him, while we could see, even at the distance and through the disturbed water, that his arms were close to his sides, and that he made no movement, except for the quick darting to and fro. After a few moments, however, the pike pole floated to the surface, but the man's body, drained, no doubt, of its buoyant fluids, remained on the deck.

"It was an hour later, with the pike pole for a feeler, before we dared approach the body, hook on to it, and tow it aft. It resembled that of the first victim, a skeleton clothed with skin, with the same look of horror on the face. We buried it like the other, and held to the poop, still drenched by the downpour of rain, hammered by the seas, and choked by ashes from the sky.

"As the shower of ashes increased it became dark as twilight, and though the three lights aloft burned out at about midday, I forbade a man to go forward to lower them, contenting myself with a turpentine flare lamp that I brought up from the lazaret, and filled, ready to show if the lights of a craft came in view. Before the

afternoon was half gone it was dark as night, and down below, up
to his waist in water, the German professor was working away.

"He came up at supper time, humming cheerfully to himself,
and announced that he had replaced his camera lens with the rock
crystal, that the lantern, with its reflector and a blue spark in the
focus, made an admirable instrument for throwing the invisible
rays on the beast, and that he was all ready, except that his plates,
which he had resensitized—with some phosphorescent substance
that I forget the name of, now—must have time to dry. And then,
he needed some light to work by when the time came, he explained.

"'Also another victim,' I suggested bitterly; for he had not been
on deck when the last two men had died.

"'I hope not,' he said. 'When we can see, it may be possible to
stir him up by throwing things forward; then when he moves der
water we can take shots.'

"'Better devise some means of killing him,' I answered. 'Shooting won't do, for water stops a bullet before it goes a foot into it.'

"'Der only way I can think of,' he responded, 'is for der next
man—you hear me all, you men—to stick your knife at the end of
the blood—where it collects in a lump. Dere is der creature's stomach, and a vital spot.'

"'Remember this, boys,' I laughed, thinking of the last poor
devil, with his arms pinioned to his side. 'When you've lost enough
blood to see it in a lump, stab for it.'

"But my laugh was answered by a shriek. A man lashed with a
turn of rope around his waist to the stump of the mizzenmast, was
writhing and heaving on his back, while he struck with his knife,
apparently at his own body. With my own knife in my hand I sprang
toward him, and felt for what had seized him. It was something
cold, and hard, and leathery, close to his waist.

"Carefully gauging my stroke, I lunged with the knife, but I
hardly think it entered the invisible fin, or tail, or paw of the monster; but it moved away from the screaming man, and the next
moment I received a blow in the face that sent me aft six feet, flat
on my back. Then came unconsciousness.

"When I recovered my senses the remnant of the crew were
around me, but the man was gone—dragged out of the bight of the

rope that had held him against the force of breaking seas, and down to the flooded main deck, to die like the others. It was too dark to see, or do anything; so, when I could speak I ordered all hands but one into the flooded cabin where, in the upper berths and on the top of the table, were a few dry spots.

"I filled and lighted a lantern, and gave it to the man on watch with instructions to hang it to the stump of the mizzen and to call his relief at the end of four hours. Then, with doors and windows closed, we went to sleep, or tried to go to sleep. I succeeded first, I think, for up to the last of consciousness I could hear the mutterings of the men; when I awakened, they were all asleep, and the cabin clock, high above the water, told me that, though it was still dark, it was six in the morning.

"I went on deck; the lantern still burned at the stump of mizzenmast but the lookout was gone. He had not lived long enough to be relieved, as I learned by going below and finding that no one had been called.

"We were but six, now—one sailor and the bos'n, the cook and steward, the professor and myself."

The old artist paused, while he refilled and lighted his pipe. I noticed that the hand that held the match shook perceptibly, as though the memories of that awful experience had affected his nerves. I know that the recital had affected mine; for I joined him in a smoke, my hands shaking also.

"Why," I asked, after a moment of silence, "if it was a deep-sea creature, did it not die from the lesser pressure at the surface?"

"Why do not men die on the mountaintops?" he answered. "Or up in balloons? The record is seven miles high, I think; but they lived. They suffered from cold, and from lack of oxygen—that is, no matter how fast, or deeply they breathed, they could not get enough. But the lack of pressure did not trouble them; the human body can adjust itself.

"Conversely, however, an increase of pressure may be fatal. A man dragged down more than one hundred and fifty feet may be crushed; and a surface fish sent to the bottom of the sea may die from the pressure. It is simple; it is like the difference between a weight lifted from us and a weight added."

"Did this thing kill any more men?" I asked.

"All but the professor and myself, and it almost killed me. Look here."

He removed his cravat and collar, pulled down his shirt, and exposed two livid scars about an inch in diameter, and two apart.

"I lost all the blood I could spare through those two holes," he said, as he readjusted his apparel; "but I saved enough to keep me alive."

"Go on with the yarn," I asked. "I promise you I will not sleep to-night."

"Perhaps I will not sleep myself," he answered, with a mournful smile. "Some things should be forgotten, but as I have told you this much I may as well finish, and be done with it.

"It was partly due to a sailor's love for tobacco, partly to our cold, drenched condition. A sailor will starve quietly, but go crazy if deprived of his smoke. This is so well known at sea that a skipper, who will not hesitate to sail from port with rotten or insufficient food for his men, will not dare take a chance without a full supply of tobacco in the slop chest.

"But our slop chest was under water, and the tobacco utterly useless. I did not use it at the time, but I fished some out for the others. It did not do; it would not dry out to smoke, and the salt in it made it unfit to chew. But the bos'n had an upper bunk in the forward house, in which was a couple of pounds of navy plug, and he and the sailor talked this over until their craving for a smoke overcame their fear of death.

"Of course, by this time, all discipline was ended, and all my commands and entreaties went for nothing. They sharpened their knives, and, agreeing to go forward, one on the starboard rail, the other on the port, and each to come to the other's aid if called, they went up into the darkness of ashes and rain. I opened my room window, which overlooked the main deck, but could see nothing.

"Yet I could hear; I heard two screams for help, one after the other—one from the starboard side, the other from the port, and knew that they were caught. I closed the window, for nothing could be done. What manner of thing it was that could grab two men so far apart nearly at the same time was beyond all imagining.

"I talked to the steward and cook, but found small comfort. The first was a Jap, the other a Chinaman, and they were the old-fashioned kind—what they could not see with their eyes, they could not believe. Both thought that all those men who had met death had either drowned or died by falling. Neither understood—and, in fact, I did not myself—the theories of Herr Smidt. He had stopped his cheerful humming to himself now, and was very busy with his instruments.

"'This thing,' I said to him, 'must be able to see in the dark. It certainly could not have heard those two men, over the noise of the wind, sea, and rain.'

"'Why not?' he answered, as he puttered with his wires. 'Cats and owls can see in the dark, und the accepted explanation is that by their power of enlarging der pupils they admit more light to the retina. But that explanation never satisfied me. You haf noticed, haf you not, that a cat's eyes shine in der dark, but only when der cat is looking at you?—that is, when it looks elsewhere you do not see der shiny eyes.'

"'Yes,' I answered, 'I have noticed that.'

"'A cat's eyes are searchlights, but they send forth a visible light, such as is generated by fireflies, und some fish. Und dere are fish in der upper tributaries of der Amazon which haf four eyes, der two upper of which are searchlights, der two lower of which are organs of percipience or vision. But visible light is not der only light. It is possible that the creature out on deck generates the invisible light, and can see by it.'

"'But what does it all amount to?' I asked impatiently.

"'I haf told you,' he answered calmly. 'Der creature may live in an atmosphere of ultraviolet light, which I can generate mineself. When mine plates dry, und it clears off so I can see what I am doing, I may get a picture of it. When we know what it is, we may find means of killing it.'

"'God grant that you succeed,' I answered fervently. 'It has killed enough of us.'

"But, as I said, the thing killed all but the professor and myself. And it came about through the other reason I mentioned—our cold, drenched condition. If there is anything an Oriental loves above his ancestors, it is his stomach; and the cold, canned food was palling upon us all. We had a little light through the downpour of ashes and rain about mid-day, and the steward and cook began talking about hot coffee.

"We had the turpentine torch for heating water, and some coffee, high and dry on a shelf in the steward's storeroom, but not a pot, pan, or cooking utensil of any kind in the cabin. So these two poor heathen, against my expostulations—somewhat faint, I admit, for the thought of hot coffee took away some of my common sense—went out on the deck and waded forward, waist-deep in the water, muddy now, from the downfall of ashes.

"I could see them as they entered the galley to get the coffeepot, but, though I stared from my window until the blackness closed down, I did not see them come out. Nor did I hear even a squeal. The thing must have been in the galley.

"Night came on, and, with its coming, the wind and rain ceased, though there was still a slight shower of ashes. But this ended toward midnight, and I could see stars overhead and a clear horizon. Sleep, in my nervous, overwrought condition, was impossible; but the professor, after the bright idea of using the turpentine torch to dry out his plates, had gone to his fairly dry berth, after announcing his readiness to take snapshots about the deck in the morning.

"But I roused him long before morning. I roused him when I saw through my window the masthead and two side lights of a steamer approaching from the starboard, still about a mile away. I had not dared to go up and rig that lantern at the mizzen stump; but now I nerved myself to go up with the torch, the professor following with his instruments.

"'You cold-blooded crank,' I said to him, as I waved the torch. 'I admire your devotion to science, but are you waiting for that thing to get me?'

"He did not answer, but rigged his apparatus on the top of the cabin. He had a Wimshurst machine—to generate a blue spark, you know—and this he had attached to the big deck light, from which he had removed the opaque glass. Then he had his camera, with its rock-crystal lens.

"He trained both forward, and waited, while I waved the torch, standing near the stump with a turn of rope around me for safety's sake in case the thing seized me; and to this idea I added the foolish hope, aroused by the professor's theories, that the blinding light of the torch would frighten the thing away from me as it does wild animals.

"But in this last I was mistaken. No sooner was there an answering blast of a steam whistle, indicating that the steamer had seen the torch, than something cold, wet, leathery, and slimy slipped around my neck. I dropped the torch, and drew my knife, while I heard the whir of the static machine as the professor turned it.

"'Use your knife, mine friend,' he called. 'Use your knife, und reach for any blood what you see.'

"I knew better than to call for help, and I had little chance to use the knife. Still, I managed to keep my right hand, in which I held it, free, while that cold, leathery thing slipped farther around my neck and waist. I struck as I could, but could make no impression; and soon I felt another stricture around my legs, which brought me on my back. Still another belt encircled me, and, though I had come up warmly clad in woolen shirts and monkey jacket, I felt these garments being torn away from me. Then I was dragged forward, but the turn of rope had slipped down toward my waist, and I was merely bent double.

"And all the time that German was whirling his machine, and shouting to strike for any blood I saw. But I saw none. I felt it going, however. Two spots on my chest began to smart, then burn as though hot irons were piercing me. Frantically I struck, right and left, sometimes at the coils encircling me, again in the air. Then all became dark.

"I awakened in a stateroom berth, too weak to lift my hands, with the taste of brandy in my mouth and the professor standing over me with a bottle in his hand.

"'Ach, it is well,' he said. 'You will recover. You haf merely lost blood, but you did the right thing. You struck with your knife at the blood, and you killed the creature. I was right. Heart, brain, und all vital parts were in der stomach.'

"'Where are we now?' I asked, for I did not recognize the room.

"'On board der steamer. When you got on your feet und staggered aft, I knew you had killed him, and gave you my assistance. But you fainted away. Then we were taken off. Und I haf two or three beautiful negatives, which I am printing. They will be a glorious contribution to der scientific world.'

"I was glad that I was alive, yet not alive enough to ask any more questions. But next day he showed me the photographs he had printed."

"In Heaven's name, what was it?" I asked excitedly, as the old artist paused to empty and refill his pipe.

"Nothing but a giant squid, or octopus. Except that it was bigger than any ever seen before, and invisible to the eye, of course. Did you ever read Hugo's terrible story of Gilliat's fight with a squid?"

I had, and nodded.

"Hugo's imagination could not give him a creature—no matter how formidable—larger than one of four feet stretch. This one had three tentacles around me, two others gripped the port and starboard pin-rails, and three were gripping the stump of the mainmast. It had a reach of forty feet, I should think, comparing it with the beam of the craft.

"But there was one part of each picture, ill defined and missing. My knife and right hand were not shown. They were buried in a dark lump, which could be nothing but the blood from my veins. Unconscious, but still struggling, I had struck into the soft body of the monster, and struck true."

The Stone Ship
William Hope Hodgson

Rum things!—Of course there are rum things happen at sea—
As rum as ever there were. I remember when I was in the Alfred
Jessop, a small barque, whose owner was her skipper, we came
across a most extraordinary thing.

We were twenty days out from London, and well down into the
tropics. It was before I took my ticket, and I was in the fo'cas'le.
The day had passed without a breath of wind, and the night found
us with all the lower sails up in the buntlines.

Now, I want you to take good note of what I am going to say:—

When it was dark in the second dog watch, there was not a sail
in sight; not even the far off smoke of a steamer, and no land nearer
than Africa, about a thousand miles to the eastward of us.

It was our watch on deck from eight to twelve, midnight, and
my look-out from eight to ten. For the first hour, I walked to and
fro across the break of the fo'cas'le head, smoking my pipe and
just listening to the quiet... Ever hear the kind of silence you can
get away out at sea? You need to be in one of the old-time wind-
jammers, with all the lights dowsed, and the sea as calm and quiet
as some queer plain of death. And then you want a pipe and the
lonesomeness of the fo'cas'le head, with the caps'n to lean against
while you listen and think. And all about you, stretching out into
the miles, only and always the enormous silence of the sea, spreading out a thousand miles every way into the everlasting, brooding
night. And not a light anywhere, out on all the waste of waters;
nor ever a sound, as I have told, except the faint moaning of the
masts and gear, as they chafe and whine a little to the occasional
invisible roll of the ship.

And suddenly, across all this silence, I heard Jensen's voice from the head of the starboard steps, say:—

"Did you hear that, Duprey?"

"What?" I asked, cocking my head up. But as I questioned, I heard what he heard—the constant sound of running water, for all the world like the noise of a brook running down a hill-side. And the queer sound was surely not a hundred fathoms off our port bow!

"By gum!" said Jensen's voice, out of the darkness. "That's damned sort of funny!"

"Shut up!" I whispered, and went across, in my bare feet, to the port rail, where I leaned out into the darkness, and stared towards the curious sound.

The noise of a brook running down a hill-side continued, where there was no brook for a thousand sea-miles in any direction.

"What is it?" said Jensen's voice again, scarcely above a whisper now. From below him on the main-deck, there came several voices questioning:— "Hark!" "Stow the talk!" "... there!" "Listen!" "Lord love us, what is it?" ... And then Jensen muttering to them to be quiet.

There followed a full minute, during which we all heard the brook, where no brook could ever run; and then, out of the night there came a sudden hoarse incredible sound:—*oooaze, oooaze, arrrr, arrrr, oooaze*—a stupendous sort of croak, deep and somehow abominable, out of the blackness. In the same instant, I found myself sniffing the air. There was a queer rank smell, stealing through the night.

"Forrard there on the look-out!" I heard the mate singing out, away aft. "Forrard there! What the blazes are you doing!"

I heard him come clattering down the port ladder from the poop, and then the sound of his feet at a run along the maindeck. Simultaneously, there was a thudding of bare feet, as the watch below came racing out of the fo'cas'le beneath me.

"Now then! Now then! Now then!" shouted the Mate, as he charged up on to the fo'cas'le head.

"What's up?"

"It's something off the port bow, Sir," I said. "Running water! And then that sort of howl... Your night-glasses," I suggested.

"Can't see a thing," he growled, as he stared away through the dark. "There's a sort of mist. Phoo! what a devil of a stink!"

"Look!" said someone down on the main-deck. "What's that?"

I saw it in the same instant, and caught the Mate's elbow.

"Look, Sir," I said. "There's a light there, about three points off the bow. It's moving."

The Mate was staring through his night-glasses, and suddenly he thrust them into my hands:— "See if you can make it out," he said, and forthwith put his hands round his mouth, and bellowed into the night:— "Ahoy there! Ahoy there! Ahoy there!" his voice going out lost into the silence and darkness all around. But there came never a comprehensible answer, only all the time the infernal noise of a brook running out there on the sea, a thousand miles from any brook of earth; and away on the port bow, a vague shapeless shining.

I put the glasses to my eyes, and stared. The light was bigger and brighter, seen through the binoculars; but I could make nothing of it, only a dull, elongated shining, that moved vaguely in the darkness, apparently a hundred fathoms or so, away on the sea.

"Ahoy there! Ahoy there!" sung out the Mate again. Then, to the men below:— "Quiet there on the main-deck!"

There followed about a minute of intense stillness, during which we all listened; but there was no sound, except the constant noise of water running steadily.

I was watching the curious shining, and I saw it flick out suddenly at the Mate's shout. Then in a moment I saw three dull lights, one under the other, that flicked in and out intermittently.

"Here, give me the glasses!" said the Mate, and grabbed them from me.

He stared intensely for a moment; then swore, and turned to me:—

"What do you make of them?" he asked, abruptly.

"I don't know, Sir," I said. "I'm just puzzled. Perhaps it's electricity, or something of that sort."

"Oh hell!" he replied, and leant far out over the rail, staring, "Lord!" he said, for the second time, "what a stink!"

As he spoke, there came a most extraordinary thing; for there sounded a series of heavy reports out of the darkness, seeming in the silence, almost as loud as the sound of small cannon.

"They're shooting!" shouted a man on the main-deck, suddenly.

The Mate said nothing; only he sniffed violently at the night air. "By Gum!" he muttered, "what is it?"

I put my hand over my nose; for there was a terrible, charnel-like stench filling all the night about us.

"Take my glasses, Duprey," said the Mate, after a few minutes further watching. "Keep an eye over yonder. I'm going to call the Captain."

He pushed his way down the ladder, and hurried aft. About five minutes later, he returned forrard with the Captain and the Second and Third Mates, all in their shirts and trousers.

"Anything fresh, Duprey?" asked the Mate.

"No, Sir," I said, and handed him back his glasses. "The lights have gone again, and I think the mist is thicker. There's still the sound of running water out there."

The Captain and the three Mates stood some time along the port rail of the fo'cas'le head, watching through their night-glasses, and listening. Twice the Mate hailed; but there came no reply.

There was some talk, among the officers; and I gathered that the Captain was thinking of investigating.

"Clear one of the life-boats, Mr. Gelt," he said, at last. "The glass is steady; there'll be no wind for hours yet. Pick out a half a dozen men. Take 'em out of either watch, if they want to come. I'll be back when I've got my coat."

"Away aft with you, Duprey, and some of you others," said the Mate. "Get the cover off the port life-boat, and bail her out."

"'I, 'i, Sir," I answered, and went away aft with the others.

We had the boat into the water within twenty minutes, which is good time for a wind-jammer, where boats are generally used as storage receptacles for odd gear.

I was one of the men told off to the boat, with two others from our watch, and one from the starboard.

The Captain came down the end of the main tops'l halyards into the boat, and the Third after him. The Third took the tiller, and gave orders to cast off.

We pulled out clear of our vessel, and the Skipper told us to lie on our oars for a moment while he took his bearings. He leant forward to listen, and we all did the same. The sound of the running water was quite distinct across the quietness; but it struck me as seeming not so loud as earlier.

I remember now, that I noticed how plain the mist had become—a sort of warm, wet mist; not a bit thick; but just enough to make the night very dark, and to be visible, eddying slowly in a thin vapour round the port side-light, looking like a red cloudiness swirling lazily through the red glow of the big lamp.

There was no other sound at this time, beyond the sound of the running water; and the Captain, after handing something to the Third Mate, gave the order to give-way.

I was rowing stroke, and close to the officers, and so was able to see dimly that the Captain had passed a heavy revolver over to the Third Mate.

"Ho!" I thought to myself, "so the Old Man's a notion there's really something dangerous over there."

I slipped a hand quickly behind me, and felt that my sheath knife was clear.

We pulled easily for about three or four minutes, with the sound of the water growing plainer somewhere ahead in the darkness; and astern of us, a vague red glowing through the night and vapour, showed where our vessel was lying.

We were rowing easily, when suddenly the bow-oar muttered "G'lord!" Immediately afterwards, there was a loud splashing in the water on his side of the boat.

"What's wrong in the bows, there?" asked the Skipper, sharply.

"There's somethin' in the water, Sir, messing round my oar," said the man.

I stopped rowing, and looked round. All the men did the same. There was a further sound of splashing, and the water was driven right over the boat in showers. Then the bow-oar called out:—
"There's somethin' got a holt of my oar, Sir!"

I could tell the man was frightened; and I knew suddenly that a curious nervousness had come to me—a vague, uncomfortable dread, such as the memory of an ugly tale will bring, in a lonesome place. I believe every man in the boat had a similar feeling. It seemed to me in that moment, that a definite, muggy sort of silence was all round us, and this in spite of the sound of the splashing, and the strange noise of the running water somewhere ahead of us on the dark sea.

"It's let go the oar, Sir!" said the man.

Abruptly, as he spoke, there came the Captain's voice in a roar:— "Back water all!" he shouted. "Put some beef into it now! Back all! Back all!... Why the devil was no lantern put in the boat! Back now! Back! Back!"

We backed fiercely, with a will; for it was plain that the Old Man had some good reason to get the boat away pretty quickly. He was right, too; though, whether it was guess-work, or some kind of instinct that made him shout out at that moment, I don't know; only I am sure he could not have seen anything in that absolute darkness.

As I was saying, he was right in shouting to us to back; for we had not backed more than half a dozen fathoms, when there was a tremendous splash right ahead of us, as if a house had fallen into the sea; and a regular wave of sea-water came at us out of the darkness, throwing our bows up, and soaking us fore and aft.

"Good Lord!" I heard the Third Mate gasp out. "What the devil's that?"

"Back all! Back! Back!" the Captain sung out again.

After some moments, he had the tiller put over, and told us to pull. We gave way with a will, as you may think, and in a few minutes were alongside our own ship again.

"Now then, men," the Captain said, when we were safe aboard, "I'll not order any of you to come; but after the steward's served out a tot of grog each, those who are willing, can come with me, and we'll have another go at finding out what devil's work is going on over yonder."

He turned to the Mate, who had been asking questions:—

"Say, Mister," he said, "it's no sort of thing to let the boat go without a lamp aboard. Send a couple of the lads into the lamp locker, and pass out a couple of the anchor-lights, and that deck bull's-eye, you use at nights for clearing up the ropes."

He whipped round on the Third:— "Tell the steward to buck up with that grog, Mr. Andrews," he said, "and while you're there, pass out the axes from the rack in my cabin."

The grog came along a minute later; and then the Third Mate with three big axes from out the cabin rack.

"Now then, men," said the Skipper, as we took our tots off, "those who are coming with me, had better take an axe each from the Third Mate. They're mighty good weapons in any sort of trouble."

We all stepped forward, and he burst out laughing, slapping his thigh.

"That's the kind of thing I like!" he said. "Mr. Andrews, the axes won't go round. Pass out that old cutlass from the steward's pantry. It's a pretty hefty piece of iron!"

The old cutlass was brought, and the man who was short of an axe, collared it. By this time, two of the 'prentices had filled (at least we supposed they had filled them!) two of the ship's anchor-lights; also they had brought out the bull's-eye lamp we used when clearing up the ropes on a dark night. With the lights and the axes and the cutlass, we felt ready to face anything, and down we went again into the boat, with the Captain and the Third Mate after us.

"Lash one of the lamps to one of the boat-hooks, and rig it over the bows," ordered the Captain.

This was done, and in this way the light lit up the water for a couple of fathoms ahead of the boat; and made us feel less that something could come at us without our knowing. Then the painter was cast off, and we gave way again toward the sound of the running water, out there in the darkness.

I remember now that it struck me that our vessel had drifted a bit; for the sounds seemed farther away. The second anchor-light had been put in the stern of the boat, and the Third Mate kept it between his feet, while he steered. The Captain had the bull's-eye in his hand, and was pricking up the wick with his pocket-knife.

As we pulled, I took a glance or two over my shoulder; but could see nothing, except the lamp making a yellow halo in the mist round the boat's bows, as we forged ahead. Astern of us, on our quarter, I could see the dull red glow of our vessel's port light. That was all, and not a sound in all the sea, as you might say, except the roll of our oars in the rowlocks, and somewhere in the darkness ahead, that curious noise of water running steadily; now sounding, as I have said, fainter and seeming farther away.

"It's got my oar again, Sir!" exclaimed the man at the bow oar, suddenly, and jumped to his feet. He hove his oar up with a great splashing of water, into the air, and immediately something whirled and beat about in the yellow halo of light over the bows of the boat. There was a crash of breaking wood, and the boat-hook was broken. The lamp soused down into the sea, and was lost. Then in the darkness, there was a heavy splash, and a shout from the bow-oar:— "It's gone, Sir. It's loosed off the oar!"

"Vast pulling, all!" sung out the Skipper. Not that the order was necessary; for not a man was pulling. He had jumped up, and whipped a big revolver out of his coat pocket.

He had this in his right hand, and the bull's-eye in his left. He stepped forrard smartly over the oars from thwart to thwart, till he reached the bows, where he shone his light down into the water.

"My word!" he said. "Lord in Heaven! Saw anyone ever the like!"

And I doubt whether any man ever did see what we saw then; for the water was thick and living for yards round the boat with the hugest eels I ever saw before or after.

"Give way, Men," said the Skipper, after a minute. "Yon's no explanation of the almighty queer sounds out yonder we're hearing this night. Give way, lads!"

He stood right up in the bows of the boat, shining his bulls'-eye from side to side, and flashing it down on the water.

"Give way, lads!" he said again. "They don't like the light, that'll keep them from the oars. Give way steady now. Mr. Andrews, keep her dead on for the noise out yonder."

We pulled for some minutes, during which I felt my oar plucked at twice; but a flash of the Captain's lamp seemed sufficient to make the brutes loose hold.

The noise of the water running, appeared now quite near sounding. About this time, I had a sense again of an added sort of silence to all the natural quietness of the sea. And I had a return of the curious nervousness that had touched me before. I kept listening intensely, as if I expected to hear some other sound than the noise of the water. It came to me suddenly that I had the kind of feeling one has in the aisle of a large cathedral. There was a sort of echo in the night—an incredibly faint reduplicating of the noise of our oars.

"Hark!" I said, audibly; not realizing at first that I was speaking aloud. "There's an echo—"

"That's it!" the Captain cut in, sharply. "I thought I heard something rummy!"

... "I thought I heard something rummy," said a thin ghostly echo, out of the night... "thought I heard something rummy" ... "heard something rummy." The words went muttering and whispering to and fro in the night about us, in a rather a horrible fashion.

"Good Lord!" said the Old Man, in a whisper.

We had all stopped rowing, and were staring about us into the thin mist that filled the night. The Skipper was standing with the bull's-eye lamp held over his head, circling the beam of light round from port to starboard, and back again.

Abruptly, as he did so, it came to me that the mist was thinner. The sound of the running water was very near; but it gave back no echo.

"The water doesn't echo, Sir," I said. "That's damn funny!"

"That's damn funny," came back at me, from the darkness to port and starboard, in a multitudinous muttering... "Damn funny!... funny... eey!"

"Give way!" said the Old Man, loudly. "I'll bottom this!"

"I'll bottom this... Bottom this... this!" The echo came back in a veritable rolling of unexpected sound. And then we had dipped our oars again, and the night was full of the reiterated rolling echoes of our rowlocks.

Suddenly the echoes ceased, and there was, strangely, the sense of a great space about us, and in the same moment the sound of the water running appeared to be directly before us, but somehow up in the air.

"Vast rowing!" said the Captain, and we lay on our oars, staring round into the darkness ahead. The Old Man swung the beam of his lamp upwards, making circles with it in the night, and abruptly I saw something looming vaguely through the thinner-seeming mist.

"Look, Sir," I called to the Captain. "Quick, Sir, your light right above you! There's something up there!"

The Old Man flashed his lamp upwards, and found the thing I had seen. But it was too indistinct to make anything of, and even as he saw it, the darkness and mist seemed to wrap it about.

"Pull a couple of strokes, all!" said the Captain. "Stow your talk, there in the boat!... Again! ... That'll do! Vast pulling!"

He was sending the beam of his lamp constantly across that part of the night where we had seen the thing, and suddenly I saw it again.

"There, Sir!" I said. "A little starboard with the light."

He flicked the light swiftly to the right, and immediately we all saw the thing plainly—a strangely-made mast, standing up there out of the mist, and looking like no spar I had ever seen.

It seemed now that the mist must lie pretty low on the sea in places; for the mast stood up out of it plainly for several fathoms; but, lower, it was hidden in the mist, which, I thought, seemed heavier now all round us; but thinner, as I have said, above.

"Ship ahoy!" sung out the Skipper, suddenly. "Ship ahoy, there!" But for some moments there came never a sound back to us except the constant noise of the water running, not a score yards away; and then, it seemed to me that a vague echo beat back at us out of the mist, oddly:— "Ahoy! Ahoy! Ahoy!"

"There's something hailing us, Sir," said the Third Mate.

Now, that "something" was significant. It showed the sort of feeling that was on us all.

"That's na ship's mast as ever I've seen!" I heard the man next to me mutter. "It's got a unnatcheral look."

"Ahoy there!" shouted the Skipper again, at the top of his voice. "Ahoy there!"

With the suddenness of a clap of thunder there burst out at us a vast, grunting:—*oooaze; arrrr; arrrr; oooaze*—a volume of sound so great that it seemed to make the loom of the oar in my hand vibrate.

"Good Lord!" said the Captain, and levelled his revolver into the mist; but he did not fire.

I had loosed one hand from my oar, and gripped my axe. I remember thinking that the Skipper's pistol wouldn't be much use against whatever thing made a noise like that.

"It wasn't ahead, Sir," said the Third Mate, abruptly, from where he sat and steered. "I think it came from somewhere over to starboard."

"Damn this mist!" said the Skipper. "Damn it! What a devil of a stink! Pass that other anchor-light forrard."

I reached for the lamp, and handed it to the next man, who passed it on.

"The other boat-hook," said the Skipper; and when he'd got it, he lashed the lamp to the hook end, and then lashed the whole arrangement upright in the bows, so that the lamp was well above his head.

"Now," he said. "Give way gently! And stand by to back-water, if I tell you... Watch my hand, Mister," he added to the Third Mate. "Steer as I tell you."

We rowed a dozen slow strokes, and with every stroke, I took a look over my shoulder. The Captain was leaning forward under the big lamp, with the bull's-eye in one hand and his revolver in the other. He kept flashing the beam of the lantern up into the night.

"Good Lord!" he said, suddenly. "Vast pulling."

We stopped, and I slewed round on the thwart, and stared.

He was standing up under the glow of the anchor-light, and shining the bull's-eye up at a great mass that loomed dully through the mist. As he flicked the light to and fro over the great bulk, I realized that the boat was within some three or four fathoms of the hull of a vessel.

"Pull another stroke," the Skipper said, in a quiet voice, after a few minutes of silence. "Gently now! Gently! ... Vast pulling!"

I slewed round again on my thwart and stared. I could see part of the thing quite distinctly now, and more of it, as I followed the beam of the Captain's lantern. She was a vessel right enough; but such a vessel as I had never seen. She was extraordinarily high out of the water, and seemed very short, and rose up into a queer mass at one end. But what puzzled me more, I think, than anything else, was the queer look of her sides, down which water was streaming all the time.

"That explains the sound of the water running," I thought to myself; "but what on earth is she built of?"

You will understand a little of my bewildered feelings, when I tell you that as the beam of the Captain's lamp shone on the side of this queer vessel, it showed stone everywhere—as if she were built out of stone. I never felt so dumb-founded in my life.

"She's stone, Cap'n," I said. "Look at her, Sir!"

I realised, as I spoke, a certain horribleness, of the unnatural... A stone ship, floating out there in the night in the midst of the lonely Atlantic!

"She's stone," I said again, in that absurd way in which one reiterates, when one is bewildered.

"Look at the slime on her!" muttered the man next but one forrard of me. "She's a proper Davy Jones ship. By gum! she stinks like a corpse!"

"Ship ahoy!" roared the Skipper, at the top of his voice. "Ship ahoy! Ship ahoy!"

His shout beat back at us, in a curious, dank, yet metallic, echo, something the way one's voice sounds in an old disused quarry.

"There's no one aboard there, Sir," said the Third Mate. "Shall I put the boat alongside?"

"Yes, shove her up, Mister," said the Old Man. "I'll bottom this business. Pull a couple of strokes, aft there! In bow, and stand by to fend off."

The Third Mate laid the boat alongside, and we unshipped our oars.

Then, I leant forward over the side of the boat, and pressed the flat of my hand upon the stark side of the ship. The water that ran down her side, sprayed out over my hand and wrist in a cataract; but I did not think about being wet, for my hand was pressed solid upon stone... I pulled my hand back with a queer feeling.

"She's stone, right enough, Sir," I said to the Captain.

"We'll soon see what she is," he said. "Shove your oar up against her side, and shin up. We'll pass the lamp up to you as soon as you're aboard. Shove your axe in the back of your belt. I'll cover you with my gun, till you're aboard."

"'I, 'i, Sir," I said; though I felt a bit funny at the thought of having to be the first aboard that damn rummy craft.

I put my oar upright against her side, and took a spring up from the thwart, and in a moment I was grabbing over my head for her rail, with every rag of me soaked through with the water that was streaming down her, and spraying out over the oar and me.

I got a firm grip of the rail, and hoisted my head high enough to look over; but I could see nothing ... what with the darkness, and the water in my eyes.

I knew it was no time for going slow, if there were danger aboard; so I went in over that rail in one spring, my boots coming down with a horrible, ringing, hollow, stony sound on her decks. I whipped the water out of my eyes and the axe out of my belt, all in the same moment; then I took a good stare fore and aft; but it was too dark to see anything.

"Come along, Duprey!" shouted the Skipper. "Collar the lamp."

I leant out sideways over the rail, and grabbed for the lamp with my left hand, keeping the axe ready in my right, and staring inboard; for I tell you, I was just mortally afraid in that moment of what might be aboard of her.

I felt the lamp-ring with my left hand, and gripped it. Then I switched it aboard, and turned fair and square to see where I'd gotten.

Now, you never saw such a packet as that, not in a hundred years, nor yet two hundred, I should think. She'd got a rum little main-deck, about forty feet long, and then came a step about two feet high, and another bit of a deck, with a little house on it.

That was the after end of her; and more I couldn't see, because the light of my lamp went no farther, except to show me vaguely the big, cocked-up stern of her, going up into the darkness. I never saw a vessel made like her; not even in an old picture of old-time ships.

Forrard of me, was her mast—a big lump of a stick it was too, for her size. And here was another amazing thing, the mast of her looked just solid stone.

"Funny, isn't she, Duprey?" said the Skipper's voice at my back, and I came round on him with a jump.

"Yes," I said. "I'm puzzled. Aren't you, Sir?"

"Well," he said, "I am. If we were like the shellbacks they talk of in books, we'd be crossing ourselves. But, personally, give me a good heavy Colt, or the hefty chunk of steel you're cuddling."

He turned from me, and put his head over the rail.

"Pass up the painter, Jales," he said, to the bow-oar. Then to the Third Mate:—

"Bring 'em all up, Mister. If there's going to be anything rummy, we may as well make a picnic party of the lot... Hitch that painter round the cleet yonder, Duprey," he added to me. "It looks good solid stone! ... That's right. Come along."

He swung the thin beam of his lantern fore and aft, and then forrard again.

"Lord!" he said. "Look at that mast. It's stone. Give it a whack with the back of your axe, man; only remember she's apparently a bit of an old-timer! So go gently."

I took my axe short, and tapped the mast, and it rang dull, and solid, like a stone pillar, I struck it again, harder, and a sharp flake of stone flew past my cheek. The Skipper thrust his lantern close up to where I'd struck the mast.

"By George," he said, "she's absolute a stone ship—solid stone, afloat here out of Eternity, in the middle of the wide Atlantic... Why! She must weigh a thousand tons more than she's buoyancy to carry. It's just impossible... It's—"

He turned his head quickly, at a sound in the darkness along the decks. He flashed his light that way, across the after decks; but we could see nothing

"Get a move on you in the boat!" he said sharply, stepping to the rail and looking down. "For once I'd really prefer a little more of your company..." He came round like a flash. "Duprey, what was that?" he asked in a low voice.

"I certainly heard something, Sir," I said. "I wish the others would hurry. By Jove! Look! What's that—"

"Where?" he said, and sent the beam of his lamp to where I pointed with my axe.

"There's nothing," he said, after circling the light all over the deck. "Don't go imagining things. There's enough solid unnatural fact here, without trying to add to it."

There came the splash and thud of feet behind, as the first of the men came up over the side, and jumped clumsily into the lee scuppers, which had water in them. You see she had a cant to that side, and I supposed the water had collected there.

The rest of the men followed, and then the Third Mate. That made six men of us, all well armed; and I felt a bit more comfortable, as you can think.

"Hold up that lamp of yours, Duprey, and lead the way," said the Skipper. "You're getting the post of honour this trip!"

"'I, 'i, Sir," I said, and stepped forward, holding up the lamp in my left hand, and carrying my axe half way down the haft, in my right.

"We'll try aft, first," said the Captain, and led the way himself, flashing the bull's-eye to and fro. At the raised portion of the deck, he stopped.

"Now," he said, in his queer way, "let's have a look at this... Tap it with your axe, Duprey... Ah!" he added, as I hit it with the back of my axe. "That's what we call stone at home, right enough. She's just as rum as anything I've seen while I've been fishing. We'll go on aft and have a peep into the deck-house. Keep your axes handy, men."

We walked slowly up to the curious little house, the deck rising to it with quite a slope. At the foreside of the little deck-house, the Captain pulled up, and shone his bull's-eye down at the deck. I saw that he was looking at what was plainly the stump of the after mast. He stepped closer to it, and kicked it with his foot; and it gave out the same dull, solid note that the foremast had done. It was obviously a chunk of stone.

I held up my lamp so that I could see the upper part of the house more clearly. The fore-part had two square window-spaces in it; but there was no glass in either of them; and the blank darkness within the queer little place, just seemed to stare out at us.

And then I saw something suddenly ... a great shaggy head of red hair was rising slowly into sight, through the port window, the one nearest to us.

"My God! What's that, Cap'n?" I called out. But it was gone, even as I spoke.

"What?" he asked, jumping at the way I had sung out.

"At the port window, Sir," I said. "A great red-haired head. It came right up to the window-place; and then it went in a moment."

The Skipper stepped right up to the little dark window, and pushed his lantern through into the blackness. He flashed a light round; then withdrew the lantern.

"Bosh, man!" he said. "That's twice you've got fancying things. Ease up your nerves a bit!"

"I did see it!" I said, almost angrily. "It was like a great red-haired head..."

"Stow it, Duprey!" he said, though not sneeringly. "The house is absolutely empty. Come round to the door, if the Infernal Masons that built her, went in for doors! Then you'll see for yourself. All the same, keep your axes ready, lads. I've a notion there's something pretty queer aboard here."

We went up round the after-end of the little house, and here we saw what appeared to be a door.

The Skipper felt at the queer, odd-shapen handle, and pushed at the door; but it had stuck fast.

"Here, one of you!" he said, stepping back. "Have a whack at this with your axe. Better use the back."

One of the men stepped forward, and stood away to give him room. As his axe struck, the door went to pieces with exactly the same sound that a thin slab of stone would make, when broken.

"Stone!" I heard the Captain mutter, under his breath. "By Gum! What is she?"

I did not wait for the Skipper. He had put me a bit on edge, and I stepped bang in through the open doorway, with the lamp high, and holding my axe short and ready; but there was nothing in the place, save a stone seat running all round, except where the doorway opened on to the deck.

"Find your red-haired monster?" asked the Skipper, at my elbow.

I said nothing. I was suddenly aware that he was all on the jump with some inexplicable fear. I saw his glance going everywhere about him. And then his eye caught mine, and he saw that I realised. He was a man almost callous to fear, that is the fear of danger in what I might call any normal sea-faring shape. And this palpable nerviness affected me tremendously. He was obviously doing his best to throttle it; and trying all he knew to hide it. I had a sudden warmth of understanding for him, and dreaded lest the men should realise his state. Funny that I should be able at that moment to be aware of anything but my own bewildered fear and expectancy of intruding upon something monstrous at any instant. Yet I describe exactly my feelings, as I stood there in the house.

"Shall we try below, Sir?" I said, and turned to where a flight of stone steps led down into an utter blackness, out which rose a strange, dank scent of the sea... an imponderable mixture of brine and darkness.

"The worthy Duprey leads the van!" said the Skipper; but I felt no irritation now. I knew that he must cover his fright, until he had got control again; and I think he felt, somehow, that I was backing him up. I remember now that I went down those stairs into that unknowable and ancient cabin, as much aware in that moment of the Captain's state, as of that extraordinary thing I had just seen at the little window, or of my own half-funk of what we might see any moment.

The Captain was at my shoulder, as I went, and behind him came the Third Mate, and then the men, all in single file; for the stairs were narrow.

I counted seven steps down, and then my foot splashed into water on the eighth. I held the lamp low and stared. I had caught no glimpse of a reflection, and I saw now that this was owing to a curious, dull, greyish scum that lay thinly on the water, seeming to match the colour of the stone which composed the steps and bulkheads.

"Stop!" I said. "I'm in water!"

I let my foot down slowly, and got the next step. Then sounded with my axe, and found the floor at the bottom. I stepped down and stood up to my thighs in water.

"It's all right, Sir," I said, suddenly whispering. I held my lamp up, and glanced quickly about me.

"It's not deep. There's two doors here...."

I whirled my axe up as I spoke; for suddenly, I had realised that one of the doors was open a little. It seemed to move, as I stared, and I could have imagined that a vague undulation ran towards me, across the dull scum-covered water.

"The door's opening!" I said, aloud, with a sudden sick feeling. "Look out!"

I backed from the door, staring; but nothing came. And abruptly, I had control of myself; for I realised that the door was not moving. It had not moved at all. It was simply ajar.

"It's all right, sir," I said. "It's not opening."

I stepped forward again a pace towards the doors, as the Skipper and the Third Mate came down with a jump, splashing water all over me.

The Captain still had the "nerves," on him, as I think I could feel, even then; but he hid it well.

"Try the door, Mister. I've jumped my damn lamp out!" he growled to the Third Mate; who pushed at the door on my right; but it would not open beyond the nine or ten inches it was fixed ajar.

"There's this one here, Sir," I whispered, and held my lantern up to the closed door that lay on my left.

"Try it," said the Skipper, in an undertone. We did so, but it also was fixed. I whirled my axe suddenly, and struck the door heavily in the centre of the main panel, and the whole thing crashed into flinders of stone, that went with hollow sounding splashes into the darkness beyond.

"Goodness!" said the Skipper, in a startled voice; for my action had been so instant and unexpected. He covered his lapse, in a moment, by the warning:—

"Look out for bad air!" But I was already inside with the lamp, and holding my axe handily. There was no bad air; for right across from me, was a split clean through the ship's side, that I could have put my two arms through, just above the level of the scummy water.

The place I had broken into, was a cabin, of a kind; but seemed strange and dank, and too narrow to breathe in; and wherever I turned, I saw stone. The Third Mate and the Skipper gave simultaneous expressions of disgust at the wet dismalness of the place.

"It's all of stone," I said, and brought my axe hard against the front of a sort of squat cabinet, which was built into the after bulkheads. It caved in, with a crash of splintered stone.

"Empty!" I said, and turned instantly away.

The Skipper and the Third Mate, with the men who were now peering in at the door, crowded out; and in that moment, I pushed my axe under my arm, and thrust my hand into the burst stone-chest. Twice I did this, with almost the speed of lightning, and shoved what I had seen, into the side-pocket of my coat. Then, I was following the others; and not one of them had noticed a thing.

As for me, I was quivering with excitement, so that my knees shook; for I had caught the unmistakable gleam of gems; and had grabbed for them in that one swift instant.

I wonder whether anyone can realise what I felt in that moment. I knew that, if my guess were right, I had snatched the power in that one miraculous moment, that would lift me from the weary life of a common shellback, to the life of ease that had been mine during my early years. I tell you, in that instant, as I staggered almost blindly out of that dark little apartment, I had no thought of any horror that might be held in that incredible vessel, out there afloat on the wide Atlantic.

I was full of one blinding thought, that possibly I was rich! And I wanted to get somewhere by myself as soon as possible, to see whether I was right. Also, if I could, I meant to get back to that strange cabinet of stone, if the chance came; for I knew that the two handfuls I had grabbed, had left a lot behind.

Only, whatever I did, I must let no one guess; for then I should probably lose everything, or have but an infinitesimal share doled out to me, of the wealth that I believed to be in those glittering things there in the side-pocket of my coat.

I began immediately to wonder what other treasures there might be aboard; and then, abruptly, I realised that the Captain was speaking to me:

"The light, Duprey, damn you!" he was saying, angrily, in a low tone. "What's the matter with you! Hold it up."

I pulled myself together, and shoved the lamp above my head. One of the men was swinging his axe, to beat in the door that seemed to have stood so eternally ajar; and the rest were standing back, to give him room. Crash! went the axe, and half the door fell inward, in a shower of broken stone, making dismal splashes in the darkness. The man struck again, and the rest of the door fell away, with a sullen slump into the water.

"The lamp," muttered the Captain. But I had hold of myself once more, and I was stepping forward slowly through the thigh-deep water, even before he spoke.

I went a couple of paces in through the black gape of the doorway, and then stopped and held the lamp so as to get a view of the place. As I did so, I remember how the intense silence struck home on me. Every man of us must surely have been holding his breath; and there must have been some heavy quality, either in the water, or in the scum that floated on it, that kept it from rippling against the sides of the bulkheads, with the movements we had made.

At first, as I held the lamp (which was burning badly), I could not get its position right to show me anything, except that I was in a very large cabin for so small a vessel. Then I saw that a table ran along the centre, and the top of it was no more than a few inches above the water. On each side of it, there rose the backs of what were evidently two rows of massive, olden looking chairs. At the far end of the table, there was a huge, immobile, humped something.

I stared at this for several moments; then I took three slow steps forward, and stopped again; for the thing resolved itself, under the light from the lamp, into the figure of an enormous man, seated at the end of the table, his face bowed forward upon his arms. I was amazed, and thrilling abruptly with new fears and vague impossible thoughts. Without moving a step, I held the light nearer at arm's length... The man was of stone, like everything in that extraordinary ship.

"That foot!" said the Captain's voice, suddenly cracking. "Look at that foot!" His voice sounded amazingly startling and hollow in that silence, and the words seemed to come back sharply at me from the vaguely seen bulkheads.

I whipped my light to starboard, and saw what he meant—a huge human foot was sticking up out of the water, on the right hand of the table. It was enormous. I have never seen so vast a foot. And it also was of stone.

And then, as I stared, I saw that there was a great head above the water, over by the bulkhead.

"I've gone mad!" I said, out loud, as I saw something else, more incredible.

"My God! Look at the hair on the head!" said the Captain... "It's growing!" he called out once more.

I was looking. On the great head, there was becoming visible a huge mass of red hair, that was surely and unmistakably rising up, as we watched it.

"It's what I saw at the window!" I said. "It's what I saw at the window! I told you I saw it!"

"Come out of that, Duprey," said the Third Mate, quietly.

"Let's get out of here!" muttered one of the men. Two or three of them called out the same thing; and then, in a moment, they began a mad rush up the stairway.

I stood dumb, where I was. The hair rose up in a horrible living fashion on the great head, waving and moving. It rippled down over the forehead, and spread abruptly over the whole gargantuan stone face, hiding the features completely. Suddenly, I swore at the thing madly, and I hove my axe at it. Then I was backing crazily for the door, slumping the scum as high as the deck beams, in my fierce haste. I reached the stairs, and caught at the stone rail, that was modelled like a rope; and so hove myself up out of the water. I reached the deck-house, where I had seen the great head of hair. I jumped through the doorway, out on to the decks, and felt the night air sweet on my face... Goodness! I ran forward along the decks. There was a Babel of shouting in the waist of the ship, and a thudding of feet running. Some of the men were singing out, to get into the boat; but the Third Mate was shouting that they must wait for me.

"He's coming," called someone. And then I was among them.

"Turn that lamp up, you idiot," said the Captain's voice. "This is just where we want light!"

I glanced down, and realised that my lamp was almost out. I turned it up, and it flared, and began again to dwindle.

"Those damned boys never filled it," I said. "They deserve their necks breaking."

The men were literally tumbling over the side, and the Skipper was hurrying them.

"Down with you into the boat," he said to me. "Give me the lamp. I'll pass it down. Get a move on you!"

The Captain had evidently got his nerve back again. This was more like the man I knew. I handed him the lamp, and went over the side. All the rest had now gone, and the Third Mate was already in the stern, waiting.

As I landed on the thwart, there was a sudden strange noise from aboard the ship—a sound, as if some stone object were trundling down the sloping decks, from aft. In that one moment, I got what you might truly call the "horrors." I seemed suddenly able to believe incredible possibilities.

"The stone men!" I shouted. "Jump, Captain! Jump! Jump!" The vessel seemed to roll oddly.

Abruptly, the Captain yelled out something, that not one of us in the boat understood. There followed a succession of tremendous sounds, aboard the ship, and I saw his shadow swing out huge against the thin mist, as he turned suddenly with the lamp. He fired twice with his revolver.

"The hair!" I shouted. "Look at the hair!"

We all saw it—the great head of red hair that we had seen grow visibly on the monstrous stone head, below in the cabin. It rose above the rail, and there was a moment of intense stillness, in which I heard the Captain gasping. The Third Mate fired six times at the thing, and I found myself fixing an oar up against the side of that abominable vessel, to get aboard.

As I did so, there came one appalling crash, that shook the stone ship fore and aft, and she began to cant up, and my oar slipped and fell into the boat. Then the Captain's voice screamed something in a choking fashion above us.

The ship lurched forward and paused. Then another crash came, and she rocked over towards us; then away from us again. The movement away from us continued, and the round of the vessel's bottom showed, vaguely. There was a smashing of glass above us, and the dim glow of light aboard vanished. Then the vessel fell clean from us, with a giant splash. A huge wave came at us, out of the night, and half filled the boat.

The boat nearly capsized, then righted and presently steadied.

"Captain!" shouted the Third Mate. "Captain!" But there came never a sound; only presently, out of all the night, a strange murmuring of waters.

"Captain!" he shouted once more; but his voice just went lost and remote into the darkness.

"She's foundered!" I said.

"Out oars," sung out the Third. "Put your backs into it. Don't stop to bail!"

For half an hour we circled the spot slowly. But the strange vessel had indeed foundered and gone down into the mystery of the deep sea, with her mysteries.

Finally we put about, and returned to the *Alfred Jessop*.

Now, I want you to realize that what I am telling you is a plain and simple tale of fact. This is no fairy tale, and I've not done yet; and I think this yarn should prove to you that some mighty strange things do happen at sea, and always will while the world lasts. It's the home of all mysteries; for it's the one place that is really difficult for humans to investigate. Now just listen:—

The Mate had kept the bell going, from time to time, and so we came back pretty quickly, having as we came, a strange repetition of the echoey reduplication of our oar-sounds; but we never spoke a word; for not one of us wanted to hear those beastly echoes again, after what we had just gone through. I think we all had a feeling that there was something a bit hellish aboard that night.

We got aboard, and the Third explained to the Mate what had happened; but he would hardly believe the yarn. However, there was nothing to do, but wait for daylight; so we were told to keep about the deck, and keep our eyes and ears open.

One thing the Mate did show he was more impressed by our yarn than he would admit. He had all the ships' lanterns lashed up round the decks, to the sheerpoles; and he never told us to give up either the axes or cutlass.

It was while we were keeping about the decks, that I took the chance to have a look at what I had grabbed. I tell you, what I found, made me nearly forget the Skipper, and all the rummy things that had happened. I had twenty-six stones in my pocket and four of them were diamonds, respectively 9, 11, 13 1/2 and 17 carats in weight, uncut, that is. I know quite something about diamonds. I'm not going to tell you how I learnt what I know; but I would not have taken a thousand pounds for the four, as they lay there, in my hand. There was also a big, dull stone, that looked red inside. I'd have dumped it over the side, I thought so little of it; only, I argued that it must be something, or it would never have been among that lot. Lord! but I little knew what I'd got; not then. Why, the thing was as big as a fair-sized walnut. You may think it funny that I thought of the four diamonds first; but you see, I know diamonds when I see them. They're things I understand; but I never saw a ruby, in the rough, before or since. Good Lord! And to think I'd have thought nothing of heaving it over the side!

You see, a lot of the stones were not anything much; that is, not in the modern market. There were two big topazes, and several onyx and corelians—nothing much. There were five hammered slugs of gold, about two ounces each they would be. And then a prize—one winking green devil of an emerald. You've got to know an emerald to look for the "eye" of it, in the rough; but it is there—the eye of some hidden devil staring up at you. Yes, I'd seen an emerald before, and I knew I held a lot of money in that one stone alone.

And then I remembered what I'd missed, and cursed myself for not grabbing a third time. But that feeling lasted only a moment. I thought of the beastly part that had been the Skipper's share; while there I stood safe under one of the lamps, with a fortune in my hands. And then, abruptly, as you can understand, my mind was filled with the crazy wonder and bewilderment of what had happened. I felt how absurdly ineffectual my imagination was to comprehend anything understandable out of it all, except that the Captain had certainly gone, and I had just as certainly had a piece of impossible luck.

Often, during that time of waiting, I stopped to take a look at the things I had in my pocket; always careful that no one about the decks should come near me, to see what I was looking at.

Suddenly the Mate's voice came sharp along the decks:—

"Call the doctor, one of you," he said. "Tell him to get the fire in and the coffee made."

"'I, Sir," said one of the men; and I realized that the dawn was growing vaguely over the sea.

Half an hour later, the "doctor" shoved his head out of the galley doorway, and sung out that coffee was ready.

The watch below turned out, and had theirs with the watch on deck, all sitting along the spar that lay under the port rail.

As the daylight grew, we kept a constant watch over the side; but even now we could see nothing; for the thin mist still hung low on the sea.

"Hear that?" said one of the men, suddenly. And, indeed, the sound must have been plain for a half a mile round.

"*Ooaaze, ooaaze, arr, arrrr, oooaze—*"

"By George!" said Tallett, one of the other watch; "that's a beastly sort of thing to hear."

"Look!" I said. "What's that out yonder?"

The mist was thinning under the effect of the rising sun, and tremendous shapes seemed to stand towering half-seen, away to port. A few minutes passed, while we stared. Then, suddenly, we heard the Mate's voice—

"All hands on deck!" he was shouting, along the decks.

I ran aft a few steps.

"Both watches are out, Sir," I called.

"Very good!" said the Mate. "Keep handy all of you. Some of you have got the axes. The rest had better take a caps-n-bar each, and stand-by till I find what this devilment is, out yonder."

"'I, 'i Sir," I said, and turned forrard. But there was no need to pass on the Mate's orders; for the men had heard, and there was a rush for the capstanbars, which are a pretty hefty kind of cudgel, as any sailorman knows. We lined the rail again, and stared away to port.

"Look out, you sea-divvils," shouted Timothy Galt, a huge Irishman, waving his bar excitedly, and peering over the rail into the mist, which was steadily thinning, as the day grew.

Abruptly there was a simultaneous cry— "Rocks!" shouted everyone.

I never saw such a sight. As at last the mist thinned, we could see them. All the sea to port was literally cut about with far-reaching reefs of rock. In places the reefs lay just submerged; but in others they rose into extraordinary and fantastic rock-spires, and arches, and islands of jagged rock.

"Jehosaphat!" I heard the Third Mate shout. "Look at that, Mister! Look at that! Lord! how did we take the boat through that, without stoving her!"

Everything was so still for the moment, with all the men just staring and amazed, that I could hear every word come along the decks.

"There's sure been a submarine earthquake somewhere," I heard the First Mate. "The bottom of the sea's just riz up here, quiet and gentle, during the night; and God's mercy we aren't now a-top of one of those ornaments out there."

And then, you know, I saw it all. Everything that had looked mad and impossible, began to be natural; though it was, none the less, all amazing and wonderful.

There had been during the night, a slow lifting of the sea-bottom, owing to some action of the Internal Pressures. The rocks had risen so gently that they had made never a sound; and the stone ship had risen with them out of the deep sea. She had evidently lain on one of the submerged reefs, and so had seemed to us to be just afloat in the sea. And she accounted for the water we heard running. She was naturally bung full, as you might say, and took longer to shed the water than she did to rise. She had probably some biggish holes in her bottom. I began to get my "soundings" a bit, as I might call it in sailor talk. The natural wonders of the sea beat all made-up yarns that ever were!

The Mate sung out to us to man the boat again, and told the Third Mate to take her out to where we lost the Skipper, and have a final look round, in case there might be any chance to find the Old Man's body anywhere about.

"Keep a man in the bows to look out for sunk rocks, Mister," the Mate told the Third, as we pulled off. "Go slow. There'll be no wind yet awhile. See if you can fix up what made those noises, while you're looking round."

We pulled right across about thirty fathoms of clear water, and in a minute we were between two great arches of rock. It was then I realized that the reduplicating of our oar-roll was the echo from these on each side of us. Even in the sunlight, it was queer to hear again that same strange cathedral echoey sound that we had heard in the dark.

We passed under the huge arches, all hung with deep-sea slime. And presently we were heading straight for a gap, where two low reefs swept in to the apex of a huge horseshoe. We pulled for about three minutes, and then the Third gave the word to vast pulling.

"Take the boat-hook, Duprey," he said, "and go forrard, and see we don't hit anything."

"'I, 'i, Sir," I said, and drew in my oar.

"Give way again gently!" said the Third; and the boat moved forward for another thirty or forty yards.

"We're right on to a reef, Sir," I said, presently, as I stared down over the bows. I sounded with the boat-hook. "There's about three feet of water, Sir," I told him.

"Vast pulling," ordered the Third. "I reckon we are right over the rock, where we found that rum packet last night." He leant over the side, and stared down.

"There's a stone cannon on the rock, right under the bows of the boat," I said. Immediately afterwards I shouted—

"There's the hair, Sir! There's the hair! It's on the reef. There's two! There's three! There's one on the cannon!"

"All right! All right, Duprey! Keep cool," said the Third Mate. "I can see them. You're enough intelligence not to be superstitious now the whole thing's explained. They're some kind of big hairy sea-caterpillar. Prod one with your boat-hook."

I did so; a little ashamed of my sudden bewilderment. The thing whipped round like a tiger, at the boat-hook. It lapped itself round and round the boat-hook, while the hind portions of it kept gripped to the rock, and I could no more pull the boat-hook from its grip, than fly; though I pulled till I sweated.

"Take the point of your cutlass to it, Varley," said the Third Mate. "Jab it through."

The bow-oar did so, and the brute loosed the boat-hook, and curled up round a chunk of rock, looking like a great ball of red hair.

I drew the boat-hook up, and examined it.

"Goodness!" I said. "That's what killed the Old Man—one of those things! Look at all those marks in the wood, where it's gripped it with about a hundred legs."

I passed the boat-hook aft to the Third Mate to look at.

"They're about as dangerous as they can be, Sir, I reckon," I told him.

"Makes you think of African centipedes, only these are big and strong enough to kill an elephant, I should think."

"Don't lean all on one side of the boat!" shouted the Third Mate, as the men stared over. "Get back to your places. Give way, there!

... Keep a good look-out for any signs of the ship or the Captain, Duprey."

For nearly an hour, we pulled to and fro over the reef; but we never saw either the stone ship or the Old Man again. The queer craft must have rolled off into the profound depths that lay on each side of the reef.

As I leant over the bows, staring down all that long while at the submerged rocks, I was able to understand almost everything, except the various extraordinary noises.

The cannon made it unmistakably clear that the ship which had been hove up from the sea-bottom, with the rising of the reef, had been originally a normal enough wooden vessel of a time far removed from our own. At the sea-bottom, she had evidently undergone some natural mineralizing process, and this explained her stony appearance. The stone men had been evidently humans who had been drowned in her cabin, and their swollen tissues had been subjected to the same natural process, which, however, had also deposited heavy encrustations upon them, so that their size, when compared with the normal, was prodigious.

The mystery of the hair, I had already discovered; but there remained, among other things, the tremendous bangs we had heard. These were, possibly, explained later, while we were making a final examination of the rocks to the westward, prior to returning to our ship. Here we discovered the burst and swollen bodies of several extraordinary deep-sea creatures, of the eel variety. They must have had a girth, in life, of many feet, and one that we measured roughly with an oar, must have been quite forty feet long. They had, apparently, burst on being lifted from the tremendous pressure of the deep sea, into the light air pressure above water, and hence might account for the loud reports we had heard; though, personally, I incline to think these loud bangs were more probably caused by the splitting of the rocks under new stresses.

As for the roaring sounds, I can only conclude that they were caused by a peculiar species of grampus-like fish, of enormous size, which we found dead and hugely distended on one of the rocky masses. This fish must have weighed at least four or five tons, and when prodded with a heavy oar, there came from its peculiar snout-shaped mouth, a low, hoarse sound, like a weak imitation of the tremendous sounds we had heard during the past night.

Regarding the apparently carved handrail, like a rope up the side of the cabin stairs, I realize that this had undoubtedly been actual rope at one time.

Recalling the heavy, trundling sounds aboard, just after I climbed down into the boat, I can only suppose that these were made by some stone object, possibly a fossilized gun-carriage, rolling down the decks, as the ship began to slip off the rocks, and bows sank lower in the water.

The varying lights must have been the strongly phosphorescent bodies of some of the deep-sea creatures, moving about on the upheaved reefs. As for the giant splash that occurred in the darkness ahead of the boat, this must have been due to some large portion of heaved-up rock, over-balancing and rolling back into the sea.

No one aboard ever learnt about the jewels. I took care of that! I sold the ruby badly, so I've heard since; but I do not grumble even now. Twenty-three thousand pounds I had for it alone, from a merchant in London. I learned afterwards he made double that on it; but I don't spoil my pleasure by grumbling. I wonder often how the stones and things came where I found them; but she carried guns, as I've told, I think; and there's rum doings happen at sea; yes, by George!

The smell—oh that I guess was due to heaving all that deep-sea slime up for human noses to smell at.

This yarn is, of course, known in nautical circles, and was briefly mentioned in the old *Nautical Mercury* of 1879. The series of volcanic reefs (which disappeared in 1883) were charted under the name of the "Alfred Jessop Shoals and Reefs"; being named after our Captain who discovered them and lost his life on them.

De Profundis
H. de Vere Stacpoole

I

The Vladivostock-Nagasaki cable was broken.

The Vladivostock-Nagasaki cable leaves Peter the Great Bay in six thousand feet of water and crosses the great ten-thousand-foot depth south of latitude 42° N.

The floor of the sea of Japan south of latitude 42° N. forms a vast saucer three hundred miles broad by four hundred miles long, or roughly, from the north of Matsu Shima to the latitude of Possiet Bay, the most southerly bay in Siberian territory.

It was at Hong Kong, where she was lying for repairs, that the *President Girling*, of the Franco-Danish Cable Company, received news of the break with orders to mend it. She was a fifteen-hundred-ton boat, new built from the yards of Stefansson and Meyerling, with geared turbine engines and everything about her of the latest from the last thing in sea valves to the last thing in grapnels— Breim's patent hold-fast all-steel grapnel, the invention of the chief cable engineer of the *President Girling*.

It was eleven o'clock in the morning when the message came on board, and Grondaal, the master of the ship, received it just as he was stepping on deck from the saloon companion-way. He came forward at once to find Breim, the chief cable engineer, who was busy over some job in the bows.

Forward of the bridge lay the electric testing room and forward of that the picking-up gear, consisting of a great drum round which the grapnel rope was wound like the line on a salmon reel, and the engine that rotated the drum. Red-painted buoys showed bright in the sunlight that flooded the deck, where coils of buoy rope were

316

being overhauled with a view to discovering defects or chafings. Breim, a big, bearded man, was superintending this business when Captain Grondaal came along to him, bearing in his hand the cablegram just arrived from the head office of the company in Copenhagen.

"We'll have to put out to-night," said Grondaal. "Lucky the stores are all aboard."

Breim took the cablegram and read it over slowly. It gave the position of the break as ascertained by the electricians at Nagasaki; that is to say, the position as regards the length of the cable; the hydrographer of the *President Girling* would work out the sea position to within a mile.

"That's a good bit north of the great dip," said Breim. "Rotten bad coral bottom too, and fifteen hundred fathoms if it's a metre."

"There or thereabouts," said Grondaal. "You have everything ready?"

"Ay, ay," replied Breim. "I have everything ready."

They were men who did not waste words. Grondaal stood for a moment watching an incoming ship taking up her moorings, then he went aft to the electric testing room to warn the electricians, and Breim turned and went on directing Steffansson, the foreman of the cable hands.

Steffansson was a gigantic, white-haired man, an Icelander with fifty years of sea experience in the cod fisheries and cable service. He had worked for the Larssen Company of Copenhagen and for the Franco-Danish Company with whom he was now employed. He had captained a boat in the Icelandic fishing fleet and had put in a season at the Alaska canneries. One might say that he had always been a fisherman, for cable mending is three-fourths of cable work and nine-tenths of cable mending is fisherman's work.

Steffansson was the right hand of Breim, and the right hand of Steffansson was Andersen, the Dane who superintended the engine of the picking-up gear.

These three men formed a corporate body, one might say that they were the three parts of an intricate mechanism. In picking up a broken cable, when the great drum of the picking-up gear was rotating, Breim on the bow balks, Steffansson at the drum and

Andersen with his hand on the lever of the engine, controlled the whole business just as the cells of a nervous ganglion control the most complicated muscular movements. A sign, a word, almost a thought of Breim's caught instantaneously by his assistants, was transmuted into tons of energy; the geared turbines of the main engines were under their control no less than the helm and the engine of the picking-up gear; a word from Steffansson to Grondaal on the bridge would cast the ship back or forward, head her to port or starboard, a sign to Andersen would rotate the great drum on which the grapnel rope was wound, paying out or hauling in.

They played with the cable once it was hooked, as a juggler plays with a ball, or a salmon-fisher with a salmon.

Breim, a well-to-do man with an instinct for sport, inherited from an English ancestor, often in his own mind compared the great picking-up drum to the reel on a fishing-rod. In principle it was, in fact, just the same. You could let out line or pull in, brake or release, and the engine worked by Andersen was better than any patent multiplier for hauling in the slack. The only difference was the size, a hook weighing a couple of hundred-weight instead of a few grains, and a wire-wove rope with a breaking strain of twenty tons instead of a twenty-thread line that a boy might snap.

Breim could have retired by this from the cable industry, and would have done so, no doubt, but for the element of sport in the business. He had caught shark with rod and line and he had once played a three-hundred-pound tuna for an hour and fifteen minutes before bringing it to gaff, but had you asked him which was the better sport, shark or cable, and had he truthfully replied, "cable" would have been the word.

The last of the men on shore leave were back by five in the afternoon, and as sunset was turning the sky behind China into the semblance of a vast stained-glass window, the *President Girling* unbuoyed.

Showing her stern to the rose-gold light of the west she slipped away from the anchorage, making less fuss over the business of departure than a trading junk. Then heading nor'-nor'-east, she passed, dissolving like a shadow in the twilight of the sea.

II

She passed the Pescadores in a rose and pearly dawn, and, pushing on up the Tung Hai Sea, entered the Sea of Japan by way of the Korea channel. From here it was a straight run to the spot against a head wind and a heavy sea.

The Sea of Japan is full of trickery. Nothing good could come from Sakhalin and the Kuriles, and a good deal of Sea of Japan weather comes from there, the great plains of Manchuria send their contingents of winds and storms, and Japan itself, though a bar to the Pacific swell, does not turn back hurricanes.

Grondaal knew this sea and its ways, and the heavy weather did not worry him. It is impossible to work cable in rough water, and the *President Girling* had often been held up for weeks on a job owing to the state of the sea; all the same the skipper was cheerful, prophesying that all this smother was the tail end of trouble, not the beginning of it, and he was right, for at daybreak on the morning that they reached the spot, the Sea of Japan lay flat as the table of a sapphire to the hard-cut horizon, flat as a dead calm can ever make the sea, from the skyline to the vague blue of the awful depths beneath the keel.

Even before sunrise, the ship was astir. With the first touch of light on the yellow funnel and the bridge canvas, the vibration of the propellers ceased. Breim on the after gratings was superintending the working of the Kelvin sounder that was paying out its lead from a bobbin carrying three miles of piano wire, whilst Steffansson stood beside him marking the depth.

Then the sewing-machine clatter of the sounder hauling in the lead filled the air.

The lead gave a depth of a mile and a quarter, and the tallow on it told that the bottom was rocky.

Then Breim went forward, and the work of putting out the first mark buoy was put in hand.

The buoy, with a mushroom anchor and over a mile and a quarter of rope, was dropped. Then the ship put away a mile to the east and dropped the second buoy. Both buoys carried lighted lamps in case of work not being over at dark.

Somewhere between these two buoys the cable would be found.

Breim had now taken command of the ship; standing on the bow balks, he gave his orders whilst the grapnel—Breim's patent all-steel, never-let-go grapnel—was bent on to the grapnel rope. This rope, with a nominal breaking strain of twenty tons, passed, after leaving the drum, under a dynamometer that registered every strain put upon it; it left the ship over a wheel in the bows between the knight-heads, just where in ordinary ships the bowsprit comes in.

When the clanking drum had ceased its revolutions and the grapnel had touched bottom, Breim raised his hand, the engine-room telegraph rang and the *President Girling*, going dead slow, began to make back along the course to the first mark buoy.

The grapnel, dragging along the sea floor in search of the cable, clutched at everything in its path, rock or coral, and every strain put upon it was registered on the great clock face of the dynamometer by the jumping indicator, which had a permanent point at two tons, that being the weight of the rope as weighed in sea water. It was now eight o'clock, and Grondaal, with the electricians and first officer, went down to breakfast, leaving Breim alone in his glory on the bow balks, and the third officer in charge of the bridge.

The saloon was a cheerful place, large, well decorated, a long table, capable of seating twenty, running down the middle. It was especially cheerful this morning, lit by the blazing sunlight, and Grondaal, at the head of the table, was in more than ordinary good spirits. He had prophesied good weather, and the brightness outside pleased him almost as much as though he had made it. They talked as they ate. Not a word about the sea. Anything but the sea. They talked of the new music-hall at Copenhagen, and the man who had built it and was likely to lose money over it; they talked of Jan Gudmundson's wife—Gudmundson was a past captain in the service, and how she spent his money and kept him in order so that he could not enter a beer hall without her apparition at the door waiting to lead him home. And then somehow—perhaps it was Jan Gudmundson's wife that suggested the subject—grapnels came on the tapis, and then, for a wonder and once in a way, a sea subject fell under discussion. Johansson, the first officer, started it.

"I've been twenty years at this business," said he, "and I've never yet seen the grapnel bring in a bit of wreck. Take the wrecks of a single year and multiply them by twenty and you will have what the last twenty years has laid on the sea floor. It ought to be paved with wrecks. Well, if they're there why don't they show up on the grapnel—give up a bit of themselves, eh?"

Grondaal went into a long argument to prove that a grapnel might go a dozen times over a wreck without detaching a plank or spar, and another to demonstrate that if it did it would be a hundred to one against it bringing its prey to the surface.

Hardmuth, the second electrician, a flaxen-bearded individual, a man with a round, innocent face and the clear, truthful eyes of a child, who had been listening to Grondaal with marked attention, now spoke up.

"I don't know anything about wrecks," said he, "but some years ago I saw the grapnel bring up something stranger than ship wreckage; it brought up a wheel."

"Steering?" asked Grondaal.

"No, the wheel of a vehicle, made of bronze."

"And where was that brought up, may I ask?"

"In the Red Sea."

Hardmuth was the ship's liar as well as second electrician; later on that day he was to have the fact borne in on him that Truth can be sometimes more fantastic than Invention.

III

The Nagasaki end of the cable was caught and buoyed by two o'clock that afternoon. At two-fifteen the hunt began for the Vladivostock end.

The weather had changed. With a steady barometer the temperature had risen, a damp, muggy blanket of heat had unrolled itself from the Manchurian plains and spread itself across the Sea of Japan. The line of the horizon had vanished in haze, the sun, with scarcely any diminution of brilliancy, had lost its sharpness, and the wind was as dead as though it had never been.

Breim, on the bow balks, was conducting operations with his coat off. Though everything was going splendidly he was out of temper on account of the heat, he was also anxious with the anxiety of a man who sees the possibility of pulling off a big coup. If they could only bring the Vladivostock end on board by, say, five o'clock, the whole job might be finished that day, and that would be a tremendous feather in the cap of Breim.

The grapnel had been lowered and the first grapple was half through when the pointer of the dynamometer, that had been indicating a strain of two tons and a quarter, rose suddenly with a flick to eight tons, held there for a moment and fell again to six.

Then it dashed up to ten tons, held there for five seconds or so, rose to fifteen and fell to seven, then rose to twelve and sank to five.

Steffansson, who rarely spoke, standing by the drum and watching these evolutions of the pointer, suddenly called out to Breim, asking him what was the matter.

Cable, once hooked, gives a slow and steady rise of strain, rock or weed tangling the grapnel may cause a sudden jump of the pointer, but when the grapnel frees itself the pointer always falls to normal.

It might have been supposed that the grapnel, dragging along the sea floor, was meeting and overcoming several obstacles in succession, but for the fact that the recessions were not to normal, but to six, seven and five tons successively.

"What's up?" cried Steffansson.

Breim made no reply. He had stopped the main engines and then put them to a few revolutions astern, taking all way off the ship. Then he bent and put his ear to the taut grapnel rope. He could always tell by the tune of the rope whether rock or cable was engaged by the grapnel. What he heard now was a new thing. A deep booming sound, like the beating of a gigantic heart at a vast distance. The rope might have been a stethoscope giving a vague hint of the beating heart of the world.

Breim straightened himself.

"Fish!" cried he to Steffansson. "We're on to a fish—look out."

"Fish!" cried Steffansson; "why, it's over a mile down!"

Breim did not seem to hear him.

"How much more rope is on the drum?" he cried.

"Not more than half a mile."

"Tell Johanssen to roust out another two mile of rope and bend it on," cried Breim. "Stand by at the engine, Andersen. Steffansson, see that the drum rope runs clear, no hitches."

The words were scarcely out of his mouth when the grapnel rope went forward, making an acute angle with the water and showing a surging ripple. The mammoth fish, or whatever it was below, had started ahead.

"Pay out slowly," shouted Breim to Andersen, then, as the leisurely clank of the drum filled the air, he reached the deck in two jumps, crossed it, and ran up the bridge ladder to the bridge.

From here he had a view of the rope ahead and of the dynamometer. Here he had the main engines under immediate control, and from here he could give his orders to Andersen at the picking-up engine. Here he had as complete dominance of the mechanism and the situation as a tuna fisherman with his rod and reel.

But it was not sport he was after in these first moments, though the sportsman in him was furiously alive; it was rope-saving, primarily, for he knew that if the thing below was not played it would break; the rope, and a mile and a half of wire-wove grapnel rope, to say nothing of the grapnel, costs money.

Eased by the slow paying out of the drum, the strain on the rope was only fifteen tons, and this despite the fact that had you looked over the side you would have seen a ripple at the ship's stern. The ship was being towed, just as the tuna-launch is towed when the tuna is making its rush, held by taut line and bending rod. Only the rush of this mile-deep monster was slower in proportion to size.

Whatever the thing was that had taken the grapnel for hook, two facts stood out concerning it. It was vast in size and sluggish for its size.

These two facts, when he recognized them together, gave Breim what he afterwards described as a "turn of the heart."

IV

Just then Grondaal came on the bridge. The thing that was happening had caused no commotion on the ship. No one knew of it but the cable men on duty. Grondaal was as ignorant as the others, and when he stepped on the bridge it surprised him to find Breim there. Then he saw the grapnel rope strutting out into the water, and for a second he was under the impression that they were going astern, an impression destroyed at once by the fact that there was no vibration of the propellers, also by the fact that the drum was paying out rope.

"Why, what's all this?" asked the astonished Grondaal.

"We're under tow," said Breim.

"Tow! What's on the grapnel?"

"The Lord He knows," replied the other, "something alive down there. The great-grandfather of all whales—seems to me. Hi, there, Steffansson, slower with the drum; put more strain on him."

Steffansson obeyed, braking the drum, and the indicator of the dynamometer steadily rose to eighteen tons, to nineteen tons, to nineteen and a half.

"Less strain," cried Breim. The drum revolved slightly quicker, and the indicator stole down to seventeen tons.

"Keep it so," cried Breim.

"Well, I'm d—d!" said Grondaal.

Breim wiped his forehead with his shirt-sleeve.

"I'm feeling that way myself," said he; "there's nothing to be done but stick on or cut, and cut's impossible with all that rope out."

"Maybe it'll disentangle," said the other; "if it's a whale it will have got the grapnel in the jaws, and then turn like a log and get bound up in the rope—"

"It's no whale," said Breim; "what I'm afraid of most is a sudden jerk, and then that rope will go like a thread; you know these wire-wove ropes and how they mushroom out like an umbrella when broken and fly back and cut everything to pieces. Lord! Look at that fool of a cable hand, climbing on to the bow balks—get off there, get clear away from the rope; what d'you think you're doing there, anyhow; get aft behind the drum."

Grondaal looked at the compass card.

"We're being taken to Vladivostock," said he. "We'll get there, maybe, at this rate, by Christmas; cold place that time of year—have you got a fur coat?"

Breim bristled.

"Well, order out the axes to cut," said he; "you're master of the ship."

"Not I," said Grondaal. "The chief cable engineer is master while cable work's on. Do as you like."

"Then I'll stick to him till I bring him aboard or alongside," replied the other; "that I swear by the great hat of Krivikur. My grapnel's hooked him, and Breim's at the other end of the rope. I'll teach the lousy brute—cut!—I'd sooner cut my hand off."

He was working himself up into a rage. The heat, the delay, Grondaal's jest, and the knowledge that the thing below had calm command of the situation, condemning him either to lose rope by cutting, or time by following, all conspired to raise his temper; his voice rose, and he was bringing his palm down with a bang on the bridge-rail when, suddenly, the dynamometer fell with a flick to two tons.

"He's off," said Grondaal.

Breim shouted to Andersen, ordering him to reel in. The engine throbbed, the drum reversed its motion and the rope came in slack and dripping, only for a moment, and then the dynamometer drove up steadily to fourteen tons, whilst the head of the ship slightly altered its pointing and the needle of the compass card fluttered.

"He's altered his course—that's all," said Grondaal. "He's making now for Possiet Bay, seems to me. Can't you liven him up?"

Breim made no reply for a moment. He was thinking hard.

The nominal breaking strain of the rope was twenty tons, but he knew it would stand a strain much above that. The worst that could happen would be the breaking of the rope. He determined on more active measures.

Leaning over the bridge-rail he gave orders for all hands to clear back into the alley-ways; all, that is to say, with the exception of Steffansson and Andersen. He told Steffansson to keep as much as possible to the rear of the drum. Andersen would have to take his chance and trust to the God of Fishermen.

He ordered the paying out of the rope to cease. The strain rose instantly to nineteen tons. He ordered Andersen at the engine to reverse the drum two revolutions. The jigger of the dynamometer dashed up to twenty tons. The thing did not register above twenty tons, what the real strain was heaven only knows. Breim put it down at twenty-five. He gave the drum another revolution.

Instead of the gun-like report of a burst rope, which he half expected, came the "flick" of the dynamometer; the pointer had fallen to normal, and then risen to two tons.

One of two things had happened: the increased strain had torn the grapnel free, or the creature below had risen owing to the strain.

"Pick up!" cried Breim.

The drum roared, and the slack came in, fathom after rushing fathom.

"You've freed the grapnel," said Grondaal.

"'Pears so," said Breim. He was disappointed. The fisherman had been roused to full life in him. Of all the fishermen in the world it had been given to him alone to fight Leviathan, using a fifteen-hundred-ton ship for a rod and a forty-foot grapnel drum for a reel, and now the fish was off.

Then suddenly his heart jumped in him.

The slack, incoming rope tautened with a snap, the sea-water on it shot out in a rainbow shower of spray; Andersen, not waiting for orders, shut off the engine, and Steffansson on his own initiative kept the drum brake released. The rope, instead of breaking, rushed out.

Breim knew what was happening below. Over two hundred fathoms of rope had come in, that meant that the thing below had risen two hundred fathoms, and it was now either running at that depth or sinking.

He let the rope run for a few seconds and then, just as the fisherman puts the brake on the line, he put the brake on the drum. Instead of breaking the rope made a more acute angle with the sea, and a swirl of water stood around it. The thing had not sunk, it was running, maybe making four knots; the ship was making the same speed, less the fraction to be deducted by the very gradual paying out of rope, for the drum, by Breim's orders, was now less controlled by the brake.

Breim was working now entirely regardless of the dynamometer, working altogether by his fisherman sense. It was inspiration pure and simple.

He jockeyed the thing below with lifting strains and alternate releases, so that at the end of an hour he judged it to be only half a mile from the surface.

The thing that filled him with wonder, and at the same time with hope, was the slow movement of the creature as compared with its undoubted bulk. If its velocity had borne any proportion to its size, the rope would have snapped in the very first minute of the struggle.

By this time the whole ship was alive to what was going on. The officers and electricians were on the bridge and the crew crowded in the alley-ways. Hardmuth had rushed below for his camera to photograph the result, whenever it was attained. As for Breim, he was unconscious of the audience about him. The bridge might have been empty for all he knew or cared; his whole soul and mind were concentrated on the struggle and on that alone.

And yet it scarcely seemed a struggle, so destitute was the business of fuss or fury, just a long, dragging strain, the drum rotating, now to pick up a bit of slack, paying out now gradually, now ceasing to rotate.

Something had gone wrong with the dynamometer; unused to such strains and such usage, it had stuck, the pointer fixed at the maximum strain, even when slack was being hauled in.

V

Half an hour before sunset, Breim had brought his prey to within a quarter of a mile of the surface, at least so he judged.

There was more than a mile of rope out, and he estimated that the thing was three-quarters of a mile from the ship.

His calculations took into consideration the depth of the sea just there, all the slack he had hauled in, all the rope he had paid out, the angle of the rope with the sea surface—or, in other words, the length of the rope between the point where it left the bow and the point where it entered the water. The thing was only a quarter of a mile from the surface, but the fact remained that it wanted, now, only half an hour to sunset. The moon would not rise till after dark. It would be the pity of the world if the great Unseen were to break from the sea under cover of darkness. It might also be dangerous.

Hardmuth, with his camera ready, was even more excited on this point than Breim. Hardmuth, the ship's liar and jester, was an earnest photographer—you know what that means.

The lower limb of the sun was just touching the sea line when the great event occurred.

Due east of the ship, and a mile away on the starboard bow, the water broke.

"Look out!" cried Breim.

The words came from him unconsciously. A horn was rising from the sea, a dark column, pointed, living, but eyeless as a worm. It rose, steadily driven up by some vast force acting from below, and stood triumphant, like the horn of Eblis, a column a hundred feet high, bulbous at the base, black as ebony, and creamed about by the sea.

The sea seemed to boil at its base, and the rays of the setting sun shone full upon the prodigy, lighting that upon which no sun had ever shone before.

The effect on the minds of the gazers might have been gauged by the utter silence that fell on the ship.

Afterwards, and putting their experiences together, the ship's company found that the dominant, heart-freezing idea, common to every mind, had to do neither with the size nor the monstrous appearance of the thing, but with the fact that it was living.

There were some who fancied it half a mile high, others who saw it in more true proportion, but there was not one who escaped the bending of the mind produced by the thought, "It is alive!"—a thought made more insistent by the sluggishness of its manner of appearance and by its calm immobility when revealed.

The fo'c'sle hands felt that, but to the keen intelligence of Breim all sorts of other considerations came crowding.

He had literally raised the dead, for what he saw was something belonging to a world long extinct, and, though it was living in the biological sense, it was extinct in the historical. It was as though some magician had reinformed with life a man of the stone age or a labyrinthodon.

Again, these vast and slow movements, this present immobility, were parts of its death struggle. The pressures under which it had been born and under which it had lived were part of the conditions of its life. They had been removed and it must die. Nay, it must now be dying.

A sound suddenly broke the stillness of the bridge, it was the click of Hardmuth's camera. The photographer had been the first to release himself from the spell.

On the sound, and as though it had been a signal, the column inclined slightly and sank, like a sword slowly withdrawn.

The last rays of sunset showed a troubled sea just there, and then, in the dusk and the haze that followed the closing of the hot day, things began to occur. Sounds came over the sea, sounds like the washing of water on a distant beach, and now and again a gurgle, like the gurgle of a vast, submerging bottle.

But the men on board the *President Girling* had other things to attend to now.

Breim's voice came bellowing from the bridge. The grapnel rope was slack. The thing had evidently freed itself from the grapnel, even before rising from the sea, and now the roar of the rotating drum hauling in the slack shut out all other sounds from over there, but it could not shut out the odour that filled the windless air, a smell of beach and ooze with a tang in it recalling tropical river mud.

It took half an hour to get the rope in; the grapnel, when it came, was hauled under the light of an arc lamp and carefully examined. It showed nothing, nothing with the exception of what seemed a tag of black leather tangled at the base of one of the prongs. The rope connection was slightly chafed.

As Breim was examining it a report like a boom of thunder came over the sea, and away over there in the half-darkness something white showed like a falling sheet of foam.

Grondaal on the bridge shouted to Breim.

"It's time to get out of here," cried he.

He had rung on the engines, and the ship, turning like a frightened thing, began to vibrate to the propellers going full speed. She had covered a mile on her new course when the sound came again, fainter this time.

They passed the light of the buoy marking the Nagasaki end of the cable, and left it spilling its amber on the water far astern.

Then, as speed was reduced, once again came the sound, faint and for the last time.

There were men on board who listened all night and watched under the light of the risen moon, but the sea had resumed its own, and, steaming close to the spot of the occurrence next morning, there was nothing to be seen, nothing but the sea surface oiling under the gentle swell away to the haze that proclaimed the birth of another hot day.

At eleven o'clock Hardmuth came out of the dark room, where he had been developing his marvellous plate.

He was as white as the foam that the propellers were kicking behind them.

He sat down on a life-buoy locker as though to take breath, and Breim, who was near by, ran to him, took the plate, and examined it, holding it up to the light.

It was the picture of a garden party at Copenhagen.

The wretched Hardmuth, disdaining kodaks and using his super-perfect single-plate camera, had employed a used plate.

It was said of Hardmuth that he never smiled or jested again— at least on board of the *President Girling*.

DEMONS OF THE SEA
William Hope Hodgson

"Come out on deck and have a look, Darky!'" Jepson cried, rushing into the half deck. "The Old Man says there's been a submarine earthquake, and the sea's all bubbling and muddy!"

Obeying the summons of Jepson's excited tone, I followed him
out. It was as he had said; the everlasting blue of the ocean was
mottled with splotches of a muddy hue, and at times a large bubble
would appear, to burst with a loud "pop." Aft, the skipper and the
three mates could be seen on the poop, peering at the sea through
their glasses. As I gazed out over the gently heaving water, far off
to windward something was hove up into the evening air. It appeared to be a mass of seaweed, but fell back into the water with a
sullen plunge as though it were something more substantial. Immediately after this strange occurrence, the sun set with tropical
swiftness, and in the brief afterglow things assumed a strange un-
reality.

The crew were all below, no one but the mate and the helmsman remaining on the poop. Away forward, on the topgallant forecastle head the dim figure of the man on lookout could be seen,
leaning against the forestay. No sound was heard save the occasional jingle of a chain sheet, of the flog of the steering gear as a
small swell passed under our counter. Presently the mate's voice
broke the silence, and, looking up, I saw that the Old Man had come
on deck, and was talking with him. From the few stray words that
could be overheard, I knew they were talking of the strange happenings of the day.

Shortly after sunset, the wind, which had been fresh during the
day, died down, and with its passing the air grew oppressively hot.

331

Not long after two bells, the mate sung out for me, and ordered me to fill a bucket from overside and bring it to him. When I had carried out his instructions, he placed a thermometer in the bucket.

"Just as I thought," he muttered, removing the instrument and showing it to the skipper; "ninety-nine degrees. Why, the sea's hot enough to make tea with!"

"Hope it doesn't get any hotter," growled the latter; "if it does, we shall all be boiled alive."

At a sign from the mate, I emptied the bucket and replaced it in the rack, after which I resumed my former position by the rail. The Old Man and the mate walked the poop side by side. The air grew hotter as the hours passed and after a long period of silence broken only by the occasional "pop" of a bursting gas bubble, the moon arose. It shed but a feeble light, however, as a heavy mist had arisen from the sea, and through this, the moonbeams struggled weakly. The mist, we decided, was due to the excessive heat of the sea water; it was a very wet mist, and we were soon soaked to the skin. Slowly the interminable night wore on, and the sun arose, looking dim and ghostly through the mist that rolled and billowed about the ship. From time to time we took the temperature of the sea, although we found but a slight increase therein. No work was done, and a feeling as of something impending pervaded the ship.

The fog horn was kept going constantly, as the lookout peered through the wreathing mists. The captain walked the poop in company with the mates, and once the third mate spoke and pointed out into the clouds of fog. All eyes followed his gesture; we saw what was apparently a black line, which seemed to cut the whiteness of the billows. It reminded us of nothing so much as an enormous cobra standing on its tail. As we looked it vanished. The grouped mates were evidently puzzled; there seemed to be a difference of opinion among them. Presently as they argued, I heard the second mate's voice:

"That's all rot," he said. "I've seen things in fog before, but they've always turned out to be imaginary."

The third shook his head and made some reply I could not overhear, but no further comment was made. Going below that afternoon,

I got a short sleep, and on coming on deck at eight bells, I found that the steam still held us; if anything, it seemed to be thicker than ever. Hansard, who had been taking the temperatures during my watch below, informed me that the sea was three degrees hotter, and that the Old Man was getting into a rare old state. At three bells I went forward to have a look over the bows, and a chin with Stevenson, whose lookout it was. On gaining the forecastle head, I went to the side and looked down into the water. Stevenson came over and stood beside me.

"Rum go, this," he grumbled.

He stood by my side for a time in silence; we seemed to be hypnotized by the gleaming surface of the sea. Suddenly out of the depths, right before us, there arose a monstrous black face. It was like a frightful caricature of a human countenance. For a moment we gazed petrified; my blood seemed to suddenly turn to ice water; I was unable to move. With a mighty effort of will, I regained my self-control and, grasping Stevenson's arm, I found I could do no more than croak, my powers of speech seemed gone. "Look!" I gasped. "Look!"

Stevenson continued to stare into the sea, like a man turned to stone. He seemed to stoop further over, as if to examine the thing more closely. "Lord," he exclaimed, "it must be the devil himself!"

As though the sound of his voice had broken a spell, the thing disappeared. My companion looked at me, while I rubbed my eyes, thinking that I had been asleep, and that the awful vision had been a frightful nightmare. One look at my friend, however, disabused me of any such thought. His face wore a puzzled expression.

"Better go aft and tell the Old Man," he faltered.

I nodded and left the forecastle head, making my way aft like one in a trance. The skipper and the mate were standing at the break of the poop, and running up the ladder I told them what we had seen.

"Bosh!" sneered the Old Man. "You've been looking at your own ugly reflection in the water."

Nevertheless, in spite of his ridicule, he questioned me closely. Finally he ordered the mate forward to see it he could see anything. The latter, however, returned in a few moments, to report

that nothing unusual could be seen. Four bells were struck, and
we were relieved for tea. Coming on deck afterward, I found the
men clustered together forward. The sole topic of conversation with
them was the thing that Stevenson and I had seen.

"I suppose, Darky, it couldn't have been a reflection by any
chance, could it?" one of the older men asked.

"Ask Stevenson," I replied as I made my way aft.

At eight bells, my watch came on deck again, to find that nothing
further had developed. But, about an hour before midnight, the
mate, thinking to have a smoke, sent me to his room for a box of
matches with which to light his pipe. It took me no time to clatter
down the brass-treaded ladder, and back to the poop, where I
handed him the desired article. Taking the box, he removed a match
and struck it on the heel of his boot. As he did so, far out in the
night a muffled screaming arose. Then came a clamor as of hoarse
braying, like an ass but considerably deeper, and with a horribly
suggestive human note running through it.

"Good God! Did you hear that, Darky?" asked the mate in awed
tones.

"Yes, sir," I replied, listening—and scarcely noticing his question—for a repetition of the strange sounds. Suddenly the frightful
bellowing broke out afresh. The mate's pipe fell to the deck with a
clatter.

"Run for'ard!" he cried. "Quick, now, and see if you can see
anything."

With my heart in my mouth, and pulses pounding madly I raced
forward. The watch were all up on the forecastle head, clustered
around the lookout. Each man was talking and gesticulating wildly.
They became silent, and turned questioning glances toward me as
I shouldered my way among them.

"Have you seen anything?" I cried.

Before I could receive an answer, a repetition of the horrid
sounds broke out again, profaning the night with their horror. They
seemed to have definite direction now, in spite of the fog that enveloped us. Undoubtedly, too, they were nearer. Pausing a moment
to make sure of their bearing, I hastened aft and reported to the
mate. I told him that nothing could be seen, but that the sounds

apparently came from right ahead of us. On hearing this he ordered the man at the wheel to let the ship's head come off a couple of points. A moment later a shrill screaming tore its way through the night, followed by the hoarse braying sounds once more.

"It's close on the starboard bow!" exclaimed the mate, as he beckoned the helmsman to let her head come off a little more. Then, singing out for the watch, he ran forward, slacking the lee braces on the way. When he had the yards trimmed to his satisfaction on the new course, he returned to the poop and hung far out over the rail listening intently. Moments passed that seemed like hours, yet the silence remained unbroken. Suddenly the sounds began again, and so close that it seemed as though they must be right aboard of us. At this time I noticed a strange booming note mingled with the brays. And once or twice there came a sound that can only be described as a sort of "gug, gug." Then would come a wheezy whistling, for all the world like an asthmatic person breathing.

All this while the moon shone wanly through the steam, which seemed to me to be somewhat thinner. Once the mate gripped me by the shoulder as the noises rose and fell again. They now seemed to be coming from a point broad on our beam. Every eye on the ship was straining into the mist, but with no result. Suddenly one of the men cried out, as something long and black slid past us into the fog astern. From it there rose four indistinct and ghostly towers, which resolved themselves into spars and ropes, and sails.

"A ship! It's a ship!" we cried excitedly. I turned to Mr. Gray; he, too, had seen something, and was staring aft into the wake. So ghostlike, unreal, and fleeting had been our glimpse of the stranger, that we were not sure that we had seen an honest, material ship, but thought that we had been vouchsafed a vision of some phantom vessel like the Flying Dutchman. Our sails gave a sudden flap, the clew irons flogging the bulwarks with hollow thumps. The mate glanced aloft.

"Wind's dropping," he growled savagely. "We shall never get out of this infernal place at this gait!"

Gradually the wind fell until it was a flat calm. No sound broke the deathlike silence save the rapid patter of the reef points, as she gently rose and fell on the light swell. Hours passed, and the watch was relieved and I then went below. At seven bells we were called again, and as I went along the deck to the galley, I noticed that the fog seemed thinner, and the air cooler. When eight bells were struck I relieved Hansard at coiling down the ropes. From him I learned that the steam had begun to clear about four bells, and that the temperature of the sea had fallen ten degrees.

In spite of the thinning mist, it was not until about a half an hour later that we were able to get a glimpse of the surrounding sea. It was still mottled with dark patches, but the bubbling and popping had ceased. As much of the surface of the ocean as could be seen had a peculiarly desolate aspect. Occasionally a wisp of steam would float up from the nearer sea, and roll undulatingly across its silent surface, until lost in the vagueness that still held the hidden horizon. Here and there columns of steam rose up in pillars, which gave me the impression that the sea was hot in patches. Crossing to the starboard side and looking over, I found that conditions there were similar to those to port. The desolate aspect of the sea filled me with an idea of chilliness, although the air was quite warm and muggy. From the break of the poop the mate called to me to get his glasses.

When I had done this, he took them from me and walked to the taffrail. Here he stood for some moments polishing them with his handkerchief. After a moment he raised them to his eyes, and peered long and intently into the mist astern. I stood for some time staring at the point on which the mate had focused his glasses. Presently something shadowy grew upon my vision. Steadily watching it, I distinctly saw the outlines of a ship take form in the fog.

"See!" I cried, but even as I spoke, a lifting wraith of mist disclosed to view a great four-masted bark lying becalmed with all sails set, within a few hundred yards of our stern. As though a curtain had been raised, and then allowed to fall, the fog once more settled down, hiding the strange bark from our sight. The mate was all excitement, striding with quick, jerky steps, up and down the poop, stopping every few moments to peer through his glasses at the point where the four-master had disappeared in the fog. Gradually, as the mists dispersed again, the vessel could be seen more plainly, and it was then that we got an inkling of the cause of the dreadful noises during the night.

For some time the mate watched her silently, and as he watched the conviction grew upon me that in spite of the mist, I could detect some sort of movement on board of her. After some time had passed, the doubt became a certainty, and I could also see a sort of splashing in the water alongside of her. Suddenly the mate put his glasses on top of the wheel box and told me to bring him the speaking trumpet. Running to the companionway, I secured the trumpet and was back at his side.

The mate raised it to his lips, and taking a deep breath, sent a hail across the water that should have awakened the dead. We waited tensely for a reply. A moment later a deep, hollow mutter came from the bark; higher and louder it swelled, until we realized that we were listening to the same sounds we had heard the night before. The mate stood aghast at this answer to his hail; in a voice barely more than a hushed whisper, he bade me call the Old Man. Attracted by the mate's hail and its unearthly reply, the watch had all come aft and were clustered in the mizzen rigging in order to see better.

After calling the captain, I returned to the poop, where I found the second and third mates talking with the chief. All were engaged in trying to pierce the clouds of mist that half hid our strange consort and to arrive at some explanation of the strange phenomena of the past few hours. A moment later the captain appeared carrying his telescope. The mate gave him a brief account of the state of affairs and handed him the trumpet. Giving me the telescope to hold, the captain hailed the shadowy bark. Breathlessly we all listened, when again, in answer to the Old Man's hail, the frightful sounds rose on the still morning air. The skipper lowered the trumpet and stood with an expression of astonished horror on his face.

"Lord!" he exclaimed. "What an ungodly row!"

At this, the third, who had been gazing through his binoculars, broke the silence.

"Look," he ejaculated. "There's a breeze coming up astern." At his words the captain looked up quickly, and we all watched the ruffling water.

"That packet yonder is bringing the breeze with her," said the skipper. "She'll be alongside in half an hour!"

Some moments passed, and the bank of fog had come to within a hundred yards of our taffrail. The strange vessel could be distinctly seen just inside the fringe of the driving mist wreaths. After a short puff, the wind died completely, but as we stared with hypnotic fascination, the water astern of the stranger ruffled again with a fresh catspaw. Seemingly with the flapping of her sails, she drew slowly up to us. As the leaden seconds passed, the big four-master approached us steadily. The light air had now reached us, and with a lazy lift of our sails, we, too, began to forge slowly through that weird sea. The bark was now within fifty yards of our stern, and she was steadily drawing nearer, seeming to be able to outfoot us with ease. As she came on she luffed sharply, and came up into the wind with her weather leeches shaking.

I looked toward her poop, thinking to discern the figure of the man at the wheel, but the mist coiled around her quarter, and objects on the after end of her became indistinguishable. With a rattle of chain sheets on her iron yards, she filled away again. We meanwhile had gone ahead, but it was soon evident that she was the better sailor, for she came up to us hand over fist. The wind rapidly freshened and the mist began to drift away before it, so that each moment her spars and cordage became more plainly visible. The skipper and the mates were watching her intently when an almost simultaneous exclamation of fear broke from them.

"My God!"

And well they might show signs of fear, for crawling about the bark's deck were the most horrible creatures I had ever seen. In spite of their unearthly strangeness there was something vaguely familiar about them. Then it came to me that the face that Stevenson and I had seen during he night belonged to one of them. Their bodies had something of the shape of a seal's, but of a dead, unhealthy white. The lower part of the body ended in a sort of double-curved tail on which they appeared to be able to shuffle about. In place of arms, they had two long, snaky feelers, at the ends of which were two very humanlike hands, which were equipped with talons instead of nails. Fearsome indeed were these parodies of human beings!

Their faces, which, like their tentacles, were black, were the most grotesquely human things about them, and the upper jaw closed into the lower, after the manner of the jaws of an octopus. I have seen men among certain tribes of natives who had faces uncommonly like theirs, but yet no native I had ever seen could have given me the extraordinary feeling of horror and revulsion I experienced toward these brutal-looking creatures.

"What devilish beasts!" burst out the captain in disgust.

With this remark he turned to the mates, and as he did so, the expressions on their faces told me that they had all realized what the presence of these bestial-looking brutes meant. If, as was doubtless the case, these creatures had boarded the bark and destroyed her crew, what would prevent them from doing the same with us? We were a smaller ship and had a smaller crew, and the more I thought of it the less I liked it.

We could now see the name on the bark's bow with the naked eye. It read *Scottish Heath*, while on her boats we could see the name bracketed with Glasgow, showing that she hailed from that port. It was a remarkable coincidence that she should have a slant from just the quarter in which yards were trimmed, as before we saw her she must have been drifting around with everything "aback." But now in this light air she was able to run along beside us with no one at her helm. But steering herself she was, and although at times she yawed wildly, she never got herself aback. As we gazed at her we noticed a sudden movement on board of her, and several of the creatures slid into the water.

"See! See! They've spotted us. They're coming for us!" cried the mate wildly.

It was only too true, scores of them were sliding into the sea, letting themselves down by means of their long tentacles. On they came, slipping by scores and hundreds into the water, and swimming toward us in droves. The ship was making about three knots, otherwise they would have caught us in a very few minutes. But they persevered, gaining slowly but surely, and drawing nearer and nearer. The long, tentacle-like arms rose out of the sea in hundreds, and the foremost ones were already within a score of yards of the ship before the Old Man bethought himself to shout to the mates to fetch up the half dozen cutlasses that comprised the ship's armory. Then, turning to me, he ordered me to go down to his cabin and bring up the two revolvers out of the top drawer of the chart table, also a box of cartridges that was there.

When I returned with the weapons he loaded them and handed one to the mate. Meanwhile the pursuing creatures were coming steadily nearer, and soon half a dozen of the leaders were directly under our counter. Immediately the captain leaned over the rail and emptied his pistol into them, but without any apparent effect. He must have realized how puny and ineffectual his efforts were, for he did not reload his weapon.

Some dozens of the brutes had reached us, and as they did so, their tentacles rose into the air and caught our rail. I heard the third mate scream suddenly, and turning, I saw him dragged quickly to the rail, with a tentacle wrapped completely around him. Snatching a cutlass, the second mate hacked off the tentacle where it joined the body. A gout of blood splashed into the third mate's face, and he fell to the deck. A dozen more of those arms rose and wavered in the air, but they now seemed some yards astern of us. A rapidly widening patch of clear water appeared between us and the foremost of our pursuers, and we raised a wild shout of joy. The cause was soon apparent; for a fine fair wind had sprung up, and with the increase in its force, the *Scottish Heath* had got herself aback, while we were rapidly leaving the monsters behind us. The third mate rose to his feet with a dazed look, and as he did so something fell to the deck. I picked it up and found that it was the severed portion of the tentacle of the third's late adversary. With a grimace of disgust I tossed it into the sea, as I needed no reminder of that awful experience.

Three weeks later we anchored in San Francisco. There the captain made a full report of the affair to the authorities, with the result that a gunboat was despatched to investigate. Six weeks later she returned to report that she had been unable to find any signs, either of the ship herself or of the fearful creatures that had attacked her. And since then nothing, as far as I know, has ever been heard of the four-masted bark *Scottish Heath*, last seen by us in the possession of creatures that may rightly be called demons of the sea.

Whether she still floats, occupied by her hellish crew, or whether some storm has sent her to her last resting place beneath the waves is surely a matter of conjecture. Perchance on some dark, fog-bound night, a ship in that wilderness of waters may hear cries and sounds beyond those of the wailing of the winds. Then let them look to it, for it may be that the demons of the sea are near them.

The Habitants of Middle Islet
William Hope Hodgson

"That's 'er," exclaimed the old whaler to my friend Trenhern, as the yacht coasted slowly around Nightingale Island. The old fellow was pointing with the stump of a blackened clay pipe to a small islet on our starboard bow.

"That's 'er, Sir," he repeated. "Middle Islet, an' we'll open out ther cove in er bit. Mind you, Sir, I don't say as ther ship is still there, an' if she is, you'll bear in mind as I told you all erlong as there weren't one in 'er when we went aboard." He replaced his pipe, and took a couple of slow draws, while Trenhern and I scrutinized the little island through our glasses.

We were in the South Atlantic. Far away to the north showed dimly the grim, weather-beaten peak of the Island of Tristan, the largest of the Da Cunha group; while on the horizon to the Westward we could make out indistinctly Inaccessible Island. Both of these, however, held little interest for us. It was on Middle Islet off the coast of Nightingale Island that our attention was fixed.

There was little wind, and the yacht forged but slowly through the deep-tinted water. My friend, I could see, was tortured by impatience to know whether the cove still held the wreck of the vessel that had carried his sweetheart. On my part, though greatly curious, my mind was not sufficiently occupied to exclude a half conscious wonder at the strange coincidence that had led to our present search. For six long months my friend had waited in vain for news of the *Happy Return* in which his sweetheart had sailed for Australia on a voyage in search of health. Yet nothing had been heard, and she was given up for lost; but Trenhern, desperate, had made a last effort. He had sent advertisements to all the largest papers of the world, and this measure had brought a certain degree of success in the shape of the old whaler alongside of him. This man, attracted by the reward offered, had volunteered information regarding a dismasted hulk, bearing the name of the *Happy Return* on her bows and stern, which he had come across during his last voyage, in a queer cove on the South side of Middle Islet. Yet he had been able to give no hope of my friend finding his lost love, or indeed anything living in her; for he had gone aboard with a boat's crew, only to find her utterly deserted, and—as he told us—had stayed no time at all. I am inclined now to think that he must unconsciously have been impressed by the unutterable desolation, and atmosphere of the unknown, by which she was pervaded, and of which we ourselves were so soon to be aware. Indeed, his very next remark went to prove that I was right in the above supposition.

"We none of us wanted to 'ave much truck with 'er. She 'adn't a comfortable feelin' 'bout 'er. An' she were too dam clean an' tidy for my likin'."

"How do you mean, too clean and tidy?" I inquired, puzzled at his way to putting it.

"Well," he replied, "so she were. She sort of gave you ther feelin' as 'er crowd 'ad only just left 'er, an' might be back any bloomin' minnit. You'll savvy wot I mean, Sir, when you gets aboard of 'er." He wagged his head wisely, and recommenced drawing at his pipe.

I looked at him a moment doubtfully; then I turned and glanced at Trenhern, but it was evident that he had not noticed these last remarks of the old seaman. He was far too busily engaged in staring through his telescope at the little island, to notice what was going on about him. Suddenly he gave a low cry, and turned to the old whaler.

"Quick, Williams!" he said, "is that the place?" He pointed with the telescope. Williams shaded his eyes, and stared.

"That's it, Sir," he replied after a moment's pause.

"But—but where's the ship?" inquired my friend in a trembling voice. "I see no sign of her." He caught Williams by the arm, and shook it in sudden fright.

"It's all right, Sir," exclaimed Williams. "We ain't far enuff to the Sutherd yet ter open out ther cove. It's narrer at ther mouth, an' she were right away up inside. You'll see in er minnit."

At that, Trenhern dropped his hand from the old fellow's arm, his face clearing somewhat; yet greatly anxious. For a minute he held on to the rail as though for support; then he turned to me.

"Henshaw," he said, "I feel all of a shake—I—I—"

"There, there, old chap," I replied, and slipped my arm through his. Then, thinking to occupy his attention somewhat, I suggested to him that he should order one of the boats to be got ready for lowering. This he did, and then for a little while further we scanned that narrow opening among the rocks. Gradually, as we drew more abreast of it, I realised that it ran a considerable depth in to the islet, and then at last something came into sight away up among the shadows within the cove. It was like the stern of a vessel projecting from behind the high walls of the rocky recess, and as I grasped the fact, I gave a little shout, pointing out to Trenhern with some considerable excitement.

The boat had been lowered, and Trenhern and I with the boat's crew, and the old whaler steering, were heading direct for that opening in the coast of Middle Islet.

Presently we were amongst the broad belt of kelp with which the islet was surrounded, and a few minutes later we slid into the clear, dark waters of the cove, with the rocks rising up in stark, inaccessible walls on each side of us until they seemed almost to meet in the heights far overhead.

A few seconds swept us through the passage and into a small circular sea enclosed by gaunt cliffs that shot up on all sides to a height of some hundred odd feet. It was as though we looked up from the bottom of a gigantic pit. Yet at the moment we noted little of this, for we were passing under the stern of a vessel, and looking upwards, I read in white letters *Happy Return*.

I turned to Trenhern. His face was white, and his fingers fumbled with the buttons of his jacket, while his breath came irregularly. The next instant, Williams had laid us alongside, and Trenhern and I were scrambling aboard. Williams followed, carrying up the painter; he made it fast to a cleet, and then turned to lead the way.

Upon the deck, as we walked, our feet beat with an empty sound that spelt out desolation; while our voices, when we spoke, seemed to echo back from the surrounding cliffs with a strange hollow ring that caused us at once to speak in whispers. And so I began to understand what Williams had meant when he said "She 'adn't a comfertable feelin' 'bout 'er."

"See," he said, stopping after a few paces, "'ow bloomin' clean an' tidy she is. It aren't nat'ral." He waved his hand towards the surrounding deck furniture. "Everythin' as if she was just goin' inter port, an' 'er a bloomin' wreck."

He resumed his walk aft, still keeping the lead. It was as he had said. Though the vessel's masts and boats had gone, she was extraordinarily tidy and clean, the ropes—such as were left—being coiled up neatly upon the pins, and in no part of her decks could I discern any signs of disorder. Trenhern had grasped all this simultaneously with myself, and now he caught my shoulder with a quick nervous grasp.

"See her, Henshaw," he said in an excited whisper, "this shows some of them were alive when she drove in here—" He paused as though seeking for breath. "They may be—they may be—" He stopped once more, and pointed mutely to the deck. He had gone past words.

"Down below?" I said, trying to speak brightly.

He nodded, his eyes searching my face as though he would seek in it fuel for the sudden hope that had sprung up within him. Then came Williams' voice; he was standing in the companionway.

"Come along, Sir. I aren't goin below 'ere by myself."

"Yes, come along, Trenhern," I cried. "We can't tell."

We reached the companionway together, and he motioned me to go before him. He was all a-quiver. At the foot of the stairs, Williams paused a moment; then turned to the left and entered the saloon. As we came in through the doorway, I was again struck by the exceeding tidiness of the place. No signs of hurry or confusion; but everything in its place as though the steward had but the moment before tidied out the apartment and dusted the table and fittings. Yet to our knowledge she had lain here a dismasted hulk for at least five months.

"They must be here! They must be here!" I heard my friend mutter under his breath, and I—though bearing in mind that Williams had found her thus all those months gone—could scarcely but join in his belief.

Williams had gone across to the starboard side of the saloon, and I saw that he was fumbling at one of the doors. It opened under his hand, and he turned and beckoned to Trenhern.

"See 'ere, Sir," he said. "This might be your young leddy's cabin; there's feemayles' things 'ung up, an' their sort of fixins on ther table—"

He did not finish; for Trenhern had made one spring across the saloon, and caught him by the neck and arm.

"How dare you—desecrate—" he almost shrieked, and forth with hauled him out from the little room. "How—how—" he gasped, and stooped to pick up a silver-backed brush which Williams had dropped at his unexpected onslaught.

"No offence, Mister," replied the old whaler in a surprised voice, in which there was also some righteous anger. "No offence. I wern't goin' ter steal ther blooming' thing." He gave the sleeve of his jacket a brush with the palm of his hand, and glanced across at me, as though he would have me witness to the truth of his statement. Yet I scarcely noticed what it was that he said; for I heard my friend cry out from the interior of his sweetheart's cabin, and in his voice there was blent a marvellous depth of hope and fear and bewilderment. An instant later he burst out into the saloon; in his hand he held something white. It was a calendar. He twisted it right way up to show the date at which it was set.

"See," he cried, "read the date!" As my eyes gathered the import of the few visible figures, I drew my breath swiftly and bent forward, staring. The calendar had been set for the date of that very day.

"Good God!" I muttered; and then:— "It's a mistake! It's just a chance!" And still I stared.

"It's not," answered Trenhern vehemently. "It's been set this very day—" He broke off short for a moment. Then after a queer little pause he cried out "O, my God! grant I find her!"

He turned sharply to Williams.

"What was the date at which this was set?—Quick!" he almost shouted. Williams stared at him blankly.

"Damnation!" shouted my friend, almost in a frenzy. "When you came aboard here before?"

"I never even seen ther blessed thing before, Sir," he answered. "We didn't stay no time aboard of 'er."

"My goodness, man!" cried Trenhern, "what a pity! O what a pity!" Then he turned and ran towards the saloon door.

In the doorway he looked back over his shoulder.

"Come on! Come on!" he called. "They're somewhere about. They're hiding—Search!"

And so we did; but though we went through the whole ship from stern to bow, there was nowhere any sign of life. Yet everywhere that extraordinary clean orderliness prevailed, instead of the wild disorder of an abandoned wreck; and always, as we went from place to place and cabin to cabin, there was upon me the feeling that they had but just been inhabited.

Presently, we had made an end to our search, and having found nothing of that for which we looked, were facing one another bewilderedly, though saying but little. It was Williams who first said anything intelligible.

"It's as I said, Sir; there weren't anythin' livin' aboard of 'er."

To this Trenhern replied nothing, and in a minute Williams spoke again.

"It aren't far off dark, Sir, an' we'll 'ave ter be gettin' out of this place while there's a bit of daylight."

Instead of replying to this, Trenhern asked if any of the boats were there when he was aboard before, and on his answering in the negative, fell once more into his silent abstraction.

After a little, I ventured to draw his attention to what Williams had said about getting aboard the yacht before the light had all gone. At that, he gave an absent nod of assent, and walked towards the side, followed by Williams and myself. A minute later we were in the boat and heading out for the open sea.

During the night, there being no safe anchorage, the yacht was kept off, it being Trenhern's intention to land upon Middle Islet and search for any trace of the lost crew of the *Happy Return*. If that produced nothing, he was going to make a thorough exploration of Nightingale Island and the Islet of Stoltenkoff before abandoning all hopes.

The first portion of this plan he commenced to put into execution as soon as it was dawn; for his impatience was too great to allow of his waiting longer.

Yet before we landed on the Islet, he bade Williams take the boat into the cove. He had a belief, which affected me somewhat, that he might find the crew and his sweetheart returned to the vessel. He suggested to me—searching my face all the while for mutual hope—that they had been absent on the preceding day, perhaps on an expedition to the Island in search of vegetable food. And I (remembering the date of the calendar) was able to look at him encouragingly; though had it not been for that, I should have been helpless to aid his belief.

We entered through the passage into that great pit among the cliffs. The ship, as we ranged alongside of her, showed wan and unreal in the grey light of the mist-shrouded dawn; yet this we noticed little then, for Trenhern's visible excitement and hope was becoming infectious. It was he who now led the way down into the twilight of the saloon. Once there, Williams and I hesitated with a certain natural awe, whilst Trenhern walked across to the door of his sweetheart's room. He raised his hand and knocked, and in the succeeding stillness, I heard my heart beat loud and fast. There was no reply, and he again rapped with his knuckles on the panels, the sounds echoing hollowly through the empty saloon and cabins. I felt almost sick with the suspense of waiting, then abruptly, he seized the handle, turned it, and threw the door wide. I heard him give a sort of groan. The little cabin was empty. The next instant, he gave out a shout, and reappeared in the saloon holding the same little calendar. He ran to me and pushed it into my hands with an inarticulate cry. I looked at it. When Trenhern had shown it to me the preceding day it had been showing the date 27th.; *now it had been altered to the 28th.*

"What's it mean, Henshaw? what's it mean?" he asked helplessly.

I shook my head. "Sure you didn't alter it yesterday—by accident?

"I'm quite sure!" he said.

"What are they playing at?" he went on. "There's no sense in it—" He paused a moment; then again:— "What's it mean?"

"God knows." I muttered. "I'm stumped."

"You mean sumone's been in 'ere since yesterday?" inquired Williams at this point.

I nodded.

"Be gum then, Sir," he said, "it's ghostses!"

"Hold your tongue, Williams!" cried my friend, turning savagely upon him.

Williams said nothing, but walked toward the door.

"Where are you going?" I asked.

"On deck, Sir," he replied. "I didn't sign on for this 'ere trip to 'ave no truck with sperrets!" and he stumbled up the companion stairway.

Trenhern seemed to have taken no notice of these last remarks; for when next he spoke he appeared to be following out a train of thought.

"See here," he said. "They're not living aboard here at all. That's plain. They've some reason for keeping away. They're hiding somewhere—perhaps in a cave."

"What about the calendar then. You think—?"

"Yes, I've an idea that they may come aboard here at night. There may be something that keeps them away during the daylight. Perhaps some wild beast, or something; and they would be seen in the daytime."

I shook my head. It was all so improbable. If there was something that could get at them aboard the ship, lying as it did surrounded by the sea, at the bottom of the great pit among the cliffs, then it seemed to me that they would nowhere be safe; besides, they could stay below decks during the day, and I could conceive of nothing that could reach them there. A multitude of other objections rose in my mind. And then I knew perfectly well that there were no wild beasts of any description on the Islands. No! obviously it could not be explained in that manner. And yet—there was the unaccountable altering of the calendar. I ended my line of reasoning in a fog. It seemed useless to apply any ordinary sense to the problem, and I turned once more to Trenhern.

"Well," I said, "there's nothing here, and there may be something, after all, in what you say; though I'm hanged if I can make head or tail of anything."

We left the saloon and went on deck. Here we walked forward and glanced into the fo'cas'le; but, as I had expected, found nothing.

After that we bundled down into the boat, and proceeded to search Middle Islet. To do this, we had to pull out of the cove and round the coast a bit to find a suitable landing place.

As soon as we had landed, we pulled the boat up into a safe place, and arranged the order of the search. Williams and I were to take a couple of the men apiece, and go right round the coast in opposite directions until we met, examining on the way all the caves that we came across. Trenhern was to make a journey to the summit, and survey the Islet from there.

Williams and I accomplished our part, and met close to where we had hauled up the boat. He reported nothing, and so did I. Of Trenhern we could see no trace, and presently, as he did not appear, I told Williams to stay by the boat while I went up the height to look for him. Soon I reached the top and found that I was standing upon the brink of the great pit in which lay the wreck. I glanced round and there away to the left, I saw my friend lying on his stomach with his head over the edge of the chasm, evidently staring down at the hulk.

"Trenhern," I called softly, not wanting to startle him.

He raised his head and looked in my direction; seeing me, he beckoned, and I hurried to his side.

"Bend down," he said in a low voice. "I want you to look at something."

As I got down beside him, I gave a quick glance at his face; it was very pale; then I had my face over the brink and was staring into the gloomy depth below.

"See what I mean?" he asked, still speaking scarcely above a whisper.

"No," I said. "Where?"

"There," he answered, pointing. "In the water on the starboard side of the *Happy Return*."

Looking in the direction indicated, I now made out in the water close alongside the wreck several pale, oval-shaped objects.

"Fish," I said. "What queer ones!"

"No!" he replied. "Faces!"

"What!"

"Faces!"

I got up on to my knees and looked at him.

"My dear Trenhern, you're letting this matter affect you too deeply—You know you have my deepest sympathy. But—"

"See," he interrupted, "they're moving, they're watching us!" He spoke quietly, utterly ignoring my protest.

I bent forward again and looked. As he had said, they were moving, and as I peered, a sudden idea came to me. I stood up abruptly.

"I have it!" I cried excitedly. "If I'm right it may account for their leaving the ship. I wonder we never thought of it before!"

"What?" he asked in a weary voice, and without raising his face.

"Well, in the first place, old man, those are not faces, as you very well know; but I'll tell you what they very likely are, they're the tentacles of some sort of sea monster, Kraken, of devil-fish—something of that sort. I can quite imagine a creature of the kind haunting that place down there, and I can equally well understand that if your sweetheart and the crew of the *Happy Return* are alive, they'll be inclined to give their old packet a pretty wide berth if I am right—eh?"

By the time I had finished explaining my solution of the mystery, Trenhern was upon his feet. The sanity had returned to his eyes, and there was a flush of half-suppressed excitement on his hitherto pale cheeks.

"But—but—but—the calendar?" he breathed.

"Well, they may venture aboard at night, or in certain states of the tides, when, perhaps they have found there is little danger. Of course, I can't say; but it seems probable, and what more natural than that they should keep count of the days, or it may have just been put forward thoughtlessly in passing. It may even be your sweetheart counting the days since she was parted from you."

I turned and peered once more over the edge of the cliff; the floating shapes had vanished. Then Trenhern was pulling at my arm.

"Come along, Henshaw, come along. We'll go right back to the yacht and get some weapons. I'm going to slaughter that brute if he shows up."

An hour later we were back with a couple of the yacht's boats and their crews, the men being armed with cutlasses, harpoons, pistols and axes. Trenhern and I had each chosen a heavy shellgun.

The boats were left alongside, and the men ordered aboard the wreck, and there, having brought sufficient food, they picnicked for the rest of the day, keeping a keen watch for signs of anything.

Yet when the night drew near, they manifested considerable uneasiness; finally sending the old whaler aft to tell Trenhern that they would not stay aboard the *Happy Return* after dark; they would obey any order he chose to give in the yacht; but they had not signed on to stay aboard of a ghost-ridden craft at night.

Having heard Williams out, my friend told him to take the men off to the yacht; but to come back in one of the boats with some bedding, as he and I were going to stay the night aboard the hulk. This was the first I had heard on the matter; but when I remonstrated with him, he told me I was at perfect liberty to return to the yacht. For his part he had determined to stay and see if anyone came.

Of course after that, I had to stay. Presently they returned with the bedding, and having received orders from my friend to come for us at day-break, they left us there alone for the night.

We carried down our bedding and made it up on the saloon table; then we went on deck and paced the poop, smoking and talking earnestly—anon listening; but nothing came to our ears save the low voice of the sea beyond the kelp-belts. We carried our guns; for we had no knowledge but that they might be needed. Yet the time passed quietly, except once when Trenhern dropped the butt of his weapon upon the deck somewhat heavily. Then indeed, from all the cliffs around us, there came back a low hollow boom that was frightening. It was like the growl of a great beast. At the bottom of that tremendous pit it presently became exceedingly dark. So far as I could judge, a mist had come down upon the Islet and formed a sort of huge lid to the pit. It was about twelve o'clock that we went below. I think by that time even Trenhern had begun to realise that there was a certain rashness in our having stayed; and below, at least, if we were attacked, we would be better able to hold our own. Somehow such vague fear as I had was not induced by the thought of the great monster I believed I had seen close to the vessel during the day; but rather by an unnamable something in the very air, as though the atmosphere of the place were a medium

of terror. Yet—calming myself with an effort—I put down this feeling to my nerves being at tension; so that presently, Trenhern offer-
ing to take the first watch, I fell asleep on the saloon table, leaving
him sitting beside me with his gun across his knees.

Then as I slept, a dream came to me—so extraordinarily vivid
was it that it seemed almost I was awake. I dreamt that all of a
sudden Trenhern gave a little gasp and leapt to his feet. In the same
moment, I heard a soft voice call "Tren! Tren!" It came from the
direction of the saloon doorway, and —in my dream—I turned and
saw a most beautiful face, containing great wondrous eyes. "An
angel!" I whispered to myself; then I knew that I was mistaken
and that it was the face of Trenhern's sweetheart. I had seen her
once just before she sailed. From her, my gaze wandered to
Trenhern. He had laid his gun upon the table, and now his arms
were extended towards her. I heard her whisper "Come!" and then
he was beside her. Her arms went about him, and then, together,
they passed out through the doorway. I heard his feet upon the
stairs, and after that my sleep became a blank, dreamless rest.

I was aroused by a terrible scream, so dreadful that I seemed
to wake rather to death than life. For perhaps the half of a minute
I sat up upon my bedding, motionless in a very frost of fear; but no
further sound came to me, and so my blood ran warm once more,
and I reached out my hand for my gun. I grasped it, shook the
clothes from me and sprang to the floor. The saloon was filled with
a faint gray light which filtered in through the skylight overhead.
It was just sufficient to show me that Trenhern was not present,
and that his gun was upon the table, just where I had seen him
place it in my dream. At that, I called his name quickly; but the
only answer I received was a hollow, ghostly echo from the surrounding empty cabins. Then I ran for the door, and so up the stairs
on to the deck. Here, in the gloomy twilight, I glanced along the
bare decks; but he was nowhere visible. I raised my voice and
shouted. The grim, circling cliffs caught up the name and echoed
it a thousand times, until it seemed that a multitude of demons
shouted "Trenhern! Trenhern! Trenhern!" from the surrounding
gloom. I ran to the port side and glanced over—Nothing! I flew to
starboard; my eyes caught something—many things that floated

apparently just below the surface of the water. I stared, and my heart seemed suddenly quiet in my bosom. I was looking at a score of pale, unearthly faces, that stared back at me with sad eyes. They appeared to sway and quiver in the water; but otherwise there was no movement. I must have stood thus for many minutes; for, abruptly, I heard the sound of oars, and then round the quarter of the vessel swept the boat from the yacht.

"In bow, there," I heard Williams shout. "'Ere we are, Sir!" The boat grated against the side.

"'Ow 'ave—" Williams began; but it seemed to me that I had seen something coming to me along the deck, and I gave out one scream and leapt for the boat. I landed on a thwart.

"Push off! Push off!" I yelled, and seized an oar to help.

"Mr. Tren'ern, Sir?" interjected Williams.

"He's dead!" I shouted. "Push her off! Push her off!" and the men, infected by my fear, pushed and rowed until, in a few moments we were a score of yards distant from her. Here there was an instant's pause.

"Take her out, Williams!" I called, crazy with the thing upon which I had stumbled. "Take her out!" And at that, he steered for the passage into the open sea. This took us close past the stern of the wreck, and as we passed beneath, I looked up at the overhanging mass. As I did so, a dim, beauteous face came over the taffrail, and looked at me with great sorrowful eyes. She stretched out her arms to me, and I screamed aloud; for her hands were like unto the talons of a wild beast.

As I fell fainting, William's voice came to me in a hoarse bellow of sheer terror. He was shouting to the men:

"Pull! *Pull! Pull!*"

THE FINLESS DEATH
Robert Ernest Vernède

Don Miguel, proprietor of the inn grown about with orange-trees, yellow and green, that grew juicily in the warm airs of the gulf, was flustered.

It could not be the heat that flustered him, for it was still before dawn; and, though at any moment the sun might come blazing out, he was not thinking of it.

"Señores!" he said, appealingly. The two Englishmen stopped.

"What does the fat fool want?" asked Flackman, impatiently.

"Don't know," said Kender. "I'll ask him"—and he put the question fluently in Spanish.

"If I might be permitted," said the inn-keeper, extending the palms of his hands in emphasis, "I would advise the Señores."

"The advice of Don Miguel is more precious than pearls," said Kender, courteously, resting the butt-end of his heavy rod on the ground, "and, without doubt, the oyster does not contain more. But in what does the advice consist?"

Don Miguel bowed to the compliment, and made answer:

"It is that the Señores should not go fishing to-day."

"For what reason?"

Don Miguel had many reasons, apparently. "The day is warm, yet on land, in the 'arbour, very cool. How pleasant to sit there and sip aguardiente. Also, Rietta will sing to the Señores. She had this morning the voice of a nightingale."

"She has the voice of six nightingales invariably," said Kender. "Also, aguardiente is good. But we came to fish."

"Consider, Señor, how easily the sun goes to the head of the unaccustomed."

355

"True," said Kender. "But the heads of both of us are thick as the rinds of pumpkins, and are protected by sombreros."

"The heads of the Señores are of an excellent proportion," said Don Miguel, hastily. "And yet—there might be a hurricane."

"I see no sign of it," Kender maintained.

The inn-keeper became yet more earnest. "Señor," he said, "you will laugh, I know it, or maybe frown, for it is Don Flackman that laughs always, thinking these things but superstitions, and of no account."

"But what things?"

Don Miguel looked about him anxiously as if he feared the presence of some supernatural agency, and crossed himself, before he answered in a low voice.

"Things that are said—in fear—the Mexicans say them. Without doubt these half-breeds are mad compared to your excellencies, and yet I, who live here and know, who am of the blood of Castile, I also am afraid. Senor, I ask you, where are the German Señores that went fishing yesterday? Them also I warned and"—again he crossed— "they have not returned."

"Warned them of what?" said Kender, eager to get to the point.

The inn-keeper dropped his voice still lower. "Of the Finless Death," he said.

Kender looked at him curiously. The man was evidently earnest in his warnings, for the sweat stood out on his face, and he wrung his fat hands as if in dread of some Impending evil. Kender himself, a scientist, a little man, but firm-lipped, unemotional, and with a chin that betokened incredulity, was the last person to take a superstition literally, or to be moved by it. Nevertheless, he hesitated a moment. It seemed to him as if something—some danger perhaps—might underlie this manifest fear.

"Aren't you coming?" said Flackman, impatiently.

He had not understood the conversation, and was longing to reach the fishing-grounds.

"In a minute," said Kender, and he turned to the inn-keeper. "What is the Finless Death?" he said, tapping him on the arm.

Don Miguel turned up the whites of his eyes. "Señor, how should I know? Only this I have heard—that at the full moon the

Finless Death moves on the lagoons, and makes men stark with fear. Last night it was almost full."

"True," said Kender, "it was undeniably almost full."

"And twice Pedro, that, as the Señor knows, is an unerring watch-dog, bayed violently."

"At what?"

"At nothing."

"And therefore at this devil?" said Kender, smiling.

The inn-keeper evaded insisting on this sequence. "The German Señores have not returned," he repeated significantly.

"Nor paid their bill?" asked Kender.

"That is no hinge," said Don Miguel, with dignity. "I have warned the Señores." He turned away hurt.

"And truly I am most grateful," said Kender; "but my friend, as you perceive, is not to be persuaded, and therefore we go to fish. Maybe we shall catch the finless thing itself."

The inn-keeper threw up his hands in an ecstasy of horror as Kender followed Flackman through the orange-groves, that led down to the creek where José, the half-breed, was getting ready the boat.

Flackman was highly amused to hear of the innkeeper's alarm.

"You refused to be warned?"

"Don't you?"

"My dear man," said Kender, "I never take warning —at least in so far as they frighten a man away from what he does know by what he does not know. It's my business to learn, just as it's my business to jest. I only told you because—well—you know you've got an imagination—it might get on your nerves."

"Nonsense!" said Flackman, and added inconsequently: "Miguel is a fat man, and all fat men are fools."

"I incline to think there's something in it."

"Some Mexican, full of aguardiente, saw a cuttle-fish at the full moon once."

"Perhaps—but it's descriptive—their name for the terror?"

"O, that I grant you," said Flackman, laughing. "They make a good case for their demons by giving them a sounding title, but they've got too many of 'em—only they seem to have impressed you, Kender?"

"Not much," said Kender, "I'm interested, I admit; I take it to be some water-devil—something connected with fish."

"But finless."

"An eel, perhaps—it's quite easy to imagine an eel without fins—or some sort of water-snake."

"Sea-serpent," Flackman suggested. He was much amused to see Kender—usually so sceptical—interesting himself in Don Miguel's supernatural absurdity. For his own part, he could think of nothing but the desire to hear his reel run again, and to hold up a fighting fish by his own skilful handling till it should be drawn to the boat-side, and the gaff, splashing faintly a hundredweight of tired silver. And it was a day of days for fishing—the sky already full of suppressed brightness, as if the sun were just behind it, and the morning unwontedly fresh. Ahead of them, Flackman could see the creek (solitary, since it was before the time when tarpon-fishing had become a fashionable amusement), and the boat and the Mexican boatman lolling beside it. He was almost annoyed with Kender that with such a view before him he would go on discussing his ridiculous subject, quite gravely too.

"But it might be some kind of sea-serpent," he was saying, "or merely a delusion, as you seem to think; for it doesn't take anything tangible to give these fellows a belief in some new devil. But I should like to know. After all, it is strange that the civilized people should be so incurious about fish, which are the ugliest things in earth or sea. Think how they were detested in bygone times! The ancients considered them not only uneatable, but unclean abominations—a part of the devilish things that lived in the sea that was always—the devil!"

"Poor old bats!" said Flackman. "They never knew what it was to fly fish. And here's José, alive and as energetic as usual. I almost expected to find he'd been swallowed by a whale!"

José's energy was not conspicuous. He began by suggesting that it was not a good day for bites.

Asked why, he said because the night before the moon was full. Flackman began to lose his temper.

"It's some trick," he said, "that the scamp has got up with Miguel. He wants to slack."

"It is a possibility," Kender admitted, thoughtfully, "but, at the same time..."

"I don't believe you want to go either."

"Never wanted to fish more," Kender said.

"It doesn't look like it."

"And if we could catch this finless beast, I should be happy for days."

"O! confound it!" said Flackman.

His spirits were mercurial, and this reiteration of an unpleasant topic was getting on his nerves. Doubtless, the whole thing was absurd; but it was unpleasant. Flackman himself thought nothing of it. He kept on assuring himself of that; but, at the same time, he was one of those who, not altogether self-reliant, liked to have their opinion corroborated by their company. And here was Kender frowning over this suggestion of peril as if he were assured there were some bottom in it, if one only knew. He wanted to fish, not to face a mystery. If he had known what they were going to encounter, he might have hung back. But he did not know, and Kender was remorseless in the pursuit of science.

"Hurry up, José," said Flackman, pettishly.

It was very sullenly that the Mexican pulled seaward, and Flackman was reduced to whistling to keep his own spirits up. The sea ran from creek to creek, lagoon-like reaches, and spaces of the bluest calm, locked in from the gulf by reefs only to be passed at certain tides and points where the rollers had forced an inlet, as sheep force their way through a hedge, by incessant pressing. They had made a good many futile casts in the open, and Flackman's spirits were at zero, before, at Kender's suggestion, they made for one of these lagoons for a last throw. Kender had relieved the Mexican at the oars, and had his back turned to the bows, so that as they shot into that reach of still water, slack and shining, except where it was criss-crossed by dull patches that looked like stains on polished walnut, it was the younger man who saw and sprang to his feet pointing to something ahead:

"What's that?" he cried. Out in the middle water, immobile, a boat floated, as though anchored in a pond. A single oar, broken at the blade, was caught in the left rollock and suspended.

As Kender stood up, he observed that there were two men in the stern, who seemed to be standing in stiff attitudes. "H'm," he said, and he sat himself down again to row for the boat, unconcernedly enough, but with a little extra speed.

Flackman remained standing: his eyes moved uneasily. "Ship your oars," he said excitedly, as they came bow to bow with the other boat. Kender shipped his oars, and sat steadying the boat in the expectation that Flackman would step across to it, if it were only for curiosity. But Flackman had no curiosity and he had gone very pale.

"Hadn't you better—hadn't we better be getting back?" he said.

Kender carefully refrained from expressing anything, but he picked up his rod which lay in the way, and stepped across past the shrinking Mexican into the other boat. Flackman was flushing now with shame at his own poltroonery.

"What's the matter with them?" he sung out, for the swing of Kender stepping across had sent the two boats apart.

The little man had rammed his rod methodically under the bow-seat, the line overboard to prevent a tangle, and was contemplating the two figures. He saw at once they were the Germans of whom Don Miguel had spoken.

"What's the matter?" cried Flackman again.

He was in an agony of uneasiness, and in the merest pretence began making casts. Again he appealed to Kender:

"You might say what's the matter with them."

"Death!" said Kender, curtly.

"Why do they look like that?"

"I don't know."

Kender sat on the thwarts and considered them. Never had he seen such dead men—in attitude exaggeratedly alive, rigid as waxworks, and hideous in their mimic intensity! One, a great bearded man, with spectacles, had his hand on the dragging oar and half knelt to it, as if he had been caught by a blinding cramp in the act of pulling; the other, of a slighter build, was bent forward standing, a gaff in his hand, menacing, as it seemed, the empty space in the middle of the boat—at least it should have been empty, but there was a slime over it, as if a great snail had crawled there. The faces of the two were indescribably afraid.

"Now, how did that slime get there?" said Kender to himself.

Almost as if in answer, Flackman gave a shout. "I've hooked something!" he said. "By gad! and a heavy one!" he went on, as the thick rod bent nearly double under the weight. "You'd better cut your line," said Kender, gruffly. "It's hardly time to fish."

"Right," said Flackman. But he didn't.

Mechanically he had struck, and equally mechanically he began to reel up. He had a semi-conscious idea of saving as much of his line as possible before he cut loose, and as he saw far down the loom of a great white fish, the zeal of sport carried him away. He reeled steadily, the rod seemed strained with a dead weight, but there was no rush or plunging. Quite suddenly the white mass was on the surface, and as Flackman tightened his hold and yelled for the gaff, it seemed to fly up into the boat. It fell, facing the bows, where the Mexican was sitting, the hook in its mouth, the line broken.

Flackman stared. From its size the fish could not have weighed less than a hundred pounds, yet it had come up without a struggle, and had been landed ungaffed. Now it lay there heaving equably—a white-bellied, shapeless thing, rotund and flabby, with the detestable lidless fish eyes.

"It's a remarkable fish," said Flackman, curiously.

"Very," said Kender.

"Did you see how it came up?"

"Yes. What are you going to do with it?"

"Chuck it over, if possible."

"I should."

They seemed unanimous in thinking it would be a good riddance.

"Hi, José! give me a hand. Hullo! what's wrong?" Flackman saw that some strange malady had seized the Mexican. He seemed to be stiffening as he crouched in the bows; his arms were stretched out fixedly, like the arms of a sign-post.

Kender started. "What's he pointing at? " he shouted.

"The fish. Ugh! it's oozing slime!"

"Slime!"

"A sort of snail slime."

Flackman drew back from the fish, disgusted. "It's too filthy to touch," he went on. "It's—by gad—Kender—it's got no fins!" His voice rose nervously. "What is it? What's it doing, and to José."

He began to stammer, frightened at he knew not what. The Mexican was growing most rigid.

"José!" shouted Kender, imperiously.

There was no answer but Flackman's. "He's—he's being poisoned, I think."

"Go and shake him!"

"I daren't."

The two Englishmen eyed each other from the boats. Then Flackman, seized with a spasm of shame or horror, snatched up the gaff and stabbed the fish through the grey-skinned back. A white ichor spurted up and took him on the arm. Kender saw him drop the gaff, clutch at his elbow, and begin to mumble wildly. It was then that a fear began to take hold of him also; he could do nothing where he sat, for there were no oars to the boat.

"Flackman!" he said, sharply. "No fins, no fins!" muttered the other.

"Come here!" commanded Kender.

Flackman looked up in a dazed manner, and took a step towards the oars. There, as his eye caught the white-bellied fish lying there, he shrank back, crying out:

"No fins, no fins!"

Even while he cried another spurt of the fluid came from the cut in the creature's back, and dribbled over his arm. He cried out, and unsheathed his knife. Before Kender could say anything, he had stuck it into his arm and stabbed again and again. Kender watched the blood stream helplessly, for he could do nothing unless Flackman would bring the boats together. He longed for an oar, longed to be able to swim. Again he shouted sharply:

"Bring her up!"

"No, no, Kender," the young man spoke in a strange voice. "I mustn't do that—I mustn't do that."

"Why not?"

"Because ..." Flackman paused, and looked out of the corner of his eyes slyly. "You understand, Kender, don't you?"

"I tell you to come here," said Kender, firmly.

"It's—no—it's impossible."

It seemed to be, for Flackman was like a child in his obstinacy. Kender changed his tactics accordingly.

"The fish will have you then," he called.

The effect was magical. Flackman sprang up, looked at the fish, shuddered, and, diving into the sea began to swim to the other boat. Kender watched. Surely it was the most peaceful scene in the world, a man swimming silently in a sea still to the horizon, scattering bubbles like diamonds before him, and leaving behind him the clear curve of his wake—a blue sky, unbeaten by any storm, a swimmer, and two pleasure-boats. And yet Kender was beginning to feel afraid. He tried to argue the fear away, but it would not go. It crept over him jointless, inexplicable, binding as a nightmare. He laughed at himself in sheer bravado, and the laugh stuck in his throat and became a shrill giggling that seemed to carry his reason with it high up above his reach. He clutched after it, to recall it, and could not. For he knew that the man that was swimming towards him had a face distorted with terror; that the boat in which he sat and giggled held two men grotesquely dead: that the blue, calm sea was vacant of human help. And in the other boat lay that monstrous fish without fins, staring the life out of the Mexican. It was with a struggle that he drew himself together, shivering, and pulled his friend on board.

Flackman fell in the bottom of the boat exhausted. He muttered continually, and was plainly delirious, for through his multifarious imaginings there ran always the vague thread of terror that haunts delirious men.

"No fins, no fins," he would moan, and clutch at the arm Kender had bound up.

It was impossible to relieve him. Kender wished for his own sake that anything could be done, for in this feeling of impotence was evil, and he was aware that his own hysteria was growing. Must they wait, then, for ever on that hateful sea? He tried the broken oar, but it would not move the heavy boat an inch. They must lie there, it seemed, and grow to knowledge of what fear could be. He sat and stared before him, and then, without warning, the last horror came. The bows of the other boat lifted suddenly, so that the Mexican rolled over and was seen to sink, while almost imperceptibly the boat itself began to glide towards them, the fish on board. As it came near, throwing no ripples before it, Kender bit his lips in agony.

There was no help—none! The boat was gliding with so swift a motion that it seemed upon them, and yet he could see still far down in the water the corpse of the Mexican, all huddled up and stiff—still twirling head over heels, round and round, deeper and deeper, to the bottom ooze. Not ten yards separated them now from the horror that blinked there in the other boat and heaved its hideous whiteness—not eight—and it was death—the death without fins—not five!

Kender shrieked aloud and ran about the boat, so that it rocked violently. For a moment it seemed an added terror, and then he saw the reason. The rod—his rod—clinched in the bows as he stepped on board, had hooked something with its dangling bait—something that went with jerks and rushes, darting ahead, towing the boat after it—some huge tarpon. It made for the opening by which they had passed into the lagoon and for the open sea. Behind, always quickening, the other boat came, drawn on by its own mysterious power. With tense eyes, Kender watched this strange race, in which he and his friend stood for both prize and spoil. Without reasoning the matter, he somehow knew (so he said afterwards) that that which reached the open sea would win away. The line taken zig-zagged for the outlet. Kender dared not stir, but he prayed to reach it, and the boat seemed to go quick with his longing.

The water flew under them—surely the outlet could not be far off—the other boat was gaining—no—yes—ah, but the outlet was before them. Their boat was through it. With a rasping noise, the ghastly boat behind drove on a sunk reef to the left. Kender, as his senses went from him in a swoon, fancied that he saw leap from it, like a great curl of smoke, the great white fish that turned in midair and plunged noiselessly into the sea...

It was towards dusk, and some seven miles off shore, that the yacht *Swallow* came on a drifting boat, noticeable for a rod bent in its bows like a bowsprit and snapped off as if by the jerk of some fish that had been hooked and had escaped. Besides this, there were on board two dead men, half standing in constrained positions, and two alive, a young man obviously raving, and another man— older—who might have been sane, except that his lips twitched continuously, and he told this story.

The Octopus Cycle
Irvin Lester and Fletcher Pratt

I

There was a long, uneasy swell on the surface of the Indian Ocean as though someone were gently rocking the floor beneath it, and a hot, moist wind blew against the face of Walter Weyl, A.B., A.M., B.Sc., as he stood against the rail of the pudgy little Messagéres Maritimes steamer, wondering whether he would dare to chance a spell of seasickness by lighting a well-cured pipe for the fourth time that afternoon.

It was hot—and off to the west, Tamatave's houses gleamed white and blistering against the green background of the Madagascar jungle, blued by the distance. Away to the north the coastline stretched illimitable. It would be another day at least before the steamer arrived at Andovorata, and Walter Weyl, A.B., A.M., B.Sc, would be able to get at the heart of the mysterious occurrences that had brought him there.

His mind traveled back to the letter from his friend of college days, Raoul Duperret, now on French government service in that mysterious land—Madagascar. He saw it again before him, the characteristic French handwriting, the precise French phrasing:

"... alas, we cannot pursue these investigations, through lack of money. To you, then, my friend, I appeal. To you belongs, permit me to say, that combination so rare of the talent for scientific investigation and the means to pursue it. To you also will appertain the credit for any discovery.

"Let me, in detail, tell you of what we know. Diouma-Mbobo is a chieftain of the blacks in the part of the island, who have never been rescued from cannibal practices. He is, as far as we know, a

366

man who rules by law and is of a truthfulness. Thus, when he accused the Tanôsy, who are the next tribe to him, of stealing people and eating them, we took measures and did not too much believe the denials of the Tanôsy. But Diouma-Mbobo's people continue to disappear, and when the commandant sent a whole company of Senegalese to preserve order, they still disappeared. What is still more distressing, is that some of the Senegalese also disappeared, and save but a solitary rifle or two found in the jungle, no trace of them remains.

"There is some fear in the island and we are in danger of losing our grip on the natives, for we cannot at all explain these disappearances nor prevent them. The commandant says, 'Send a battalion of chasseurs,' but it is my belief that a battalion of chausseurs would likewise fail, and I send for you, for I believe the agency that destroys men thus is not human. No human would neglect the rifles.

"As you know, Madagascar is a country apart. We have here the giant spiders, large as bats; the lizards, large as sheep, and no, not a single snake. All our animals are outré, impossible even, and what if one more impossible than all...? And thus it is to you, my rich American friend, I appeal for myself and my country."

It had offered precious little real information, that letter, but enough to have caused Walter Weyl to drop a learned monograph on the ammonites of the Upper Cretaceous and hurry across ten thousand miles of ocean with microscopes, rifles and all the equipment of the modern scientist, to the aid of his friend.

The sun went down suddenly, as it does in the tropics, and the sea was purple darkness all at once. The lights of Tamatave twinkled away behind and were blotted out; off to the west was only the menacing blot of the huge island, forbidding and dangerous in the gloom. Weyl sat musing by the rail, listening to the hushed voices of a couple of men in the bows.

Forgetting his dinner below, he fell into a half-doze, from which he was suddenly awakened by a sense of approaching evil, definite, yet which could not be located. He looked about lazily. The Southern Cross hung brilliant in the sky; there was no other light but the flare of portholes on the water, and no sound but the slap of waves against the bows. Yet the night had suddenly become dreadful. He struggled lazily to put a name to the sense of impending doom, and as he struggled there was a sudden and terrible scream from the bow—the cry of a man in mortal anguish and fear.

"Oh—o—o—u—" it went, running off into a strangled sob, and through it cut the shout of the other sailor, "Secours! Secours! Ferent ..." and the sound of a blow on soft flesh.

Weyl leaped to his feet and ran forward; there was the sound of a slamming door, and a quick patter of feet behind him. In front was the blackness of the bows, out of which emerged a panic-stricken man who charged against him, babbling incoherent French, and bore him to the deck. As he went down he caught a glimpse of two waving prehensile arms, like lengths of fire-hose, silhouetted against the sky.

Somebody ran past him, the deck leaped into illumination as lights were switched on, and he picked himself up to see—nothing. The bows were empty. There was a babble of conversation:

"Where is Ferentini?"

"What is the trouble?"

"Who is there?"

There was confusion, stifled by the appearance of the captain, a eupeptic little man in a blue coat and a tremendous moustache which swept his shoulders. "This uproar—what does it mean?" he said. "Let the sailor Dugasse come forward."

A big Basque, obviously panic-stricken and with rolling eyes, was shoved into the light. "Tell us the reason for this," demanded the captain.

"Ferentini and I," he gasped, "we were talking, so, in the bow. One, two big arms, like a gorilla, seize him by the neck, the chest, and zut! he is gone. I strike at them, but he is gone."

"Assassin!" said the captain briefly, "Confess that you quarreled and you threw him over."

"No, no. He was taken. I swear it. By the Holy Virgin, I swear it."

"Put this man in the lazarette, you Marulaz, and you Noyon. There will be an investigation. Take his knife away from him."

"His knife is gone, monsieur," said one of the seamen who had stepped forward to take charge of the sailor Dugasse.

"Without doubt, he stabbed the other. Put him in irons," was the captain's succinct reply, as he turned toward the cabin and his interrupted dinner.

Walter Weyl stepped forward. "I think the man's story is true," he offered. "I think I saw something myself."

"Permit me to inform you, monsieur, that I am the commandant of the vessel," remarked the eupeptic captain, with the utmost courtesy. "There will be an investigation. If the man is innocent it will do him no harm to spend a night in the lazarette." And again he turned away.

Dissatisfied, but realizing that he could do nothing, Weyl walked toward the bows, to see if he could find any trace of the strange encounter. There was nothing, but as he was about to return and go below, his foot struck something, which on investigation with a flashlight, proved to be the knife of the sailor Dugasse.

The blade was wet, and as he picked the weapon up there dripped slowly from it a pale, greenish oleaginous liquid, totally unlike human blood. With this bit of evidence in his hand, he started thoughtfully for his cabin.

II

Two days later the friends sat under the giant mimosa, in whose shade Raoul Duperret had built a little cottage on the height overlooking Andananarivo. A table had been dragged outdoors and was now piled with a miscellaneous collection of instruments, papers and microscope slides.

Weyl leaned back in his chair with a sigh and lit his pipe.

"Let us see what we have, after all this study," he said. "Check me if I go wrong. Diouma-Mbobo's people and about a dozen of the Senegalese have disappeared mysteriously. So did the sailor Ferentini on the boat that brought me here. In no case was any trace found of the man after he disappeared, and in the cases on the island when anything was found it was always a knife or a rifle.

"This report," he ruffled the papers, "from one of the Senegalese, says that he saw his companion jerked up into a tree by a huge black rope, but when he rushed to the tree he could see nothing. It was late in the evening. Now this account agrees singularly with that of the sailor Dugasse—and moreover, if natives were responsible for the disappearances, they would at least have taken the knives, if not the guns.

"Therefore, I consider that the disappearance of Ferentini, the Senegalese and the natives was due to the same agency, and that the agency was not human; and, therefore, I think the Tanôsy and the sailor Dugasse, although he is still in jail, should be acquitted."

Duperret nodded a grave assent.

"But I am sure it was nothing supernatural. I saw something on that boat, Duperret, and the Senegalese saw something. Moreover, there is Dugasse's knife. I have analyzed that liquid which dripped from it; it is blood, indubitably, but blood different from any I have ever seen. It contains a tremendous number of corpuscles of a new character, not red, but greenish yellow, and the liquid in which they float is similar to that of all other bloods. More than anything, it resembles the blood of an oyster, which is impossible, as oysters do not lift men into trees. Therefore, I accuse some hitherto unknown animal of these deaths.

"But what kind of an animal are we dealing with?" Weyl went on without paying any attention to an interruption from Duperret. "Evidently a very swift and formidable one. It killed Ferentini in a few seconds. It dragged a powerful Senegalese, who was provided with a rifle, off with equal swiftness, and the stabs of Dugasse were as futile against it as the rifle of the other black boy.

"In both cases, the attack came from above, and I am inclined to think, since we were attacked some distance off the coast and the natives some distance inland, that the animal possesses extraordinary mobility—probably wings. This would make a bird of it; which is impossible because of the blood; therefore, making the whole thing absurd... But in any case, the hunt for this animal, or animals, for there may be more than one, will be a dangerous business."

"All is decided then?" asked Duperret. "Very well, let us depart. I am eager for action, my friend." And he stood up, stretching his muscular frame toward the towering tree.

"Done," said Weyl.

He rose. "You have same influence with the military authorities, you of the civil arm? If the matter were put to the commandant in the proper way, do you suppose we could get an escort? I need not conceal from you that this big-game hunt is likely to be a serious business. Any animal that devours live men..."

"The commandant and I were at St. Cyr together," replied Duperret. "He will doubtless appoint a lieutenant and a demi-company of African chasseurs to assist us."

III

A week later found them with a dapper French lieutenant, Dubosc by name, making the best of insufficient pup tents and canned French sausage by a dank, slow stream a few miles out of Fort Dauphin. Around them lay or squatted a perspiring group of black soldiers in the uniform of the Chasseurs d'Afrique, while round them again, further from the sun of the white men's presence, were as many natives, equally sable of hue, and with no uniforms at all. These were the guides lent by Diouma-Mbobo, silent and somewhat scared men, for that portion of the jungle had earned a bad reputation from the repeated disappearances.

Weyl was annoyed. "If we only knew what we were looking for and where to find it," he said to Duperret that evening, "but here we are three days out, with our labor for our pains. Hunting for one animal in this jungle is like the old needle and haystack saying."

"Yes, and I'm afraid for the guides," the Frenchman had answered. "They'll desert unless they are given something to do."

Night found them as restless as the guides. Weyl woke to a sense of something impending, looked out and saw only the calm sentries speaking in low tones as they encountered each other at the end of their rounds. He felt reassured, and dropped off into another hour or two of slumber punctuated by fierce dreams, woke again and saw a moonlit shadow on the flap of his tent. "Raoul!" he called softly.

The Frenchman bent and entered.

He was fully dressed.

"Nerves keep you awake, too?" said Weyl. "I've been awake before, but everything's quiet. But why are you dressed?"

"I have a premonition. Also, I hear something unusual. You hear that strange whistling? No, you would not. You are not used to jungle noises. To me it is very much to notice. Something..." and he looked at his friend, who, though in a strictly unofficial manner, was recognized as commander of the expedition. "Shall we rouse the soldiers?" he questioned.

"They'll need sleep if we're to march all day," Weyl answered.

"But I am thinking we will not need to march. However—" Raoul was about to dismiss his feeling as a fancy and threw another glance over his shoulder through the open tent flap.

In an instant he was on his feet, almost tearing the tent from its pegs, a half cry escaping his lips that caused Weyl to leap up beside him, seizing the revolver that lay by his hand.

Three, four, half a dozen snakelike arms, mysterious in the moonlight, hovered for an instant over the heads of two sentries who had met at the edge of the trees, and before they had comprehended their danger, before they could be warned, they were gripped, lifted from their feet and their cries stifled before they reached the gloom of the branches fully ten feet above.

Weyl, with a horror such as he had never felt before, seemed to clutch at his throat, fired rapidly into the tree. Something dropped with a crash of leaves; a veritable chorus of whistlings and swishings rose around the camp, and in the tents and along the sentry line there were sudden lights and activity, shouts of "Qui vive?" "Aux armes!" and the thick note of a hastily blown bugle as its owner was roused from sleep.

Men ran from their tents to stand gazing. "Raoul!" shouted the American. "It's here! The machine gun!" and, pistol in hand, in his sleeping garments, he dashed for the tree.

He glanced up. A subdued rustling gave no clue to its source, nothing to shoot at, but out of the tail of his eye he caught a glimpse of motion among the giant ferns, and the peculiar whistling again became audible.

He turned, and was suddenly conscious of an insane disbelief in his senses. What he saw resembled nothing so much as an enormous umbrella, standing ten feet high on stilt-like, but prehensile arms, while at the point where they gathered, a huge, bulbous head

rose and fell rhythmically as the thing emitted that singular, high-
pitched whistle. There was something unspeakably loathsome,
some touch reminiscent of putrefaction and decay about it.

An arm, like a huge snake, lifted from the ground and swung
aimlessly about under the leaves. Abruptly, another animal, the
duplicate of the first in all respects, came from behind a tree to
join it, and the two, despite their clumsy form and lurching uneven movement, began to advance toward him with a rapidity that
was astonishing.

Weyl awoke to the necessity of flight. He raced back toward
the camp, where Lieutenant Dubosc, aroused by the shots and cries,
and aware that something was impending, had formed the
Senegalese in a rough, slanting angle of a line, the men facing the
jungle, while behind them Diouma-Mbobo's natives crouched in
frightened curiosity.

The American turned as he reached the line. Behind him, into
the clearing, with an odd semblance of order, came a half-dozen, a
dozen, twenty of those terrible umbrella-like shapes, moving deliberately, but covering the ground as fast as a man runs.

A shot was followed by an order, a bugle note, and the irritat-
ing crash of the volley, which shaded into the rattling drum of the
machine guns. When his eyes again became used to the dark after
the flame of the rifles, Weyl saw that the giant, shapeless beasts
were moving forward as swiftly and imperturbably as before. Had
all the shots missed?

Another volley collapsed into a frantic and spasmodic burst of firing, as no effect was visible on the hideous shapes that came on swiftly.

Weyl aimed his revolver carefully at one bobbing head, and the
shot was drowned in a crashing chorus of fire; the beast came right
on. He was dimly conscious of shooting again and again in a kind
of frenzy at those horrible bulby umbrellas that kept coming closer,
dim figures of horror in the green moonlight, huge and impreg-
nable, towering over the little group of humans who shouted and
cursed and fired impotently.

One man, half maddened, even ran forward, waving his bayonet, and was gathered gently up by two of those big arms as a child
might be picked up by its parent.

A thrill of wavering ran down the line; one or two threw away their rifles, when suddenly, right at their feet, one of the monsters collapsed. There was a chorus of whistling and they moved backward, apparently without turning, as rapidly and silently as they had come...

A feeble cheer rose from the Senegalese, a cheer that was silenced instantly, for a glance revealed that half the hastily formed line was missing, the men gone as completely as though they had never been.

Weyl was aware that he had been clicking an empty pistol, that his throat was dry, that Duperret sat at his feet, his face in his hands, seemingly without power of motion. Senegalese and natives, frightened to the verge of madness, babbled like children all around him. The iron voice of Dubosc rose:

"Silence, my children!"

Out in the clearing before them was no sign that men had battled for their lives, save one ugly, loathsome shape, that sprawled on the ground and twitched feebly in the gloom.

IV

The survivors of that unbelievable, one-sided battle dragged themselves back into Fort Dauphin five days later. One man was violently insane, tightly bound, and as for the rest, it seemed that only remnants of sanity remained. The emotional blacks had almost collapsed under the strain, and nothing but incoherent gibberings could be extracted from them by the soldiers who cared for the exhausted, weaponless, starving and almost naked remainder of the trim company of Chasseurs who marched out with drum and bugle only a fortnight before.

Weyl begged off from an immediate report to the commandant, and went to bed, where he slept the sleep of exhaustion for twenty hours on end, and Duperret did likewise.

Weyl woke vastly refreshed, and with the horror that had been dragging at his mind relieved, though with such a feeling of weariness as he had not known since college football days. The black boy at the door obligingly brought him the latest newspapers, now not quite a month old, and he re-established his touch with the world of men by reading them over the tiny breakfast of coffee and rolls which was all the fort physician would allow him.

An item in one of them caught his eye, and caused him to sit up in his chair with a whoop of joy, that brought a scandalized glance from Major Larivet, the white-moustached old Alsatian who was in command of the fort, and a grin from Duperret, the first since that dreadful night of the attack.

The item, in bad French, was a translation from the bad English of a New York newspaper telling of Weyl's departure for Madagascar. It was filled with the exalted pseudo-science of which newspapers are fond and contained much ingeniously sketchy biographical and geographical data, but its appeal was obvious.

The American leaned forward over the cups.

"Does your fort boast a typist?" he asked. "Lieutenant Dubosc has probably already told you of the terrible experience we have had. I am anxious to make my report on it through the newspapers."

"Monsieur," said Major Larivet, gravely, "he died an hour ago by my side. I know nothing but that I have lost many men from my command."

"So..." said Weyl, "All the more reason I should make my report in writing. I need not conceal from you the fact that we are facing a danger which threatens not merely Fort Dauphin and Madagascar, but the entire world."

There was incredulity on the major's face, but he replied courteously, "My means are entirely at your service, gentlemen."

Beginning his report with scientific exactitude, Weyl included Duperret's letter, noted the sudden midnight attack on the steamer and went on to the details of the expedition:

".... For hours after the attack," he wrote, "we were unable to get anything like control out of the chaos in the camp. I think another attack of these unspeakably loathsome 'Umbrella Beasts' would have brought complete panic; certainly hardly any rifles but Duperret's and mine would have met them.

"We could not hope to escape by an immediate dash for the fort, though it was less than thirty hours' march away. The beasts seemed to be on every side, and they would have every advantage in the jungle, where we would have been instantly swept into the trees by their swinging tentacles.

"Fortunately, these hideous monsters appeared to have gathered their fill of human food for the time being, and meanwhile the idea of fire occurred to us. All the wood we could gather without too closely approaching the trees was collected and heaped in piles about five feet apart in a complete circle. These were set alight, and we huddled in the center of the blazing ring, almost roasted by the heat, but feeling infinitely safer. With the coming of day, the heat was almost intolerable, but we gained confidence as it became apparent that the beasts would not dare the fire, though we could hear them whistling in the trees.

"Our situation was bad. The supply of wood was not inexhaustible, and that of water was already used up. I am convinced that these beasts were possessed of a comparatively high intelligence. The manner of their attack, the character of the one killed in the battle, led to this conclusion; and they were evidently deliberately laying siege to us with the intention of starving us out of our refuge.

"Our rifles were useless, and to make a sudden dash through the lines would certainly involve the sacrifice of most of those present—perhaps all. So we sat down to plan a way out. Obviously, we had to find a means to make ourselves immune to their attacks.

"I thought I had it when I remembered that no barbarian, beast or insect, would tolerate castor oil. Desperate as was our situation, the idea of escaping a deadly and horrific death by means of that homely remedy made me want to laugh hysterically. I remember Duperret watching me trying to smother the urge, looking queerly at me, quite obviously doubtful of my mental balance. His speculative and startled glance added to the absurdity of the thing, and I almost lost my self-control. I realized we were all on the edge of madness.

"The idea had, of course, to be discarded. We had castor oil among our medical supplies, but barely enough to discourage the insects of the tropical jungle; certainly not enough to smear ourselves from head to foot to keep off those giant monstrosities menacing us from all sides.

"The solution we hit upon finally may not have been the best, but it was simple, and like many another, did not occur to us till we were ready to give up in despair. Duperret, Dubosc and I had spent the entire first day of our siege discussing and rejecting ways and means, and we had just about decided that the only thing to do was to make a concerted dash into the jungle, firing into the trees, and trusting to luck and mobility to carry us through, when the lieutenant startled us with a sudden leap, and shouted something wild, something we did not understand.

"We feared for his sanity as mutely we watched him dashing about furiously from spot to spot in the clearing, tearing up handful after handful of liana grass and throwing them on the fire.

"When, however, a dense cloud of thick, choking, black smoke rolled up, and when Dubosc turned to us with a triumphant light in his face, we understood dimly what his idea was, and in a frenzy of relief several of us danced foolishly in a circle about the fire and its column of smoke.

"In a council that followed, we decided that our attempt to escape had better be made during the day, once we had all noticed that there was less activity among our besiegers during the hours when the heat was most intense. We kept our fires burning, then, throughout the night until dawn. Nobody slept; we were too apprehensive, and too busy improvising torches for our protection during the march. The beasts, evidently fearful of the fire, remained in their trees all that night, and though they continued to whistle about us (this seems their sole mode of communication) there seemed to be less whistling from the side to which our smoke drifted. This assured us that our lieutenant's plan would work.

"At dawn, bearing our smoking flambeaux, we set out. Arms and equipment were useless; they were discarded. To prevent the panic that appeared imminent among the men, Dubosc threatened to shoot down any man who left the formation, and to insure obedience, only Duperret, he and myself were allowed to retain revolvers.

"As we neared the trees, there was crowding among the men, but a few sharp words brought them to their senses. We halted just at the edge of the clearing, and Duperret and I leading the shivering company, threw our branches down under the trees and piled more wood on to make a little blaze. There was a discernible commotion in the foliage above us, but we could see nothing. When the noises subsided, we ventured in a hundred yards or so and built another fire.

"This scheme was resorted to at intervals all along our march. Progress was necessarily slow. At some dark spots, where the jungle was thick, it was necessary to proceed in narrow files, and these were the most dangerous, not only because of the 'Umbrella Beasts' but also because of the fright and impatience of the men.

"It was in one of these places that a casualty occurred. One of the chasseurs suddenly broke from the line and ran, shouting madly, to wave his torch at a vinous growth hanging from a tree, which he must have taken for a tentacle of one of the beasts. He stumbled, his torch flying from his hand as he fell. His danger then evidently deprived him of what senses he had remaining, for, regaining his feet, he ran, not back into the line but deeper into the jungle. We heard a strangled cry in a few moments. That was all. None of us dared to leave the company to bring him back.

"Another time, a man went raving mad, and made a violent attack on Dubosc. Before he could be caught, he stabbed that brave man twice in the breast.

"Now, as to the animals which attacked us. I had one before me for some sixty hours, though with little opportunity to examine and none at all to dissect it. My observations, though somewhat scanty, lead me to the conclusion that we are dealing with a hitherto unknown member of the great mollusk family. The family includes the octopus and oyster, neither with red blood, and it was the nearly colorless fluid that puzzled me about the blood of the beast that attacked the ship.

"The beast that was killed at the camp had a larger body than any known member of the family, and tentacles at least fifteen feet in length and correspondingly powerful. A protective covering of chitin appears to have been developed, and due to the lack of any internal skeleton and the fact that the muscles must base on it, this protective covering to its body is of a thickness and strength sufficient to be quite impervious to rifle bullets. The one we killed had received a bullet full in the eye, which passed through into its brain.

"It is this brain that offers the most remarkable feature of these creatures. A brief investigation shows me that their brains are certainly larger than those of any animals except the big apes, and probably as large as those of the lower races of man. This argues an intelligence extremely high, and makes them more than ever dangerous, since they can evidently plan acts and execute them in concert.

"They have eight tentacular arms, covered on the lower side with the usual cephalopod type of suckers, the center of each sucker being occupied, as in some species of octopus, by a small, sharp claw. The thickness, and therefore the muscular strength of these arms is enormous. It is no wonder men proved utterly powerless against them.

"I am unable to say anything about either their method of breeding or what device they have arrived at for breathing air; probably some protective covering keeps the gill-plumes moist, as in the crayfish, making access to water at times necessary.

"In the face are two very large eyes, capable of seeing well in the dark and located directly in front of the large brain. The mouth consists of a huge beak, razor-edged. There are no teeth. Add this formidable beak to their extraordinary powers of swimming, their swift progress on land, their giant strength and their great intelligence, and it becomes evident that the human race is faced with a great peril.

"There is nothing whatever to prevent these animals from swimming the ocean or attacking the greatest city. One of these beasts could kill a hundred people in an hour and hardly any weapon we possess would be of the slightest use..."

As he wrote, Weyl's mind was again filled with the terror of that mad march through the jungle with the "Umbrella Beasts" whistling on every side, and his imagination shuddered at the picture of London or New York under an invasion from those grim Madagascar jungles; all business stopped, every door barred, the octopuses triumphantly parading the streets, breaking in here and there and strangling the last resistance of families cowering in corners, powerless against the invulnerable and irresistible animals. Here and there some squad armed with dynamite or some other weapon more powerful than rifles, would offer a brief resistance, but they too would go down in time. Civilization throttled, and in its place a ghastly reign of animalism...

V

Major Larivet was inclined to skepticism over Weyl's report. In a brusque, but kindly way, he had suggested that it be delayed, "... till you have had time to think it over. Perhaps, when the effect of your experience has—ah—worn off—"

Weyl gazed at him in astonishment at this suggestion, but he was to remember it forty days later.

Meanwhile, there was nothing to do but wait till the report reached the outer world, and some echo of it in the form of men, aeroplanes, scientists with their instruments and death dealing concoctions arrived to wipe out that terrible blot. And during the waiting, even Major Larivet's skepticism vanished under the pressure of events.

The octopuses, as Weyl called them, had confined their raids to isolated districts up to the time of his expedition, but now, acting apparently upon a well-formed plan, they became bolder and began a systematic extermination of every native in this part of the island.

Three days after the return of the expedition, a native runner dashed in half-crazed with fright to report a twilight raid on a whole village, from which hardly a soul escaped. As the days drew on, this ominous news was followed by such demonstrations of the power and intelligence of the octopuses as confirmed Weyl's darkest fears.

A village on the coast was attacked, and the natives, taking to their clumsy boats to escape the terror by land, found themselves no less helpless on the water, the only news of the dreadful event coming from some native who had gone there and found only a circle of empty huts.

Alarm of panic proportions spread like wildfire among the Malagasy, and in a stream that became a torrent they poured into Fort Dauphin for protection.

Daily the reports of depredations showed that the octopus terror was spreading and coming nearer, and Major Larivet found himself faced with the problem of feeding several hundred hungry and frightened natives with means wholly inadequate.

The climax came with the arrival of four men, or rather, shadows of men, who babbled that they were the last of the great tribe of the Tanôsy. Fighters to the core, instead of flying, they had stood out in battle array against their antagonists. The result had been unspeakably horrible—they had seen their comrades torn to pieces before their eyes, and the women and children hunted down.

It was while things were in this state that the little tin-pot mail boat arrived with its cargo of supplies and European newspapers.

Weyl's heart rose as he marched off to his quarters eagerly with the papers under his arm, but it sank like lead when he and Duperret opened journal after journal, in quick, disappointed perusals.

Not one, they perceived, took the matter seriously. Weyl's phrase, "Umbrella Beasts," had been seized upon by humorous commentators with gusto, rolled on their tongues and spun off their pens to tickle the ribs of readers. Of serious acceptance there was not a sign. The general tone of the papers was one of howling derision. It was suggested that Weyl had gone crazy, that he was a publicity-mad mountebank. But the more usual spirit of the papers was that of the French wit who blared: "Weyl's Umbrella Beasts; Inseparable companions for that rainy-day walk. No one acquainted with the dictates of fashion can afford to dispense with this novel combination of household pet and Protective Implement!"

And the cartoons...!

Weyl looked up from the papers to meet Duperret's glance. There were actual tears in the Frenchman's eyes.

"It seems to be up to us," said Weyl, after a moment. "Well—I am not a rich man, as it is reckoned in America, but I can command a considerable amount of money, and can borrow more. I will write a cable-gram to be sent off immediately, and have every cent spent for materials to fight this thing."

Together they composed the carefully worded message to Weyl's assistant in the laboratory in New York, and together they took it to the dock and delivered it to the captain of the boat with the most urgent instructions to send it the moment he arrived at Andovoranbo.

VI

Not long after daybreak the American was roused from his sleep by a confused shouting under the window. Hurrying into his clothes, he dashed out to see the little mail boat wallowing crazily off the jagged rocks that guarded the entrance to the harbor, her funnels silent and smokeless. Within ten minutes she was right among the breakers, pounding in the surf, but there was no sign of officers, crew, or lifeboats.

It was late in the afternoon before he could secure a native dhow to get out to the wreck. When he stepped on the slanting deck of the wrecked boat, Weyl found what he had feared. There was no one on board—only a blood-stain here and there.

Every man in the settlement was quite capable of visualizing what had happened. Writhing, black-grey tentacles reaching up out of the midnight sea, the swarming of hideous bodies over the ship, relentless groping arms searching out the screaming seamen, the fatally prehensive embrace of repulsive flesh...

That very night Fort Dauphin received notice that it was under close siege. A mile out on the northeast beach two natives were taken by an octopus that came unexpectedly out of the water on them, and on the opposite side of town a soldier was pursued along the sand right up to the walls of the fort. Later the report ran in that one of the sentinels on the west side had disappeared.

But neither Weyl nor Major Larivet was quite prepared for the bold attack on the fort two days later.

Twilight was just bluing the edges of the jungle a quarter mile from the bastions of the fort, and the three white men were smoking gloomily over their coffee, when a shot and a shout from the sentry brought them to their feet.

They hastened to the bastion. Out of the jungle in the same regular, military order they had preserved on that fatal night of the first attack, came the octopuses, huge ugly heads bobbing above, undulating tentacles below.

Larivet, with a gleam in his eyes at being at last able to come to grips with the enemy, snapped sharp orders as the artillerymen swung the two "seventy-fives" into position. Duperret and Weyl watched breathlessly, heedless of the wild cries of alarm that issued from the natives who had seen the octopuses. The mouth of the gun swung down slowly. An order. Brief motions, the crash of the discharge, and right in the center of the advancing line a terrific burst of flame and dust.

An octopus staggered, stumbled with wildly flailing arms and flopped inertly to the ground.

Crash! The bright flames from the two guns mingled, and in the flare of the explosions three more of the monsters went to oblivion. They were not invulnerable, then! There was a ray of hope!

Weyl found himself cheering frantically. He felt a pressure at his shoulder and saw a couple of natives beside him, their courage revived. The black artillerymen worked like mad. They could not miss at that point-blank range.

All down the octopus line were gaps, and the wounded beasts strove to right themselves. They wavered, broke, and in disorderly flight headed back into the jungle, pursued by the avenging shells of the seventy-fives till they had passed from sight.

The natives were crowding about, shouting with emotion and hurling epithets after the retreating monsters. They were saved— at least for the time being.

But the conference of the three white men that night was grave.

"We have not really accomplished very much," said Weyl, "except to show them that we have weapons against which they are not invulnerable. I don't think they will attempt to rush the fort again, but they are terribly intelligent. They may try a surprise attack at night or from the sea, or may even give us a regular starvation siege."

"No, they will not soon approach your guns again," agreed Duperret, "but what are we to do if they attack the town from the other side. The fort surely cannot hold all the people you have here."

"Gentlemen," said Larivet gravely, "in that case we can only do our duty. I shall have one of the guns moved to the other side of town. Meanwhile we can do nothing but wait till someone comes to help us."

"Or until we go to them," from Weyl.

Duperret paled slightly, and stood up. "I offer myself as a messenger," he said. "I will take a dhow out. If I am attacked, well, I know where to shoot them—in the eyes. I—"

"No, Raoul, no," said Weyl, "let me try it. It would be simply—"

He was interrupted. A native servant entered excitedly.

"Him one piece boat in town," said the black. "White man comes."

"Boat? White man?" queried Larivet, puzzled. A cheery voice in the doorway answered him, "I say, is anybody here?" it said, and in marched an extraordinary figure of a man.

A large sign saying "Englishman" could not have stamped his face more effectively than his expression of cheerful vapidity. His clothes were white, scrupulously clean, and meticulously pressed, and in one hand he bore what looked like a small fire extinguisher. He extended the other toward Weyl.

"You're Weyl, aren't you?" he said. "Mulgrave's my name; Henry Seaton Mulgrave. Earl of Mulgrave and Pembroke, and all that rot. At your service."

"Of course I remember," said Weyl cordially. "You gave that extraordinary paper on the Myxinidae before the British Association. Ah, that paper! Allow me," he said, and translated into rapid French for the benefit of Larivet, "to present the Earl of Mulgrave, one of the most distinguished of living scientists."

There were bows, a drink offered and accepted, and the visitor, carefully placing his fire extinguisher in the corner, curled his lanky frame up in a chair.

VII

"Seriously, though, y'know," Mulgrave said after finishing his whisky and soda, "if it hadn't been that I was a bit in the doldrums at the time your report came out, I believe I would have joined the rest of the world in thinking you somewhat—er—balmy, despite your excellent reputation. But I needed a cruise anyway, and came on the chance there was something in it; sort of a sporting venture, d'y'see? It did seem quite a bally cooked-up sort of mess, the way those journals played it up, y'know."

Weyl's nod of understanding was followed by an inquiring look at the queer contrivance the Englishman had placed in the corner.

"Flammenwerfer," Mulgrave answered the silent query. "Germans used 'em in the war. Superior bit of frightfulness. Shoots out fire. And really quite effective, even against your bally octopuses, I assure you."

"But," Weyl exclaimed, "you can't possibly—"

"Oh, yes, I have," Mulgrave smiled. "The ruddy animals hadn't the decency to wait for a proper introduction, and paid us a visit on the *Morgana*—my yacht, y'know—just outside the harbor. I fancy when we got through with them they were rather scorched. *Morgana* was war-built and has steel decks, so we didn't mind putting the Flammenwerfer to work against them. We've got what's left of one stretched out on the deck. Others got away."

Weyl breathed a sigh of relief and thankfulness that this casual Englishman had come prepared. How easily the mail boat disaster might have been duplicated! He shuddered.

"Well then, part of our horrible problem seems to be solved, thanks to your foresight, Mulgrave. At least we have a means of wiping them out. But here's the difficulty. It will take years, killing them off one by one, as we'll have to do with your pump gun. I tell you, they infest the whole island, thousands of 'em. They're increasing and multiplying faster than we could possibly kill them off. That's the only way I can explain this recent outbreak. They were few enough in number, before this, to remain in obscurity except in isolated districts, and known only to ignorant and superstitious natives." Weyl's forehead creased in perplexity and worry. "If they keep on—well, they'll need the whole globe. And that means only one thing; man will have to get off it to make room for them. They're powerful enough, and intelligent enough, to have their own way about it, too. Don't doubt it. Unless—"

Mulgrave evidently did not share Weyl's anxiety, though he did not seem to underestimate the danger. "I'll finish that last sentence of yours, Weyl, although I'll admit things are a bit worse than I had thought. But meanwhile, let's look over our resources, and try to find out a bit more about the nature of the beast we're up against. The post-mortem of that lamentably deceased visitor on the *Morgana*'s deck ought to tell us something of his weak points. Do you want to go out there now?"

With chairs tilted back against the cabin of the *Morgana*, the three men regarded the sundown sky in a moody and depressed

386

silence. Their dissection of the octopus killed by Mulgrave's pump-gun had added little to their knowledge of the anatomy of the menacing brutes, save a confirmation of Weyl's hypothesis that their breathing, while on land, was conducted by means of the same gills which supplied them with oxygen in the water, protected, like the lobster's, by a covering of chitin.

Mulgrave's chair scraped on the deck. "Well, let's get back ashore," he said. "Can't do any more now I fancy, unless they decide to stage a party for us this evening."

"It comes down to this, then," said Weyl, continuing the conversation which had been abandoned with the end of their anatomical researches. "Fire, or some kind of guns heavier than the ordinary service rifle, are the only things that will do any particular good."

"Have you thought of gas, my friend?" asked Duperret.

"Huh," answered Weyl shortly. "Airplanes? Chemicals? And what about all the men on the island—for we should have to cover it all with gas to be of any use."

"The time is rather short, too, I fancy," chirped Mulgrave. "How long will provisions last?"

"Not long," agreed Duperret, moodily. "A week, or perhaps a little more."

"Then, within seven days, or at the most ten, we must concoct a plan and put it into force—a plan that will wipe out God knows how many of these unearthly enemies of the earth. It must be extermination, too, for if one pair were left to breed... I'm more than half convinced that the thing is hopeless. Yet I don't like to show the white flag. These are, after all, only beasts. Super-beasts, it is true, but the equals and heirs of man? I hate to believe it."

"But, my friend, you forget the force of mere numbers," said Duperret. "So many rats could easily overpower us, guns and all, from mere lack of time to kill them as fast as they came on. Comparative values, as of man and beast, are insignificant."

Weyl nodded a pessimistic agreement.

"There's only one chance," he said. "If we could find some way to attack them in the water—they must go there to breed at least, and I fancy they must make periodic visits to the water to wet their gill plumes in addition."

VIII

It was three days later.

Another octopus attack on the little fort had met with a bloody repulse, and a score of the great bodies lay at the edge of the jungle in varying stages of decomposition, where they had been blown to extinction by the swift shells of the seventy-fives. A conference was in progress on Major Larivet's verandah; a conference of beaten men.

"As a last resort," Duperret was saying, "there is the open sea and Mulgrave's yacht."

"Why, as for that," Weyl answered, "it wouldn't hold a tenth of us, even crowded to the rails. Besides, leave those natives behind? Damn it, they trust us."

"It would hardly be cricket," said Mulgrave. "What of the mail steamer? Aren't they apt to send someone to look us up when she does not appear?"

"Not even yet is the boat due at Andovoranto, said Major Larivet, "and there is the time for the news to reach Andananerivo... The lack of news to them will be but a token that we have pacified the Tanôsy and are in need of nothing.

"Yes," Duperret agreed, "I know these officials. They are aware of something unusual only when they have seventeen dossiers, each neatly tied in red tape and endorsed by the proper department head. My friends, we are alone."

"Which means," Weyl continued, "that we have about a week more to live before the food runs out or they overwhelm us. And then—good-by world of men!"

There was little silence, broken only by the sound of Mulgrave puffing at his pipe. It was ended by a shot and a shout from one of the sentries at the western side of the fort; the signal of another attack.

During that night the great octopuses twice fought their way down to the fort, and twice were repulsed, though the second effort, bigger and more violently sustained than the first, only ended when Mulgrave, called in the crew of his yacht and their flammenwerfer.

As the following day drew on, the unrest in the jungle about the army post became more pronounced. Major Larivet, Duperret,

and Weyl, worn with lack of sleep, kept vigil by the little counter-
scarp, listening to the innumerable whistlings and rustlings so near
to them, while the soldiers and natives, visibly shaken, were difficult to keep in line.

When evening came, it seemed as though the octopuses had
concentrated their forces for a great drive. The whistlings had increased to such a volume that sleep was nearly impossible, and as
soon as the sun went down, the movements of dark forms could be
observed where the animals were silhouetted against the sky along
the beach

The first attack came half an hour later. It was a sporadic out-
burst, apparently, consisting of only three or four individuals, and
these were quickly dispersed or slain by a few bursts from the seventy-fives. But it was followed by another, and another, the numbers of the attackers ranging all the way from three to fifteen or
twenty. Unlike the previous attempts on the fort they were frenzied and unorganized as though the directing intelligence behind
them had suddenly failed. Immune to fear, the living octopuses
came right on, through the hail of fire and died at the foot of the
rampart, or dashed over it even, to be wounded to death by bayo-
nets fixed on long poles with which the black soldiers reached and
stabbed frenziedly at eyes and softer parts.

Once, during a lull in the combat, the commandant and Weyl
were called to witness a monstrous dud, at the very edge of the
fort between two of the hideous beasts. The ungainly creatures
locked in each others' tentacles, rolled hideously together, tearing
at each other with their great beaks, till a Senegalese reached over
with one of those improvised bayonet pikes and dealt first one and
then the other mortal stabs. Weyl felt a singular sensation of nau-
sea.

Toward dawn it became evident to the exhausted artillerymen
and their wearied leaders that the octopuses were now aiming not
so much at conquest, as at escape. They no longer blundered into
the fires that had been built about the fort and village; no longer
hurled themselves upon Mulgrave's crew of flame-throwers and
the shells of the seventy fives. They seemed to be heading for the
beach, to be striving to reach the water.

And when dawn broke, the men in the enclosure saw a few stragglers from the hideous army at the edge of the jungle, making their way, like the others, with ungainly flappings and swishings, always toward the beach. It was impossible to watch them without feeling an almost physical sensation of illness, of sinking. But what did it mean? No one among the harassed defenders of Fort Dauphin was prepared to say.

IX

Mulgrave's wearied crew had gone aboard with their ship, and the white men, refreshed by a few hours' sleep and a bath, were discussing the question. "I am of the opinion," Weyl was declaring, "that they have certain periods when they must wet their gill-plumes again, and last night's disturbance represents one of those periods. If we could only attack them at such a time—"

He was interrupted by the arrival of an excited Senegalese, who addressed Major Larivet:

"The boat she is smoke. She go."

"How?" "What?" cried the four, leaping to their feet and starting down the road in the direction of the pier.

It was too true. The *Morgana*, out beyond the reef line, was marked by a tiny plume of smoke from her funnel, and as they gazed, she seemed to move a bit.

"Quick!" shouted Weyl, "let's push off a dhow."

Followed by the Englishman, and at a longer distance by Duperret, he raced for the pier and leaped into the little craft. "Grab a sweep," he called to Larivet.

Propelled by sail and oar, the little craft began to swing out from the pier, and then catching the land breeze in its full strength, heeled over. Duperret drew in his sweep, useless at that speed. He shaded his eyes and looked toward the *Morgana*. Suddenly he turned with a short bitter laugh.

"Look," he said, pointing. A few hundred yards ahead of the dhow, Weyl and Mulgrave saw a globular grey shape among the waves. From it, lying flush with the water, radiated—tentacles. Weyl put the tiller over to avoid it, and as the craft swang saw another, and then another. It was the end.

But even as he prepared to wear the little ship round and run back for the pier, if indeed they could make that temporary safety, they saw out beyond the loathsome globular head and spreading arms a triangular fin-shape that cut the water with hardly a ripple.

It was charging straight at the octopus, and as they watched, there was a swift turmoil in the water, the flash of a sleek, wet, black body, a vision of dazzling teeth, had the globular head of the octopus disappeared into a boil of water from which rose two tentacles, waving vainly. Off to the right, another of those knife-like fins was coming, followed by more—a half dozen, a dozen, a score; and suddenly around each of them there gathered the whirl and flush of a combat.

The dhow drew ahead, right toward the center of one of the tumultuous whirlpools. Out of it dissolved an octopus that was only half an octopus, its tentacles torn and a huge gash across that inhuman parody of a face—an octopus that was striving vainly to escape from a flashing fate that ran behind it.

Weyl shouted—Duperret began to weep; the unaffected tears of joy of the emotional Frenchman and Mulgrave, stirred from his imperturbability, was shouting, "Killer whales!" to an audience that had eyes and ears only for the savage battles all about them.

Everywhere, they could see through the clear tropical water that the killers, stronger and swifter, if less intelligent, were the victors. The octopuses, routed, were trying to get away as vainly as the natives had tried to escape from them.

"Let the bally yacht go," shouted Mulgrave to Weyl. "I want to enjoy this."

For fifteen, twenty minutes, they watched, until they saw the vanishing fin of a killer moving off to northward, signal that that part of the battle was over, and that the killers were departing for new fields of triumph. Three men, with hearts lighter than they had known them for weeks, manoeuvred the boat back to the pier.

X

"They seem to be gone, sure enough," said Weyl, tossing down on the table a brace of the native pheasants. It was only two days later, but he had returned from a four hours' trip into the jungle.

"I didn't even come across the traces of a single one of them—unless you can call a trace the fact that they seem to have cleaned out about all the animals in this district. Even the monkeys are gone."

"Do you think they will come back?" asked Major Larivet.

"I am sure they will not," said Weyl. "There seem to be perfect shoals of killer whales off the coast, attracted no doubt by the octopuses, which are their favorite food. You may be sure they would hunt down every one, as the killers are very voracious."

"But what made them appear in the first place?"

"God knows. It is, or was, since they are now gone, some phenomenon allied to that which produces the lemming migrations every twenty-eight years. You, Mulgrave, are a biologist. You know how, once in twenty-eight years, these little rat-like animals breed in such numbers that they overrun whole districts, and then migrate into the ocean where they are drowned by the thousand.

"These octopuses would have plenty of opportunity to develop their extraordinary size and intelligence, as well as their quality of breathing air by life in the shallow, deserted lagoons all around Madagascar, and if they were actuated by a life-cycle similar to that of the lemmings, they would breed in the vast numbers which we saw. It seems the only logical hypothesis.

"In any case, there is nothing for the rest of the world to fear. A sort of wireless telegraphy seems to exist among animals with regard to neighborhoods where food can be obtained in quantities, and just as you will see the condors of the Andes flock to where food is, the killer whales gathered around this visitation of giant cuttlefish.

"It is one of Nature's numerous provisions to right the balance of things on the earth when they threaten to get out of joint in any direction. If any other enemy of man were to multiply as these octopuses did, you may be sure he would find an animal ally.

"We were merely panic-stricken and foolish to think we could accomplish anything. We should have waited."

"And now, my friend," said Duperret, "I suppose I must bid you farewell."

"Yes. I am anxious to get back to my monograph on the Ammonites of the Upper Cretaceous. It will astonish the scientific world, I think."

Speculative Fiction

INVERTEBRATA ENIGMATICA

GIANT SPIDERS, DANGEROUS INSECTS, AND OTHER STRANGE INVERTEBRATES
IN CLASSIC SCIENCE FICTION AND FANTASY

INVERTEBRATA ENIGMATICA
Giant Spiders, Dangerous Insects, and Other Strange
Invertebrates in Classic Science Fiction and Fantasy

ISBN 1-930585-65-9

Coachwhip Publications
CoachwhipBooks.com

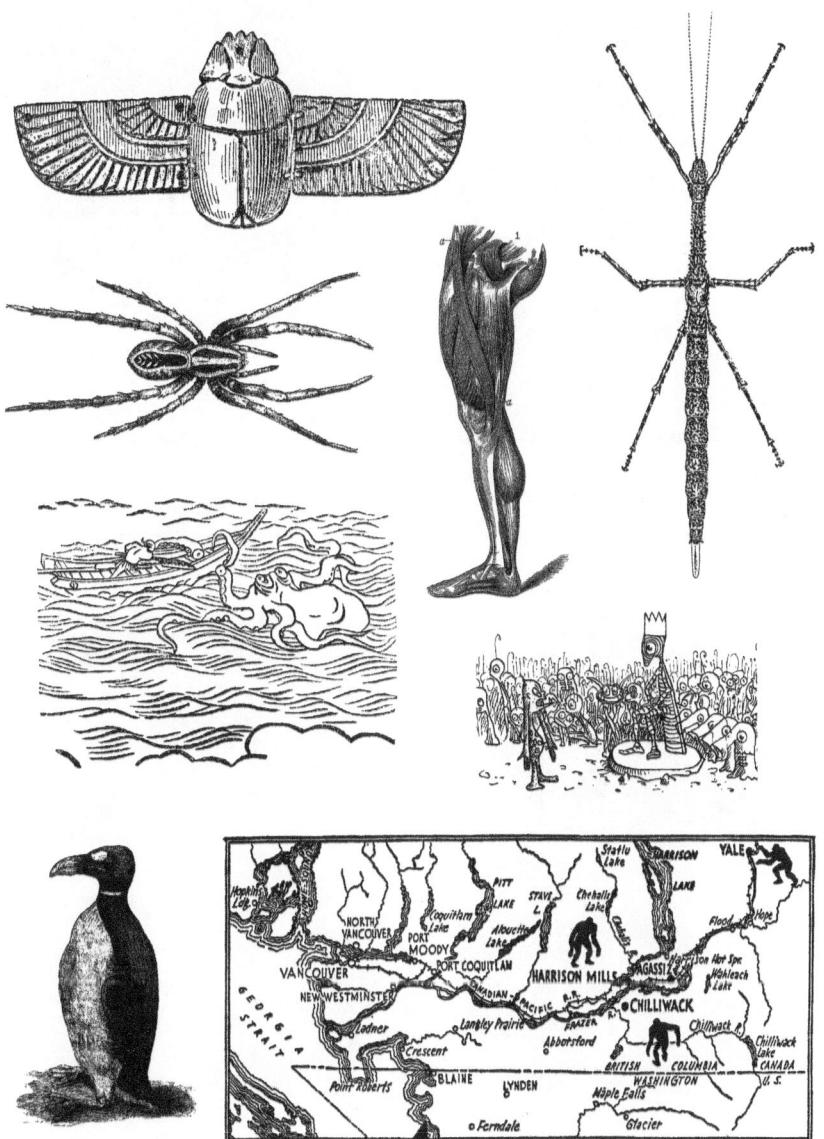

COACHWHIPBOOKS.COM

SPECULATIVE FICTION

Plants in Science Fiction
and Fantasy

Supernatural Stories in the
Christian Tradition

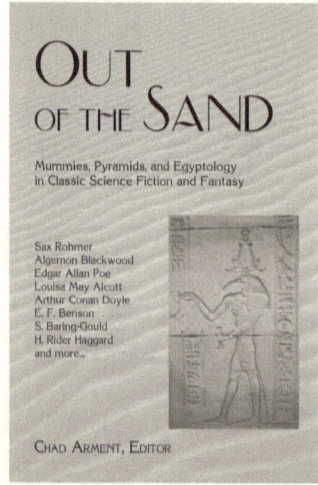

Egyptology in Science
Fiction and Fantasy

Time Travel in Science
Fiction and Fantasy

SHADOWS FROM A VEILED CREATION: Classic Tales of
Supernatural Fiction in the Christian Tradition
ISBN 1-930585-26-8

ABOUT TIME: The Forerunners of Time Travel and
Temporal Anomalies in Science Fiction and Fantasy
ISBN 1-930585-55-1

FLORA CURIOSA: Cryptobotany, Mysterious Fungi,
Sentient Trees, and Deadly Plants in Classic
Science Fiction and Fantasy
ISBN 1-930585-56-X

OUT OF THE SAND: Mummies, Pyramids, and Egyptology
in Classic Science Fiction and Fantasy
ISBN 1-930585-58-6

THE FANTASTIC IMAGINATION OF GEORGE MACDONALD I:
Essays, The Portent, At the Back of the North Wind,
The Flight of the Shadow
ISBN 1-930585-61-6

THE FANTASTIC IMAGINATION OF GEORGE MACDONALD II:
Phantastes, The Carasoyn, The Wise Woman, and Lilith
ISBN 1-930585-62-4

THE FANTASTIC IMAGINATION OF GEORGE MACDONALD III:
The Princess and the Goblin, The Princess and Curdie,
The Light Princess, The History of Photogen and Nycteris,
Short Stories
ISBN 1-930585-63-2

PYM: The Narrative of Arthur Gordon Pym
of Nantucket / An Antarctic Mystery
ISBN 1-930585-57-8